A CLEAN KILL

A sound out in the dark hallway made him look up. He saw a figure coming toward him. The person stopped in the open doorway.

He put the receiver back in the cradle.

"You came back," he said. "Why?"

There was no answer.

"It doesn't matter. We have to talk anyway."

The figure in the doorway slowly brought up a hand.

He saw the gun.

He tried to stand.

He heard the shot.

The bullet shattered his right temple, propelling him back against the leather chair.

He felt nothing, but he saw a blaze of light, like an exploding sun. Then he fell onto the desk, twisting as his body slumped forward.

He lay there, his head cocked at an angle. The blood seeped slowly out of his brain, onto the yellow legal pad and onto the purple blotter, a slow river of red spreading outward, settling into the dents and cracks of the old cherry desk. . . .

Books by P.J. Parrish

DARK OF THE MOON

DEAD OF WINTER

PAINT IT BLACK

THICKER THAN WATER

Published by Pinnacle Books

THICKER THAN WATER

P.J. Parrish

PINNACLE BOOKS
Kensington Publishing Corp.
http://www.kensingtonbooks.com

PINNACLE BOOKS are published by

Kensington Publishing Corp.
850 Third Avenue
New York, NY 10022

All Kensington Titles, Imprints, and Distributed Lines are available at special quantity discounts for bulk purchases for sales promotions, premiums, fund-raising, and educational or institutional use. Special book excerpts or customized printings can also be created to fit specific needs. For details, write or phone the office of the Kensington special sales manager: Kensington Publishing Corp., 850 Third Avenue, New York, NY 10022, attn: Special Sales Department, Phone: 1-800-221-2647.

Pinnacle and the P logo Reg. U.S. Pat. & TM Off.

First Pinnacle Books Printing: January 2003

10 9 8 7 6 5 4 3 2 1

Printed in the United States of America

For Jim DeGraci and Ray Recchi.
They loved a good mystery.

Acknowledgments

We would like to thank some special people who took the time to help us with the creation of this story: Kara Winton of the Fort Myers Police Department; Lisa Steinlage of the Broward County Medical Examiner's Office; Carl "Bud" Haemmerle of the Broward County Sheriff's Office crime laboratory; and Sarah Nell Hendry Gran of the Fort Myers Historical Society.

And a debt of gratitude is owed to all our lawyer friends: Jim Norman of Teaneck, N.J., James Norman of Fort Lauderdale, Fla.; Cameron Cohick, Dennis Harraka, Jeremiah Healy, and Peter Lent.

And to Susan, who let us steal her life.

"The first thing we do, let's kill all the lawyers."

"Nay, that I mean to do. Is not this a lamentable thing, that of the skin of an innocent lamb should be made parchment? That parchment scribbled o'er should undo a man? Some say, the bee stings: but I say, 'tis the bee's wax, for I did but seal once to a thing, and I was never mine own man since."

—King Henry VI, Part II.

November 1986

Chapter One

He stood at the window, looking down at the dark street below. In the orange glow of the streetlight, he could see the black tops of the trees waving in the wind. It was late and a storm was blowing in from the gulf. There was no one out tonight. He didn't even see the homeless man who usually slept on the bus bench across the street.

The wind gusted, catching a wad of newspaper. He watched it as it swirled and twisted in the orange spotlight, like a madman performing a desperate dance to the demon music in his head.

He turned away and pressed his palms into his eyes. *Jesus.* . . . He was so tired.

He looked at his desk, at the files and papers covering it. His brain was telling him to go home, get some sleep. But there was so much to do yet, so many things he hadn't taken care of. And sleep, the real sleep that made you whole again, was something he had given up on years ago.

Going back behind the desk, he sat down in the old leather chair. The corned beef on rye and cream soda were still there, untouched. He sat there, hands heavy on the armrests, eyes unfocused, brain working.

What was he worried about?

Cade wouldn't do anything. Even if he took his threat seriously, the man wasn't stupid enough to try something. Except sue. He could still do that. The statute of limitations had run out, but with a good lawyer and a sympathetic judge, Cade could still make his life a hell.

But what did he care? It was over anyway. He was tired of keeping the lies to himself, tired of carrying the whole thing around for the last twenty years.

He didn't care what would happen to him if it all came out. He'd be disgraced, disbarred for sure. He'd lose a fortune. But he just didn't care anymore.

His wife, she would care. And his partner, he would too. But he didn't care about them either. Or about anyone anymore.

He shut his eyes.

That wasn't true. There was still one person he loved, one person who loved him.

He opened his eyes. They focused on the far wall, on an arrangement of framed photographs. No people, no children, just sepia-toned street scenes of old Fort Myers as it looked in the forties, and one picture of a pale yellow Victorian cottage on a sugar-white beach against a cloudless blue sky. *Remembering how nice the world can be. . . .*

Not anymore. It was over now. Twenty years . . . gone.

One decision, one moment, and his whole life had gone down a different road.

He felt his throat constrict. He could make it right

though. He could still do right by Cade, try to make up for what he had done. But first, he had to tell someone. He wanted some peace, some absolution, and there was only one person who would give it to him. He glanced at his watch. Nine-thirty.

He picked up the phone.

A sound out in the dark hallway made him look up. He saw someone coming toward him. The person stopped in the open doorway.

He put the receiver back in the cradle.

"You came back," he said. "Why?"

There was no answer.

"It doesn't matter. We have to talk anyway."

The figure in the doorway slowly brought up a hand.

He saw the gun.

He tried to stand.

He heard the shot.

The bullet shattered his right temple, propelling him back against the leather chair.

He felt nothing, but he saw a blaze of light, like an exploding sun. Then he fell onto the desk, twisting as his body slumped forward.

He lay there, his head cocked at an angle. The blood seeped slowly out of his brain, onto the yellow legal pad and the purple blotter, a slow river of red spreading outward, settling into the dents and cracks of the old cherry desk.

His eyes were still open, fixed on the picture of the yellow beach cottage on the far wall.

Chapter Two

There was so much red. It streamed out from the center in slender little arteries, bleeding across the purple backdrop.

He had been standing here for ten minutes now, waiting for just the right moment to do what he had come here to do. He didn't know much about taking photographs. But he knew that he had to wait until just the right moment.

The red was deepening, spreading.

Finally, he brought the camera up to his eye, aimed and took a picture of the sunset.

A smile tipped the corners of Louis Kincaid's mouth. Finally. He had finally done it. He didn't even need to wait for the film to come back this time. He knew this time the picture wouldn't be blurry, the colors pale or the damn horizon crooked. This time he had finally nailed it.

He looked back out over the gulf. The sun hovered

just above the horizon for a second. Then, as if pricked by a pin, the red ball suddenly deflated and melted into the water.

He heard someone applauding and turned to see a couple standing about a hundred yards or so down the beach. They were applauding the sunset. He always thought it was funny that people did that. It was the tourists mainly, who came down to the beach at dusk, wine glasses in hand, to pay homage to Mother Nature or God or whatever deity they thought was behind the light show.

The sunset. He used to notice it. No matter where he was—in his cottage or his car, sitting at a bar or buying groceries. Every day without fail, right around five, his eyes wandered to the west and he would wonder what it was going to be like that night.

But things were different now. He had been here six months and sunsets were now just a scientific phenomenon to be taken for granted, like rain or snow. Nothing but slanting sunlight shooting through a prism of dirt, gas molecules and water vapors.

But he wouldn't tell Frances that.

He would just send her and Phillip the photograph and tell them that this was what he saw when he stepped out of his cottage and that, yes, he was very happy and no, they didn't need to worry about him.

The colors were fading and the couple had disappeared. He watched the dark green waves crash and foam. The storm last night had left the water still churning and the tide line was rimmed with rotting kelp, broken shells and dead fish. He turned and started back toward the cottage.

He paused at the crest of the low dune. The sun had turned the weather-beaten gray boards of the cottage to umber, making it look like some rustic hideaway on Cape Cod. He stared at the cottage—*his* cottage—

for a minute then brought the camera up to his eye and took a picture.

The photograph wouldn't show the torn screening on the porch or the mildew in the shower stall, but, hey, Frances wouldn't know that. His foster mother would just be happy that he finally had settled into such a nice place.

At the door, he paused to knock the sand off his flip-flops, then went in. His eyes wandered over the old rattan furniture with its faded blue cushions, up over the terrazzo floor to the pale green walls decorated with matching prints of two crazed-looking pink cockatoos.

Settled . . . was he settled? He liked his cottage. He liked taking his cup of coffee out to the beach in the morning and getting surprised by the sight of a dolphin's fin breaking the glass-smooth water. He liked Captiva Island. More than he thought he could have.

But *settled?*

That wasn't the right word. Not with that little something that kept gnawing at him inside, that voice that kept telling him twenty-six-year-old men didn't settle into sleepy little beach towns where the only things keeping a person connected to the real world were cable television and a causeway bridge.

Twenty-*seven*. Today was his birthday. He had almost forgotten.

Louis set the camera on the bar and went to the refrigerator to get a Dr Pepper. As he closed the door, his eye caught the card that hung there under the seashell magnet. It was a birthday card with a picture of a golden retriever wearing a big red bow. He took it down and opened it, reading the short note again from Frances and Phillip. They had never forgotten his birthday, not once since he had first come to live with them when he was eight. Every November, a week before his birthday on the eighteenth, no matter where he was, the card would find him—always with the twenty-dollar bill tucked inside.

He put the card back under the magnet. Leaning back against the counter, he took a drink of the Dr Pepper, watching the shadows growing in the corners of the kitchen.

Shit, his birthday. Maybe he would go over to the Dodies'. He had just been to see them over the weekend, but hadn't thought to mention his birthday was coming up. He glanced at his watch. After six. They'd already have had supper, but Margaret would surely fix him a plate.

No, he had been sponging off Sam and Margaret too much lately. He couldn't afford to wear out his welcome. Even on his birthday.

A cricket started to sing somewhere in the cottage. His stomach rumbled, and he knew without looking there was nothing but a couple cans of Beefaroni in the cupboard. He finished the Dr Pepper and tossed the can in the trash. He'd walk down to Timmy's and grab an early dinner, maybe a few beers.

He threw on a clean T-shirt and left the cottage. Next door, at number four, a family was dragging their suitcases out of their car and stopped to look at him. Louis gave them a smile and mumbled a good evening. The two teenaged boys stared at him sullenly. Louis hoped they weren't like the last ones who had rented number four. Those kids had blasted their boombox into the night and he finally had to go over and tell them to stop.

He hadn't really cared about the loud music. But the other guests did and it was his job to do something about it.

Louis shook his head as he headed out to the road. Security for Bransons on the Beach cottages. An ex-cop couldn't get much lower than that. Even if it did mean he paid next to nothing for a gulf view others paid three hundred a day for.

The lot of Timmy's Nook was nearly empty. It was too early for the locals and Timmy's was too rustic looking for most of the tourists.

Bev looked up from behind the bar and gave him a smile. "You're early. You hungry or just bored?"

"Both," he said, taking a seat at one of wood tables covered with red checkered vinyl.

Bev was up to her thin elbows in soapy water. "It'll be a minute or two. Carlo's just fired up the fryers." She cocked a head toward the cooler. "You know where it is."

Louis got up, went behind the bar and got a Heineken, taking it back to the table. He watched Bev as she finished washing the bar glasses. He came into Timmy's a couple times a week and Bev was always there to serve him his fried grouper sandwich with fries and slaw, but they had never gotten beyond friendly banter. Outside of what he saw of her here, he didn't know much about her, and she sure as hell knew nothing about him, other than his tastes in food and that he lived down the road. And what had been in the newspapers.

Bev dried her bony hands. She looked maybe sixty, a spindly Lucille Ball with her upswept dark-rooted blond hair, bright red dime-store lipstick, always dressed in the same black capri pants and black tops. He liked her. She was like his cottage. Old-fashioned, a little musty, but homey.

She came over to lean against the wall near his table and eyed his Miami Dolphins T-shirt.

"Nice shirt," she said.

"What's wrong with it?" Louis asked.

"The Bucs ain't good enough for you?"

"The Bucs aren't good enough for much of anything."

"All we need is a couple of good draft picks."

"Shit, Bev, even Bo wouldn't come to Tampa for seven million. The Bucs stink. They will always stink."

She started to sulk, but Louis knew it was fake. They had been having this same argument since the first day he walked in. She was a die-hard Bucs fan and hated the Dolphins just on general principle. It was what passed for personal talk between them.

"Fucking Fish," she muttered. "What kind of colors is that for a football team? Pool colors. You don't look good in aqua, you know. No man looks good in aqua."

Louis smiled, shaking his head.

"You want your usual?"

"Yeah. Extra tartar."

Bev went back to the kitchen. Louis took a swig of beer. She was right about the aqua T-shirt. Six months ago, he wouldn't have been caught dead in one. Hell, he never used to wear T-shirts out in public. Same with the khaki shorts and the flip-flops he was now wearing. He took another drink of beer. Was it because of Florida, like Dodie switching from flannel to those guayabera shirts? Or was it because he wasn't a cop anymore? Even when a cop was off-duty, he usually dressed like he wasn't. The humidity had probably just melted the starch out of him.

Bev wandered back, bringing silverware wrapped in a paper napkin. "Haven't seen you in two days," she said. "Where you been?"

"I had a job down in Bonita Springs," Louis said.

"Another cheating, dirt-bag husband?"

"Cheating, dirt-bag wife this time."

"How'd you nail her?"

"Photos. Coming out of the Days Inn."

"Cheap bastard. He couldn't spring for the Marriott?"

Louis knew Bev liked hearing the details whenever he had a surveillance case. But he didn't really want to give them.

"Boring case, Bev," he said. "Nothing juicy this time."

"Damn." She retreated to the kitchen. Louis took another drink of beer, his eyes wandering out the window. It was too dark now to see much further than the dock, but out in the black channel he could make out the red and green running lights of a boat making its way south.

His thoughts drifted to the husband of the woman he had busted in Bonita Springs. The poor guy had looked at the photographs, taken out his checkbook, slid the check across the table to Louis and left. All without saying a word.

Louis stared out at the black water. God, he hated it. He hated that woman, he hated that man, he hated sitting in a hot car waiting for people to prove they were human. He hated being a PI. He hated not being a cop.

"Excuse me."

Louis looked up. A man was standing at his table. Tall, thin, wearing jeans and a faded green T-shirt.

"Are you Louis Kincaid?" he asked.

Louis nodded warily. It had been months since anyone had recognized him and he had begun to hope the notoriety was finally wearing off. He didn't want to spend the rest of his life answering questions from strangers who got off hearing about serial killers. The press had dubbed it the "Paint It Black" killings, after the Rolling Stones song. Once, when he was sitting at a bar, a drunk came up and even started singing it. Louis had almost punched the guy out. He just wanted to forget it, wanted his fifteen minutes to be up.

He looked up now into this man's eyes. What was the question going to be this time?

"I'm Ronnie Cade. I heard about you."

Louis saw Bev looking at them. She had come to be a little protective of him.

"I went to your house," the man said. "Some weird French guy said you were probably here."

Great. Leave it to Pierre . . .

"Can I sit down?" the man asked.

"Look, man, I don't mean to be rude, but I'm getting ready to eat," Louis began.

"I want to hire you."

Louis blinked in surprise.

"I know you caught that paint guy and that you're doing private investigation stuff now." The man looked around at another couple taking a nearby table. "Can I sit down?"

Louis hesitated. He needed the work. There wasn't a helluva lot of cases for a PI to take on here. But this guy looked like he was a little too desperate.

He caught Bev's eye again. And Carlo, the sumo-sized cook, had come out. Louis gave them a small wave to signal he was okay. His eyes moved back to the man standing in front of him.

His dark hair was pulled into a ponytail and he had an eagerness in his expression that at first made him seem young, but from the fine web of lines around the eyes and the leathery skin of his arms, Louis guessed him to be in his late thirties.

Cade was bouncing lightly on his toes, his lips moving back and forth between a smile and grimace, like he couldn't decide if he wanted to be tough or friendly.

"All right. Sit down," Louis said.

Ronnie Cade dropped into a chair, started to extend a hand, then drew it back. He crossed his arms and leaned forward on the table.

"I know you must get real good money for what you do," Cade said, "but I was hoping maybe you would take what I got and let me make payments on the rest."

Louis stared at him. *Good money?* He rubbed the

condensation off his beer bottle. "First things first. What kind of investigation do you want me to do?"

"My father's been arrested. They've charged him with murder."

Louis took a drink of his beer and waited just long enough to not look eager. "You want a beer?" he asked.

Cade nodded quickly. "Bud."

Louis called over to Bev, trying to sound casual, but inside his heart was quickening. This was promising.

"Who did your father allegedly kill?" Louis asked.

"That lawyer Spencer Duvall."

Louis straightened slightly.

"I thought that would get your attention," Cade muttered.

Bev brought the beers. Louis ignored the questions in her eyes. After she left, he asked, "How much can you pay to start?"

"Five-hundred dollars," Cade said.

"Shit, man . . ."

Cade's hand shot out and he grabbed Louis's wrist. Louis jerked his hand back and Cade threw his hands in the air.

"I'm sorry," he mumbled. "I'm sorry, okay?"

"Does your father have the same temper, Mr. Cade?"

"I said I was sorry," he said, his eyes low, his voice strained.

Louis shook his head slowly. "Five-hundred dollars is a day's work in a homicide investigation, Mr. Cade. Doesn't your father have a lawyer?"

"Yeah, court-appointed. Everyone knows how hard they work for people like us."

"People like who?" Louis asked.

Cade paused to take a drink and wiped his mouth with the back of his calloused hand. "Look, I do lawn maintenance for a living. My kid and me live in a double-wide over on Sereno. I ain't had many breaks in my life and I don't blame anybody for that. But the law don't work the same for everybody." He paused again. "Do I have to start singing a sad song for you here?"

Louis glanced around the restaurant. He had seen the news about Spencer Duvall on TV. A big-shot lawyer getting gunned down in his own office late at night would be news anywhere, let alone Fort Myers. He had seen the film of a man being hauled away in handcuffs, the talking head saying the suspect had been recently released from prison. Louis had just chalked it up to a revenge thing gone bad. Now here was the guy's kid, begging for someone to believe his dad didn't do it. Interesting. But not interesting enough that he could afford to work for near free.

"Look, Mr. Cade, I don't think I—"

Cade leaned forward. "He's my *father*," he said. "I'll give you anything I have." He reached in a pocket and slapped a business card on the table. "Look, I've got my own business, I got a truck—"

Louis shook his head. "Sorry, man."

Cade stared at Louis for a long time, then grabbed his beer and quickly drained it. He stood up slowly, digging for money in the pocket of his jeans.

"Forget it," Louis said. "It's on me."

Cade didn't move. His eyes flitted around the restaurant, then came back to Louis. "I lost him," he said tightly.

"What?" Louis said.

"My father. He went to prison. I lost my father for twenty years." Ronnie Cade's eyes glittered in the florescent lights. "My father wasn't there when I graduated high school, when I got married or when I had my boy. Twenty years, man. He just got out and now this."

Louis didn't reply, the sounds of the restaurant suddenly dull and thick.

Cade shook his head slowly. "Fuck, you haven't got the faintest idea what the hell I'm talking about, do you?"

He started away.

"Hey, Cade," Louis called out.

The man turned.

"I'm not making any promises, okay? But I'll look into it."

Cade stared at him for a moment, then nodded briskly. He left, the screen door banging behind him. Louis picked up the business card. J.C. LANDSCAPING. It was dirt-smudged and the phone number was inked out and a new one scribbled in. He slipped it in his shorts pocket.

Bev came over, setting the grouper sandwich down in front of him. "What was that all about?" she asked.

"A job offer," Louis said, picking a fry out of the basket.

"For what?"

"The guy's father was arrested for murdering a lawyer."

Bev's eyes darted to the door where Ronnie Cade had disappeared. "That was Jack Cade's kid?"

"I guess. He didn't say what his father's name was."

"Jack Cade. He just got out of prison and now they're saying he killed Spencer Duvall," Bev said, excitement creeping into her voice. "What, you don't watch the news?"

"I saw it." Louis took a bite of the sandwich.

"Don't you think it's kind of weird?" Bev pressed.

"Bev, I think all cons dream of killing the guy who put them away. Maybe this one made his dream come true."

"But why would Jack Cade kill his *own* lawyer?"

Louis looked up at her, wiping his chin with a paper napkin. "Duvall was Cade's *defense* lawyer?"

She nodded. "Twenty years ago. When Cade was on trial for murder."

Louis set his sandwich back in its plastic basket. "Who did Cade murder?"

"A girl." Bev's brow furrowed. "Kathy something, I think. No, Kitty, her name was Kitty. She lived over in Fort Myers. It was big news around here at the time. I was working at the HoJo's on Cleveland and the cook had this TV in the back and we followed it on the news. It was pretty bad stuff. That girl . . . he raped her, too, and left her body in a dump." She paused. "So you gonna take the case?"

Louis looked up at Bev. "I'm not sure."

"Why not?"

"He can only pay me five hundred."

Bev shook her head slowly. "You should have taken it."

"Why?"

"End of the month. I gotta collect on your tab, hon. Five hundred bucks can buy a lot of grouper sandwiches."

"I'll settle up at the end of the week, I promise."

Bev picked up his empty Heineken bottle. "I'll bring you another." She stopped. "Kitty Jagger, that was her name." She shook her head absently. "Wow. Twenty years. I can't believe that was twenty years ago. Where's the time go?"

She went back to the kitchen. Louis picked up his sandwich, took another bite and set it aside. He looked out the window, out at the black moonless night and the inky water of the channel lapping against the dock.

Twenty years was a long time. But not long for rape and murder. Spencer Duvall apparently had done a good enough job to have kept his client out of the chair. Why would Jack Cade turn around and kill the guy who had saved his neck?

He fished out the business card Cade had left. J.C. LANDSCAPING. Louis guessed the J.C. stood for Jack Cade. Twenty years ago, Ronnie Cade would have been, what?—fifteen maybe? What goes through a kid's head when he finds out his father is a rapist and murderer? How the hell do you forgive that?

He's my father. I lost him. . . .

A green bottle appeared in front of him. Louis looked up at Bev.

"Today's my birthday," he said.

"No shit?" Bev said.

Louis took a quick swig of beer. "Yeah, no shit."

Chapter Three

The glass doors to the Lee County jail reflected the sun like mirrors and Louis paused on the sidewalk, still not used to seeing himself in what he had come to think of as his new "uniform." This morning, it was fresh khaki slacks, a yellow polo shirt and a blue blazer. It was what he always wore when he was meeting a client for the first time.

Not that he was sure Jack Cade was going to be a client.

He had spent a fitful night turning Ronnie Cade's situation over in his head. He couldn't afford to take a charity case, that much was certain. He had just deposited the check from the Bonita Springs case, but there was nothing else on the horizon and he knew he'd have to live off that money for a while. He glanced back at the white '65 Mustang parked at the curb.

He shouldn't have spent so much getting it fixed. New brakes, new transmission, and the body work and paint job. It had taken a huge chunk out of his meager savings. He should have listened to Dodie and junked the old thing and bought something new and reliable.

He shook his head. "Man, I'll walk before I have to drive a damn Civic," he muttered as he started for the door.

He stopped, spotting the *News-Press* box. The Spencer Duvall murder was the lead story again. This time, however, there was a picture of Jack Cade.

Louis popped in a quarter and pulled out a paper. Jack Cade looked to be on the downslope of fifty, with the same long, thin face and hooded eyes as his son. Louis knew you couldn't read much from a mug shot. Except when the person was innocent. Then you could see it in the eyes, the indignation, shock or bewilderment of the falsely accused. Jack Cade looked simply blank—bored, if anything.

He knew what had kept him tossing and turning all night. It wasn't the money. It was that he didn't think he could get past the fact that Jack Cade had been convicted of rape and murder. But he had made a promise to Ronnie Cade. Maybe if he met the father face to face he could find a good reason to walk away from this.

Folding the paper under his arm, he went in. At the glass window, he tapped lightly on the wall microphone to get the clerk's attention.

"Morning, Zach."

Zach turned and keyed the mike on his side. Reddish-blond spikes of hair sprouted from a sun-burned square head that melted into the collar of his dark green shirt. Zach Dombrowski was a dead-ringer for Barney Rubble.

"Hey, Louis. Haven't seen you for a while. How goes it?"

"Okay," Louis said as he picked up a pen to sign in.

Zach leaned close to the mike so the other deputy behind the glass could not hear him.

"I heard a rumor we might be adding guys in February, Louis. Why don't you put in?"

Louis looked at Zach in surprise. The others around here weren't usually so friendly. "I don't think I could work for Mobley."

Zach nodded. "He has an Eight Ball on his desk. He uses it to make decisions. 'Should I take a shit? Signs Point To Yes.' "

Louis smiled and tossed the pen down.

Zach looked at the log. "You here to see Jack Cade?"

"Is that a problem?"

Zach shrugged. "Well, I guess not, except the Sheriff left orders to be notified when anyone visits Cade."

"Then notify him."

"He's off duty but he's over at the Dinkle Center."

"Lucky break for me."

"I better call him anyway. Hold on a minute."

As he waited, Louis read the Duvall story. It recapped Cade's arraignment with a few comments from the prosecutor, State Attorney Vern Sandusky, assuring Southwest Florida "that the case was progressing as expected and that I will do everything in my power to make sure that Jack Cade spends the rest of his life in prison."

Zach tapped the glass. "Sheriff says you can go up, but he wants to see you at O'Sullivan's in an hour."

Louis nodded, tucking the newspaper under his arm as he headed to the elevator.

The doors opened and a deputy stepped in. He gave Louis the once-over, focusing on his VISITOR badge. Louis glanced at the deputy's name plate. LOVETT. He remembered Lovett had been the arresting officer on a deadbeat father case he had worked several months ago. He felt Lovett's eyes on him and wondered if the deputy remembered him, too.

"Kincaid, right?" Lovett asked.

Louis nodded. He waited, but the deputy's eyes stared straight ahead at the closed doors.

"You remember that case we worked together on a few months back?" Louis said finally.

Lovett's eyes didn't waver. "No."

Great. The silent treatment again.

"What about Jack Cade? What's the talk?" Louis asked.

Lovett's eyes slid to Louis, then snapped back to the doors.

"The way I see it, killers like Cade are no better than garbage, and lawyers like Duvall are no better than the maggots that feed off it."

The doors opened. Louis moved to step off.

"You working for or against that asshole?" Lovett asked.

"Neither," Louis said.

The doors closed with a wheeze of air. The deputy posted on the fourth floor saw Louis and jerked his head to the right. Louis followed him down a dim hall done in the same chipped beige paint as the iron-bar door that clanged shut behind them. The deputy stopped at a metal door and motioned for Louis to go inside.

"He's in five, down at the end."

A long table split the room, a plexiglass divider running its length with privacy partitions. Louis stopped at the end and looked at the man seated behind the glass.

Jack Cade's head was down, his stringy, ink-black hair shading his face. His arm was slung across the back of the wooden chair and his ankle was propped on his knee. Louis cleared his throat.

Cade lifted his head, running thick fingers through his hair to move it from his forehead. His gray-green eyes peered at Louis from under lazy lids for several seconds before dropping away. He drew his thin lips into a grimace.

"I told them I didn't want to see any reporters."

His voice sounded hollow, strained through the small holes in the plexiglass.

"I'm not a reporter."

"Funny. You look like one."

"I'm a private investigator, Louis Kincaid. Your son Ronnie wants to hire me to help in your defense."

"Kincaid? Yeah . . ." Cade cocked his head. "Ronnie told me you were too expensive. What changed your mind?"

"Your son makes a compelling argument for family values."

Cade narrowed his eyes, then flicked his hand toward the empty chair. Louis sat down, studying Cade.

His eyes were dulled with disinterest and his large body, all sinew and muscle beneath the orange jumpsuit, was draped over the chair like he was home watching a football game. Except for his right foot. The foot, propped on his left knee, was moving in a nonstop, rhythmic jerking motion.

"You got any smokes?" Cade asked.

"Sorry."

"So you working for me or not?"

"I don't know. Talk to me."

"What do you want to know?"

Louis pulled a small notebook from his back pocket. "I'm coming in cold, Mr. Cade, so you're going to have to start at the beginning. All I know is Spencer Duvall was shot Monday night around nine-thirty in his office and you were arrested the following afternoon."

Cade didn't reply.

"So why did they arrest you?" Louis asked.

"I went to see Duvall that morning."

"Why?"

"I went there to tell him I was going to sue him. I had an appointment. You can check."

"Sue him? For what?"

"He fucked up some legal work he did for me a few years back."

"What kind of legal work?"

Cade was studying his hands. He began to pick at the skin around his nails. "Criminal."

"You mean when he defended you twenty years ago?"

Cade snickered. "Can't call what he did a defense, not by any stretch. The asshole cost me twenty years."

"It could have been worse," Louis said.

Cade didn't blink. His eyes seemed darker now, the color the gulf had been after the storm.

"The rape and murder," Louis said. "Tell me about it."

Cade pressed his lips together and shook his head. "Not important."

"Tell me or this is over now."

Cade shut his eyes slowly, like he was tired to the bone. Or bored. His right foot kept up its steady jerking. "I was sent up for raping and killing this girl. There were things that should've been brought up, motions and shit like that. Duvall didn't do any of it and I got fucked. That's why I was going to sue him."

"How old was '*this girl*'?"

Cade shrugged. "Fifteen. Sixteen."

"How did you kill her?"

"I told you—"

"How was she killed?"

"Who cares?"

"How was she killed?" Louis demanded.

"She was stabbed." Cade dragged his foot off his knee and turned away, rubbing a hand over his rough chin.

"Mr. Cade—"

Cade spun back. "What the hell difference does it make? This is about Duvall. This is about today."

Louis stared at Jack Cade, his fingers working gently against the metal clip on the ballpoint pen. *Man, get the hell out of here. You don't need this loser or the five-hundred dollars.* But he wanted to know.

"Did you do it?" Louis asked.

"I didn't kill that cocksucker lawyer."

"I mean the girl. Did you kill the girl?"

"Why you digging up old stuff no one cares about?"

"Did you kill her?"

Cade leaned forward, the pupils of his eyes barely visible under the heavy lids. "The only thing you need to know is that I didn't kill Duvall."

Louis was amazed to see a small smile creep into the corners of Cade's mouth.

"You know what?" Cade said. "I should answer your question just because I find your need to know . . . amusing."

"This isn't funny, Cade."

The tipped corners of his mouth grew into a grin. "That depends on your vantage point." He tapped on the plexiglass between them. "You ever looked at anything through six inches of plastic? You ever seen the world through greasy hand prints and scratches and dried spit? Try it sometime. Try it for twenty years. It kind of . . . clarifies things."

Cade's smile faded.

"Answer the question," Louis said.

Cade dropped his head, picking again at his ravaged cuticles.

"What you say your name was again?" he asked, without looking up.

"Louis Kincaid."

"How you spell that?"

Louis spelled his last name and when Cade looked up he was grinning. "Thought maybe we had a distant relative in common for a minute there. Kin-CADE . . . get it?''

"I asked you a question, Cade," Louis said. "Did you kill her?"

But Cade ignored him again. "Ronnie said he offered you five-hundred bucks," he said. "That's barely enough to put macaroni on your table, right?"

Louis didn't answer him.

"Would you be so curious about whether I killed that girl if I paid you five thousand?"

"Yes, I would."

"What if it was ten thousand? Or a hundred thousand?"

Louis just stared at him.

"At what dollar amount does my value as a human being reach the defendable level? How much would it take for you *not* to be so curious?"

Louis closed the notebook. Cade's eyes flitted to it and back up to Louis's face.

"I didn't kill that girl," he said finally.

Louis locked on Cade's chameleon eyes, hoping to see some hint of the truth there. There was nothing.

A steel door on Cade's side opened and a guard emerged. Cade glanced at the guard and smiled. "Well, I guess the maids are finished with my room." He unfurled his body from the chair.

"So," he said to Louis, "you staying for the macaroni?"

Louis rose, slipping the notebook in his back pocket. "I don't know yet. I need to do some research on your case."

"Yeah, you do that." Cade turned away.

Louis started back toward the steel door at the other end of the room.

"Kincaid."

Louis looked back. He could see Cade's face at the plexiglass again.

"Don't ever ask me about that dead girl again," Cade said.

He disappeared from view. Louis walked back to the steel door and hit a buzzer. Back out in the hall, Louis drew in a deep breath.

"Hey, your name Kincaid?"

Louis turned to the deputy who had called out. "Yeah."

"Zach says there's someone downstairs who wants to know who's seeing Jack Cade."

"Who is it?" Louis asked.

"Cade's lawyer. And she's mad as hell."

Chapter Four

There were only two women in the lobby when Louis got out of the elevator. One was an old blue-hair with a grandkid in tow. The other was a black woman in a dark red suit carrying a slim briefcase. Her eyes immediately lasered onto Louis and she came forward.

"You're Louis Kincaid?"

"Yes, and you are—?"

"What was your business with my client?" she asked.

"His son wants to hire me—"

Her brows knitted. "Ronnie? Ronnie hired you to do what?"

"I'm a private invest—"

"What?"

"I—"

"He hired a PI? Damn it!"

Louis glanced at Zach behind the glass; he was

watching intently. Louis knew he had keyed the mike so he could hear every word.

"Look," Louis said, holding up a hand, "maybe we should—"

"I can't believe it," she said, shaking her head. "I told him to stay out of this, to keep his damn mouth shut." Her dark eyes shot suddenly to Louis's face. "What did my client tell you?"

"Nothing. Look, lady—"

"Nothing he told you can be used against him—"

"Hold it, I'm not even sure I'm going—"

"How much is he paying you?"

"How much is he paying *you?*" Louis shot back.

She pushed a strand of hair back from her forehead. "Nothing. I'm his public defender."

Louis gave her a wry smile. Her expression remained icy.

"Let's start over," Louis said. He held out his hand. "Louis Kincaid."

She hesitated, then gave him a curt handshake. "Susan Outlaw. Now what exactly did my client tell you?"

Louis looked again at Zach. His face was practically pressed against the plexiglass.

Louis glanced at her. "Why don't we go somewhere where we can talk in private?" he said.

She looked at the slim watch on her wrist. Louis could tell she was mulling something over. What? Whether he was going to waste her time? Shit, what was it with lawyers? They all thought they were the only ones with schedules to keep. Not that he had anywhere else to go today, except to see Mobley, and he wasn't in any hurry to do that.

"All right. Let's go," she said, pivoting to the door.

"Yes, ma'am," Louis said.

She led Louis to a wood-and-fern bar near the court-house called The Guilty Party. Susan left to make a call. Louis waited, stirring three packets of sugar into his coffee. He glanced around the cramped room. It was packed with blue-suited lawyers and grim civilians wearing jury buttons.

When she came back to the table, she sat down with an irritated sigh and took a quick drink of her coffee.

"Problem back at the office?" Louis asked politely.

"Look, Mr. Kincaid, I don't have time to sit around in cafes sipping cappucinos."

"It's just bad bar coffee."

"Let's just get to the point," she said. "What did Jack Cade tell you?"

Louis sat back in his chair. "Not much. That he didn't kill Spencer Duvall."

"Anything else?"

"That he didn't rape and kill that girl twenty years ago either."

She was sitting with her back to the window and he couldn't make out much of her features in the glare of the sun—except for her frown. That he could see clearly.

"Why would you ask him about that?" she asked.

"The man was convicted. Why wouldn't I?"

"It's totally irrelevant. Surely, even a PI can see that."

He let the barb go. "Curiosity then, I guess."

She was squinting at him, like she thought he was crazy. She started to say something but was interrupted by her beeper going off. With an impatient sigh, she grabbed it. Her expression changed as she read the number, her mouth dropping open slightly. In the back light, Louis couldn't tell if she was upset or just surprised.

"Excuse me," she muttered, rising quickly.

Louis watched as she went to the pay phone again. She punched in a number and with a look at Louis, turned her back. A minute later she was back.

"I'm sorry—" she began.

"Would you mind moving your chair?" Louis asked.

She looked at him. "What?"

He pointed at the window. "The glare from the window. I like to see who I'm talking to."

She craned her neck to look at the window then back at Louis. When she shifted her chair into the shadows Louis could see that something had changed, like a mask had slipped, leaving her face unprotected.

Back in the police station lobby, she had seemed older, pushing forty or so. But he could see now she was probably younger, with one of those hard-to-guess faces that some women were blessed with. Smooth skin maybe a half-shade darker than his own tan, a round face with a high forehead, generous mouth and eyes the shape and color of toasted almonds. Her hair ... maybe that was what made her look older. It was black with brown streaks, swept up in one of those hard French twisty things, but with pieces of it falling out the back, like she hadn't had a lot of time to work on it that morning.

Susan Outlaw ... shit, what a name for a defense attorney.

"I'm sorry for the interruption," she began again.

"Boss got you on a short leash?"

"No, it was my son. Or his principal rather."

She seemed distracted. Louis started to ask if the kid was in trouble at school, but something in her expression told him not to. He remembered suddenly the time his foster mother Frances had been summoned to school when he was in the sixth grade. A kid had called him an orphan and Louis had taken a swing at him with a geography book, splitting his lip. Later that night, as Louis picked at his dinner, Phillip spoke to him quietly but firmly.

You didn't even know what the word 'orphan' meant,

Louis. Next time, make sure you know what you're fighting for. Learn to use your brains, not your fists.

And Frances: *I don't know, Phil, sometimes a good punch in the mouth is more effective.*

"Now look, Mr. Kincaid," Susan said, drawing him back.

"Louis. It's Louis, okay?"

She stared at him. He had the feeling he wasn't going to be invited to call her Susan any time soon. He glanced at the gold band on her left hand and found himself wondering what Mr. Outlaw called her. Somehow she didn't look like she'd answer to Sue or Susie.

"I've had two days—just two days—to get up to speed on Jack Cade's case," she said. "I can't be wasting time worrying about you or anyone else getting in my way."

"Getting in your way?" Louis said. "I would think you'd welcome the help."

"I don't need help," she said evenly.

"I never saw a public defender that didn't need help."

She was staring at him again, daggers this time, like she was sizing him up—age, experience—and finding him lacking. It irritated the hell out of him, but he wasn't about to take the bait.

"How long have you been in the PI business?" she asked finally.

"Almost a year," he said.

She gave a short scornful laugh, reaching in her briefcase for something.

"I was a cop before this," he said. Probably too quickly.

She froze, then slowly shook her head. "I should have known," she said.

"What's that supposed to mean?"

"It's written all over you."

"Bullshit." Now he was getting pissed.

She waved a hand of dismissal. "The walk, the talk. The eyes. Yeah, especially your eyes."

She snapped the briefcase closed and he realized she was getting ready to leave. He didn't want her to leave; he needed her to tell him things about Jack Cade. Like a good reason why he should take his case.

"Do you think your client is innocent?" Louis asked.

Susan was half out of the chair and she leveled her eyes at him and slowly sat back down.

"Lawyers have to believe their clients," she said.

"No they don't. They just have to believe in the law."

"Now you're sounding like a lawyer," she said.

He thought about telling her that he was pre-law in college, but there was no way it wouldn't sound like chest-beating at this point.

"But you're a cop, with a cop brain," she added. She rose, smoothing back the wayward strand of hair again. She was standing in that back light again and he had to squint to look up at her. She was tall, maybe five-nine, with a generous body that he suspected she thought boxy dark suits could hide.

"Which means what?" he asked.

"Which means that you think if he is arrested he must surely be guilty. And like the rest of the scum who make cops' lives miserable, he should probably rot in hell."

"I haven't even decided to take this case," he said.

She slipped the strap of her purse over the shoulder of her red suit. "Well, I can't stop Ronnie Cade from hiring you," she said. "Just don't get in my way."

She turned, her heels clicking on the terrazzo floor as she headed out the door. He picked up the mug and took a drink, grimacing at the taste of the muddy coffee.

It hit him then that she was right.

His first impression of Jack Cade had been that he was probably guilty. Not just of the rape and murder of the girl twenty years ago but also of shooting Spencer Duvall.

He had been a cop for only three years, but it had left its mark, making him turn a deaf ear to the protests of dirtbags as he shoved them into the backs of patrol cars. They were thieves, druggies, wife-beaters and murderers. The harmless ones were liars who cut corners, and the worst ones were sociopaths who cut their evil swathes through other people's lives. But they were all dirtbags who broke the law and still got a good night's sleep afterward. And yeah, every single one of them was innocent.

Other people, civilians, didn't see it the way cops did. Neither did people like Susan Outlaw. She was an attorney. No, a *defense* attorney, who had to see the world and its lowlifes in a different light just so she could collect a paycheck and pay her rent. He had always wondered how defense lawyers did it. What, did they count leeches to get to sleep at night?

The walk, the talk. The eyes. Yeah, especially your eyes.

Louis took another drink of coffee.

Okay, so he still had cop eyes.

But he wasn't a cop any more.

He glanced at his watch. Shit. It was twelve-thirty. He was supposed to meet Mobley at O'Sullivan's. A ripple of laughter drew his attention to a nearby table, where a clot of men in suits were huddled over beers, sleek briefcases sitting at their feet like obedient pet dogs. Lawyers.

Louis shook his head. It hit him in that second: If he took Jack Cade's case, he would have to go over to the other side for the first time in his life.

Maybe that was why he hadn't slept last night.

He tossed some bills on the table and left.

Chapter Five

He walked the four blocks to O'Sullivan's. The old bar was a stone's throw from the police station and walking distance from the sheriff's office, an easy stop for deputies after shifts.

Louis eased inside, blinking to adjust to the darkness. He had been in the bar a few times before, when he first arrived in Fort Myers. He had come hoping to find some conversation and a sense of camaraderie. And at first, when he was riding the wave of the serial killer case, he had found acceptance among the cops.

But his stature had faded quickly when the *News-Press* had run a follow-up profile on him. In the article, the whole Michigan thing had come out and suddenly conversation in O'Sullivan's wasn't so friendly. Zach back at the sheriff's office was the exception; most the cops were like Deputy Lovett in the elevator, treating him like he didn't exist.

Louis scanned the crowd for Mobley. He spotted

him leaning over the jukebox. Mobley's blond hair was wind-blown, his tan face glowing blue in the jukebox lights. He was off-duty, wearing a white polo shirt and creased black trousers that looked like they had been req'd from the uniform room at the sheriff's office.

Louis moved through the crowd toward him. Mobley glanced at him, then looked away.

"I expected you a half-hour ago," Mobley said.

"Got tied up."

Mobley fed a dollar bill into the jukebox and started punching numbers.

"What's your interest in Cade?" he asked without looking up.

"His kid, Ronnie, wants to hire me."

Mobley's finger paused over a button, then he poked at it hard. "Didn't think the Cades had any money."

Louis didn't reply. Mobley picked up his beer off the top of the jukebox and started back to his table, nodding at Louis to follow. The table in the back was cluttered with empty beer bottles, crumpled napkins and ashtrays brimming with butts. The two cops sitting there looked up at Louis, then their eyes slid to Mobley.

"Since when did this table go civilian, Sheriff?" one asked.

"Since I said so. Take a piss break, guys."

The men ambled off toward the pool table. Mobley motioned for Louis to sit down.

"What do you drink?" Mobley asked.

"Heineken."

Mobley went to the bar and returned with two beers. He slid in the booth across from Louis and finished off his first beer in one long drink then reached for the fresh one.

"What's this about, Sheriff?" Louis asked. "You going to bust my chops just because I saw Cade?"

"There's a lot of interest in this case, from Tallahassee on down. Sandusky wants to know who the players are, that's all.'' Mobley eyed him over the lip of the bottle. ''Are you a player?''

Louis hesitated. He didn't like Lance Mobley. Worse, he didn't respect him. The guy was a political animal who ran his department like a personal fiefdom. Louis was tempted to use this Cade thing just to piss him off.

''It sounds like you're circling the wagons, Sheriff.''

''You didn't answer my question.''

''I don't know.''

''You don't know? You don't *know* if you're working for Cade?''

Louis took a drink of beer.

Mobley sat back, laying his arm across the back of the booth. ''Have you done any homework on this yet, Kincaid?''

''Not much.''

''Well, let me give you a quick history lesson then,'' Mobley said. ''Jack Cade raped and murdered a girl named Kitty Jagger back in 1966. They had him dead to rights. His slimeball lawyer, the late Spencer Duvall, managed to finagle a plea bargain for him for manslaughter.''

Louis remained silent.

Mobley shook his head. ''The asshole should've fried to a crisp for what he did to that girl. Instead, he gets a lousy twenty years. A fucking gift. Then what does he do? Gets out and one week later shoots the goddamn lawyer who saved his ass in the first place.''

''He says he didn't do it.''

''Yeah, he said that twenty years ago, too, but he took the plea quick enough.''

''What do you have on him?''

''His lawyer has all that. Talk to her,'' Mobley said.

''I'd rather hear it from you.''

A slow grin came over Mobley's face. ''So you've met Susan Outlaw.''

"Yeah, this afternoon."

"We don't like her much around here, you know."

"She's just doing her job," Louis said.

Mobley's smile faded. "Yeah, I suppose. But no one's going to plead Cade down this time. Not even by a day. He's going to fry this time."

Louis leaned forward, resting his elbows on the table. "What do you have?"

"Why should I give you anything?"

"Professional courtesy?"

"You're not a professional. You don't have a badge. You don't even have that PI license yet."

"Look, I know you don't like me—"

"Most the guys in here don't like you."

"That shouldn't change how you do your job, Sheriff," Louis said.

Mobley leaned back in the booth again, considering him carefully. Louis took advantage of the pause.

"All right, just tell me what I'm up against," he said.

Mobley glanced around the bar, then he let out a long, beer-scented sigh. "We got witnesses who heard him threaten Duvall the morning of the murder. We got a witness who says he saw Cade that night hanging around the building. We got his prints on Duvall's desk."

"He doesn't deny being in the office. He had an appointment."

"We also found his prints on the credenza *behind* Duvall's desk."

"What about other prints?"

"Hundreds. Other lawyers, the secretary and the partner, the wife. But no one suspicious."

Louis picked up his beer.

"Plus," Mobley added, "we got one of his Raiford buddies telling us Cade bragged about how he was going to get back at Duvall when he got out."

"Did Cade offer an alibi?" Louis asked.

"Yeah, a real dandy. He and his kid were home watching TV."

Louis took a drink, averting his eyes.

Mobley leaned forward. "You know what you're really up against, Kincaid? The dirtbag factor. Jack Cade was, is, and always will be a dirtbag. He killed once and he did it again. People can't get beyond that. And our esteemed prosecutor, Vern Sandusky, knows it. He's on his white horse, making up for the shitty system that let Cade off so light twenty years ago."

Louis picked up the napkin and wiped the condensation off the side of the Heineken bottle. "Sounds like a slam-dunk."

"That's for sure."

Louis stood up slowly. "Thanks for the info."

"Don't get yourself dirty with this, Kincaid."

Louis paused, looking down at Mobley. He could see the Busch logo in his pupils.

"You looking for more clippings for your scrapbook, Kincaid, is that it?" Mobley said. "Well, you might get some more headlines working this case, but you're not going to win any popularity contests defending that asshole."

"I'm not out to win anything, Sheriff."

"Suit yourself," he said, picking up his beer.

Louis started away.

"Get your fucking PI license, Kincaid," Mobley called out, loud enough for the whole bar to hear.

The rain was moving in. Louis could see it, advancing across the gulf like a pale gray scrim falling across a stage. When it reached shore, it brought a cool breeze that wafted through the screens and set the auger shell wind chimes clicking like old bones.

Louis had been watching a small brown lizard do

pushups on the screen, and as the rain hit, it sent the lizard scurrying for cover. Issy launched herself at the screen after it.

"Hey, knock it off," Louis yelled at the cat. But both creatures had disappeared.

Louis stared dismally at the sagging screen. It had torn free of the wood frame in the corner. He debated whether to go in and get a knife and try to poke it back in, but he knew Issy would just tear it up again.

Damn Pierre. The little weasel landlord expected him to act as a security guard for a break in the rent, but the damn cottage was falling apart and he wouldn't repair a friggin' thing.

The rain was picking up force, pounding on the roof now. Louis's eyes drifted upward. If this kept up, he would have to move the bed again.

With a sigh, he put on his glasses and turned his attention back to the newspaper clippings he had just started reading.

After leaving Mobley, he had gone to the public library and pulled copies of everything to do with the Duvall murder case. It wasn't much, but he needed to get the basic facts and there was no way he was going to get his hands on any police files. Neither Mobley or Susan Outlaw were going to help that account.

He turned his attention back to the *News-Press* articles. Spencer Duvall's body had been found by his secretary, Eleanor Silvestri, when she came to work at eight A.M. the next morning. According to the medical examiner, Duvall had been shot once in the head, the time of death estimated around nine-thirty P.M. Duvall and his secretary had been alone in the office, working late, but she left at about nine. Jack Cade had visited Duvall's office earlier in the day and been overheard making threats to the attorney.

Louis moved on to the most recent article about Cade's arraignment. He paused, seeing Susan Outlaw's name. She said she would not seek a change of venue, even given Cade's history. "What happened twenty years ago has no bearing whatsoever on my client's current legal situation," she was quoted as saying.

Man, was this woman naive or just plain dumb?

There were other older articles about Spencer Duvall, including a feature that detailed his rise to one of the state's highest-profile criminal lawyers, with an estimated net worth of 5.3 million. His professional style had earned him the nickname The Tortoise. He was plodding and thorough—and he never lost.

Finally, there was an old copy of *Gulfshore Life*. It was a heavy glossy that advertised itself as "The Magazine of Southwest Florida" but was more a bible of the good life, stuffed with ads for art galleries, plastic surgeons and financial advisers.

The magazine had an article about a renovation at the Thomas Edison House, led by the historical society. The Duvalls were mentioned as the project's leading contributor, coughing up a cool quarter mil.

The librarian had also marked another page in the back. It was a society column called *The Circuit*, and it took Louis a minute to find the Duvalls in one of the color group photographs. It was one of those typical society snaps, a line-em-up-shoot-em-down, with the subjects posed, champagne glasses in hand, faces frozen in smiles.

It was a Christmas party of some kind, and there were eight people in the photograph, all in gowns and tuxes. He picked out Candace Duvall in the front—small, tanned and attractive with blond hair sleekly upswept, a big toothy smile, dressed in strapless red with diamonds at her neck and ears. Spencer Duvall towered at her side, a good-looking man of about forty-five, with thinning sandy hair over a wide forehead and intelligent dark eyes behind stylish wire-rimmed glasses. In contrast to his wife, he was somber, unsmiling. He looked more like a befuddled physics professor than a dogged defense attorney.

Louis set the articles aside and looked out to the gulf. The rain was letting up, the afternoon sun slanting low through a slit in the gray clouds. The odor of low tide hung in the air, that familiar brew of kelp, brine and rotting things.

Why was he doing this? He didn't want this case. Why was he even reading these damn articles?

He felt something touch his bare ankles and looked down to see Issy staring up at him.

"What?" he said.

The cat didn't move.

"Food? Is that it?" He pushed himself out of the chair and the cat followed him into the kitchen. He shook some Tender Vittles into a bowl on the floor. He leaned against the sink, thinking of Ronnie Cade, about what he had said about losing his father for twenty years.

Shit, at least Jack Cade was still alive.

The dampness was creeping through the cabin. Louis rubbed his hands over the thin cotton of his T-shirt. He went into the bedroom to get a sweatshirt.

At the dresser, he rummaged through the drawers until he found an old University of Michigan sweatshirt. He pulled it on. He was about to close the drawer when he paused.

The manila envelope was tucked under some old shirts. He had forgotten that he had put it there.

He pulled it out and undid the clasp. He upended the contents onto the top of the dresser. There were only a handful of photographs, a couple from college, a few of Phillip and Frances Lawrence, one of Bessie, the old woman who had rented him a room in Black Pool, Mississippi. A faded portrait of his mother when she was eighteen, a snapshot of his sister, Yolanda, and another of his brother, Robert.

Then, he found it. A small square in black and white, its edges pinked in the old style of the fifties. A white man, standing on a porch, wearing overalls and a straw hat that shielded his face. The image was blurred slightly, like the man had been moving just as the picture was snapped.

He hadn't looked at the photograph in a long time, so long in fact that he half-expected the man in the picture to age. But he never did. He was always exactly the same.

Louis stared at his father, his thumb rubbing the slick surface.

Then he gathered up the photos and put them away. Going back to the kitchen, he scanned the counter and spotted the business card laying next to the phone.

He picked up the phonc and dialed Ronnie Cade's number.

Chapter Six

The sky was still bruised with clouds by the time Louis made his way across the causeway to Sereno Key. The Dodies lived on the key, so he knew his way around, and he headed the Mustang quickly through the small town center and up to the north end, looking for Mantanzas Trail. Sereno Key was a small island, comprised of trailer parks, marinas and neat little canal-laced retiree neighborhoods like where the Dodies lived. The key also was the home to half a dozen wholesale nurseries that grew native palms for the landscapers replanting the scorched-earth tract-home developments springing up around Fort Myers. There was a building boom going on in Southwest Florida, and money was being made digging up century-old oak trees and replacing them with scraggly palms.

But prosperity had apparently bypassed J.C. Landscape. The sign that greeted Louis outside the chain-link gate said WE MEET ALL YOUR LANDSCAPING NEEDS, but what he saw suggested Ronnie Cade's business could barely meet its own.

The grounds, puddled from the rain, were dotted with scrubby palm trees and plats of plants struggling to stay upright. A five-foot pile of black plastic pots was heaped against a shed next to pallets of mulch rotting in their faded bags. A small tan and black dog was laying near the door, chained to the shed, and it raised its snout to sniff the air as Louis got out of the Mustang, then went back to sleep. The smell of gasoline and manure hung in the air.

Ronnie Cade had heard the Mustang's door and came out of the shed, wiping his hands on a dirty rag.

"You found the place," Ronnie said.

"It wasn't hard." Louis looked around. There was a double-wide trailer parked behind the shed. It was fronted by a small concrete patio that held a barbecue grill and some plastic chairs clustered around an old wooden electrical spool. Huge purple thunderheads were piling up again in the west.

"You have a lot of land here," Louis said.

Ronnie squinted out over the grounds. "Yeah, ten acres," he said flatly. "Come on inside. We can talk while I finish up."

Louis followed, stepping over the comatose dog. Inside, it was cool and smelled of cut grass. The shed was filled with bags of fertilizer, compost, power mowers, edgers and other gardening tools. Ronnie went to a workbench, where the guts of a gas-powered leaf blower lay exposed under the glare of a florescent light.

"I was surprised when you called," Ronnie said, picking up a screwdriver. "I thought when I didn't hear from you, you decided to blow me off."

"I went and saw your father," Louis said.

Ronnie turned to look at him, but then went back to poking the screwdriver in the blower. "So?"

"He didn't give me any compelling reason to take your case."

"Then what are you doing here?"

"Maybe you can."

"Can what?"

"Give me a reason."

"I already did. I told you, my father is innocent."

"What about twenty years ago?" Louis said.

Ronnie turned and stared at him. "I don't want to talk about that."

"Well, I need—"

Ronnie pointed the screwdriver at Louis. "Look, it doesn't matter. I don't want to talk about it."

Louis heard a motor outside and the sound of air brakes releasing. He looked out the door and saw a yellow school bus pulling away down Mantanzas Trail.

A moment later, a boy came to the door, stopping in the threshold when he saw Louis. He was about thirteen, gangly, with unruly dark hair and sunburned arms exposed in his Van Halen T-shirt.

"Hey, Dad, what are you doing home? I thought you were cutting Bay Beach today?" he asked, eyeing Louis.

"Got rained out. What about you?"

"Teacher work day. Half day." The dog had come in, and the boy dropped his backpack to scratch its ears.

"Go get changed," Ronnie said. "I need some help loading that sod before it starts raining again."

"Oh, man . . ."

"No lip, you hear?"

He heaved a sigh. "I'm hungry."

Ronnie wiped a hand over his brow. "Okay, there's some of those pizza things left. Then get back out here, okay?"

"Do I nuke 'em on high?"

"No. Half-power or they splatter up the inside."

With a lingering look at Louis, the boy left, the dog trailing after.

"Your son?" Louis asked.

Ronnie nodded, concentrating again on the leaf blower.

Louis was thinking how much the boy looked like Jack Cade. He remembered that Ronnie had said he lived with his son and wondered if the boy's mother was in the picture. He had the feeling she wasn't; there was something about this place that had the forlorn aura of men living alone.

"He helps you around here, I take it?" he asked.

"Eric? Yeah. He's a good kid. Not like me when I was his age. I gave my dad a lot of shit. He even had to bail me out of jail once when I did something stupid. But he kept me straight after that. Maybe that's why I feel I owe him this now."

Ronnie glanced at him. "You got any kids?"

Louis shook his head quickly.

"I raised Eric by myself," Ronnie said, his fingers deep in the blower's greasy bowels. "His mother split when he was seven. Hand me those pliers, will you?"

Louis scanned the bench and held out the pliers. Ronnie's face was screwed in concentration as he took another stab at the wounded motor. Finally, he threw the pliers down.

"Fuck! The fucking thing is stripped. Shit!"

He ran a hand over his brow and took a step back, staring at the mess of metal on the bench. He looked at Louis and gestured to the bench. "The fucker's shot!"

Ronnie spun and kicked at a metal stool, sending it crashing against the wall. He stood there for a moment, hands on his hips, head bowed. Then he turned to Louis.

"I can't pay you," he said, his voice strained.

Louis held out his hand. "Look, Cade—"

"No, you're not hearing me. That five hundred I said I'd pay you?" Ronnie was shaking his head. "I haven't got it, man! I have two-hundred and thirty-three dollars in my checking account and if I don't use it to buy a fucking new blower, I can't go to work tomorrow!"

Louis saw something move in the corner of his eye and glanced over to see Eric Cade standing at the door. He had changed into cutoffs and a frayed man's dress shirt that looked too big for him. He was holding a pair of leather work gloves, staring at his father.

Ronnie saw him and look a deep breath. "Eric, go get started. I'll be there in a minute."

The boy hesitated.

"Go! Now!"

The boy spun and disappeared outside. A low rumble of thunder came from the west.

"Shit," Ronnie whispered.

Louis stood there, not knowing what to say.

"I'm sorry, man," Ronnie said. "I lose it sometimes." His lips twisted into a grimaced smile. "Brat attacks, Cindy used to call them."

Ronnie's eyes focused again on the leaf blower on the bench and came back to Louis. "They want half a million bail for my dad," he said.

"You'd only have to come up with fifty thousand," Louis said.

"Fifty thousand," Ronnie said softly, his eyes still on the leaf blower. "I was thinking I could get a mortgage. The land's free and clear. It's the only thing I own, except my truck and that piece of shit trailer."

Louis didn't know how mortgages worked, but he suspected that it would be tough for a man like Ronnie to get a bank to even listen to him. It started to rain, a soft tattoo on the roof of the woodshed.

"I don't want to lose this place," Ronnie said.

"I can understand that," Louis said.

"My dad bought this land in the fifties after he got back from Korea," Ronnie said. "There was nothing on the key in those days, but he knew it was going to be worth something someday. He was always good at taking care of plants, so he started growing some palm trees. We were the first landscaping business on Sereno."

Ronnie picked up the screwdriver again, making a half-hearted poke at the metal. "It was tough at first, but Dad and me, we made it work. After a couple years, we had contracts at the golf courses and built up a good client base taking care of the yards over in Hyde Park."

Louis recognized the name. It was a neighborhood of old homes along the Caloosahatchee River, an enclave of grace that had survived the financial vagaries that plagued Fort Myers' downtown core.

"What happened?" Louis asked.

Ronnie's hand paused over the metal, but he didn't look up. "What happened?" he said. "They found that girl's body in the dump, that's what happened. Everything changed after that day."

Louis wished he had more details about the Jagger case. "What made them think your father killed her?" he asked.

Ronnie was silent.

"Ronnie?"

"A tool," he said. "They found one of his tools next to her body."

The rain had stopped. Louis could hear a grunting sound out in the yard. Through the open door, he caught a glimpse of Eric Cade stacking slabs of sod onto a flatbed.

"He didn't do it," Ronnie said softly. "I don't know much else about what happened but I know that much. He didn't do it."

Eric Cade appeared at the door, the front of his shirt

streaked with mud. "Dad, you want that Bahia grass loaded too?"

"Yeah, we gotta take it over to Frencko this afternoon."

Eric was staring at Louis, brows knitted slightly.

"Go finish up," Ronnie said quietly. When the boy didn't move, Ronnie added, "Go finish up and I'll let you drive out to the corner."

Eric's face lit up. "You mean it?"

Ronnie smiled slightly. "I'll be there in a minute and we'll head out."

Eric left. Ronnie put down the screwdriver and turned to Louis. "Look, I don't know what the bank is going to say about the mortgage thing. If that doesn't pan out, there's this developer that's been bugging me. If I have to, I'll sell off some of the land." He paused. "I'll find a way to pay you."

Louis hesitated. "All right. I'll see what I can do."

Ronnie didn't smile, but wiped his hand on his jeans, then held it out. Louis shook it; it was hard and calloused, the grip firm.

"I need your help with something," Louis said.

"What's that?"

"Susan Outlaw," Louis said. "I need you to run interference for me."

Ronnie nodded slightly. "I'll talk to her."

A truck's engine roared to life outside, followed by a horn beeping. Louis looked out the door and saw Eric Cade sitting behind the steering wheel of the truck.

"I gotta get going," Ronnie said.

Louis followed him out into the yard. Ronnie paused by the passenger door of the old truck, his eyes traveling over the grounds of the nursery. "I was just trying to keep things afloat until Dad came back," he said. "Things are rough right now, but they'll get better. I'll get you your money."

"I believe you," Louis said.

Ronnie got in. Eric gunned the engine. Ronnie leaned out the window and gave a tentative smile. "Thanks, man."

Louis nodded. He watched the old Ford bump out of the lot and jerk slowly up Mantanza Trail, the brake lights blinking every few feet. He took a final glance around the downtrodden nursery. He had the feeling that J.C. Landscaping wasn't the only thing Ronnie Cade was trying to keep afloat.

Chapter Seven

The elevator jerked to a stop and the door wheezed open, letting Louis out on the ninth floor. He was in a plain, uncarpeted hallway. A sign with an arrow pointed left to DUVALL AND BERNHARDT, ATTORNEYS AT LAW.

He had expected a hotshot lawyer like Spencer Duvall to have an office in one of the new buildings on Jackson Street overlooking the river. But Duvall's address turned out to be an old building on a side street just off Martin Luther King Boulevard.

He found the entrance and went in. It was nice inside compared to the exterior. Hushed, tasteful, lots of dark mahogany and framed prints of English hunting scenes. The blue carpet gave like a sponge. The receptionist's desk was empty, but there was a lipstick-ringed Garfield coffee mug on it.

Louis went to the window. Nothing to see but the tarred and tiled roofs of downtown Fort Myers with a glimpse of the green-gray Caloosahatchee beyond. No view for the hotshot either.

"Can I help you?"

Louis turned and looked down at a tiny woman with a fluff of gray hair. She was in her sixties, wearing a tan suit with glasses dangling from a chain around her neck.

"I'm Louis Kincaid. I have an appointment with Mr. Bernhardt," Louis said.

The woman's eyes swept over him. "Mr. Bernhardt had to leave early. I called your office but there was no answer."

Office . . . it was his home phone. He had to get an answering machine. He stifled a sigh at the wasted trip. He was hoping to at least get a look at Duvall's office. He glanced at the closed door over the secretary's shoulder. Damn Bernhardt. He was probably in there, ducking him.

He thought about trying a smile, but then realized it wasn't going to break the ice with this old biddy. "Look," he said, "I really need to see Mr. Bern—"

"Ellie?"

The secretary jumped to her desk and punched a button.

"Yes?"

"Is Pearson here yet?"

"Is that your boss?" Louis asked.

The old lady ignored Louis. "No, he's not, Mr. Bernhardt," she said into the phone, "but Mr. Kincaid is."

There was no answer. The secretary hung up and gave Louis a frown. "I hate lying for him," she said.

Louis was about to speak when a man in a blue suit appeared. He was short, overweight, about fifty but looked older, with thin gray-blond hair and the ashy skin of a future coronary patient.

"Lyle Bernhardt," he said briskly, extending a hand.

Louis accepted the soft, damp handshake. "Louis Kincaid."

"I don't appreciate being strong-armed," he said.

"I had an appointment," Louis said calmly.

Bernhardt frowned. "Well, come in, then," he said, motioning Louis toward his office.

"I was hoping I could see Spencer Duvall's office," Louis said.

Bernhardt hesitated. "What? Why?"

"It's just routine, Mr. Bernhardt. Part of any investigation."

Bernhardt pursed his lips and glanced at the secretary. She was watching him closely.

"I don't think that would be proper," he said. "Besides, it's all been cleaned up now anyway."

"The scene's been cleared?" Louis asked.

"Yes, thank God. Terribly distracting, if you know what I mean. Our clients were most uncomfortable. Why don't you come into my office?"

Bernhardt led Louis into a large office done in the same pseudo-English manor style as the reception area. Louis took a chair across from Bernhardt's imposing desk. The desk was heaped with papers and fat legal files. Bernhardt stared at the piles for a moment, as if confused.

"Sorry for the mess. Things have been in such an uproar since . . ." Bernhardt's voice trailed off. "The police don't seem to appreciate the fact that business must go on no matter what."

"It was just you and Mr. Duvall, right?" Louis said.

Bernhardt nodded. "That's the way it's been for almost twenty years now. I wanted to expand, but Spencer wouldn't hear of it. Now I'm left with all of it."

"You could hire someone now," Louis offered.

Bernhardt looked at him like he was nuts. "You don't just go out and find someone overnight. At least not someone who can handle the kind of cases Spencer did.''

He was rubbing the spot between his eyebrows. ''What a mess he left me with,'' he muttered, staring at the files on the desk.

Finally, he looked up at Louis. ''Ellie said you're a private investigator. For whom?''

''Ronnie Cade.''

''Ronnie? He doesn't have any money. He's nothing but a lousy mow-and-blow guy. And his father is broke. You're wasting your time, son.''

Bernhardt made a point of looking at his watch. Louis felt himself starting to bristle.

''Just because a man's broke doesn't mean he isn't entitled to a decent defense,'' Louis said.

Bernhardt's expression was piteous. ''Oh, come on. Don't start with that liberal claptrap.''

''Jack Cade—''

''—is a lying, murdering sonofabitch who should have been electrocuted twenty years ago. If he had, my partner would still be alive right now.''

Bernhardt began rubbing vigorously at the spot between his eyebrows again.

''Your partner was the one who got Cade the plea bargain that kept him alive,'' Louis said. He could hear his words, but it was almost like someone else was saying them. Being on the other side was going to take some getting used to.

''I don't need you or anyone to remind me of that.'' Bernhardt leaned forward. ''Look, Cade is an ungrateful moron. He should have gotten down on his knees and kissed Spencer's shoes. Do I think Cade shot him? Yes, I do. He's as guilty of shooting Spencer as he was of killing that girl twenty years ago.''

''You weren't involved in that case, Mr. Bernhardt?'' Louis asked.

Bernhardt shook his head. ''Spencer was working

alone in those days. We got together about a year later. I would have never defended a man like Jack Cade. But Spencer, well, he never could resist a challenge.''

"Do you think Cade really intended to sue your partner?''

"No, he intended to kill him. Revenge is a powerful, primitive emotion, and Jack Cade is a primitive man.''

The phone intercom beeped. Bernhardt punched the button. The secretary's voice came on. "Mr. Pearson's here.''

"Send him in,'' Bernhardt said. He rose. "I'm sorry, but I have a client to see.''

Louis pushed himself out of the chair. "Thanks for your cooperation,'' he said, not bothering to keep the sarcasm out of his voice.

"Of course.''

Louis left, passing a burly man in a business suit. The door closed behind him. Louis stood there for a moment, collecting his thoughts. What there was to collect anyway.

He felt someone's eyes on him and looked over to see the secretary staring at him.

"Do you want to make another appointment?'' she asked.

"Think it will do me any good?''

"Nope.'' The intercom buzzed. "Yes, Mr. Bernhardt?''

"Ellie, where's my Rules of Court?''

"On the shelf where it always is, Mr. Bernhardt.''

"No, it's not. I looked—''

"The shelf to your left, Mr. Bernhardt.''

"What? Oh. Here it is.'' He clicked off.

She looked up at Louis. "His regular secretary is out on maternity leave. I'm filling in.''

Something clicked in Louis's head. Ellie . . . he remembered the name from the newspaper articles. Ellie Silvestri had been Duvall's secretary.

Louis watched as she busied herself with some papers. It occurred to him that she had the air of someone in mourning. The newspaper article said she had been with the firm for twenty-five years ... a long time to work for one man, longer than most marriages. He suddenly remembered that Ellie Silvestri had found Duvall's body when she came to work the next morning. Gunshot to the head. He knew what that could look like.

"Mrs. Silvestri—"

She looked up at him, surprised he knew her name. "It's Miss."

She had clear green eyes, unclouded by age. Eyes that probably didn't miss much.

"I was wondering if you'd be willing to answer a few questions," Louis began.

"About what?"

"Your boss."

Something shifted in her expression. Then, suddenly, she teared up. She yanked a Kleenex from the box on her desk.

"I'm sorry," she said.

"No need to apologize," Louis said.

She blew her nose. "What did you want to ask me?"

He wanted to ask her about finding Duvall's body, what the scene had looked like, but that was out of the question for the moment. "That elevator," he said, pointing out the glass doors. "Is it locked after hours?"

"No, the building is filled with attorneys and they come and go at all hours. The downstairs lobby is always open too."

"Did Mr. Duvall normally work late?"

She smiled wanly. "A man doesn't become a legend working a mere forty hours."

"Besides Jack Cade, did Mr. Duvall receive any threats recently? Maybe from dissatisfied clients?"

The secretary shook her head slowly. "The police

already asked me that, and that woman defense attorney.''

''What can you tell me about the relationship between Mr. Duvall and Mr. Bernhardt? How did they meet?''

''In law school at Tallahassee, I think. But they didn't become partners until 1968.'' She sighed. ''It was just Mr. Duvall and me in the beginning. It was very hard in those days, let me tell you. Mr. Duvall did all his own investigative work. He was very good at it, better than Matlock, I think. Some weeks I didn't get paid. We both ate a lot of baloney sandwiches.'' She fell silent again, lost in memories.

''But business picked up,'' Louis prodded.

She smiled slightly. ''Oh yes. Mr. Duvall was very, very good at what he did. Word got out, especially after the Cade case.''

She teared up again.

''I don't know what's going to happen now,'' she said softly, staring off at the rooftops. ''I mean, I don't know what we're going to do.''

She hadn't said it, but he could see it there in her eyes. She meant she didn't know what *she* was going to do.

''Miss Silvestri,'' Louis said gently, ''are you going to lose your job here?''

She grabbed another Kleenex. Louis felt like kicking himself. ''I'm sorry,'' he said. ''That was—''

She waved a hand. ''No, it's all right. Fact is, I'm an old dinosaur here. Lyle will let enough time go by to look decent, then he'll hire some young thing with big boobs.'' She grimaced. ''Lyle is big on appearances.''

He noticed she had switched to calling Bernhardt by his first name. ''And Spencer Duvall wasn't?'' Louis asked.

She smiled slightly as she shook her head. ''Not at

all. I mean, even after the money started coming in, Mr. Duvall didn't change. He was born and raised here. He never got the sand out of his shoes.''

Her eyes drifted to the hallway, toward Lyle Bernhardt's closed door. ''Come with me,'' she said.

''Where?''

''You said you wanted to see Mr. Duvall's office.''

He followed her down the hall, passing Lyle Bernhardt's door. At the end of the corridor, she slipped a key from her pocket and unlocked the door. She ushered Louis quickly inside, shutting the door behind them.

The office was larger than Bernhardt's, but it couldn't have looked more different. A massive old cherry desk dominated the room, with a pair of well-worn wing chairs and a small round table facing it. The floor had been left uncarpeted and the rich oak planks were covered with a softly faded Persian carpet. The lamps were brass, the walls a sun-bleached moss green paper. On the wall behind the desk, there was a framed degree from Florida State School of Law. On the wall opposite the desk was a group of old photographs of Fort Myers street scenes and a Victorian beach house. There was a scarred wood glass-front bookcase, its shelves filled not with books but with carefully displayed conch shells. The place looked more like the den of somebody's eccentric old uncle than a law office.

''Nice,'' Louis said, turning.

Ellie Silvestri was staring at the room. ''My God,'' she said softly.

''What's the matter?''

''I've never seen it this . . . clean.'' She came forward, scanning the old furniture and walls. ''Mr. Duvall was a pack rat and he hated it when I tried to tidy up. He didn't even like the cleaning lady coming in here.''

Ellie moved to the desk. It was clean; the crime scene technicians had taken everything. She was looking at the powder smudges.

"That's from the fingerprint techs," Louis said, feeling the need to explain.

Ellie nodded slightly, her eyes still scanning the room. Again, Louis wondered what Ellie Silvestri had seen that morning when she walked in.

He glanced behind the desk, trying to visualize the scene. There was an old credenza, marked with smudges. The chair was gone; the police probably had it.

The newspaper article said only that Duvall had been shot in the head. A big chunk of the Persian rug under the desk had been cut away, a bloodstain probably. Louis looked at the desk. He spotted something dark in a crack and bent down for a closer look. It was blood. Which meant Duvall probably had fallen forward.

"Damn," he said under his breath. There was nothing here to see, nothing to give him a sense of what had happened.

He smelled smoke. He turned and was surprised to see Ellie Silvestri lighting a cigarette.

"I'm sorry, do you mind?" she asked softly. "Lyle doesn't let me smoke in the office. Mr. Duvall never cared. He always let me come in here when I needed my fix."

"Go right ahead."

She drew on the cigarette, her eyes wandering over the office. Louis went to the window and pushed back the curtain. The view was of a dilapidated building next door. At least you could see the river from the lobby window. There was nothing to look at from here. But maybe that's the way Duvall wanted it; some driven people worked better with nothing pretty to distract them.

"Miss Silvestri, can we talk about the night Spencer Duvall was killed?" Louis asked, letting the curtain fall.

She looked at him beseechingly. "I already told the police . . ."

"I know. But sometimes things can be missed." Or at least he hoped so, in this case.

"You were here when Jack Cade came in for his appointment that morning?" Louis asked.

She nodded, her eyes darkening. "It was just before lunch. It was so strange seeing him. I mean, I hadn't seen that man in twenty years. He looked so different. His hair was longer. And his face had changed so much."

"Did you hear anything that was said?"

"Spencer's door was ajar so—" She paused. Louis was amazed to see her blush. Then he realized it was the first time she had called Duvall by his first name.

She pulled in a deep breath. "Jack Cade was furious. I heard him say he was going to sue Spencer for legal malpractice."

"How did Mr. Duvall react?"

"I couldn't really hear what Spencer told him because Spencer didn't raise his voice at all. Which was unusual because he could bellow back on occasion. But Spencer was quiet."

"Then what happened?"

"Cade got louder, so I went in and asked Spencer if he wanted me to call security."

"Did you?"

"I didn't have to. Jack Cade started to leave." She paused, tears springing to her eyes. "But he stopped and looked back at Spencer and said, 'I'll get you, Duvall, one way or the other.' Then he was gone."

She snuffed her cigarette out in the ashtray on the small round table.

"What happened after Cade left?"

"Nothing really. We all went back to work."

"No one else came to see him?"

"He had one appointment after Jack Cade left, but

he told me to cancel it. Spencer was in here with his door closed the rest of the day. We were preparing for the Osborne case and I figured that's why Spencer didn't come out. I stayed late to finish typing the brief.''

"What time did you leave?"

"Just before nine. I remember because I was thinking that I was going to miss *Matlock.*''

"Was there anyone else in the office?"

"No, everyone was gone."

"Did Mr. Duvall say anything to you before you left?"

"He said he was staying over and asked me to order him a sandwich from Moe's across the street."

"Staying over?"

"Spencer kept an apartment here in town. He often stayed there when he worked late because he hated driving home to Sanibel."

"So you got him a sandwich?"

She nodded slowly. "Corned beef on rye with thousand island dressing and a cream soda, same as always. Then I left."

She paused. "No, wait. That isn't right. After I brought the sandwich back, Spencer asked me to go down and get the Cade file."

Louis had been looking around the room and he turned. "He asked to see Jack Cade's old file?"

Ellie nodded. "We store the old files downstairs. I went down and got it." She nodded to the desk. "Last time I saw the Redweld, it was right there."

"Redweld?"

"Redweld. That's what we call them. It's a brand name for the file folder."

"You told the police this?"

She nodded. "I guess they took it, with all the other files and stuff that was in here."

Louis had a million other questions, but he knew Ellie Silvestri couldn't answer them. He had to get his hands on the police file, and he knew the only way he was going to do that was to go through Mobley.

Ellie was staring at the desk, arms wrapped around herself. Louis knew she was seeing Duvall's shattered head lying on top of the file.

"Miss Silvestri," he said gently, "did Mr. Duvall tell you why he needed the old file?"

She shook her head slowly. "That was the last time I saw Spencer. I mean, besides the funeral. But the casket was closed."

Suddenly, she looked tired, every bit her sixty-some years. He had one more question. He touched her arm and she looked back at him.

"Why do you think Mr. Duvall asked you to get him that old file?" Louis asked.

"I told you, he didn't say."

"I know. I was asking your opinion."

She drew in a deep breath and let it out slowly. "I've been asking myself that same question. Spencer knew Cade would get nowhere with a suit because of the statute of limitations. He had nothing to worry about from that old case." She paused, shaking her head.

"What is it?" Louis said.

"But he *was* worried," she said. "Maybe worried isn't the right word. I mean, he was fine that morning, then after Jack Cade left he stayed in here all day and I didn't even see him until I brought him the sandwich. He was upset about something."

"What do you think it was?" Louis asked.

"I thought it was because Cade threatened him. But I don't know. When he asked me to go get that old file, it was more like he was just . . ."

"What?" Louis prodded gently.

She looked at him. "Sad," she said.

Her eyes drifted to the closed door. "I'd better get back out front," she said.

He followed her back past Lyle Bernhardt's door

and out into the outer office. Ellie paused behind her desk. Louis realized she was looking at him oddly.

"You're working for Jack Cade, aren't you," she said.

Louis hesitated.

"Everybody thinks he did it," she said.

There was something in her voice and Louis had to ask, "Do you?"

"I think Jack Cade killed that girl twenty years ago. But Spencer kept Jack Cade out of the electric chair." Her brows knitted. "Why would you kill the man who saved your life?"

Louis was silent for a moment. "Miss Silvestri, you probably knew Spencer Duvall better than anyone on earth. If you were me, who would you talk to?"

"What do you mean?"

"Who else would want Spencer Duvall dead?"

Ellie trained her green eyes on Louis. "Candace?"

Louis tried not to let his disappointment show. The old thing had seen too many episodes of *Matlock.* "What makes you suspect Mr. Duvall's wife?"

"She wasn't very good to him," Ellie said, her mouth pulling into a thin line. "Personally, I think she's crazy."

Oh great. Overly protective secretary secretly in love with powerful boss and hates his wife. Episode 502.

"Spencer was going to divorce her," Ellie said.

Louis couldn't hide his surprise. "He told you this?"

"Well, no, but I knew something was wrong between them," Ellie said. "He had been staying at the apartment more and more." She paused. "She was here that morning."

"The day Spencer was shot?"

Ellie nodded. "I was shocked to see her. She never came down here unless she had to. She never even called. Not like she used to when they were first married. He married her right after college, you know. I thought it was strange to get divorced after all that time.''

Louis shook his head. "But you have no proof your boss was getting a divorce."

Ellie was staring at the desk. "Wait," she said. "I made an appointment for him. It was with another lawyer here in town, a man named Brian Brenner. He handles a lot of divorces."

"They could have just been meeting for lunch," Louis said.

Ellie looked dubious. "No, I knew Spencer. Something was wrong at home."

"Did Mr. Duvall keep the appointment with the other lawyer?" Louis asked.

"No, it was for the following week. I'd look it up for you, but the police took Spencer's appointment book."

Louis heard voices and turned to see Bernhardt coming down the hall, leading his client out. Bernhardt's eyes darted between Louis and Ellie.

"I need to see you. Now," he said to Ellie. Bernhardt went back down the hall to his office. Ellie let out a big sigh.

"Are you going to get in trouble for this?" Louis asked.

"I don't care," she said with a shrug. "I could never work for a man like Lyle. Maybe I'll retire. My daughter lives over in Clewiston and says she has a room ready for me." She paused, her green eyes hopeful. "I've never been there. Have you?"

Louis shook his head.

"Clewiston," she said softly. "I think I'd miss the water." She started toward Bernhardt's door.

"Thank you," Louis said.

"For what?"

"For helping me. You didn't have to, and I appreciate it."

She hesitated. "Do you believe Jack Cade killed Spencer?"

"I believe a man has a right to be believed until the evidence proves he shouldn't be."

She gave him a small smile. "That sounds like something Spencer would say."

Chapter Eight

When Louis called Brian Brenner's office, his secretary told him that Brenner had already left for the day and wasn't expected back in the office for several days. Louis quickly concocted a lie that he was an old college friend in town only for a day. The secretary obligingly offered up the information that Brian had gone to the family home on Shaddlelee Lane to meet a real estate appraiser and that Louis could still catch him there if he hurried.

Shaddlelee Lane turned out to be just south of downtown, in an old residential enclave sandwiched between McGregor Boulevard and the river. The lane, paralleling the river, was dense with old-growth trees and lined with gracious homes. Most weren't large, but their lots were, great sweeps of tamed jungle that buffered them from their neighbors' windows and brought back an air of a slower time.

Louis drove slowly, looking for a FOR SALE sign. He

didn't see one, but saw a wrought iron gate with a large B on it. There was a small weathered tile plaque on one of the stone pillars that said CASA COLIBRI. The gate was open and at the end of the long driveway, Louis could see a large home with a black BMW parked in front.

"What the hell," he murmured, and swung the car in. He pulled up next to the black car and killed the engine.

He got out. He saw no one, but the Beemer's vanity plate said B2. He thought about calling out Brenner's name, but the quiet was so intimidating he decided against it. He looked around.

The grounds were a riot of tropical vegetation—thickets of purple bougainvillea, gaudy crotons, hibiscus trees with their pink ballerina-skirt blossoms, orange trees stooped with fruit, and palms of every size and shape. It looked like Eden after everyone had left.

The house itself was three stories, Mediterranean in style, with wrought iron balconies, arched doorways and fanciful turrets. The white stucco was peeling and many of the windows were shuttered. It was obvious that someone had once taken great care to build it—it was there in the details, the Spanish tile borders, the leaded windows, the coral fountain topped with a hummingbird. But like the grounds, there was a forsaken feel about the house.

The sound of footsteps on the crushed shell drive made him turn.

"It's about time," the man said firmly.

He was tall, in his mid-thirties, thinning brown hair around a large tanned face. Stylish Bolle sunglasses and a suit that looked too expensive for a real estate appraiser. Brian Brenner, Louis decided.

"Mr. Brenner?"

"I thought Janice was coming," Brenner said.

"I'm not the appraiser," Louis said. "I'm a private investigator."

Brenner stared at him through the iridescent sunglasses.

"I called your office," Louis said, "but they said you were going out of town and I had to talk to you."

"About what?"

"Spencer Duvall."

Not a twitch in Brenner's face.

"You have time to talk now?"

Brenner consulted his gold Patek Philippe. "I'm afraid I don't. I have to take care of this." He flapped an impatient hand up at the house.

"Well, it looks like your appraiser is running a little late," Louis said.

Brenner adjusted his sunglasses. "You're a PI? I've never seen you before. Where did Susan find you?"

Okay, he would let him think he was working for Susan Outlaw. Lawyers ran in packs, even if they were on opposite sides.

"I've only been in town a couple months."

"Who did you say you were?"

"Kincaid. Louis." He was glad that Brenner didn't seem to recognize his name.

"All right," Brenner said, "but we'll have to talk while I walk. I've got to check out the inside. We've had some break-ins here since it's been vacant."

Louis waited while Brenner unlocked the heavy wood front door. They stepped into the dim, cool interior.

The small, circular foyer had an iron staircase spiraling upward. Beyond, Louis could see a living room with large arched windows, shuttered against the light. The place smelled musty and wet. Louis thought of his cottage with its leaky roof.

Brenner had taken off his sunglasses and was scanning the walls. "Jesus," he said softly. "I'd forgotten what a mess this place was."

"Nice old house," Louis said, trying to prick Brenner's impatience with some small talk.

Brenner didn't say anything.

"Why are you selling it?"

Brenner was picking at some crumbling plaster and he looked over at Louis. "You're kidding, right?"

Louis shrugged. "I like old things."

"The land is worth about two-point-five in this market. The house is a tear down."

Brenner walked away, heading to the living room. Louis followed.

"Look at that," Brenner said. "Damn kids."

Someone had spray-painted an obscenity on the wall.

Brenner's gaze came back to Louis. "What did you want to know about Spencer Duvall?"

"He had an appointment to see you," Louis said.

Brenner was staring at the coral rock fireplace, dusty with soot and cobwebs. "Yes, but then he was murdered."

"Were you handling his divorce?"

Brenner turned. "Who said Spencer was getting a divorce?"

Louis cocked an eyebrow at him.

Brenner sighed. "Okay, Spencer was coming in to draw up the papers."

"Did his wife know?"

Brenner let one beat go by. "No."

"Why not?"

"I can't take this," Brenner said, pulling out a Kleenex. "I'm allergic to mold. Let's go outside."

Brenner unlocked a French door. It creaked open and they stepped back out into the sunshine. Brenner paused on the flagstone patio to blow his nose. A broad, overgrown lawn sloped gently away from the house.

Beyond, Louis could see a dock with a small boathouse on the river.

"I guess I better go see if the seawall is still there," Brenner said, starting down the lawn.

Louis followed. "Why didn't Duvall tell his wife he was initiating divorce proceedings?" he asked.

"You'd have to know Candace to understand," Brenner said as he walked. "She was hell to live with. Spencer was going to tell her, but he wanted to get his financial ducks in order first. He didn't want to put up with her moods any longer than he had to."

"They knew each other since college," Louis said. "I find it hard to believe she didn't know her husband was dumping her."

"Spencer was an attorney. He knew how to keep a secret."

"Like another woman?"

Brenner stopped and looked at Louis. "Spencer?" He smiled slightly. "No, there was no other woman in Spencer's life."

"You were good friends?"

"Not particularly. We crossed paths socially, but nothing more really." Brenner started toward the river.

"So how can you be so sure?"

Brenner stopped again. With his big head and sunglasses, he looked like a fly. "Spencer wasn't the type, believe me."

They were standing near a swimming pool, half-filled with still, green water. Brenner's eyes drifted to the cabana. The broken windows of the cabana stared back forlornly.

"Kids," Louis said.

"What?" Brenner said, looking at him.

"Kids," Louis repeated, nodding toward the broken windows.

"Yeah," Brenner muttered.

The faint sound of a car horn carried out to them

from up by the house. Louis and Brenner both looked back. A moment later, a blond woman in a green suit appeared at the open French door. She was holding a hand over her eyes, looking their way.

"I have to go," Brenner said.

He didn't wait for Louis to answer. He hurried back up the path to where the appraiser waited. They disappeared into the house.

Louis stood there, squinting in the bright sun. Well, at least he knew for sure about the divorce. Now he just had to find out if Candace Duvall did.

At the Sanibel-Captiva toll booth, Louis stopped to show his resident badge and then drove on over the causeway. He turned off Periwinkle Way, looking for the Duvall home. Bayview Lane turned out to be a secluded street, buffered on one side by mangroves and lined with waterfront homes on the other.

He slowed the Mustang in front of an open gate. He had considered calling ahead, but he had finally decided to just show up. He wanted to meet Candace Duvall cold, with no time for her to prepare neat little answers.

He turned into the drive, stopping the Mustang and letting out a low whistle. Before him loomed a huge three-story house. It gleamed white in the sun, aggressively modern, with big empty windows. All the native sea grapes had been cleared, leaving a patch of Astro Turf–like lawn and two new royal palms, propped up with tripods of two-by-fours.

Louis stared at the place in disbelief. He had been expecting something else, maybe a nice old beach place with the same pleasantly seedy elegance of Duvall's office. This place was a monstrosity, madly out of proportion with the homes around it. Zero-lot-line McMansions crowding out picturesque bungalows. And they called it progress.

So much for sand in the shoes, Louis thought as he pulled in the drive.

He parked next to a canary yellow Mercedes convertible. The vanity tag read CANDY 1. A second car was parked nearby, a modest older-model blue Toyota.

At the massive bronze doors, Louis found an intercom and rang. He waited, his eyes wandering up to the small camera above. A woman's accented voice came back.

"Deliveries around the side, please."

"I'm here to see Mrs. Duvall," Louis said. He looked directly up into the camera lens. "My name is Louis Kincaid."

There was a pause. "Mrs. Duvall is expecting you?"

"No. But I'm here on behalf of Mr. Duvall's lawyer, Brian Brenner." Another lie. It was becoming frighteningly easy.

It was at least a minute before the door opened. A small bronze-skinned woman in a white uniform motioned him in.

"Wait here, please."

The woman disappeared, her Aerosoles squeaking on the marble like sneakers on a gym floor. It gave Louis a chance to look around.

He was standing in a soaring circular foyer, right in the center of an elaborate mosaic of stars made of onyx, lapis and some kind of gold stone. A twin staircase curved up around him, a sinuous U of glass and chrome. Under it, the foyer opened onto what he guessed was the living room, a cathedral of blinding white light dotted with sleek pale blue furniture. Through the huge windows beyond, he could see a turquoise rectangle— the pool. And beyond that, a shimmer of blue that was San Carlos Bay.

He turned at the sound of squeaking soles.

"Mrs. Duvall says to wait for her in the living area."

Ah. Living *area*.

Louis followed the maid into the white light.

The maid left him alone again. He looked around, debating whether to actually sit in one of the unforgiving silk chairs. He decided to remain standing. His eyes wandered over the room's severely elegant furniture and down to the white carpet with its little gold star design. This wasn't a place people lived in; it was some designer's wet dream. Everything was perfect. The perfect pleats of the white sheers. The perfect fingerprint-free glass tables. The perfect slant of the white orchids in their crystal vase.

He was trying to reconcile all this with Duvall's cozy old office when a waft of cold air caused him to turn. Candace Duvall was standing at the foyer.

He knew Candace Duvall was in her mid-forties but she was trying real hard not to look like it. She had a tumble of heavily frosted blond curls around a small, deeply tanned face with big eyes and a pug nose. Her body was just thin enough to be called lush instead of plump, and ill-concealed in a loosely belted robe. The robe was white silk dotted with little gold stars. He wondered if she always coordinated her clothes with her carpet.

"Luisa didn't tell me your name," she said.

"Louis Kincaid."

She was leaning against a pillar, a languid pose. More Mae West than mourning wife.

"You work with Brian?"

Brian? Well, Brenner had said they were social acquaintances.

"I've never seen you before," she said.

"I'm new," he said.

She came slowly into the room. From her pocket, she extracted a cigarette and a blue Bic. She lit the cigarette and drew quickly on it.

"You don't look like a lawyer," she said, her eyes locked on his. They were brown and puppy-like. Her face had the shiny taut look of a recent peel. Coupled with the eyes, it made her look like one of those little Pekinese dogs.

"What are lawyers supposed to look like?" he asked.

"You know, Brooks Brothers. Or Savile Row, in Spencer's case."

Savile Row? That didn't square with sand in the shoes either.

Suddenly, Candace moved toward him, stopping just inches away. Louis resisted the urge to move back. Her smell—a potent brew of flowers, cigarettes and something musty he couldn't quite place—filled his nostrils.

She took a step back. "You don't smell like a lawyer either," she said.

"Lawyers have a smell?"

"Everyone has a smell, their own unique human perfume," she said. "My first boyfriend, he smelled like sawdust and Necco wafers. Not unpleasant, really."

She went to a sofa and sat down, crossing her well-muscled, tanned legs. "Spence, he smelled like shoe polish." She drew heavily on the cigarette as she stared up at him.

He suddenly could remember the smell of the shoe polish he used to shine his shoes with when he was a cop. Okay, he'd play along.

"Roll-on or paste?" he asked.

"What?"

"Shoe polish. Roll-on or paste? The roll-on stuff smells like burnt tires. The paste smells more like turpentine."

She stared at him for a moment, then laughed. She leaned forward to tap her cigarette in a crystal ashtray. The robe opened to a clear view of her tanned left breast and a large brown nipple. Louis didn't look away. She leaned back, still smiling slightly.

"You're not a lawyer, are you?" she said.

"No."

"You don't work with Brian either, do you?"

"No."

"What are you doing here then?"

"I'm a private investigator."

She nodded, pursing her lips. "Working for who?"

"Jack Cade."

She stared blankly at him for a moment, then leaned forward and snuffed her cigarette out. When she sat back again, her eyes weren't so puppy-like anymore. "You work for the man who killed my husband and you come to my home expecting me to talk to you? What, are you nuts or just stupid?"

Okay. Fun and games were obviously over.

"I'm just trying to get to the bottom of some things, Mrs. Duvall," he said. "I'd like to just ask you a few questions—"

"I'm sure you would."

"Did you know your husband was divorcing you?"

He waited, watching Candace Duvall's face. Damn. Nothing. No surprise, no flinch, no nothing. If the woman knew anything, she was a hell of an actress.

A flash of color caught Louis's eye and he looked to the large windows over Candace Duvall's shoulder. Someone had come onto the patio. A young man in a red Speedo. Tall, tanned, lithe as an Olympic swimmer, with flowing dark hair. He stood at the pool for a moment, then dove in, slicing the water as cleanly as a dolphin.

"I think you should go."

Louis looked back at Candace Duvall. There wasn't a trace of warmth left in those brown eyes now.

"Mrs. Duvall—"

She jumped to her feet. "Luisa!" she bellowed.

"Hey, calm down—"

"I gave my statement to the police," she said. "I don't have to talk to you. Now get out. Luisa!"

Louis put up his hands. "All right, I'm going."

The maid appeared.

"Show this man out," Candace said. "If he won't go, call the police."

Louis went quickly to the door, the little maid at his heels.

"You better go," she whispered, opening the bronze door.

Louis put up a hand to prop the door open over the maid's head. He glanced back at the foyer. Candace Duvall had disappeared.

"Who else is staying here?" he asked the maid.

"What?" she said.

"Who was that guy out at the pool?"

The maid frowned. "There is no one else here." She pushed on the door.

"Is that your car?" Louis pointed at the blue Toyota.

The maid looked like he had asked her if that was her hearse. "No! Is not mine. Now, please leave! Or I will—"

"Okay, okay."

The door closed. Louis stood for a moment on the tiled portico. With a glance up at the security camera, he went back to his Mustang. He got in, sitting there without starting the engine. He looked back at the huge white house.

He hadn't expected the place to be draped with black cloth or anything. But Spencer Duvall had been killed just before filing for divorce and his widow wasn't exactly putting out grief vibes.

Hell, what kind of vibes had Candace Duvall been putting out? She hadn't been flirting; he knew when a woman was coming on to him, and she certainly wasn't. But there had been something clearly sexual about her.

The guy out at the pool. Did Candace have a lover?

Louis stared up at the white house, his mind and senses working. Her look, her hair, her smell—damn, that was it—her smell. Shit, he knew that smell. Candace Duvall had just been clearly, unquestionably, royally, laid.

Louis pulled out a notebook and jotted down the license number of the blue Toyota, noting it was from Dade, not Lee County. He started the Mustang and threw it into reverse. But then he paused.

Something was bugging him. His senses were clicking back, trying to recall what he had seen. What he had smelled.

The slender figure in the red bathing suit came into his head again.

Oh geez . . .

Candace Duvall had a lover all right. But it wasn't a man.

Chapter Nine

Louis leaned back against the headboard and put on his glasses. He was going through the newspaper clips again and he focused now on the feature about Spencer Duvall, the one with the local-boy-makes-good angle. He had only skimmed it before, but now, after what Ellie Silvestri had told him and what he had seen at the Duvall mansion, he wanted to try to get a better picture of the man himself.

Spencer Duvall, the article said, was from Matlacha, a tiny island north of Fort Myers. Matlacha was barely bigger than the two-lane causeway road that connected it to Pine Island on the west and the mainland on the east. Matlacha—it was pronounced Mat-la-SHAY, for some reason—was home to some old motels, a few downtrodden marinas, a number of psychics and more than a few colorful watering holes, including the infamous Lob Lolly and Mulletville. Louis only knew Matlacha because Dodie was always dragging him out there to his favorite restaurant, the Snook Inn.

Duvall's mother had been a waitress and his father a charter boat worker and fishing guide. Duvall's older brother had served time for armed robbery and died in a car accident when he was just twenty-three. Duvall, on the other hand, had gone to Florida State on scholarships and come home to open his law practice in downtown Fort Myers.

Duvall had married his college sweetheart, Candace Kolke, from Quincy, a small town up near Tallahassee. They had lived in Fort Myers until 1969, when they moved to a home on Bayview Lane on Sanibel Island. Two years ago, they had razed the old house, bought the lot next door and built the white monster. It had recently been on the cover of *Florida Design* magazine. The Duvalls also had a ski lodge in Aspen and a "small villa" overlooking Baie de Saint Jean on St. Barts.

Louis took off his glasses. Baloney sandwiches and sand in the shoes, Ellie Silvestri had said. Why was he getting the feeling *he* was the one being fed a bunch of baloney?

It was starting to rain again, just as it had almost every night this week. He tossed the article aside and got up off the bed. In the kitchen, he exchanged the empty Dr Pepper for a Heineken and shut the refrigerator, leaning against it.

Spencer Duvall might have started out humble, but it looked like he got used to living the good life pretty easily, no matter what Ellie Silvestri chose to believe.

He took a drink of beer. Rich people. He had dealt with them before—many of his PI clients had more money than God. And then there were the Lillihouses back in Mississippi, putting on a facade as fancy as the one on their antebellum mansion. The rich he had known went around making their messes and then hiring other people—people like him—to clean them up.

He took another drink of the beer. Why was he in such a sour mood? He knew the answer. The deeper he got into the case, the more disgusted he was getting with the players in it.

Spencer Duvall, the warrior lawyer who made a bundle getting killers and rapists off. Candace, his bitchy-itchy wife. Lyle Bernhardt, the squirrely partner, and Brian Brenner, the weasel house-wrecker. And the Cades . . . pathetic Ronnie and his creepo father.

God, what a bunch of losers.

The rain was beating on the roof. Palmetto pounders, that's what they called big storms here. He looked back at his hand, flexed it and started back to the bedroom.

He heard the slam of the screen door and quickly after, a woman's voice.

"Kincaid?"

Louis squinted, seeing a shadow in the gloom out on the porch.

"Kincaid? It's me, Susan Outlaw."

He moved to the open front door. She was standing on the porch, soaked, her hair matted to head, water running down her face.

"Mrs. Outlaw," he said, stepping back to let her enter.

She didn't move. "Just what the hell are you and Jack Cade trying to pull?" she said.

"What?"

"What did you tell him?"

Damn, he had forgotten that he had told Ronnie Cade to run interference.

"What did you tell him?" she repeated. "What did you tell him you could do for him that I couldn't?"

Louis put up a hand. "I didn't tell him anything. I haven't talked to Jack Cade."

"Well, somebody sure the hell did!"

A puddle was forming at her feet. Her mascara had left streaks down her face.

"Come on in," he said. "I'll get you a towel."

She came inside. Louis didn't know if she was shaking because she was cold or angry. He moved toward the bathroom, snagged a towel off the rack and came back to her.

"What did Jack Cade say to you?" he asked, holding out the towel.

She grabbed it. "He told me he would fire me if I didn't take you on," she said.

Great . . .

"That's not all," she said. "He also said women didn't have the balls to do what it would take to get him off."

She wiped her face with the towel. "Tell me you didn't put those thoughts into his head," she said.

"I didn't," he said simply.

"Bullshit."

Louis had to fight not to match her anger. What was it with this broad, anyway? He was willing to meet her halfway; that's all he wanted when he had asked Ronnie Cade to intercede. He took a drink of beer.

"Well, answer me," she said, her voice rising.

"I don't have to answer to you. Or anyone else," Louis said.

She glared at him, then threw the towel at him. He caught it against his chest. She stalked off toward the porch.

"Wait," Louis called out.

She turned.

"Look, Cade has spent the last twenty years in prison working up a hate for the legal system and all lawyers." He tipped his beer toward her. "That includes you, lady."

Susan's body remained rigid.

Louis took a breath and made an effort to soften his voice. "I went to see Ronnie Cade yesterday," he said.

She took a step back in the room. "Ronnie? Why?"

"I asked him to talk to you, to get you to . . ." he hesitated just long enough.

"To *what?*"

"Man, to back off," he said, shaking his head. "Look, we're on the same side here!" He paused. "I've decided to take the case."

She was just standing there, staring at him. Then he saw her shoulders relax some and she brushed the wet hair from her face. Her skirt was wrinkled and she had a run in her stocking. He wondered if she had come straight from the jail to his cottage. He motioned toward a chair. She shook her head.

"I'll get it wet," she said.

"It doesn't matter. The whole place leaks. Sit down."

She slumped into the chair. "Why'd you change your mind about the case?"

"I don't know."

She gave him a withering look.

"It's the truth," he said. "I don't know why I changed my mind. Maybe I feel sorry for Ronnie."

She snorted out a laugh.

"Maybe I'm bored, maybe I'm broke," Louis said. "Maybe I'm crazy."

She didn't reply and he noticed her eyeing the bottle. "You want one?" he asked.

She nodded.

When he returned from the kitchen, she had taken off her sodden high heels and was rubbing her toes. He set the beer on the table next to her and waited while she took a long drink. He watched a tiny rivulet of beer trickle from the corner of her lips. She wiped it away and looked up at him.

"Look, I could use some help on this," she said. "I fought to get this case and I want to keep it. I've been working like a dog, but I haven't got anything."

He could see this was hard for her. "Can Cade fire you?" he asked.

"It takes some maneuvering, but yes, he can." She hesitated. "I could use some more help."

"You want me to work for you?"

She looked him in the eye. "Yes, I do."

Louis went to the kitchen and came back with a fresh beer.

"So where were you planning to start?" she asked as he took a drink.

"I already have," Louis said, sitting on the sofa across from her. "I went and saw Bernhardt this morning."

"A real prince, isn't he. You get anything useful?"

"Not from him. But Duvall's secretary told me she thought Duvall was getting ready to divorce his wife."

"The secretary? She didn't mention anything like that when I talked to her."

"I saw Duvall's lawyer to make sure, some guy named Brenner."

"Scott or Brian?"

"There's two?"

She nodded. "Brothers. They come from good lawyer stock. Their father was an attorney here for centuries and went into politics as a state senator. He died a while back. The sons stayed local, kept the family practice going. They've made a fortune in civil work, suing doctors, insurance carriers and pharmaceutical companies."

"Brian Brenner confirmed that Duvall was getting ready to draw up papers," Louis said. "But get this— he claims Candace didn't know about the divorce."

"Oh, right," Susan said. She was frowning slightly, like she was perturbed she had missed all this.

"I found out something else," Louis said. "Candace Duvall has a lover."

Susan's eyes shot up. "Who is he?"

"She. It's a she."

It took Susan a second before his comment registered.

"Fuck a duck," she whispered. "How do you know?"

"I went to her house."

"She let you in? How in the hell did you find out she has a lover? Did you see them?"

"Not exactly."

"She told you?"

"No."

Susan sat forward. "Well, how, damn it? This could be important stuff."

Louis shifted slightly, playing with the Heineken label. "It's hard to explain."

"Try," Susan said dryly.

"I smelled it."

She burst out laughing and fell back in the chair. She looked back at him. "You're kidding me, right?"

"No. It's true. Believe me, I know what I'm talking about here."

She picked up the beer bottle, still chuckling.

"Look, I saw a woman at the house," Louis said. "She was out at the pool, topless."

Susan arched an eyebrow.

"Well, if Candace does have something going on the side and if she knew she was about to be dumped, wouldn't you say that could give her motive?" Louis asked.

"Motive is not a requirement to prove your prima facie case," Susan said.

"But money is important to Candace and Florida is not a community property state," Louis said. "Spencer could have divorced her and not given her a dime, right?"

"Theoretically," Susan said slowly.

"I thought all you needed was to dig up something to prove reasonable doubt. This doesn't do it?"

"Only if we can prove Candace has a lover. And last time I looked, smells were not admissible evidence, Kincaid."

She was smiling. She was enjoying this.

It took a moment, but he finally smiled. "Okay, so I'll find the topless babe."

Susan was still smiling. "Kind of gives new meaning to the term 'the other woman' doesn't it."

"No shit." Louis took a swig of beer.

Susan pulled out a business card and set it on the table. "Call me in the morning at my office and we'll work out a way to pay you."

"I'll go see Cade tomorrow and set him straight," Louis said.

She nodded, like she still wasn't quite comfortable accepting his help. The rain stopped. The sudden silence was deafening.

"I gotta get home," she said, slipping on her shoes.

Louis followed her out to the porch. A strong breeze swept in from the water, catching him full in the face. He turned to look at her. Her hair was a mess, plastered to her head, but her face looked clean and smooth.

"You sure you can do this?" she asked.

"What?"

"Work the other side of the fence?"

Louis hesitated.

"If you take this job," Susan said, "you've got to operate under the assumption that Jack Cade is innocent."

"He killed once before. Hard for me to forget that."

"He served his time," Susan said.

"Twenty years isn't near enough justice."

"That's your cop brain talking, Kincaid. Cops have their own warped idea of justice and how it should be served up."

"That's because they see firsthand the damage these assholes do."

"Cops seem to forget they don't work for the prosecutor."

Louis leaned against the door jamb. "If you believe that, why are you hiring me?

She cocked her head. "I'm not sure. I get the feeling you operate with a different kind of compass. One that keeps you from crossing certain lines."

"You don't know me, counselor."

"I know what happened to you. I know why you're not the most popular guy in O'Sullivan's."

Her eyes were steady on his, and he felt his chest tighten. He took a quick drink of beer to stay cool.

"Who told you?"

"A deputy I know. Then I went and did some research, read some old newspaper articles. I know that you killed a cop to protect a kid, a punk kid no one cared about."

Louis looked past her, out at the swaying dark palms, lost in a wave of images he had thought were long buried. A blue uniform in the snow. A gun, cold in his hand.

"It was a long time ago," Louis said.

"It cost you a lot."

When he didn't say anything, she asked, "Do you ever think what would've happened to you if you hadn't done what you did?"

He didn't like talking about this. He hadn't talked to anyone about it, except Sam Dodie. But something made him answer.

"I don't think I could've put on a uniform again, for one thing."

"You haven't."

He shrugged. "I will, when the time's right."

Susan was silent.

Louis sighed, then looked at her. "Look, I've got to be honest here. I don't like dirtbags like Cade. I don't like lawyers either. But I'm a good investigator and that's what you'll get.''

''What about Kitty Jagger?''

''What about her?''

''Can you forget that Cade was convicted of killing her?''

Louis hesitated. ''Let's put it this way—I won't let it get to me.''

''Then I think we can do business.''

Susan extended her hand. Louis shook it without returning her smile.

''Christ, Kincaid, you look like you're making a deal with the devil,'' Susan said.

Louis finished off his beer in one gulp. ''Maybe I am, counselor.''

Chapter Ten

Louis sat in the hard wooden chair, waiting for Jack Cade. His gaze wandered around the visitation room. Standing near the back was a deputy, his green uniform crisp but his eyes limp with boredom. The florescent light flickered as the rattle of a fan suddenly filled the room. Louis could feel a spray of cold air from the vent above him.

He watched the plain black and white clock on the wall over the deputy's head. The thin red second hand made its way slowly around the stained face.

To Louis's left was a heavyset black woman in a brightly patterned cotton dress. She was speaking in a soft foreign accent to a weary-looking man on the other side of the dirty plexiglass. The man's eyes locked briefly on Louis's.

He had been behind bars himself once. It was brief, but he had never forgotten the soul-numbing feel of it. How did men stand it for decades? He looked away from the man's gaze.

The back door opened and a deputy escorted Jack Cade in, shoving him down into the chair across from Louis. Cade didn't even shrug off the deputy's hand. Just took it, like he was used to it or it no longer mattered.

Cade was cuffed and he settled into the chair uneasily. His hair was hanging in eyes, and he tossed his head slightly to throw it back. He peered at Louis through the scarred plexiglass.

"I see Miz Outlaw took my advice," Cade said.

"Let me tell you something, Cade. You have nothing to gain by pissing off Susan Outlaw or me."

"Well, you're here, ain't you?"

"For the time being. You pull anything like that again, I walk. And you better hope she doesn't walk with me."

Cade didn't look at him. The prisoner next to them was starting to talk excitedly, his accent so heavy Louis couldn't understand what he was saying. Cade was staring at him.

"Did you hear me, Cade?"

"Why would I care if the bitch walks?"

Louis leaned close to the plexiglass. "Because she's probably the only person in Lee County who thinks you didn't kill Duvall. How's that grab you?"

Cade's eyes slid back to Louis. "You don't?"

Louis didn't answer.

"How the hell can you help me if you think I'm guilty?"

"Convince me otherwise."

Cade looked away again. He was picking at his cuticles, scratching at them with the hard, dark nails of his other hand.

The prisoner in the next cubicle raised his voice,

his speech slipping now into a foreign language that sounded like slurred French.

"Talk to me, Cade," Louis said.

Cade was staring at the black man and his girlfriend.

"Cade," Louis said sharply.

Cade shook his head slowly. "Fucking foreigners. Can't even get away from them in jail."

He finally let his eyes drift back to Louis. "Haitians. Washing up on the beach like goddamn fish. They ought to toss them off a boat in the Bermuda Triangle and see if they can swim home past the sharks."

Cade was waiting for Louis's reaction. But Louis wasn't going to give him the satisfaction of seeing his disgust.

"Tell me about the night Duvall was killed," Louis said. "Why did you go back to his office that night?"

"I didn't."

"They've got a witness who ID'ed you."

"A homeless drunk." Cade smiled.

"Why were you going to sue Duvall?"

"I told you."

"You said he was incompetent. How?"

"I never said he was incompetent. Incompetent means somebody doesn't know what they're doing. Duvall knew exactly what he was doing."

The Haitian prisoner was getting more agitated. His girlfriend was crying. Cade's eyes lasered onto the couple.

"What do you mean?" Louis asked.

"Duvall sold me out."

"How?"

Cade shook his head.

"Cade, look at me."

Cade shifted, his breathing turning hard. "It's fucking over. I got no way to get anything back now. My life is down the drain because of Duvall and I got no way to get anything back because the sonofabitch is dead!''

The guard was eyeing Cade.

''You've got to calm down here, Cade,'' Louis said. ''Shit . . .''

''You've got—''

Cade leaned into the plexiglass. ''Don't tell me what I gotta do,'' he said. He took a deep breath and leaned back, running a hand over his hair.

''My kid was here yesterday,'' Cade said. ''He's lost most the yards on his routes,'' Cade said. ''Folks are telling him they don't want their lawns paying for his scumbag father's defense.''

Louis let out a long breath. ''Look, Cade . . .''

''That sonofabitch lawyer took away my life and now he's taking away my kid's. He owes me.'' Cade leaned forward, his eyes glistening. ''You hear me? He owes me!''

Louis was quiet for a moment. He decided to play his card.

''You couldn't have sued Duvall anyway,'' he said.

Cade looked up at him.

''Statute of limitations on legal malpractice is two years in this state,'' Louis said.

Something passed over Cade's eyes momentarily and was gone, like a final dissipating swirl of smoke from a dying fire.

''You didn't know that, did you?'' Louis said.

Cade was silent for a long time, head bowed as he picked at his hands. The Haitian's creole mixed in with the hum of the florescent lights.

Suddenly, a hard twisted smile came to Cade's face. ''I should have known, man, I should have known.''

''Known what?'' Louis asked.

''That it wouldn't work,'' Cade said. ''The cards aren't stacked that way for guys like me.''

The black woman in the next cubicle started to cry softly again. The Haitian man just sat there.

"When I was in the joint," Cade said, "this guy who knew something about the law told me I could sue Duvall for a million bucks when I got out. I didn't believe it. I mean, a fucking jury giving a guy like me a million bucks."

He looked up at Louis. "Then I got out and saw how bad things were for Ronnie and I figured what the fuck, what do I got to lose?"

He gave a sharp laugh. "Now you tell me I couldn't have gotten anything anyway. Ain't the legal system fucking great?"

Louis was silent. The Haitian man had started up again. But his angry chattering was muffled, pushed to the back of Louis's mind.

If Cade thought he stood to get a big settlement from Duvall, he was the last person who wanted Duvall dead. But there was something else here, too. Cade represented a part of the past that a lot of people wanted to forget. Suing Spencer Duvall would have brought back bad memories for a lot of people, no matter how hard the courts tried to keep the focus on Duvall's alleged malpractice and away from the evidence that convicted Cade in the first place. The media alone would retry the case. He wondered if Jack Cade looked at it from that angle.

"What do you think would have happened if you could have sued Duvall?" Louis asked.

Cade just looked at him.

"The evidence would have been reexamined, Cade," Louis said. "Other people, the newspapers, would retry it all over again, outside of the courtroom. Things would come out that have nothing to do with Duvall's ability or intent. Hell, other lawyers would step forward with new technology, raise questions. It would have been a circus."

"Told you, it doesn't matter now."

"Not to you, but maybe it did to someone else."

Cade looked up at him. "Who?"

"The person who really killed Kitty Jagger?"

Cade gave a snort, shaking his head. "Now you're saying you believe me, that I didn't do it?"

Louis hesitated. "Let's just say I believe that if someone thought Duvall could be sued, they'd be worried about what might come out."

The Haitian man raised his voice and Cade looked over at him.

"Who did you tell that you planned to sue Duvall?" Louis asked.

"Everyone from here to Raiford for the last year."

"Did you see a lawyer?"

Cade shook his head, his eyes still on the Haitian. "No money."

"Then we'll have to go another direction," Louis said. "We have to talk about Kitty Jagger."

Cade looked back quickly. "Fuck that, man."

"It's a believable defense for the mess you're in now," Louis said.

Cade was silent. The Haitian man was ranting, his girlfriend's crying growing louder.

"You'll have to tell me everything that happened twenty years ago," Louis said.

Cade sucked in a slow, long breath that expanded his chest under the orange jumpsuit.

"The only thing I'm going to say is that I was set up."

Louis didn't reply.

Cade raked at his hair with both hands, glancing again at the Haitian. Suddenly, he spun toward the man. "Hey, shut the fuck up!" he yelled.

The Haitian man and his girlfriend froze, staring at Cade.

Louis tapped on the plexiglass.

"Cade, forget them. Look at me."

Cade's eyes shot back to him.

"Now tell me about Kitty Jagger," Louis said.

Cade shook his head slowly. "It's over, man."

"How did you lose the garden tool?"

"Look, I told you I don't know nothing about it."

"Who else had access to your tools?"

"I said I didn't do it, man."

"But someone—"

"I told you!" Cade spat out. "I told you I don't know who killed that girl!"

Louis's eyes flicked up to the deputy watching Cade's back, then he looked back at Cade.

"She had a name, Cade. Her name was Kitty."

Louis was amazed to see a small smile tip Cade's lips.

"Kitty," he said slowly. He cut Kitty's name into two sharp syllables, holding each between his teeth before spitting them out.

Louis felt something tighten inside his chest.

"I didn't kill Kitty," Cade said. "Kitty killed *me,* man."

Cade sat back in his chair, staring at Louis. His eyes had gone opaque in the florescent lights. The Haitian man had started up again, his voice ricocheting off the concrete walls.

Louis rubbed the bridge of his nose. Suddenly, the room seemed to close in on him, the stale stench, the clang of a door, the muted bellow of a deputy and the desperate babbling of the Haitian man.

Louis rose sharply and pushed back his chair.

Cade looked up. "Where you going?"

"Think about what I said, Cade," Louis said. "Think about Kitty Jagger. She might be the only person right now who can save your ass."

Louis didn't look back as he walked away. At the door, the deputy buzzed him through.

Out in the hall, Louis paused. He could still see Cade's eyes, as murky as that damn plexiglass between them. He pulled in a deep breath. Nobody should have eyes that you couldn't see into.

Chapter Eleven

Louis took off his glasses and rubbed his eyes. When he put them back on, the screen of the microfiche machine came back into focus. He had been at the Lee County Library for nearly two hours, tracking down anything he could find on Kitty Jagger's murder.

"Excuse me."

Louis looked up into the face of the librarian.

"We're getting ready to close."

Louis looked at his watch. It was only five.

"We close early the day before Thanksgiving," she said.

Thanksgiving? Man, he had forgotten. He punched a button and the machine spit out a copy of the article on the screen.

Outside the library, he paused, then decided to go to the bar across the street. He ordered a Coke and arranged the clips in chronological order. He started with the earliest one, from the *Fort Myers News-Press*, dated April 11, 1966. The headline said, GIRL FOUND DEAD AT DUMP SITE.

It reported that the unidentified body of a young woman had been found at the city dump by two garbage men making an early-morning run. It was only a couple paragraphs on the bottom of the front page. Other news had taken precedence that day: Frank Sinatra had married Mia Farrow in Las Vegas.

Louis took a sip of the Coke.

He knew the dump site; he had passed it on the drive down to Bonita Springs. The locals called it Mount Trashmore. It was a giant landfill that had been sodded over to make it look nice for the new subdivision that was just a mile downwind. If it weren't for the steady stream of garbage trucks and the gulls circling overhead, you could almost believe it was just a pretty hill. If South Florida had hills.

The next article was dated April 12th. Police had used a gold locket found on the body to help identify the girl as a local teenager named Kitty Jagger, age fifteen. The medical examiner's report said she had been stabbed, beaten and raped. She had been dead about two days when found. Police had no suspects but had located a bloody garden tool that appeared to be the stabbing weapon.

He set the article aside and turned to the next one dated a week later.

It said Kitty Jagger had last been seen on April 9th, the day of her death, by her boss at Hamburger Heaven, a drive-in where she was a carhop. She had worked her usual five-to-eleven night shift and had left to walk to the bus stop as she always did. There was an interview with Kitty's widowed father, Willard Jagger, an unemployed roofer on disability who said that when his daughter did not come home, he called the police to file a missing person's report.

The article was illustrated with a small black and

white picture of Kitty Jagger. It looked to be a yearbook photo, a blow-up from a group shot, probably Kitty's freshman class. In it, Kitty Jagger was staring straight ahead, a small smile tipping her lips. From what Louis could tell, she looked like your average pretty high school girl, with long blond hair parted in the middle and hanging straight around her round face.

Louis moved on to the next article, heavy with a black headline: SUSPECT ARRESTED IN JAGGER MURDER.

This was the first mention of Jack Cade. There was a photo of Cade being led into the Lee County Courthouse. He was wearing a jumpsuit like the one Louis had seen him in yesterday, but his face was that of a very different and younger man.

Cade's hair was flat and black, combed straight back away from a striking face. He was thinner, sinewy, the muscles in his upper arms tight against the grip of the deputy's hands. The difference was the eyes. Cade's eyes in this picture registered anger and bewilderment; they were nothing like the hard, flat eyes that stared back at him from behind the plexiglass.

Louis moved to the story. A bloody garden tool, recovered with the body, had been traced to Cade, who, like all lawn maintenance workers, regularly dumped his trash at the site where Kitty Jagger's body had been found. The article also revealed that a pair of semen-stained panties had been found in Cade's truck, and that the O blood-type, derived from the semen stain, matched Jack Cade's type.

Louis sighed. Ronnie Cade hadn't mentioned that.

The article finished up with a description of the damage done to Kitty's body: blunt trauma to her head and twelve stab wounds to the chest and shoulders. Louis set the clip aside and looked down at his arm.

About halfway up his forearm was a long thin scar. He ran his fingertips over it, feeling the faint ridge. Then he turned his hand over and looked at the knife scar that marked the fatty part of his palm, cutting sideways to the center. His little finger was still numb at the tip, and sometimes when it was cold and wet, he could feel the muscles in his hand tightening beneath the skin.

He finished the Coke and took off his glasses. If he was going to start digging into this, he would be facing some tough opponents. Mobley and the prosecutor, Vern Sandusky, were sure to fight it.

And Susan. God, he wasn't looking forward to telling her what he was thinking.

The bartender ambled over. "You want another one?"

"No thanks. Where's your phone?"

"By the john. But it's out of order.

Louis gathered up the clips. It was just as well. This was something he was going to have to do in person.

Louis pulled the Mustang to a stop in front of the yellow bungalow, double-checking the address he had written on a scrap of paper. It was a neat little house, tucked in the shadows of some swaying banana trees on Sereno Key. Susan Outlaw's car, an old silver Mercedes sedan, was in the drive and a bicycle lay in the yard.

At the front door, he knocked and waited. The door opened and a small brown face with black-rimmed glasses appeared behind the screen.

"Hello," the boy said.

Louis smiled down at him, but the boy did not smile back.

"Hi, is your mother home?"

"Benjamin, who is it?"

"Just some guy, Ma!" he hollered over his shoulder.

"I told you never to open the door—" Susan

stopped, coming up behind him. Her face registered first surprise, then irritation.

"How'd you get my address?" she asked.

"I'm a PI."

"He probably looked it up in the phone book, Ma," Benjamin said.

"You should've called," she said.

"Sorry. I took a chance. We need to talk."

She nudged Benjamin aside and stepped to the screen. Her hair was pulled back in a tight knot and there was a white powder sprayed across the front of her red T-shirt. The front of the shirt read: A Woman Needs a Man Like a Fish Needs a Bicycle.

"Is this a bad time?" Louis asked.

Susan pushed open the screen. "Come on in. But don't look at the house. It's a mess. I'm baking."

Louis stepped inside, expecting to see a messy house, but the living room was neat, furnished with a trim blue sofa and a wooden rocking chair with a quilted seat pad. The pale yellow walls were bare except for a large, black-framed poster of the Eiffel Tower. There was a scattering of magazines on the coffee table along with a Clue board game. A small entertainment center with a TV took up one wall, flanked by bookcases overflowing with novels, law books, and a set of Encyclopedia Britannica. As Louis followed Susan through the small dining room, his eyes traveled over the table. It was covered with stacks of folders, yellow legal pads, books and an open briefcase— except for one end where an arithmetic book lay open next to a *Star Wars* looseleaf binder.

Nice house. Tidy, attractive, but all business. *Just like the lady herself,* Louis thought as he followed her into the kitchen.

The kitchen was painted a bright green in an attempt to match the ugly '50s tile. There was a Winn-Dixie bag on the floor with some groceries still stacked on the counter—a box of Stove Top stuffing, a can of cranberries, some potatoes. Louis could see a frozen turkey sitting in one side of the double sink.

"You shouldn't let that sit out," he said.

Susan was standing at the counter and turned. "What?"

"The turkey," he said, nodding.

"It needs to defrost by tomorrow and it won't fit in the refrigerator," she said.

"Put it in some cold water."

"What, you working for the Butterball hotline now?" Louis shrugged.

She went back to ripping away at something sticky in a big bowl. The stuff vaguely resembled cookie dough.

"Looks too dry," Louis said.

She threw him a look as she struggled to work the wooden spoon through the dough. "I followed the recipe," she said.

"Recipes don't always work," Louis said. "Add some water."

Susan grabbed a measuring cup, turning to the sink to fill it. She leaned down, watching the water carefully as it rose to the line.

"How much are you going to add?"

"Enough to make it look normal."

"Then you don't know how much you're going to add?"

"No."

"Then why bother to measure it?" Louis asked.

She turned. "Look, you came to talk, not cook. So talk."

Louis watched her pour the water into the dough. She began to work it in, her hips swaying in sync with the rotations her hand made around the bowl.

"I went and saw Cade," Louis said. "He knows now that we're a package deal."

She nodded slowly. "I talked to my boss. He said I can add you to the payroll as an investigator. You are now an agent of the PD's office."

Louis looked up at her, not comfortable with the title, especially with the name Jack Cade attached to it.

"Hold on," Susan said. She left and returned a minute later. She held out a beeper.

"I'm not wearing that," Louis said.

"Don't be crazy. I have to be able to get ahold of you." She slapped it down on the table and returned to the sink.

He picked up the beeper, turning it over in his hands. "Does this mean we're going steady?"

She threw him a look and went back to the cookie dough. Louis saw something out of the corner of his eye and turned. Benjamin was leaning against the door jamb, watching them. He was a skinny little thing, huge brown eyes behind the big glasses, twig-brown arms poking out of a *Star Wars* T-shirt.

"You really a PI?" he asked.

"Kind of."

"You track down murderers and stuff?"

Louis looked at Susan for help, but she was busy.

"What kind of gun you got?"

"I don't carry a gun right now," Louis said.

The boy made a face. "What kind of car you got? Sonny Crockett has a Ferrari Spider but it's not really his—"

"Ben, go do your homework," Susan said.

"I did it already."

"Then go watch TV."

The boy made a suffering face. "Oh man, I wanna stay in here."

"No. Get."

"Can I lick the bowl first?"

"I told you before it's not good for you."

Louis suddenly recalled something his foster mother Frances used to say to him, and he turned to Benjamin.

"It'll give you worms," he whispered.

Benjamin trudged off and fell to the floor in front of the television. Seconds later the *Jeopardy* theme song came on. Louis watched as Susan opened the oven door. The sweet scent of chocolate chip cookies filled the kitchen. He knew he needed to tread carefully. This was her case, after all, and he had to respect that. He had to find out what her plan was before he tried to force one of his own on her.

Susan started cleaning up the mess on the counter.

"Can I have the bowl?" Louis asked.

She turned. "What?"

"The bowl."

She gave him a weird look, then brought the bowl over to the table, sitting across from him. He scraped the spoon around the rim and began to eat the dough.

"That junk's not good for you," she said.

"Yeah, I know, it gives you worms. I need to know what your trial strategy is going to be," Louis said.

She swiped a finger in the bowl and nibbled at the dough, like she was afraid to experience it all at once. "My strategy is that Jack Cade didn't shoot Duvall. Someone else did. A powerful man like Duvall had lots of enemies. My staff, such as it is, is working on his financials now to see if there was anything hinky there."

"What about that witness who saw Cade at Duvall's office?"

"A bum named Quince," Susan said. "He hangs out at the bus stop across the street and he said he saw a man leave Duvall's office just after nine-thirty. Never saw Cade's face, just said he looked out of place. He described a black leather jacket. They never found a similar jacket when they searched Cade's house.

Quince doesn't know what he saw. He's a homeless drunk who served time."

"Being an homeless ex-con makes him blind?" Louis asked.

"There you go, thinking like a cop again."

"Okay, what about the fingerprints? Mobley said Cade's prints were on the credenza, like he was looking for something."

"Cade was in the office that morning. Says he leaned against things."

"They find the weapon?"

"No, and Cade doesn't own a gun. He can't."

"Not legally anyway."

"Well, they don't have anyone stepping forward to say they sold him one illegally either."

"What caliber was the gun used on Duvall?"

Susan thought for a minute. "A seven-point-six-two by twenty-five."

"A what?"

She chuckled at the puzzled look on his face. "It's a Tokarev. It's Chinese, an old semi-automatic. It shoots a 30-caliber bullet from a nine millimeter cartridge. It's probably a collector's gun."

"Doesn't sound like something Cade would have," Louis said.

"My thought exactly. He'd be lucky to snare something off the street."

"Alibi?"

"His son Ronnie. Says he was home watching *Star Trek, the New Generation.*"

"Next," Louis said.

"What?"

"It's called *Next Generation,* not New."

She shrugged and took another swipe at the cookie dough.

"I take it the cops don't believe Ronnie," Louis said.

"They can't disprove it. And even though Ronnie *is* the son, he's pretty credible."

"Did they find anything when they searched Cade's trailer?"

"No."

Louis put the spoon back in the bowl. He was silent, staring at the squiggles in the Formica surface of the table. He didn't realize he was shaking his head. But Susan saw it and bristled.

"What?" she demanded.

He looked up. "What?"

"That look. If you've got something to say about how I'm handling this, say it." She crossed her arms across her red T-shirt.

Louis drew in a slow breath. "I think you've got to reconsider the Jagger case as a motive in Duvall's murder."

Susan's expression was stunned. "You're kidding, right?"

"No, listen to me," Louis said. "I've been giving this a lot of thought since talking to Cade. He told me the only reason he wanted to sue Duvall was to get big money so he could put his life back together. Ronnie is broke. He owes money all over the place. The nursery business is about to go under. Cade was looking for money, that's all."

"So?" Susan said.

"So, he had everything to gain if the Jagger case was examined in the context of a civil suit."

"He couldn't have sued him anyway. The statute of—"

"Cade didn't know that. His intent was to sue, not kill."

"How do you know Cade didn't know?"

"He told me."

Susan gave a derisive laugh.

"You believe him when he said he didn't shoot Duvall. Why can't I believe him?"

"I never said I believed him. It's just the story I have to proceed with."

Louis shook his head. "He wanted money, not revenge."

"I don't like it," she said. "You'd have to be able to prove Cade really intended to file the suit and that he didn't know it was futile."

Louis nodded.

"And you'd have to be able to show someone else could have had something to lose if the Jagger case was reopened."

"Well," Louis said, "There's always Bernhardt. If Cade brought suit, the practice would be liable to any claim."

Susan said nothing.

"And there's Candace," Louis said. "She was the starter wife, remember. Maybe Duvall was looking to upgrade and she knew it." He paused. "Spencer had a place in town. Maybe he had something going on the side, like Candace. And maybe Candace knew." He took another lick of the cookie dough. "Even if Candace had a lover, she still had something to lose if Spencer divorced her."

Susan was quiet. He thought she was probably angry. But maybe she was just tired. It occurred to him that her prickliness probably came from the stress of the case, not from any real part of her personality. He had asked around, trying to find out more about her and had been told by a source at the courthouse that she was just a couple years out of law school and was trying real hard to make an impression. She had landed a big case with Cade, but now she was treading water and she knew it. He took a breath. He had one more point to press.

"And of course, there's the person who really killed Kitty Jagger."

Susan shook her head. "Do you have any idea how long it would take to solve a twenty-year-old murder?"

"Yes, I do, in fact," Louis said.

Susan held his gaze for a moment, then a sudden frown creased her face.

"Shit!" she blurted out. She spun to the oven and jerked open the door. Smoke filled the kitchen. Louis didn't have to look to know the cookies were black. He knew the smell. Frances could never get the hang of cookies either.

Susan pulled out the cookie sheet and tossed it into the sink. "Dammit!"

"You burn 'em again, Ma?"

Susan and Louis both turned to see Benjamin standing at the door. She didn't say anything. Benjamin came in and looked down into the sink. He gingerly picked out a cookie and bit into it. He was trying hard not to grimace and Susan was trying hard not to look upset.

"How was *Jeopardy?*" Louis asked, to break the silence.

Benjamin glanced at him suspiciously. "I missed Final Jeopardy."

"What was the question?"

He shrugged. "It was dumb. Something about a shot heard around the world. The category was baseball. I don't know a lot of sports stuff."

"Ralph Branca," Louis said.

Benjamin's eyes widened. "Yeah, that was it! That was the answer! How'd you know that?"

Benjamin looked up at Susan, who was standing, hands on hips, staring at Louis. She still looked angry, maybe about the cookies, but more likely about what he had suggested about the Jagger case.

"I'm going to go see Mobley tomorrow. I need to see the Jagger file," Louis said.

"You're on my payroll now, Kincaid," she said. "Don't waste the taxpayers' money digging up the past."

"If I work for you, I work my way," Louis said evenly.

Susan was silent. Benjamin looked up at her, over at Louis, then back at his mother. He grabbed another burnt cookie out of the sink and bit into it.

"Mom, these are okay, see?" he said quickly. "The outside is bad, but the inside is still okay. We can use some of them. Ma? Look . . ."

Susan's hand went out to cup Benjamin's head, pulling him to her waist. She was still staring daggers at Louis.

"This isn't going to work," Louis said, rising.

"Take the pager," Susan said.

He looked at her in surprise.

"I want to win this," she said. "Bring me something I can use."

"We striking another bargain here, counselor?"

"Call it what you want," she said. "Just bring me something I can use."

Chapter Twelve

Louis set the *Sports Illustrated* aside and stood up, glancing at his watch. Mobley had kept him waiting over thirty minutes. He went to the reception desk. A bronzed blonde in a sleeveless mint green dress looked up.

"Can you buzz him again?" Louis asked her.

"I told you. He gets mad if I do that," she said.

"Buzz him. I'll protect you."

The blonde gave him a smirk. She didn't need protecting; her biceps rivaled his own. If he remembered correctly, Mobley kept a bench press in his office. He wondered if she worked out with him.

While he waited, Louis scanned the portraits on the far wall. It was a gallery of all the Lee County Sheriffs from the last two decades, all tight-lipped old white guys. A parade of pale stale males . . . until you got to Lance Mobley with his windsurfer hair and Robert Redford jaw. Louis's eyes went to the middle portrait.

It was larger than the others with a fancier gilt frame. The gold plaque beneath read HOWARD DINKLE, SHERIFF 1962–1970.

Dinkle looked to be in his late fifties. He had been sheriff during the Kitty Jagger case. Probably dead by now.

"The sheriff will see you now."

Louis went down the hall and tapped on the door. Mobley hollered back and he went inside.

Mobley's leonine head was bent over his desk, a file spread in front of him. Louis glanced at the weight bench and he had a sudden image of the secretary laying flat on her back, dressed in hot pink spandex, sweating to the oldies. He had a second vision of Mobley on top of her.

He turned back to Mobley. On the wall behind him were the standard community recognition certificates and plaques, plus something that looked like a college degree. Louis squinted and could read the name of the school. Florida State University School of Law.

Mobley sat back, swinging gently in his chair. "This is interesting reading."

"Is that the Jagger case file?"

Mobley nodded. "Had a damn hard time finding it after you called. Locating something in that shack they call a warehouse is like digging through an outhouse for used toilet paper."

"Nice analogy," Louis said.

"Why did you ask me to pull it?"

Louis pulled up a chair. He wasn't sure how much to tell Mobley. He was no expert at legal maneuvering and wondered if he could hurt Susan's case. "Cade claims Duvall gave him a lousy defense," Louis said. "I just wanted to take a look."

"You don't believe him, do you?"

Louis shrugged. "I don't know."

Mobley closed the file and stacked it on top of two others. He pushed the folders toward Louis.

"Okay, here's the copies you wanted. Take a look—a quiet look, if you get my drift—but I doubt you'll be able to tell whether Duvall did a good job or not. Takes a legal mind to be able to do that."

Louis glanced at the diploma on the wall. Massage the ego.

"How about some help?" Louis asked.

Mobley caught the look at the diploma. "I'm not the person to ask, Kincaid. I'm on the other side here, remember?"

"Your part is done, Sheriff. It's up to the lawyers now."

"The lawyers," Mobley said quietly. "Ever wonder what the world would be like if we didn't have any lawyers?"

Louis ignored the comment.

"Okay, then let me ask you this," Mobley went on. "Did you ever stop to think about what happens if you find out Duvall *did* fuck up the Jagger case? That gives your client more motive to kill him, doesn't it?"

"Not if somebody else had a better reason."

"You're wasting your time."

"What if he didn't do it?"

"He's out now anyway, so who cares?"

"I do," Louis said. "And you should."

Mobley's jaw twitched, but he just leaned back in the chair and leveled his eyes at Louis. "I don't question any conviction without evidence to the contrary. Especially a case that happened when I was too young to care about anything other than getting laid."

Louis had a thought. "You were here then?"

Mobley rose and went to the bench. "Yeah, I grew up here." His eyes snapped to Louis's face. "I didn't know her, Kincaid."

"This is a small town," Louis said. "It was even smaller then. Why *didn't* you know her?"

"I was a senior, she was a freshmen. Big gap in those days, even at a small school like Fort Myers High. Plus we just ran in different crowds. You know how cliques can be."

Mobley was rolling his hand gently over the circular weights.

"You don't remember anything about her?"

Mobley drew a breath, letting it out slowly. "I remember she was pretty. We never got it on with the greasers."

"Greasers?" Louis said.

"Frats and greasers. That's what the world was divided into in my salad days, Kincaid."

"Greaser? You mean like John Travolta?" Louis asked.

Mobley was smiling slightly, enjoying his trip back in time. "Yeah. Guys in black leather who took shop, dropped out or got drafted."

"What about the girls?"

"They got pregnant."

Louis was silent. Somehow that didn't jive with the picture he was building in his brain of Kitty Jagger.

"But you remember the murder?" Louis asked.

Mobley's hand dropped from the weight bench. "Yeah. They made an announcement over the PA system. Some of the girls were crying." He shook his head. "I remembering thinking what phoneys they were because none of them ever looked twice at Kitty Jagger."

Mobley looked at Louis. "He killed her, Kincaid. We all know it."

"I still want to take a look. At everything."

Mobley walked to a credenza and opened a large cardboard box. On the side was written: #4532, Homicide, LCSO, Florida, April, 1966, Jagger, K.

He pulled out some plastic bags and a stack of photos, spreading them on his desk. Louis moved to it. The plastic bags held some bloody clothing, some torn clothing that looked like red cotton, and a pair of girl's panties, turned inside-out. They appeared to have droplets of brown blood and several large yellowish stains, along with some discoloring Louis assumed was from the lab testing.

"Is this semen?" Louis asked.

"Yeah, that's how they pinned the panties to Cade. He's a secretor."

Louis knew that meant his blood group could be typed from any body fluid. "So's eighty percent of the population," Louis said. "What's Cade's blood type?"

"O positive."

"Most common type. Did they break it down into subgroups? Proteins?"

Mobley shook his head. "It was 1966, the dark ages for serology. I doubt they went beyond seeing that big O come up."

"Could they now?"

Mobley was getting irritated. "Hell, I don't know. That shit's awful old. Samples break down."

"Did Cade offer an alibi?" Louis asked.

"Yeah, some guy named Atterberry. But they were never able to find him."

"What about the weapon? You have it?"

Mobley reached into the cardboard box and pulled out another large plastic bag. He extracted a tool and laid it on the desk between them. It looked like a pickaxe, about a foot and a half in length with a wooden shaft.

Louis picked it up, his eyes drawn to the forged steel double head. "Jesus, what is this?" he asked.

"Gardeners use it to loosen hard dirt. Cade's—and only Cade's—fingerprints are all over the handle."

Mobley gave a twisted smile. "It's called a Clot-Buster. Catchy name, huh?"

Louis turned it over in his hands. It was heavy, one end of the steel blunt-edged and coated with rust. The other metal end had three thick prongs, covered with a brown grit that Louis was sure was dried blood. It was hard to think of the evil-looking thing being used for something as innocent as gardening.

"She was stabbed with this end?" he asked, nodding at the three prongs.

"Yup. I was reading the autopsy report when you came in," Mobley said. "The wounds all showed that three-prong profile."

"How did they know this was Cade's?" Louis asked.

Mobley pointed to a blurred mark on the handle. "It's hard to see, but there's a phone number there, done with a laundry marker. It was Cade's business phone."

"Anybody could have put it there."

"Cade's wife admitted she marked his tools with their phone number because she was tired of him losing them. Cade claims this one went missing a couple days earlier."

Louis set the Clot-Buster on the desk.

"What else you got?" he asked.

Mobley picked up a stack of photos and handed them to Louis. They were crime scene photos, each labeled with an evidence number from the trial. Louis went quickly through the first ones, which showed the dumpsite and wide-angles of the body.

He flipped to the next series of photos, all shots of Kitty Jagger's body. Blood smeared across her bare, bruised thighs. A close-up of her hands. And a shot of her torso with its gaping wounds in a slender chest.

He paused at the next photo. He was staring into Kitty's face. He was trying to see some resemblance to the smiling girl of the newspaper photo. But this face wasn't even human-looking anymore. The body had lain in the dump for two days and he knew from experience what that could mean.

It was blood-streaked, the eyes open, the corneas milky with death. Rigor had frozen her lips into a horrible grin, revealing her small teeth. The left part of her cheek had been pecked away, probably by the gulls that he had seen circling over the dump.

He set the photos down, running his hand over his eyes. Mobley had walked back to his desk and was sitting when Louis turned to face him.

"Why are you wasting your time with this?" Mobley said. "From what I hear, Outlaw hasn't got anything that's going to help Cade beat this Duvall thing. I'd think you'd be working on that."

Louis was still looking down at the photograph of Kitty Jagger's ravaged face.

"It was twenty years ago. Let it go, Kincaid," Mobley said quietly.

The door opened and the secretary poked her head in. "Sheriff, Vern Sandusky is on hold."

Mobley picked up the receiver, finger poised over a button as he looked at Louis. Louis was still staring at the photo of Kitty.

"Kincaid."

Louis looked up.

"Forget her. She's dead and her killer has been convicted. There's nothing you can do for her now."

Mobley jabbed at the phone and swung his chair around away from Louis.

Louis gathered up his files and left. When he walked out, the Amazon was looking at him.

"How'd it go?" she asked.

"Hard to convince your boss of anything, isn't it?"

She smiled. "Not if you know how."

Louis's beeper went off, and he tried to shift the

files so he could turn it off, but she beat him to it, reaching across her desk to his hip.

"Need to use the phone?" she asked, leaning on the desk.

Louis shook his head, seeing Susan's number. "Nah. It can wait."

"Let me know if there is anything else I can do for you."

The look in the Amazon's eyes wasn't hard to translate. Okay, he'd use it. "What about a transcript from Jack Cade's 1967 trial?" he asked.

"You don't want much, do you?"

He tried a smile. "It would be a big help to me."

She cocked her head, tapping her pen against her cheek. "Okay, give me your number," she said. "I'll call you if I can get it."

Louis rattled off the pager number. The Amazon waved the paper between two long pink fingernails. "Got it."

He was going to ask for her name, but he had the feeling it would open doors he didn't want opened right now.

"Thanks, I owe you one," he said.

"I'll collect later," she said.

Chapter Thirteen

It shouldn't have bothered him. It was just a normal wound chart—the simple line drawing of a generic female body that pathologists used to record injuries to the deceased. Louis stared at the sketch. The body portion of the drawing was oddly neutered with no nipples or pubic area. The pathologist had dutifully drawn in the twelve stab marks on the torso.

But something about it was bothering him.

Then he saw it. The drawing's face. Unlike the body, it was detailed, with eyes, hair—*shit,* and a smile.

Jesus. He had heard about these old wound charts, but he had never seen one before. They had been phased out years ago when someone finally realized how grotesque they were.

He tossed the diagram aside, hoisted himself off the bed and went to the kitchen. He returned with a Dr Pepper and it was several minutes and half a can later before he returned to Kitty Jagger's autopsy report.

The pages of the twenty-year-old report were yellowed, some even mildewed from lying in the damp bowels of the municipal filing system. A musty odor rose up to him as he carefully turned the pages.

Katherine Lynn Jagger. DOB: 2-29-51. Height: 5 ft. 5. Weight: 122 lbs.

Cause of death: cerebral hemorrhage.

Manner of death: blunt trauma to the skull.

Mode of death: homicide.

Issy jumped up on the bed. The cat stared at him for a moment, then laid down on one of the open folders.

He was looking for something that might provide a clue about where she had been killed before being dumped. But so far there was nothing.

Contents of stomach: partially digested beef, potatoes, bread, unidentified sugar liquid, alcohol.

Louis shifted his weight and the bed creaked. He was trying to see her now, trying to imagine where she had been, what she looked like, what she had done the night she died. She had worked that night at Hamburger Heaven. She had probably eaten a hamburger, fries and a Coke sometime during her shift.

Tissue analysis: nothing unusual.

Lung analysis: nicotine, potassium monopersulfate.

Okay, she was a smoker. And she had at least one drink about an hour before she was killed.

Mobley had said she was a "greaser," the wilder crowd, the kids who smoked, drank, dropped out, got pregnant.

Louis flipped the page back to the internal organ analysis. She hadn't been pregnant.

But she definitely had been raped. Semen had been found in her vagina and on her thighs. Coupled with the extensive bruising on her inner thighs, everything pointed to rape, not consensual sex.

He started to set the report aside but paused, something registering that had not struck him before. He flipped back to the lung analysis. Potassium monopersulfate. What the hell was that?

He pulled his notebook closer and made a note to call Vince Carissimi, the medical examiner, in the morning.

The low rumble of thunder pulled Louis's attention to the window. A cool breeze, smelling of rain, wafted in through the jalousies. He glanced up at the wet stain in the ceiling above his bed. It had rained almost every night in the last week and he knew he was living on borrowed time before the whole damn roof gave way.

He set the autopsy report aside and scanned the bed, looking for the police report. Issy was sleeping on it. He tried to ease it out from under her.

"Off, cat," he said.

With a quick move, he jerked it out. The cat didn't even look up at him.

He opened the folder. He was looking for the lead investigator on the case and finally zeroed in on a Detective Robert Ahnert. His signature appeared on all the reports. Ahnert's own accounts, including his initial call to the dumpsite, were written in a concise, unemotional style. Even his report of going to the Jagger home to deliver the news that Kitty's body had been found was handled in the same detached manner.

Louis started to gather it all up but then paused. Something in his memory was nagging him. He went to his dresser and got the file that held the newspaper clips about Kitty's murder. He found the interview with her father, Willard Jagger.

Damn. There it was. Willard Jagger said he had reported his daughter missing on April 9th. Two days before her body was discovered in the dump.

So where was the missing person's report? He knew that cops usually let twenty-four or even forty-eight hours go by before they acted on a missing person's report. But this wasn't a big city where teenagers normally went missing. This was a small town where the disappearance of a fifteen-year-old girl would probably send up a red flag. Why hadn't Ahnert acted when Willard Jagger reported his daughter missing?

Bernhardt and Candace Duvall would have to wait, no matter what Susan thought. He needed to talk to Ahnert. If the guy was still alive.

Louis leafed through the rest of the material, but there was nothing unusual. It was all there, complete, professional—and as impersonal as the wound chart.

Kitty Jagger . . . reduced to the ultimate generic.

It had started to rain. He could hear it beating on the roof. A moment later, he felt a splatter on his head and his eyes darted up.

"Shit," he muttered.

The stain was starting to drip. Louis jumped up and dragged the bed a foot to the left. He went to the kitchen and returned with a pot, setting it under the drip. Issy had retreated to a mound of dirty clothes on the floor.

Louis stared at the mess of papers and folders on his bed. The blowup copy of the black and white yearbook picture of Kitty Jagger was lying on top.

He hadn't noticed it the first time, but he realized now that she looked vaguely like a girl who used to babysit him. Amy . . . that was her name. She lived three doors down from the Lawrence house and she used to bring a little blue case of 45s with her. He remembered she came over one night with a burn mark on her forehead from ironing her hair. All the white girls had wanted stick-straight hair in those days, like the Beatles' girlfriends.

Amy was fifteen. He was ten. She taught him to do the Boogaloo. She called him "little soul brother."

He paused, then went to his bureau. He opened a drawer, pulling the worn envelope out from under his underwear.

He sifted slowly through the pictures, pausing at the portrait of his sister Yolanda. Hand on hip, cocky tilt to her head, flirtatious smile. He wished he could remember her that way. Not the way she had looked the last time he saw her. She had been standing on the porch, screaming, crying, as the social services woman put him in the big green car.

His sister . . . he could still remember her touch when she washed him, her voice when she rocked him to sleep. His sister had been there for him.

Louis picked up another faded photo. It was of his mother Lila, the one taken when she was eighteen and still beautiful. Where had she been that day? He remembered she was sleeping. Or had she been passed out?

He picked up the faded snapshot of the white man in the straw hat.

And where were you, you sonofabitch?

Louis lifted his eyes to his reflection in the dresser mirror.

I don't even know what you really look like. Or if I have any part of you in my face.

Louis dropped the photo to the dresser and turned away from the mirror. He rubbed his face and glanced at his watch. It was after midnight and he needed some sleep.

He moved back to the bed and started to gather up the files. Finally, he gave up and just shoved them aside, crawling up against the pillows and leaning his head back against the headboard.

The rain was beating a steady rhythm on the roof, and he tried to relax, but there was too much junk swimming in his head. Too many pictures of girls' bruised faces and shadowy men in straw hats.

He heard a noise and sat up.

The creak of his screen door. He moved quickly off

the bed, to the bedroom door and peered out into the dark living room. There was someone there.

Louis reached around the doorjamb and flipped on the light.

Jack Cade squinted at him, his black hair matted to his head, rain streaking his face.

"What the fuck?" Louis said. "What are you doing here?"

Cade brushed his hair off his forehead. "Ronnie sold some land. I got bail."

"I don't care. Get the fuck out."

Cade slowly peeled off his windbreaker, water puddling at his feet.

Louis took a step toward him. "Hey, man, I said get out."

Cade eyed Louis through thick-lidded slits. He tossed the sodden jacket on a chair.

"When I'm ready."

Louis grabbed the jacket, opened the screen door and tossed it to the porch.

"Leave," he said, holding open the door.

"You're starting to annoy me, Louie."

"Look, you don't just walk in someone's house in the middle of the damn night."

"You afraid of me?"

"Fuck no."

"Good. We need to talk."

"Not here. You want to talk, call me at Susan Outlaw's office."

Cade didn't move. Louis stared at him, debating whether he should try to throw him out. But Cade probably had at least twenty pounds on him.

"I'm dripping on your floor here, Louie," Cade said. His eyes were traveling around the small living room, finally focusing on the bedroom door. He moved quickly to it.

"Hey!" Louis yelled. He followed Cade, letting the screen door slam.

Cade didn't stop or look back. He went through the bedroom and disappeared into the bathroom. He emerged with a towel. He vigorously rubbed his face and hair dry then tossed the towel on the floor.

"Get out of here," Louis said evenly.

But Cade just looked at him, his face shadowed by the dim light. "I could sure use a beer or something."

Louis shook his head. "I'm out. You got thirty seconds."

Cade gave a small shrug. His eyes were moving slowly over the bedroom now. Louis felt himself tense, unnerved by the intimacy of Cade's gaze as it moved across his clothes, his books, his bed. Cade's eyes came to rest on Issy. The cat was lying in the pile of clothes on the floor, its ears flattened back as it stared up at Cade.

"That your kitty?" Cade asked.

Louis didn't answer. The thunder rolled overhead, fading away. Cade was looking at the files on the bed now. He cocked his head to try to read the top one.

"Don't touch anything," Louis said.

Cade's eyes zeroed in on the blurry blowup of Kitty Jagger. He looked back at Louis. "That's my old file, ain't it?"

Cade bent and gently opened the file. Louis took a step toward him and Cade drew back, letting the folder close.

"I'd like to read it."

"Not tonight."

"I always wondered what Ahnert's take on me was."

Louis hid his surprise. "Detective Ahnert?"

"Yeah. Good old Bob."

"Forget Ahnert. You need to leave," Louis said sharply. He moved to the bed and started gathering up the files.

Cade picked up the picture of Kitty and held it out. "Forgot something," he said.

Louis grabbed the picture and stuffed it in a folder. "Look, Cade," he said. "We're going to get something straight. You don't come here unannounced and not at night. You don't ever just drop in on Miss Outlaw, either. You—"

Cade had moved away. Louis spun around.

Cade had stepped to the dresser. He picked up the old snapshot.

"Who's this?" he asked.

Louis started to grab it, but Cade was too quick. He pulled away, taking a few steps back as he looked at the picture, then back up at Louis.

"This your old man?" he asked.

"None of your fucking business."

"He still alive?"

Suddenly Louis didn't care what his chances were. He didn't want Cade touching that picture. He tensed, ready to lunge, but before he could, Cade tossed the snapshot back on the dresser. He was staring at Louis now, and Louis had a sickening feeling Cade could read his mind.

"I didn't know my old man either," Cade said. "I had my mom, but the old man, well, he was in Raiford and some bastard stuck a fork in his belly."

Cade pointed to his own chest. "Leaves a hole, you know, a hole right here."

Cade's eyes were moving slowly over the bedroom again. "Yup, fathers are important, Louie, no matter what they are. You can't separate from them, even if you want to. It's important for a man to know where he comes from, what kind of blood runs through his veins."

Louis moved quickly, grabbing Cade's arm and shoving him toward the living room. Cade jerked away, backing up.

"Let me say what I came here to say," Cade said.

"Make it quick."

"I've been thinking about what you said the other day, about that girl. I've decided I don't want you digging around in it. There's nothing there. Leave that girl dead and buried."

Louis knew Cade could probably break his neck, but he didn't care. He just wanted him out. He shoved Cade and he stumbled toward the screen door.

"Get out," Louis hissed. "You ever come here again, I'll have your ass arrested. After I kick the shit out of you."

Cade looked back at Louis, amused. He scooped his windbreaker off the porch and took a quick step toward Louis. He poked his finger in Louis's chest.

"A hole," he said. Then he smiled. "You hang onto that picture, Louie."

Cade turned and hit the screen door. It slapped closed behind him. Louis watched him disappear into the shadows of the trees.

Chapter Fourteen

It wasn't hard finding Ahnert. He was still with the Sheriff's Department, working out of a substation in a place called Corkscrew Bend. But when Louis phoned, he was told Ahnert was off for the Thanksgiving weekend. In the phone book, Louis found a Robert Ahnert living down in San Carlos Park. When he called, a cheerful woman named Brenda told him her father-in-law loved visitors and that Louis should come on by.

When Louis pulled up to the pink house, a young man came out the front door, the sun glinting off something silver on his chest. He was just a silhouette in the brightness, but Louis recognized the crisp blue sleeves, the bulge of a holster and the swing of the baton at his hip.

"Can I help you?"

Louis walked to the porch, stepping into the shade of a palm tree so he could see the officer's face. He was definitely Fort Myers police, and his face still had that eager look that went with being new. He wasn't a detective, so why was he here? As far as Louis knew, no one at the department cared about Kitty Jagger.

"My name's Kincaid. I'm here to see Bob Ahnert."

The officer grinned. "Oh yeah, Dad's been waiting on you. He's been excited all morning, thinking someone wanted to come ask about some old case."

"You work for Chief Horton?" Louis asked.

"Yeah, just passed my six-month mark. You know Horton?"

Louis nodded. "Met him last March."

Suddenly, the officer's face changed. "You're *that* Kincaid." He recovered enough to stick out his hand. "Dave Ahnert, pleasure to meet you."

Louis shook his hand, wondering what Dave Ahnert had heard about him.

Dave Ahnert turned to the open front door. "Dad! You got company!" He turned back to Louis. "I gotta get going. Let yourself in."

Louis watched him trot to the curb, where a blue and white cruiser was pulling up. When Louis turned back to the house, Bob Ahnert was standing on the porch.

He was a big guy, pushing sixty, with a silver brush-cut atop a fleshy sunburned face. Black-rimmed glasses circled piercing blue eyes.

"Mr. Ahnert?"

"That's me," he said.

"I'm Louis Kincaid, I called earlier."

Ahnert stared at him through the glasses, his lips drawn in a line.

"I called Sheriff Mobley," Ahnert said. "Asked him if he knew what you might want with me. He said you were looking into the Kitty Jagger case. That true?"

Louis nodded, feeling the sun on his back.

"Why?" Ahnert asked.

"I think the Spencer Duvall case and Kitty's murder might be related."

"Jack Cade was convicted of killing Kitty. That isn't good enough for you?"

Louis shook his head. "No, it isn't."

Ahnert stared at him a long time. Louis squinted at Ahnert, trying to read his face. "You going to talk to me or not?" Louis asked finally.

Ahnert nodded toward the house. "Come on in," he said.

Louis followed Ahnert through the living room and into a dimly lit den. Louis paused at the doorway, struck by the smell of stale cigar smoke. The blinds were drawn and the television was on, tuned to a rerun of *Barney Miller*.

The walls were covered with framed pictures, lots of family portraits that showed a young Ahnert with his brunette wife and two kids, and then a succession of portraits capturing the kids as they grew. A second wall was given over to photographs of cops in various color uniforms and group photos of the Lee County Sheriff's Office. There was a portrait of a very young Ahnert in his uniform. He looked remarkably like his son Dave, the same eagerness there in the eyes.

Ahnert settled into a frayed green chair stained at the headrest. He picked up the remote and muted the sound but didn't turn it off.

"Take a seat," Ahnert said. "I don't like looking up at people."

Louis took the chair next to him. On the small table between them was the remains of a turkey sandwich and an ashtray that held a dead cigar and a book of matches from O'Sullivan's Bar.

"Did you read my case file?" Ahnert asked.

Louis nodded. "Once through."

"Then you see what I saw."

"There's more to a case than ink and paper. You were there. You spoke with people. You saw the crime scene. You must have gotten a sense of Kitty's case."

Ahnert snorted softly, looking toward the television. "A sense? What good are senses? It's evidence that convicts, not ESP."

Louis leaned forward. "Jack Cade asked about you."

Ahnert's eyes shot to Louis's face. "Why would he do that?"

"You tell me," Louis said. "He wondered what your 'take' on him was. Why would he care? What kind of relationship did you have?"

Ahnert picked up the matchbook. Louis hoped he wasn't going to light the cigar.

"I didn't care about him, and the relationship as you call it was non-existent," Ahnert said. "I was a cop, he was a suspect. I never gave him any reason to think I wanted anything but the truth."

"Did you get it?"

Ahnert looked back at the television again. "I've worked thirty-five years for this department, Mr. Kincaid. It was and is a good department, with good officers. We did everything right on that case. We did it by the book. We had everything we needed to charge Jack Cade and get him convicted."

"I know. I saw the evidence. But I still have questions."

Ahnert nodded, flipping the matchbook open and closed with his fingers as he stared blankly at the TV screen. "All right then. Go ahead and ask."

"I read that Kitty's father reported her missing around midnight the night she didn't come home. There's no missing person's report in the file. Did you take one?"

Ahnert didn't look at him. "Procedure was twenty-four hours."

"Small town in the sixties, a minor girl?" Louis paused a beat. "So why didn't you take a report?"

Ahnert didn't answer. Louis was about to ask again when suddenly Ahnert pushed himself out of the chair and went to the far wall. He took down one of the framed pictures and held it out to Louis.

"This is why," Ahnert said.

Louis took it. It was a color portrait of a teenaged girl with long dark hair, aged seventeen or eighteen. It was probably a class portrait, but the girl wasn't wearing the usual prim blouse or sweater. She was dressed in a rainbow tie-dyed dress, a bright green headband tied across her forehead. She was wearing a collar of white beads. He'd seen the beads before. Amy, his baby-sitter, used to wear them, along with those big hoop earrings and heavy mascara that made her look like a very young Cher. What did they call those damn beads? Peace beads? Puka beads, that was it.

"That's my daughter, Lou Ann," Ahnert said. "She ran away from home on Thanksgiving night. Ran off to San Francisco to be a goddamn hippie. 'Make love, not war,' they said. Called me—her own father—a pig the night she left."

Louis handed the photo back.

"Her mother died a couple years later," Ahnert said, hanging the photo back up. "Lou Ann didn't even send a card."

"Kids can be self-centered."

Ahnert didn't answer. He came back and sat down in the chair, his eyes going back to the television. Louis waited, watching Detectives Fish and Dietrich mouth an argument.

"You thought Kitty Jagger was a runaway?" Louis said finally.

Ahnert gave a small nod. "When that call came in, I didn't see much sense in pulling overtime to chase down an ungrateful teenager who was probably out smoking dope.''

Louis could feel his anger welling up inside. Willard Jagger reported Kitty missing one hour after she left work. If she had been abducted—or even gone willingly with someone—there was a good chance she was still alive when Ahnert got the call.

"You made a mistake, Detective," Louis said. "She might have still been alive at midnight."

Ahnert's shoulders visibly tightened. "I don't believe she was."

It's easier to believe that, Louis thought. But he said nothing. He should have known Ahnert would protect his procedure. And his case. Anything less would make him look incompetent. There was nothing left to try but a little fishing.

"Did you know Kitty?" Louis asked.

Ahnert's fingers paused on the matchbook. "I knew of her."

"Enough to believe she was a runaway," Louis said, not bothering to keep the sarcasm out of his voice.

Ahnert didn't look at him. "I knew she was Willard's daughter. I had seen her around town." He paused. "I found out more about her when we got into the investigation."

"Like what?"

Ahnert's eyes came back to Louis's face and rested there for several seconds before going back to the matchbook.

"She lived with her old man, took care of him, just the two of them in that house over in Edgewood Heights." Ahnert was staring at the TV again. "Edgewood was a part of town that no one paid attention to, kind of low class. I think because of that people maybe thought Kitty was too. There wasn't the outrage that would have come with the murder of, let's say, the prom queen or a big-shot's daughter."

Louis had the feeling Ahnert was including himself in that damnation.

"But there was a quick arrest," Louis said.

"Folks were afraid Cade might start hunting in better neighborhoods."

Louis sensed a softening in Ahnert's voice. "Do you believe Jack Cade killed her?"

"Sheriff Dinkle felt we had our man," he said.

"What about you?"

Ahnert hesitated. "I believe every piece of evidence should be examined and explained. Things that aren't explained leave doubts. Doubts that don't go away."

Louis let Ahnert's words hang in the air as they both stared at the television. A clock ticked somewhere in the room.

"Detective, what were the doubts?" Louis finally asked.

Ahnert seemed frozen in the chair, but his fist closed slowly around the O'Sullivan's matchbook.

"Dinkle was a good sheriff. He just liked to keep things simple for the lawyers."

Louis leaned forward. "Are you saying you withheld evidence?"

Ahnert shook his head. "Of course not. The lawyers had every piece of paper I collected."

"Then *what* happened?"

Ahnert unwrapped his fist and looked down at the matchbook, taking a deep breath. "I just had a few more questions to ask and I wasn't allowed to ask them."

"Dinkle stopped you?"

Ahnert shrugged. "It was probably nothing. Nothing that would prove Jack Cade innocent. Just a few loose ends."

Louis clenched his jaw. Excuses from a cowardly old cop.

"If you couldn't ask the questions twenty years ago,

let me ask them now," Louis said. "What's the harm? Dinkle's dead. You're about to retire—"

Louis heard a car pull into the drive. Ahnert stood up and went to the window, bending a slat in the blinds.

"My daughter-in-law is home."

"Detective," Louis said, "I think you want to tell me something."

"You'd better leave now, Mr. Kincaid."

Louis stood up. "Okay, I get it. You got a lot of uniforms looking up to you. Maybe you don't want your name brought up in this mess. I can understand that. But don't leave me hanging on this. Jack Cade was convicted of killing Kitty Jagger. And this whole damn town is about to convict him for another murder."

Ahnert looked suddenly very tired. Louis drew in a breath, angry at himself for getting angry.

"Detective, please," Louis said.

Ahnert pursed his lips, then nodded. "There are two things in the file you should look at."

"I don't have the time to keep going through a file looking—"

Ahnert's hard blue eyes silenced him. "You have more time than I had, Kincaid."

Louis took a breath, forcing himself to calm down. "Okay, what about the file?"

Ahnert hesitated. "There is something in there that should make you ask *why is this here?* And the other is something that should be there, but isn't."

Louis felt his anger rising again. "Come on, man, don't pull this Deep Throat act with me."

The front door opened. A moment later, a woman appeared at the door of the den, her arms filled with grocery bags. Her eyes went from Louis to Ahnert and she smiled.

"Hey Dad, I see you got a visitor," she said.

"Yeah, but he's just leaving," Ahnert said. "Let me help you with those, Brenda."

"There's more in the car," she said, heading off to the kitchen.

Ahnert went out the front door. Louis followed him out to the station wagon in the driveway. As Ahnert was about to reach in for a bag, Louis grabbed his arm.

"Give me something real, someone to talk to," Louis said.

"Talk to Kitty," Ahnert said.

"Come on, Detective."

"That's all I'm saying," Ahnert said. "Talk to Kitty."

Louis let go of Ahnert's arm. He thought of the sign outside Vince Carissimi's autopsy room: *Mortui Vivos Docent.* The dead teach the living.

"What, the autopsy report?" he asked.

"Talk to Kitty," Ahnert repeated. "But be careful."

"Of what?"

Ahnert hoisted a bag of groceries up into his arms. "That you don't start hearing Kitty talking back to you."

Chapter Fifteen

The beeper went off. Louis grabbed it off his belt and tossed it on the passenger seat. He knew without looking that it was Susan again. He would eventually have to break down and call her. But not now.

Now he wanted to calm the demons that had been swirling around in his brain since leaving Bob Ahnert's house, and he didn't want Susan yanking on his chain trying to reel him back to the Duvall case, deal or no deal.

Talk to Kitty. Okay, he would go back and look at the autopsy report again. But he knew Ahnert meant more than that. Ahnert knew what every detective knew: Walk in the dead person's shoes and you'll find the killer.

So now he was on his way to find Kitty Jagger's home. And her father—if he was still alive.

It didn't take Louis long to find Edgewood Heights. It was north of downtown, an old neighborhood of small homes with the cookie-cutter, slapdash look of the Levittown boxes that had sprung up in the '50s. It might have been a nice neighborhood in its day, populated by young couples just starting out. But now most of the homes needed work and had iron bars on the windows and rusted trucks in the drives. Louis suspected it had probably looked much the same when Kitty lived here.

Louis pulled up in front of 5446 Balboa. The house was a small rectangle, a faded gray that had probably been blue once. There were empty flower boxes under the plain windows. As he went up the cracked sidewalk, Louis noticed the overgrown shrubs and bare flower-beds, the brick edgers scattered in the dirt. A sun-bleached plastic flamingo lay by the front door.

He knocked. He was about to give up when he heard the lock turn. The door opened and an old man squinted in the sunlight.

"Yeah?"

Louis knew from the police reports that Willard Jagger had been only forty-five when Kitty was murdered. This guy looked at least eighty.

"Mr. Jagger?" Louis asked.

The man retreated behind the door. "What you want?"

"My name is Louis Kincaid. I'm an investigator and I'd like to talk to you about your daughter."

"Daughter? Ain't got no daughter."

"You're Willard Jagger, Kitty Jagger's father?" Louis asked.

Something passed over the man's face. "Kitty?" he said. "You're here about Kitty? Something happened to Kitty?"

Louis hesitated. The guy was really confused, or sick maybe.

"Mr. Jagger, may I come in?" Louis asked gently.

Willard Jagger's milky blue eyes were searching

Louis's face, like he was desperately trying to recognize him. He started to close the door. But Louis realized he was just unhooking a chain. The door swung open. Louis went in.

Willard Jagger was standing in the middle of a small living room, looking back at Louis. He was wearing old baggy pants, a short-sleeved sports shirt and beat-up slippers.

"I'm sorry. I get mixed up sometimes," he said. He rubbed his stringy gray hair vigorously, his eyes moving around the room and coming back to Louis.

"Who'd you say you were again?"

"Louis Kincaid. I'm a private investigator."

"Like Mannix? Don't care for that show too much. Too much violence . . ."

Louis wasn't sure how to handle this. It was clear Williard Jagger wasn't well.

"Can I get you an apple juice?" Willard said suddenly.

Before Louis could say no, Willard shuffled off to the kitchen. Louis sat down on the worn sofa, letting his gaze travel around the living room while he waited for Willard to come back.

The furniture was old Danish modern, the cushions a threadbare turquoise, the drapes a pattern of orange and turquoise squiggles. The carpet was worn orange shag, and a turquoise vinyl Barcalounger sat in one corner, guarded by a goosenecked floor lamp that looked like something out of *The Jetsons*. Over the sofa hung a large fake oil painting of Venice and every surface was covered with little ceramic dogs. There was an old blond Zenith console TV, a stack of albums resting against its side. Off in one corner, a large rotating fan sent the stale air swirling around Louis's ankles.

The room wasn't dirty. But it felt like it was, like it hadn't been opened to sunlight in years.

Willard returned empty-handed. "I'm out," he said.

"That's okay," Louis said.

Willard looked upset, but he settled into the Barca-lounger across from Louis.

"Could we talk about your daughter, Mr. Jagger?"

"My daughter?"

"Kitty . . . can we talk about Kitty?"

Willard's eyes were wandering around the room. "The home care lady comes once a week. On Fridays. I'll have to tell her to get apple juice. The fella who brings me the box food, he never remembers the apple juice." He was sitting rod-straight in the lounger, eyes on the dead TV, hands tapping lightly on the armrests.

The fan whirred, stirring the fetid air.

Louis hung his head. He wasn't going to get anything out of this. He was about to get up when Willard spoke again.

"Kitty . . ."

Louis looked up at Willard.

"She didn't call," he said. "She always called when she was going to be late. But she didn't call."

Louis leaned forward. "She was working at the drive-in that night," he said gently.

Willard nodded. "Took the bus. She gets it right at the corner of McGregor and Linhart. Leaves her off at Evans Street. Only three block walk from there. She always took the bus. The number five down Mac-Gregor. Only three blocks . . ."

"Maybe she went out with friends that night after work?" Louis prodded.

Willard shook his head. "She always called."

"What about boyfriends?"

Willard shook his head harder. "No dating 'til she's sixteen . . . we agreed on that."

Louis slid his notebook out of his jeans. "You and your daughter were close, Mr. Jagger?"

He looked at Louis, a slight frown on his waxy face. "Huh?"

"You cared about each other?"

A small smile tipped Willard's lips and he nodded. "Kitty took care of me," he said. His eyes wandered back to the blank TV. "After Rosalie died, Kitty took care of me. Washed my shirts, made me grilled cheese sandwiches, took care of Rosalie's flowers."

Rosalie was Kitty's mother, Louis recalled from the police reports. She had died when Kitty was twelve.

"What was Kitty like, Mr. Jagger?" Louis asked.

Willard looked at Louis. "Like? Like her mother, I guess." He smiled, his eyes brightening for a moment. "Pretty. God, Rosalie was pretty."

Louis shut his notebook with a sigh. He rose, his eyes traveling one last time around the room. This was such a lonely house, filled with shadows, memories and ghosts.

He had a thought. "Mr. Jagger? Could you show me Kitty's room?" he asked.

Willard looked over at him, like he was seeing him for the first time. Then, he hoisted himself out of the lounger and started off down a hallway. Louis followed.

They stopped at a closed door. There were some bright green and orange flower decals on the cheap wood. Louis waited, but Willard was just standing there, staring at the decals.

"Close the door when you're done," he said, leaving Louis alone.

The door stuck; Louis had to put a shoulder against it to open it. The air wafted out, musty but strangely sweet.

The curtains were shut, casting the room in a pink glow. Louis reached inside and flipped on the light.

Small, maybe ten-by-ten. Pale pink everywhere. A single bed, a tiny night stand and dresser. A small wire stand in the corner holding a record player.

Louis went in. The bed was unmade, a nightgown left in the tangle of pink chenille and flowered sheets.

A tattered sock monkey and a stuffed pink cat lay at the foot of the bed. A pile of clothes lay on the floor, mixed in with some scuffed white tennis shoes, a geography textbook and a blue looseleaf binder.

His eyes swept over the walls. A poster of the Beatles in Gay 90s bathing suits, another from the surfing movie *The Endless Summer,* a garish psychedelic poster for Moby Grape at the Fillmore, and one from the movie *Goldfinger.*

He went to the night stand. A tiny white lamp, a cheap transistor radio, two bottles of pink nail polish and a magazine. Louis picked it up. It was the February, 1966 issue of *16* Magazine: BEATLES 66 WOW-EE PIX! DC5 ON THE LOOSE! PETER & GORDON'S UNTOLD SECRETS!

Louis put the magazine back in its place. He turned to the record player. It was an old model that played only 45s. Louis craned his neck to read the top one on the spindle. Leslie Gore's "You Don't Own Me."

The sweet smell was getting to him.

He turned to the dresser. The top was a mess of brushes, rollers, makeup, perfume bottles and plastic jewelry. Spilled white dusting powder covered everything like a fine layer of snow.

He slowly opened the top drawer. Maybe there would be a diary; girls wrote secrets in diaries. He picked carefully through the tangle of jewelry and junk. Nothing. He went on to the second drawer, gingerly moving aside the underclothes. The third drawer was just more clothes. Nothing . . .

He turned his attention back to the mess on the top of the dresser. There was something touching about it, like all the paraphernalia was the stuff of some grand experiment. Girl metamorphosing to woman.

Louis picked up a tube of lipstick. Yardley's Peppermint Kiss. He slowly twirled it open. Frosty pink, like the inside of a shell.

He set it down and picked up one of the half a dozen perfume bottles. It was called Heaven Scent. He brought it up to his nose and drew back.

It was cloying sweet. It was the smell that still clung to the room after twenty years.

He set the perfume down, letting out a long breath. *Jesus...*

Time had stopped. He could almost see her, jumping out of bed, late for school, coming back and dumping her books, changing into her uniform before hurrying off to work.

His eyes traveled slowly around the tiny room again. They had just left everything. Why hadn't anyone packed her things away? And that old man sitting out in his lounge chair, like he was still waiting for her to walk in the door and make grilled cheese. It would be sick if it weren't so damn sad.

What about you, Kincaid? What are you doing in here, lurking around like some vulture picking at the bones?

The sweet smell was making him sick. He wanted to get this over with and get out.

But get *what* over with? He didn't even know what he was looking for. He rummaged through the mess on the top of the dresser again. There was a small jewelry box. It was one of those boxes with the little twirling plastic ballerina inside, but the figure didn't move when he opened it.

More junk. Buttons. Flower Power. Don't Trust Anyone Over Thirty. I Am a Human Being: Do Not Bend, Spindle or Mutilate.

Snapshots at the bottom. Louis pulled them out. There were five, mostly shots of another girl, a plump redhead, taken at a beach. Louis briefly considered keeping them and trying to track down the girlfriend, but discarded the idea as futile.

He stopped and pulled in a slow breath.

It was a color snapshot of Kitty Jagger. She was laying on her side on a towel in the sand. Her skin was tan and she was wearing a two-piece bathing suit, pink checks with a band of ruffles across the bra top. Large brown eyes, full lips. Her hair hung in long yellow ribbons over the pink ruffles. She was smiling up at whoever had snapped the picture, her head propped up by one hand, her other hand draped over the deep curve of her bare brown waist.

Louis eased himself down onto the edge of the bed, staring at the picture.

Fifteen . . .

This was the first real picture he had seen of her. The blurry copy from the old newspaper article, that had shown a pretty girl in a sweater smiling obediently for a class photo.

But this . . . this was not a girl.

Louis squeezed his eyes shut. His head was starting to hurt from the smell. He opened his eyes.

It would have been a seductive pose. If she had known. But Kitty Jagger didn't know. He was sure; he could see it there in the guileless smile. She had absolutely no concept of her power.

He rose slowly from the bed. He started to put the photo back with the others in the jewelry box. He hesitated, then slipped it in his back pocket.

The bedroom door would not close. He had to give it a hard shove. When he went back out in the living room, Willard Jagger was still sitting in the turquoise lounger. The television was on to a soap opera, the sound turned low.

Willard looked up at him blankly. Louis was afraid he wasn't going to remember him.

"You still here?" Willard said.

Louis nodded. "Mr. Jagger, do you remember Kitty's friends?"

Willard just looked at him blankly.

"Kitty had a girlfriend with red hair?" Louis prompted.

Willard blinked several times, like something had suddenly registered. "Joyce," he said.

"You remember Joyce's last name?"

Willard just stared at him. "Joyce," he said softly. The light went out in his eyes.

Louis took a last look around the small living room. "I'm leaving now, Mr. Jagger," he said. "Thank you for talking to me. And for letting me in her room."

"Did you close the door?"

"Yes."

Willard nodded, his eyes locked on the television.

Louis quickly let himself out the front door.

His head was pounding as he got in the Mustang and headed back downtown. He couldn't get that sickly sweet smell or the picture of Kitty out of his head. Or the idea that had just started to build. Did Kitty have another side to her that others didn't see? Could she have elicited her killer somehow? A boyfriend, an unknown admirer? Shit . . . or Cade?

He turned onto First Street. Damn, Susan would take his head off if he even brought this up. Blaming the victim because she was attractive was neanderthal brain thinking. It was also cop brain thinking. No one liked to admit it, but the vestige of sexual bias was still there.

No dating, Willard had said. And Ahnert's reports had not mentioned any boyfriends. That still didn't mean boys . . . men . . . didn't see what he himself saw in the photo.

The beeper went off. He ignored it.

How was he going to get Susan to let him stay with this? Especially when he had no leads.

At McGregor and Linhart, he stopped at a light. Linhart Avenue. That's where Kitty got on the bus after work.

The light changed and Louis swung across the left

lane, cutting off a truck. The guy leaned out to give him the finger. Louis turned onto Linhart.

He drove slowly past a stripmall, a medical complex and the Driftwood Motel. He braked hard.

Damn . . .

There it was. Hamburger Heaven. It was still there.

It had been remodeled, he guessed. The drive-in spots had been blacktopped over, the speakers taken out, the fifties-style architecture tarted up with tropical pastels. But it still had an old neon sign that advertised "Best Fries In Florida."

He parked and went in, taking a stool at the counter. When a young waitress approached with a menu, he realized he had not eaten all day.

"Can I help you?" she asked.

"Only if you were about twenty years older," Louis said.

She frowned.

"Sorry. Bring me a cheeseburger, fries and a Coke, please."

The place was nearly deserted even though it was lunch time. Louis saw the white cap and black face of the cook. The smell of frying meat filled the cool air.

Louis thumbed through the countertop jukebox while he waited. It was a mix of oldies and new stuff. "Big Girls Don't Cry" by the Four Seasons. "Papa Don't Preach" by Madonna.

The waitress brought his food. The fries were a golden mound next to a plump-bunned burger.

"Looks great," Louis said.

"If you like grease," the waitress said.

"A quick question," Louis said.

She looked suspicious.

"Is there anyone here who was working here twenty years ago?"

"Ray was, I think. I mean, he's really old."

"Is Ray the owner?"

"No, the owner's dead. Ray is his son." She paused. "You looking for a job? Ray's looking for a cook. I'll go get him."

She was gone before Louis could say anything. He tried a fry. It was delicious. He dug into the burger. It was cooked just right.

A man emerged from the back. He was about forty-five, red-faced, his big belly wrapped in an apron.

"You the guy asking about the cook's job?" he said, coming up to Louis, wiping his hands on the apron.

"No, the waitress misunderstood," Louis said. "I'm an investigator. I'm looking for some information."

"Investigator? What you investigating?"

"Kitty Jagger's death."

Ray was silent for moment. "I guess this has something to do with that Cade guy?"

"Why do you say that?"

"I read in the paper he got arrested again. He kill another girl?" He shook his head. "Man, they should've never let that bastard out."

Louis let it go. "Were you here when Kitty worked here?"

Ray nodded. "My dad owned the place then. I was working for him, learning the business. I was only nineteen."

"So you knew Kitty?"

Ray smiled slightly. "Oh yeah. Kitty was a great kid."

"Were you here the last night she worked?"

Ray's smile faded. "Yeah, but I left early. I wish I hadn't. I wish I had given her a ride home."

"You gave her rides home?"

"When she'd let me. Mostly she walked down to the bus stop."

Louis paused, wondering where to go with this. "What kind of girl was Kitty?" he asked.

"What you mean?"

"Did she have a lot of friends?"

Ray shrugged. "I guess. I mean, she wasn't one of the real popular kids, you know, the inner circle. You know how bad things can be in high schools with the cliques. There was only her and Joyce. They were like joined at the hip."

"Joyce? Did she have red hair?"

Ray nodded. "She worked here with Kitty."

"You remember her last name?"

"Crutchfield. I don't know if she's still around, but I remember she dropped out in her senior year and married some guy named Novack. I think he was from Immokalee."

"What about boyfriends?" Louis asked. "Did you ever see Kitty with anyone?"

Ray hesitated. "Not really."

"What does that mean?"

"I mean, there wasn't one guy she was interested in. Though the guys that came in here, they sure were interested in her." He paused, seeing the look on Louis's face. "She was beautiful," he said. "I mean, not just pretty like some girls. Kitty was beautiful. She could've been a model or something."

"These guys," Louis said. "Any of them try to pick her up?"

Ray looked uncomfortable. "Yeah. But she never went."

Louis had to ask. "Did you?"

"Did I what?"

"Try to pick her up?"

Ray's beefy face got redder.

"Ray, I'm not a cop," Louis said.

"Okay, I asked her out once. She turned me down, all right?"

Louis had a vision of the fat teenaged Ray sweating up the courage to ask Kitty Jagger out. He hoped she had been kind.

"She give you any reason?"

Ray frowned. "Yeah, in fact she did. And you know what? I still remember. Twenty years later and I still remember exactly what she said."

Louis waited.

"She said, 'I'm saving myself for a rich guy.' " Ray shook his head. "Shit, like she was going to find a way out, going home every night to her crippled old man."

The tone of Ray's voice had changed. "What a waste," he said.

A phone rang. The waitress called Ray's name and told him he had a call.

"I gotta go," Ray said to Louis. He pointed at the fries. "What do you think?"

"Best in Florida," Louis said.

Ray gave a wry smile. "Lot of good it does me. The high school is only two blocks away, but they all go to McDonald's now."

Louis popped the last fry in his mouth and stood. "Thanks for your help."

Ray went in the back. Louis left money on the counter with a nice tip for the waitress. Outside, he paused, his headache gone now, but the images of Kitty's bedroom still a swirl in his head. He had to find Joyce Novack.

He paused to put on his sunglasses and his eyes drifted down to the newstand by the door. The headline in that morning's *News-Press* couldn't be missed.

HAITIAN PRISONER KILLED IN JAIL

Louis bought a paper and scanned the story. Jesus. The man who had been sitting next to him and Cade the other day had been stabbed to death. An investigation was ongoing, according to Mobley.

Louis got in the car. He was just starting the car

when the beeper went off again. He grabbed it off the seat and got out, going to the pay phone. He dialed Susan's office.

"Where the hell have you been?" she demanded.

"Never mind that right now."

"Never mind? Look—"

"Susan, we have to talk."

"Damn right we have to talk. We had a deal—"

"Not now. I'll meet you at O'Sullivan's in fifteen minutes."

"Screw that. I can't—"

"Be there, Susan. This is important." He hung up.

Chapter Sixteen

O'Sullivan's was nuts-to-butts cops. The Tampa Bay Bucs were battling the Bears to a soundtrack of clacking billiard balls and the swoosh of the bar dishwasher.

Louis made his way to the bar, the newspaper under his arm. He scanned the smoky room for Susan but didn't see her. He hoped she hurried.

The football game broke for half-time and Louis looked up as a news update came on the screen. A small picture of a Haitian man came on the screen and the bar went silent.

"Sheriff's officials are remaining silent on the death of a Haitian inmate Friday night in the Lee County jail. In a statement released this morning, the sheriff's department said Lucien Faure was found dead in the inmates' shower facilities. Officials stated Faure bled to death, but no weapon has been found. Officials have not named any suspects."

"Who the fuck cares?" someone hollered from the back.

The man next to Louis shook his head. "The lawyers will be all over this. I heard the Haitian Liberty League is already beating down Mobley's door."

Louis didn't comment. He pulled the newspaper from under his arm and stared at the face of the dead Haitian.

Someone touched his shoulder. He turned to see Susan. She was dressed in jeans and a sweater, her face icy in the flat light given off by the bar. He motioned for her to follow him into a dim hallway back by the restrooms. He handed her the newspaper folded to the article.

She looked at it, then back at him. "So?"

"I think Jack Cade killed him."

"What makes you think so?"

"Last time I saw Cade at the jail, this same guy was next to us, talking to someone," Louis said. "Cade got pissed at them, wanted them to shut up, said they were annoying him."

Louis waited while a man pushed between them, headed for the john. "Then last night, Cade showed up at my house."

"He came to your house? Why?"

"He gave me this bullshit story about wanting to talk about Kitty Jagger, but while he was there, he told me his old man was killed by a fork to the belly. Leaves a hole, he said."

She looked at him blankly.

He poked a finger at her chest. "A hole, he said."

"Cade's been out since . . . what? Saturday afternoon?"

"The guy was stabbed Friday night."

Susan frowned. "That doesn't mean Cade killed—"

Louis raised a hand to silence her until another man moved past them.

"All right, we know he's despicable, Louis," she

said, her voice lower. "But there's nothing we need
to do about this. There's no evidence, and Cade's not
a suspect or I would have been the first to know." She
held out the paper. "I'd say it's not our problem."

He took the paper back. "We have to tell Mobley."

"The hell we do. Besides, you can't even if you
wanted to."

"Why not?"

"Excuse me," someone said.

Susan stepped aside to let a man pass, then leaned
close to him. "You're an official agent of the public
defender's office. You're bound by confidentiality.
Anything Cade says to you is privileged."

"Bullshit. Not if he was planning to commit another
crime. Even I know that."

"Did Cade threaten the Haitian man? Did he make
any move toward him?"

"No."

"When he came to your place, did he tell you he
did it?"

Louis was getting pissed. "No."

"Then we have no legal obligation," she said.

"What about a moral one?" Louis snapped.

"Morality doesn't come in to play here. Besides, do
you know what an accusation like that would do to
our case at this point? We have a big enough problem
with Cade's image as it is."

Louis tightened, turning away. "I don't believe
this."

Susan gave him a minute, then touched his arm. "It's
just your cop brain kicking in, Kincaid. It'll pass."

"It's wrong."

"It's the law."

"Aren't you the least bit worried Cade will get pissed
at me or you and put a hole in one of us?"

Susan was trying to keep a steady gaze, but it

wavered slightly as she spoke. "I've been threatened before. Goes with the territory."

He leaned back against the wall.

"Look, forget this," Susan said. "What else have you got? Did you hunt down Candace's girlfriend yet?"

"No," Louis said, folding the newspaper slowly.

"What about Bernhardt? Or the divorce? Anything new?"

He was silent.

"Damn it, Kincaid, what the hell have you been doing all day? I paged you four or five times."

"I went to see Bob Ahnert and Willard Jagger."

Susan's mouth drew into a line. "Who is Bob Ahnert?"

"The detective who worked Kitty's murder."

She was silent. Louis could almost see her counting to ten. Or thinking of a way to take his head off while twenty cops watched.

"Well, that's just great," she said finally. "I'm grasping at straws and you're out chasing irrelevant shit."

Louis glared at her. "Ahnert is important."

"For what?"

"Background. It's important to show Duvall may have manipulated Cade's case. It's important to Cade's motive."

"Cade doesn't *have* a motive because we're trying to show he didn't do it!"

Another man tried to push past them and Susan turned on him. "Can't you wait?"

"Screw you, lady," the man mumbled.

Louis took her by the shoulders and moved her aside. When the man passed, she shook her head.

"Reasonable doubt, Kincaid, reasonable doubt. That's all I need to show. I'm not Perry Mason, for God's sake. Real lawyers don't prove who else did it, only that someone else *could* have. We can't waste time—"

Louis heard Mobley's name and looked over Susan's head toward the front door. Mobley had come in and was chatting with some of his deputies at the bar.

Susan was still talking. ". . . and Bernhardt and the wife are certainly more believable as suspects—"

"Excuse me," Louis said.

Susan spotted Mobley and grabbed Louis's arm. "What are you going to do?"

"I don't know."

"Don't tell Mobley anything, please. You could take both of us down."

He pulled away from her and walked to the bar, edging up to Mobley.

"We need to talk, Sheriff."

"Well, it's the Lone Ranger," Mobley said. "Where's Tonto?" He saw Susan approaching and raised a hand. "How," he said solemnly.

She didn't even look at either of them as she swept by.

"That woman could use a charm course," Mobley said.

Louis saw Susan pause at the door and look back at him before she left. Louis looked back at Mobley.

Damn it. She was right. What was the point? The Haitian wasn't going to get any deader. But Mobley could make life miserable for Susan, and Cade's case could end up in the toilet. Okay, it could wait for now. God help them, though, if Cade got a burr up his ass because someone else pissed him off.

"What do you want, Kincaid?" Mobley asked.

"Never mind."

"Good. It's assholes and elbows at work and I don't need any shit from you."

Louis motioned to the bartender to bring both

Mobley and himself a beer. When it arrived, Mobley looked at him.

"If that's a bribe, I don't come that cheap."

"Not a bribe. Just incentive."

"For what?"

Louis leaned on the bar, moving closer to Mobley. "I saw Bob Ahnert today."

"I heard."

"He indicated he wasn't allowed to ask all the questions he needed to ask in the Kitty Jagger case. Said Dinkle stopped him."

"Look, Kincaid, Howard Dinkle is like God in this town. And as much as I hate hearing about the golden days of Dinkle, I'm not going to let you pin a misconduct medal on a fellow cop, even though I hear you're pretty good at that kind of thing."

Louis let the comment pass. "Ahnert also said there is something in the file that can get those questions answered."

Mobley shook his head. "Let me tell you something about Robert Ahnert. I pulled his jacket after he called me about you. Ahnert was a lot like you, always digging too deep and too long. He caught the Jagger case because our other detective was on leave of absence. He was reprimanded during that case for inappropriate behavior, so it's no wonder he blames Dinkle for not being able to do his job."

"What was the inappropriate behavior?"

Mobley eyed him. "That's confidential."

"I'm getting to hate that word."

Mobley snickered. "All right, I'll tell you, just so you know how little stock to put on his investigation. He stole an item that belonged to the victim."

Louis looked over. "What was it?"

"A gold necklace. Some kind of heart-shaped locket. Guess Ahnert needed the money."

"Why? Did he pawn it?"

Mobley shook his head. "Someone else found it in his cruiser before he could pawn it. But if he wasn't going to pawn it or sell it, why the fuck would he take it?"

Louis resisted the urge to touch his own back pocket. He knew the picture he had taken from Kitty's bedroom was still there.

"I've got to go," Louis said suddenly. "Thanks, Sheriff."

"You owe me again, Kincaid," Mobley said. "And like I said, I don't come cheap."

Chapter Seventeen

Louis sat in the Mustang a long time, Monday's newspaper folded on his lap. He had not wanted to come out here to J.C. Landscaping again. The place had a sadness about it that drained him. But the questions couldn't wait.

He wanted to know about why Cade had asked about Bob Ahnert. He wanted to know more about Kitty and what Cade told Spencer Duvall during the trial. And he wanted to know about the Haitian man.

He got out of the car. It was almost December, but the temperature was still in the mid-eighties, the air sticky and thick. He looked at the lopsided trailer, sitting in the brush, baking under the mid-day sun.

As he started to the door, Ronnie came around the back of the trailer, carrying a small tree, its roots wrapped in burlap. It looked dead.

Ronnie stopped and put the tree down. He ran his forearm across his forehead and smiled nervously.

"Hey, Mr. Kincaid."

Louis took off his sunglasses. "Is your father here, Ronnie?"

"Yeah, inside." Ronnie nodded to the trailer but made no move toward it. Louis suspected he was embarrassed to have him inside.

Finally, Ronnie wiped his hands on his jeans and led Louis to the trailer. The door stuck and Ronnie had to jerk on it to get it open.

"Come on in," Ronnie said.

The trailer was dark, sunlight kept out by tinfoil duct-taped to the windows. The paneling on the walls was a faded brown, warped from the humidity and streaked with some kind of dried liquid. The place smelled of dirty clothes, dog food and something fried. A chugging wall unit a/c was not making a dent in the heat.

The kitchen was just an alcove off the living room, dimly lit by a flickering fixture over the sink. The appliances were the same vintage as the trailer, Louis suspected, old avocado things with chipped corners and missing dials.

Ronnie's son, Eric, was sitting at the small table in the kitchen, finishing a sandwich. His dark eyes settled on Louis's face and for an instant, Louis saw Jack Cade in him again. Eric's face had the pink smoothness of a boy, but his eyes the dead glaze of someone who had already given up.

Benjamin Outlaw's face came to Louis's mind, with its bright curiosity and hope.

"Dad?" Ronnie called. "Louis Kincaid is here to see you."

Jack Cade came down the narrow hallway, zipping his pants. His well-muscled arms were exposed by the white T-shirt he wore. His hair was ragged and he had two or three days growth on his jaw.

"You just come around without calling?" Cade

asked, reaching for a beer can on the counter. "You threw me out of your place for that."

"I need to talk to you."

Cade took a long swallow of the Budweiser, then belched. "I'm listening."

Louis glanced at Eric. "Outside," Louis said to Cade.

"What? You don't like my home?"

"It's private."

Cade looked at Eric. "Up, kid."

Eric hesitated just a moment too long and Cade gave him a light cuff to the head. "I said, move."

Eric got up, glaring at Cade, then moved over to the couch.

Cade pulled a fresh can of Budweiser from the refrigerator and sank into a chair at the small table. He waved at the other chair and Louis reluctantly sat down, moving Eric's plate to the side. He laid the newspaper on the table, pushing it toward Cade.

"Did you have anything to do with that?" he asked.

Cade glanced at the newspaper. He took a drink of beer and set the can down, rubbing it with his calloused fingers.

"Next question."

"I didn't hear an answer to my first one."

Ronnie had come in from the back and was standing near the sink. Louis knew he could see the headline from where he stood.

Cade sniffed, running his arm under his nose. "Hate this fucking weather. Can't breathe."

"Answer me, Cade."

Cade shrugged. "If I tell you I did or didn't, what does that change?"

"It would make me feel a helluva lot better."

Cade leaned forward, his fingers gripping the can so tight, it cracked. "You're *working* for me. You don't have to feel better. I do."

Louis sat back, his chest tight. Man, he should've trashed this case right from the start.

"You're thinking about walking out on me now, ain't you?"

"I think about it every day, Cade."

Cade smiled. "But you can't now, because of her, right?"

Louis's first thought was that he wasn't sure who Cade meant—Kitty Jagger or Susan Outlaw?

"Who?" he asked.

"The bitch lawyer."

Louis wanted to punch him.

Ronnie jumped forward. "Can I get you a drink, Mr. Kincaid?"

Louis forced himself to look at Ronnie. He knew Ronnie was in his late thirties, but he looked pretty young right now. And embarrassed.

Louis shook his head, pissed. Sweat was trickling down his back and he could feel his shirt clinging to his skin. It was like a frickin' oven in here.

Forget it, Kincaid. He's just trying to rattle you. Ask him what you came to ask and get out of here.

"Tell me why you asked about Bob Ahnert?"

"I told you to leave that shit alone."

"And I told you it's the heart of your case. And unless you tell me right now that you killed Kitty Jagger, then I'm keeping at it. Now answer me."

Louis looked up at Ronnie. His face was like stone. Cade's was glistening with sweat.

Cade wet his lips. "Ahnert came to see me one day. It was just after the trial started. He wasn't supposed to talk to me without fucking Duvall there. But he did anyway."

"What did Ahnert want?"

"He asked me what chemicals I worked with. And he wanted to know if I knew where Atterberry might have gone to."

"Your alibi witness?"

"Yeah."

Louis hesitated. Why was Ahnert still asking questions after the trial had already started?

"What did you tell Duvall?"

"I told him I didn't know where the hell Atterberry was. I only knew him because he hung out at the same bar as me. He worked seasonal, stayed in motels. Anyway, we ran out of cash and Atterberry said he had some beer back at his motel. So he drove us over there and that's where we stayed."

"Watching TV?"

"Watching *Star Trek*," Cade said, taking a drink.

"What did Spencer Duvall tell you about Atterberry?"

"That they couldn't locate him," he said bitterly.

"Did you know where he was?"

Cade shook his head. "I didn't know then, but I learned later. Atterberry moved on to Texas, to the next job. He wouldn't have been hard to find."

"What about the chemicals? Did Bob Ahnert tell you why he wanted to know?"

Cade crushed the empty beer can and tossed it across the kitchen to the overflowing trash can. It rolled to the floor and Ronnie picked it up.

"Nope. I gave him a list. He never got back to me and I never heard about no chemicals brought up in the trial."

"When did you agree to the plea bargain?"

Cade got up and jerked open the fridge. Ronnie moved out of his way, looking at Louis apologetically.

"A couple weeks into the trial," Cade said.

There was only one question left, the one Louis had wanted to ask Cade from day one.

"Why did you take the plea bargain?"

Cade hesitated, standing in the center of the kitchen,

his fingers on the beer pop-top. "Twenty years or the chair."

Cade looked over at Ronnie, who immediately averted his eyes. "Blood is thicker than water, man," Cade said.

Ronnie went over to Eric, who had been watching the exchange intently.

"Come on, we got work to do," Ronnie said. Eric got up and they left.

Louis ran his hand across his face, wiping away the perspiration. The air was thick with the smells of the trailer. He stood, picking up the newspaper. "I have to go."

Cade looked up at him. "Leave that girl's case alone or I'll fire you."

"You fire me and I'll tell the sheriff's office about that little confrontation you had with the Haitian. Mobley ought to like that, don't you think?"

"Don't fuck with me, Kincaid."

Louis turned and walked out, jerking the door shut behind him. He stopped to pull in a deep breath of fresh air and saw Ronnie and Eric near his car.

Eric was looking at the Mustang, running a hand lightly over the fender. He looked up as Louis approached, his dark eyes almost hidden by the hair falling over his forehead.

"Eric likes your car," Ronnie said.

Louis looked down at Eric. For the first time, Louis thought he saw some life in the kid's eyes.

"This a sixty-six?" Eric asked.

"Sixty-five. I've had it since high school."

"This is a classic. Is it worth a lot?"

"Only to me, probably." Louis got in the car.

Eric walked around the car, peering in the windows. Ronnie leaned in the car's open window.

"He didn't mean none of that stuff he said in there,"

Ronnie said. "Not about Miss Outlaw or that Jamaican guy. Dad's just . . . angry."

"Angry and stupid," Louis said. "I'm trying to help him."

Ronnie lowered his voice. "He's scared. He's scared they're going to get him for this Duvall thing. He's scared of going back to prison."

Louis wanted to tell Ronnie what he was thinking. That Ronnie didn't know his father, that the man who had left when Ronnie was fifteen was dead and a different man had come back. A man who was capable of things a son couldn't imagine.

Louis started the car.

"Is he?" Eric said suddenly.

Ronnie turned to look at his son. "What?"

"Is he going back to prison?" Eric asked.

Ronnie turned to his son. "Well, Mr. Kincaid is going to do everything he can—"

"Is he?" Eric repeated.

Ronnie looked at Louis. But Louis was looking at Eric's eyes. There was no sadness in them, no fear that his grandfather might be going to prison. Just something that hadn't been there before—cold, hard hope.

Chapter Eighteen

It was four A.M. and he was looking for something that wasn't there.

The entire Jagger case file was spread on his bed, floor and dresser, the contents divided into statements, evidence logs, photos and interviews. He had found a statement Ahnert had taken from Horace Atterberry that backed up what Cade had said: He and Atterberry were watching *Star Trek* in a motel room. Louis set it aside.

Odd. That was almost the same alibi Cade offered for the night Spencer Duvall was shot, that he was home watching *Star Trek, the Next Generation*. Same show, twenty years apart. Was this what Ahnert was talking about?

It couldn't be that simple.

Hell, maybe Atterberry was still alive. He would try to locate him tomorrow, despite the fact that Susan expected him to follow up on Candace's lover.

He continued to read, staring at the typed words and gruesome photographs until they were blurry. He could find nothing else.

Thunder rolled overhead and as rain began to patter the roof, Issy ran in from the living room and jumped on the bed. Her fur was wet. She had probably gotten outside through the torn porch screen. He had to get the thing fixed or one day he'd come home and find her flattened on the road.

She rubbed up against him and he nudged her away.

She came back, and again he set her aside. She moved to the end of the bed and stared at him. He took off his glasses and stared back. It occurred to him that in the nearly two years he had owned the cat, he had never felt anything but obligation toward it.

Is that your kitty?

Louis reached for her, but she scampered off, disappearing into the bathroom.

He went back to reading. Another report. Another piece of evidence. All of it seemed in order, everything a prosecutor would need to convict a murdering rapist.

Interviews with Willard Jagger, the owner of Hamburger Heaven, Jack Cade's customers. He even found Ahnert's statement from Joyce Crutchfield, but it said only what Ray had already told him, that Kitty had no boyfriends and pretty much led a quiet life, going to school, working and taking care of her father.

Damn it, what was missing?

Talk to Kitty.

Louis looked around the room for the autopsy report and saw it lying on the floor near the dresser. There was water dripping from the ceiling right over the top of it.

He snatched it up and shook the water free. He moved back to the bed, crawled up against the pillows and reached for his glasses.

At the lung analysis he stopped.

Potassium monopersulfate. He had tripped on it the first time he read the report but had forgotten about it. Ahnert said to look for something that was missing, so this couldn't be it. What else had Ahnert said? *Something is there that shouldn't be.* Was this it?

He looked at his watch. It was almost dawn. He couldn't call Vince Carissimi, the ME, for a couple hours yet.

He crawled off the bed and went to the closet. He had not fully unpacked, even after a year, but he knew he had a dictionary somewhere. He rifled through a box of books. College texts, old notebooks, a yellowed police manual from Ann Arbor and his high school yearbook. Nothing.

Well, his generic dictionary probably wouldn't have the sulfate thing in it anyway. He looked at the phone, hesitated, then walked to it. He dialed Susan's number.

It rang once and he was surprised she picked up so quickly, but she was probably used to getting late-night calls.

"Hello . . ." She sounded drugged.

"Susan, I need you to look up something for me."

"Huh?"

"This is Louis. That big dictionary on your dining room table—"

"I . . . what time is it?"

"It's almost morning," Louis said.

"The hell it is. Wait a minute . . ."

He heard her sheets rustle, then she came back to the phone.

"Tell me first what you said to Mobley."

"I didn't say anything to him."

"You swear?"

"I swear."

There was a pause. He could hear her breathing.

"Susan, I swear."

"Okay, what do you need a dictionary for?"

"There was something in Kitty Jagger's lungs that wasn't explained. Look it up for me."

There was a long pause. Then a sigh. "Kincaid, I thought you were going to find Candace's girlfriend."

"Come on, Susan. Please."

"Hold on."

The phone went down with a clank in his ear. A minute later, she was back.

"Spell it."

Louis read off the letters.

He could hear pages turning. "Okay. Here it is. All I see here is potassium sulfate . . . no mono-thing."

"Okay, what is potassium sulfate?"

"You're not going to like this, Kincaid."

"What is it?"

" 'Potassium sulfate: A white crystalline compound used especially in fertilizer'."

Louis closed his eyes. Who more likely to use fertilizer than a damn landscaper?

"Are you thinking what I think you're thinking?" she asked.

"Yeah."

"Maybe she got it from the dumpsite."

"It was in her *lungs,* Susan. Dead people don't inhale anything."

Susan was silent for a moment. "Maybe she wasn't dead when she was dumped."

"No blood at the dumpsite. She bled and died somewhere else."

Susan sighed tiredly. "Sorry, Kincaid."

"Not your fault." He tossed the autopsy report to the bed. "Thanks anyway."

"No problem. I know what it's like."

He stared at the puddle of water near the dresser. "Sorry I woke you."

"Don't worry about it. I think better on five hours sleep."

"Thanks for understanding."

"I'm not understanding, I'm just groggy. I still think you're chasing ghosts. Get some sleep, Kincaid. You've got to go lezzie hunting tomorrow."

"Right." He hung up.

He started to gather up the files, then stopped, looking again at the autopsy report.

There's something missing that should be there. Damn, what was he looking for?

Louis took the report back to the bed. Issy was curled up on the pillow, giving herself a bath. He started to move her aside, then stopped. He eased himself in next to her.

A bird had started up somewhere outside his window. The light was graying up. He put on his glasses and started reading again.

Chapter Nineteen

The tape player was going. It was the Doors, but it took Louis a moment to recognize the song "People Are Strange." The autopsy room was empty. Not even a corpse on the table.

The smell of brewing coffee defused the room's normal must. Louis's eyes went to the Mr. Coffee on the counter, dripping out a mud-black stream. He was about to help himself to a cup when the door opened and Vince Carissimi came in, tying an apron over his green scrubs.

"Hey, Kincaid, long time no see," he said, smiling. "What brings you down here so early?"

"I need help," Louis said.

"Looks like you need coffee." Vince pointed to the coffee pot. "If that doesn't jumpstart the ticker, nothing will."

Louis poured a cup and went to a desk, where Vince was looking at a clipboard.

"Okay," Vince said. "I got some time before I have to start on Mrs. Piccoli. What you need?"

Louis held out Kitty Jagger's autopsy report. "I need you to take a look at this for me."

Vince took it, pursing his lips. "Kitty Jagger. Wow, moldy oldie. This have anything to do with the Cade case? I heard you're working for his defense."

There was a slight coolness to Vince's voice. Or was Louis just hearing something that wasn't there?

"It might," Louis said.

Vince was looking at the wound chart, shaking his head. "Man, I haven't seen one of these in years. This one looks a little like June Allyson."

"Vince . . ."

"Sorry, what did you say you needed?"

"The detective who worked the case told me there is something missing from this report that should be there. He told me to 'talk to Kitty.' "

Vince gave him a weird look.

Louis took a sip of the coffee and tried not to grimace. "I was up all night looking at the thing but I can't see it."

Vince was already flipping the pages. Jim Morrison had moved on to "I Can't See Your Face in My Mind."

"Looks pretty standard, Louis," he said. "No *anguis in herba* that I can see."

"What?"

"Snake in the grass. Nothing weird lurking."

Louis let out a tired sigh. "You sure?"

"I am always sure." He hesitated. "Wait, here's something interesting. Look at this."

Louis moved closer.

Vince had flipped back to the first page. "Cause of death: cerebral hemorrhage due to blunt trauma. Not possible."

"Why not?" Louis asked.

"Because according to this, she lost most the blood from her body. Dead people don't bleed like that."

"So the stab wounds killed her?"

Vince nodded. He was reading something else.

"Was she hit or stabbed first?" Louis asked.

"I'd guess hit and knocked out. She had a skull fracture. Then someone stabbed her. The pathologist got it backward. *Humanum est errare.*"

Louis shook his head. "The detective didn't say something was wrong. He said something was missing. *Missing.*"

Vince ran a hand through his salt-and-pepper hair and flipped back a page. He was silent for a moment. The Doors had moved on to "When the Music's Over."

"Whoa," Vince said softly.

"What?"

"According to this, they took two semen samples, one from the panties, the other vaginal. Standard procedure," Vince said. "See this? This is the lab report on the sample from the panties—blood type O positive."

"Yeah, I know about that."

Vince looked up.

"What?" Louis asked.

"There's no lab report from the vaginal sample," Vince said. "The lab would routinely type all samples to eliminate the possibility of multiple perpetrators or partners. You know, in case she was having sex with a boyfriend."

"Her father says this girl didn't have a boyfriend," Louis said.

"Right . . ."

"She was fifteen, Vince."

Vince gave him a look.

"I don't think Kitty was the type to fuck around," Louis said.

Vince just stared at him. "Calm down, Louis, I'm

not knocking your lady's reputation. *De mortuis nil nisi bonum,* bud.''

"Is there any way to track this down?" Louis asked.

"The second sample or the report itself?" Vince handed him back the autopsy report. "Hard to say. State lab did the tests. Who knows if they still have the results or the sample."

Louis looked at him. Vince sighed.

"You're going to find a way to follow up on this whether I help you or not, aren't you?" Vince said.

"Yeah, I am."

Vince hesitated. "You know, when I heard you were working the other side, I didn't believe it. I mean, Jack Cade—"

"Save it, Vince."

Vince crossed his arms over his chest, then nodded.

"So can you get that report?"

Vince was quiet.

"Come on, Vince. I wouldn't ask if it weren't a big deal."

He shrugged. "I'll make a call, but don't get your hopes up. Twenty years is a long time."

"Thanks." Louis rubbed a hand over his face.

"You all right?" Vince asked.

"Yeah, yeah. Just didn't sleep last night, that's all."

A haunting bass line was coming out of the tape player, echoing off the tile walls. Jim Morrison singing "You're lost, little girl, you're lost . . ."

Louis grabbed a pen and scribbled a number on the desk blotter. "Here's my beeper. Would you call me if you hear anything?"

"Yeah, sure." Vince paused. "Look, you wanna go get some breakfast? Mrs. Piccoli isn't going anywhere."

"Haven't got time." Louis started toward the door.

"Louis?"

He turned back.

"I wasn't getting on you, about Cade I mean," Vince said. "In my line of work, you come to think everybody gets their due eventually. I forget sometimes you guys can't wait for that. I'll call as soon as I get that report."

Louis nodded.

"Fiat justitia, ruat coelum," Vince said. "Let justice be done, though the heavens may fall."

Chapter Twenty

Louis pulled up to Susan's house and cut the engine. He sat for a moment in the dark, thinking about his wasted day.

It had started out promising enough. After Vince had told him about the semen sample, he had spent the morning trying to track down Kitty's friend Joyce. There was no one listed in the Immokalee phone book under Novack, but there was a Stan Novick. Louis got an answering machine with a woman's voice but didn't leave a message. He had been about to drive out to Immokalee when Susan beeped him.

"I ran the Toyota's plate," she said when he called her office. "It came back to Harold Lieberman of Dade County."

He had stayed silent, thinking about losing the whole day driving to Miami.

"There's six Liebermans in the directory. You need to call them," Susan said. "I'd do it myself, but I'm in court all day. You got a pen?"

So Louis had called five Harold Liebermans in Dade County, looking for someone who fit the description of the woman he had seen on Candace's patio. He hit on the sixth call. A woman answered and told him yes, she had a daughter named Hayley and Hayley had wrecked her own car and was using her father's Toyota, and if he saw her, tell her to bring it back because Harry was going to be pissed off when he got out of Mt. Sinai and found out it was gone. The woman said she didn't know where her daughter was living, and Louis had the feeling she didn't want to.

A breeze wafted in from his open window. Louis leaned forward and glanced out the windshield. The clouds were moving over the moon. It smelled like more rain was coming.

He leaned back against the headrest, looking at Susan's dark windows. She wasn't going to be happy about the Lieberman dead end, and he had been thinking all day that he wasn't earning his pay and they should part ways. For her sake—and for his.

He shifted, reaching in his jeans pocket. He pulled out the picture, holding it so he could see it in the streetlight.

Kitty Jagger smiled back at him.

She would be thirty-five now. Maybe she would have found her rich knight and he would have whisked her off to a pink palace in Palm Beach. Maybe she would have found a way to get to college or be a model. Or maybe she would have just married a nice guy, had a couple blond kids and lived in a house over in Cape Coral, driving over on the weekends to take care of Dad's flowers and bring him apple juice.

The smell of something sweet came in the car window, carried by the breeze. Louis looked up, almost expecting to see someone. Just darkness. He rubbed his hand over his face. He put the picture away and got out of the car.

The sweet smell followed him as he went up the walk. He knocked on the front door. When he heard nothing, he peered in the small diamond-shaped window on the door. The living room was dark. He looked at his watch. It was only nine. Who went to bed at nine?

The heady perfume was swirling around him. A porch light went on. That's when he saw the big plant by the door, its delicate white flowers swaying in the wind.

Shit. It was just Night Blooming Jasmine.

The deadbolt clicked open and then the door. He smiled. Susan didn't.

"You were supposed to call me," she said, walking away. She was barefoot and wrapped in a fuzzy white robe. Her hair was pulled to the top of her head, spraying out like a small fountain.

Louis could hear soft music coming from the back of the house. Elegant. Classical. Handel's Water Music. Frances used to play it sometimes to make him sleep. It used to make him think of palaces and chandeliers. Susan faced him, her face scrubbed clean of make-up. She looked different; fresh, younger . . . cuddly. Like a polar bear cub.

His eyes went to the hallway. He could see the dim flicker of candlelight on the walls. Oh man, he was interrupting something.

Say something.

"You weren't asleep, were you?" he said.

"No." Susan turned, walking into the kitchen, returning with a glass of wine. "So did you track down the Lieberman thing?"

"Yes."

"Who is she?"

"Her name is Hayley."

Susan waited.

"That's all I found out."

"No address?"

"Not yet." The last word came out too close to an apology.

Susan gave him a long look. He was trying to figure out how to bring up the idea that he wanted to quit the case when Susan spoke again.

"So what else did you do today?" she asked evenly.

He hesitated. "I went to see Vince Carissimi."

"The M.E.? Why?"

"I wanted him to take a look at Kitty Jagger's autopsy report. There was a second semen sample."

"A what?"

"A second semen sample taken from Kitty, other than the one on the panties."

"What panties?"

Louis forgot she had not reviewed Kitty Jagger's case. He knew she didn't want to hear about this, but he needed to tell someone.

"The biggest piece of evidence against Cade was the semen on Kitty's panties that the cops found in Cade's truck," he said. He could hear the eagerness creep into his voice, an eagerness he wanted her to share.

"It was blood type O," he went on. "There was also semen inside her. The sample was probably tested, but there is no report on the results."

Susan was standing there, hand on hip, staring at him. He knew what was coming.

"And what does this have to do with Spencer Duvall?" she said.

"The report is missing, Susan," he said. "What if it was taken out of the police files for a reason? What if it turns out to not be O positive, what if—"

"Kincaid . . ." she said.

"Susan, listen," he said. "I got a lead today on Kitty's girlfriend and—"

"Kitty's girlfriend?"

"She's living in Immokalee and I think if I talk to her about Kitty—"

"Kincaid, stop," she said more firmly.

He looked at her. She was shaking her head, her eyes tired. She dropped down on the sofa, holding the wine glass between her hands, head bowed.

"Susan," he began, "I know I promised to—"

"Yes, you did," she said. "We made a bargain, remember? You told me you'd find me something, but you're running around chasing some damn ghost."

He just stared at her.

She set the wine glass aside. "You have got to get off this Jagger thing."

"It's important to the case," Louis said.

"No, it's important to *you,* Kincaid." She shook her head. "I can hear it, I can hear it in your voice when you say her name now."

"That's nuts, Susan."

"No, it's not," she said. "I'm going to say this one more time, okay? You are trying to keep Jack Cade out of the electric chair. You are not trying to solve that girl's murder."

It was time to tell her he wanted out. But then he took a good look at her face. He knew she had been in court all day, but she had never looked this beaten down before. He sat down in a chair across from her.

"What happened today?" he asked.

She rubbed her temples. "I lost all three of my motions."

She began to gather up a bunch of drawings and colored markers, putting them back in their case. She looked up. Louis followed her gaze.

Benjamin was standing in the hallway in his pajamas. He gave Louis a curious glance, then disappeared down the hall.

Susan waited until she heard a door close. "There's something else, too."

"What?"

"Sandusky told me today he's seeking the death penalty for Cade."

Louis was silent for a moment. "Any way around it?"

"I don't know. He might reconsider if Cade pleads and saves him the trouble of a trial."

"Cade will never do that."

"Sometimes the thought of death can quickly alter how you look at life, even if it's behind bars."

She stacked the papers neatly on the table and put the markers on top. She ran a hand over her hair, staring vacantly at the coffee table. A toilet flushed and a moment later, Benjamin reappeared.

"Nite," he muttered.

"I'll be there in a minute, honey."

Benjamin went back to his bedroom. The phone rang. Susan went into the kitchen, switching on the light.

Louis glanced down the hall. He could see the open door of Benjamin's room.

"Dammit," Susan said into the phone.

He looked toward the kitchen.

"I'm not on call tonight." Susan was leaning against the doorjamb, head in hand. "Don't you throw this up at me again."

Louis looked back at the hall. Benjamin had ventured out and was listening to his mother. Susan hung up, her back to Louis.

"You okay?" Louis asked.

She nodded stiffly. "Idiot."

"Who?"

"My boss," she said, facing him. She saw Benjamin. "Get dressed, Ben. You're going to April's."

Benjamin let out a whine. "I don't wanna. I hate April."

"Get dressed. You have to go. I have to go see a client."

"I can stay alone," he said.

"Benjamin, don't argue, please," Susan said, ripping the scrunchie from her hair. "Get dressed and pack up your clothes for tomorrow."

Susan swept past Benjamin and disappeared down the hallway. Louis watched the boy as he slumped against the wall. Apparently he had been wrong; there was no Mr. Outlaw around. Not tonight, anyway.

"I'm not going," Benjamin yelled.

"Don't be a butt, Ben," Susan yelled back. "Get dressed."

Benjamin sank down to the carpet, burying his head in his arms. The kid looked miserable, pulled up into a tight little ball. Louis watched him, listening for tears, but he wasn't making a sound. The Handel stopped abruptly.

"Ben!" Susan called out.

Louis stared at the kid, shaking his head.

Oh man . . . don't do this. You don't even like kids.

Louis rose and went to the hallway. "Susan? I'll stay with him," he called.

Benjamin looked up at him. Susan came out of her bedroom, brush in her hand but still in her robe.

"What?" she said.

"I said I'd stay with him. No sense in dragging him out at this time of night."

Louis looked down at Benjamin. The gratitude on the kid's face was almost painful to see.

"I can't ask you—"

"I don't mind," Louis said, motioning toward the sofa. "I'll just sit here and watch TV. It's no problem."

"No, it's not right." She disappeared into her room, half-closing the door.

Louis looked at Benjamin. "Sorry, buddy."

With a sigh, Benjamin dragged himself up off the floor and trudged off toward his room.

Louis could hear them both rustling around in their rooms. Finally Susan reappeared, wiggling her arms into a beige jacket. Her hair was pulled back into a knot, and she had put on lipstick.

"I'll only be an hour," she said.

"I thought—"

"I changed my mind. Make sure he's in bed by ten and that he brushes his teeth after you give him that pudding in the fridge that he'll con you out of ten minutes after I leave."

"Okay," Louis said.

Benjamin had come back out. He had put on jeans and T-shirt but was still barefoot.

"You can stay here," Susan said to him.

"Yes!" He made a pumping motion with his scrawny arm.

"But don't give Mr. Kincaid any lip, you hear?"

She was stuffing things into her briefcase. "You have my pager number. I'll be at the jail." She paused. "You look tired. If you feel like it, take the sofa. There's a blanket in the closet at the end of the hall."

"Thanks."

She started to the door.

"Susan?"

She turned.

Louis hesitated. "I'll find Hayley Lieberman."

She nodded and opened the door.

"Take an umbrella," Louis said, "it's getting ready to rain again."

She stared at him for a moment, then grabbed the umbrella.

"Thanks," she said softly. Then she was gone. Louis locked the door behind her and stood looking out the window, watching her old Mercedes chug off into the darkness.

He turned. Benjamin was standing there, staring up at him.

Louis looked at his watch. "You got a half-hour. What's on?"

Benjamin scrambled onto the sofa, dug the remote from under a cushion and started punching it. A.J. Simon was giving his slob brother Rick grief as they drove down yet another San Diego freeway in pursuit of yet another dirtbag.

"You like this show?" Louis asked, sitting down next to him.

Benjamin shrugged. "It's junk. I'd rather watch *Miami Vice*. Mom won't let me. Too much drugs."

Louis nodded. "Where's your bathroom?"

Benjamin pointed down the hall.

Louis started down the hall toward the bathroom, but then paused. Her bedroom door was open. He took a step, trying to see inside without being too obvious.

It was painted an off-white, with a ceiling border that swirled with browns and deep reds. The furniture was old, borderline antique. Her bed was unmade, the comforter a big, billowy thing that matched the border. There was a pile of black clothes on the floor, something lacy looking, and a wad of pantyhose.

He spotted the tape player on the bureau, and could pick up the strong scent of vanilla. He saw a candle burning on the night stand.

"Hey, Benjamin," Louis called.

"What?"

"Your mom left a candle going in her room. Come here and blow it out."

"Your legs broke?"

"Just get in here, please."

Benjamin went in and blew out the candle. He gave Louis a "you're nuts" look and started off to his own room.

"I thought you wanted to watch TV?" Louis asked.

Benjamin gestured to his clothes. "Can't sleep in this."

Louis followed him to the bedroom and stood at the door.

"You don't have to watch me every minute," Benjamin said as he wriggled out of the jeans.

"Yes I do."

"I'm not going to run away or something."

"Well, I'm responsible. I'm not taking any chances."

Benjamin gave him another withering look.

Louis's eyes wandered over the boy's bedroom. It was beige, like his mother's, with a brown spread, tan carpet and shelves of books and toys. The ceiling was studded with little green stars that probably glowed in the dark, and eight papier-mache replicas of the planets were strung from the ceiling. There was a small telescope at the window, *Star Wars* posters on the walls and a gleaming saxophone sitting in a stand. The room was surprisingly neat. Nothing like his own room back at the Lawrence house had been.

"Nice room," Louis said. "Very neat."

"I'm not a slob," Benjamin said. He was buttoning his pajamas, one eye on Louis as he ventured farther into the room.

"You make those?" Louis asked, pointing at the planets.

"Yeah. Science project."

"I thought there were nine planets."

Benjamin shook his head. "Pluto is technically not a real planet. They think it's really an asteroid. So I left it out. I only got a B because of it. But I'm right. It's just an asteroid."

Louis nodded. He noticed a framed photograph on the dresser. It was of a striking black man with close-cropped hair and serious eyes. He was wearing a dark suit.

He had to ask. "That your dad?"

Benjamin was folding his clothes and he paused to glance at the photo. "Yeah. His name is Austin. He's in England."

So now you know, Kincaid.

"What's he do?"

"For work? He does financial stuff, kinda like working for a bank, but he like sets up companies in foreign places. He has a lot of money, but can't use it 'cause it's like tied up in big buildings and Ma says he's cash poor. Whatever that means."

Louis was still looking at the photo. "How often does he get home?"

"Never," Benjamin said. He tossed his sneakers into the closet. "You wanna look at Venus?"

Louis shook his head.

Benjamin plopped down on his bed. "Probably too many clouds tonight anyway."

Louis came in and sat on the edge of the bed. "So . . . your mom and your dad . . ."

Don't ask, Kincaid. It's not right.

"They got divorced when I was little," Benjamin said, rolling over onto his stomach. "I don't remember him really, not in my real brain, but he sends me stuff. He sent me the telescope for Christmas and fifty dollars for my birthday. And that." He pointed to a cast-iron replica of a double-decker bus.

"I wanted a Nintendo Super Mario, but it's like two hundred dollars. Guess he's too cash poor to get that. But the bus is kinda cool."

Louis sensed a sadness in Benjamin's voice. "You want some pudding?"

Benjamin hesitated, looking at Louis. "Can I show you something first?" he asked.

Louis shrugged. "Sure."

"You promise not to tell my mom?"

"I don't know. What if you show me drugs or cigarettes or—"

"Oh man . . . it's just a book."

Great. Was the kid going to show him pornography? Maybe it was only *Playboy*. Bare boobs, that was normal, wasn't it? But damn, the kid was only eleven.

Benjamin was rooting through his closet.

"Has your mom ever seen stuff like the stuff in this book?"

"All the time."

Benjamin emerged with a large hardcover book. He brought it back to the bed and sat down next to Louis, laying the book on his small knees.

Louis had a hard time not letting his mouth hang open. The book was titled *In the Presence of Evil, Mass Murderers and Serial Killers*.

"Where did you get this?" Louis asked, trying to gently wrestle it away.

Benjamin held tight. "From the swap meet. I told the man my mom was a lawyer and she needed it for work."

"Have you read it?"

"Four times."

"Jesus, kid. You shouldn't be looking at that sh—" Louis stopped himself.

"You can say shit. Ma says it. Anyway, I wanted to ask your opinion on some of these cases."

Louis stared at him.

"You know about these cases, don't you?"

"Well, yeah, I've read about some of them."

Benjamin flipped the book open. "This guy here says that the Boston Strangler probably wasn't guilty. Did you know there's some people who think another guy in prison killed all those women and that DeSalvo just wanted to be important so he took the blame?"

Louis found himself staring at a black and white photo of a woman the caption identified as Mary Sullivan.

"What do you think?" Benjamin asked. "You think he really killed her?"

Louis rubbed his face and slowly stood up. "Put the book away, Benjamin."

"Yeah but I wanted to—"

"Put it away."

Benjamin heaved a huge sigh. "I thought you were a private investigator."

"I am."

Jesus, when did he finally admit that to himself?

"So you solve murders, right?"

Louis wanted this conversation to end real quick. "Yeah, I do."

"Is it hard to do?"

"Yeah, it's hard. Now—"

"Do they ever tell you why?"

"Who?"

"The killers."

"What? No. Well, yeah, sometimes. Look, Benjamin—"

"Well?"

"Well what?"

"Why do they do it?"

Louis was silent. He wasn't any expert, but this had to be weird for a kid to be asking these questions.

"Maybe you should ask your mother about this," Louis said.

"I did. She said she doesn't know."

Benjamin was looking up at him, waiting.

"I don't know either, Benjamin," he said.

Chapter Twenty-One

The beeper was buzzing against his side. He waited until he stopped at a light to look at the number. He was hoping it was Vince. It took him a moment to recognize the number as the Sereno Key Police Department, the chief's private line.

He pulled into a 7-Eleven, got a coffee to go, and called Dan Wainwright.

"I have an address for you on that Lieberman woman," he said. "Got a pen?"

"Yeah, hold on, Dan." Louis set the coffee down on the phone ledge. Wainwright read off an address. Louis wrote it on the styrofoam cup.

Louis knew Wainwright was not supposed to run numbers for a civilian. "I owe you one, Dan," he said.

"No problem. How's things going for you, Kincaid?"

"It's going," Louis said.

Wainwright was silent for a moment. "Call me. I'll buy you a beer some night, okay?"

"Yeah, yeah. I'll do that." He clicked off.

Louis stood there for a moment, watching the traffic crawl by on Cleveland Avenue. He hadn't seen Dan Wainwright in months, not since they had worked together on the Paint It Black case. The case had created a bond between them—the kind of bond that sparked between cops in the adrenaline-drench of a dangerous case. But Louis had not stayed in touch afterward. Maybe it was because the Sereno Key chief was one of the few people who knew how much Louis hated PI work, knew how badly he wanted to wear a uniform again. He didn't like it when people knew too much about him, especially when it came with a dose of pity.

Louis glanced at his watch. He was tempted to go over to the medical examiner's office; it was only a couple blocks away. But he knew if Vince had found out anything about the semen sample, he would have called. He was also tempted to drive out to Immokalee to find Joyce Novick.

He picked up the styrofoam cup and looked at the address. But a promise was a promise. He would go find this Lieberman woman.

The address turned out to be one of the new developments out by the airport. This one was called The Villas of Lancaster Lakes, the lakes being a green-water pit scooped out of the limestone and the villas just more of the soulless gulags that were springing up all over the old pasture lands. Louis found building E and apartment 322, but there was no answer when he knocked. There was also nothing covering the windows.

He peered in. The apartment was vacant. Recently vacant, if the little bits of debris on the carpet and nails on the walls were any indication. He found the rental office and the landlord who told him that Hayley Lieberman had moved out three days ago.

"She broke her lease," the man said. "Didn't give me any notice."

"She didn't say where she was going?" Louis asked.

"They never do. They just pull a Robert Irsay on me. Just backed up the van in the middle of night and split. Women are the worst. They sign a lease, then three months later they find some guy to sponge off and they move in with him. And I gotta paint the place all over again."

Louis nodded. "Thanks for your help."

"If you see her, tell her she can kiss her security goodbye."

Louis got back in the car. Another dead-end. Nothing to do but report back in to Susan. He glanced down at the county map he had spread out on the seat. He was right near Immokalee Road, only about a half-hour drive to the town. At least it wouldn't be a total waste of time.

He drove out to Immokalee Road, but as he waited for the light, a thought hit him, something the landlord had said about women finding some guy to sponge off of.

Hayley Lieberman had found someone to sponge off of, all right.

Damn. Joyce Novick would have to wait. He turned left, heading back toward Fort Myers. It was just a hunch, but he owed it to Susan to follow up on it.

He drove over the Sanibel-Captiva causeway and turned off Periwinkle Way, heading to the Duvall home.

Bingo. The old Toyota was there in the drive of the big white house. And Candace's yellow Mercedes convertible wasn't. Dumb luck.

At the front door, Louis paused, looking up at the security camera. No way was he going to get past that little maid. With a quick look around, he left the porticoed porch and followed a flagstone path around the side of the house. There was a small iron gate with a DELIVERIES sign on it. He opened it and went in.

The huge house butted right up against the lot line, leaving just a small walkway to the back. He followed it toward the back yard.

"You've scraped bottom, Kincaid," he muttered to himself as he crouched down to get by a window.

He could see San Carlos Bay beyond the hibiscus hedges. At the corner of the house, he heard something and stopped. A splash.

He looked around the corner. Hayley Lieberman was doing laps in the pool. He looked around the patio. No sign of anyone else, just a towel, a book and some lotion on a lounge chair.

He ventured onto the patio. It took Hayley another lap before she looked up and saw him. She stopped, squinting up at him as she treaded water.

"You need me to get out?" she asked.

She looked like a sleek dark seal, and she was smiling.

Louis shrugged. "It would help," he said.

She went to the side and hoisted herself out. She was wearing the little red bathing suit bottom and nothing on top. She didn't look back at Louis as she went to the lounge and grabbed the towel.

"You're using too much chlorine," she said, turning.

"Excuse me?" Louis said.

She nodded at the pool. "Chlorine."

She was looking at him oddly now. He was trying hard to look at her face.

"You're not the pool boy?" she asked.

Louis shook his head. "My name is Louis Kincaid. I'm a private investigator."

It took her a moment, but she smiled again. "Oh, sorry," she said. She rubbed the towel over her dark hair and tossed it aside.

She was maybe thirty, tall, almost his height, with a taut dancer's body—boyish hips, finely muscled legs and no tits. Definitely good looking.

Definitely not his type, he thought with relief as she nonchalantly stretched out on her back on a lounge chair, arms behind her head.

"So, what are you investigating?" she asked. Her tone was almost playful.

"Spencer Duvall's death," he said. Something told him to let her take the lead in this.

She put on sunglasses. "Poor Spence," she said.

"Why 'poor Spence'?"

"Kind of . . . sad, don't you think?"

"Murder is rarely happy."

"I mean *him*. He was kind of sad."

Louis heard a door and looked back to see the maid coming toward them carrying a tray.

"Candace should be back soon," Hayley said. "She's getting her nails done."

"I'd rather talk to you," Louis said.

The maid stopped abruptly when she recognized Louis. "Mrs. Duvall told you not to come back here," she said.

Hayley raised an eyebrow at Louis, then waved the maid forward. "Never mind, Luisa," she said, "just give me the drink and go away."

The maid scowled at Louis and left.

"I'm sorry," Hayley said to Louis. "You want a Long Island iced tea? I told her to use the Belvedere this time. It's really good."

"No thanks. Tell me more about Spencer. How well did you know him?"

She took a sip of the drink. "Not well. We moved in different circles."

"Your circles intersected," Louis said.

Hayley smiled and gave a small shrug. "I flunked geometry."

There was nothing to do but go for the throat. "How long have you and Candace Duvall been together?" he asked.

He couldn't see her eyes behind the dark glasses, but she was still smiling.

"About a year," she said finally. "We met at the Body Works. I teach yoga and aerobics there."

"Did her husband know about you?"

She shrugged again. "Candy didn't want me coming over here when he was home. One time he came home early when I was here and she introduced me as her personal trainer." Her smile had faded.

"So Candace isn't . . ." Louis hesitated.

"Out of the closet?" Hayley reached for the suntan lotion. "Nope."

Something sour had crept into Hayley's voice. "Are you?" Louis asked.

"Since high school."

Hayley was rubbing lotion on her chest. Louis was trying not to look at her.

"Did Candace know her husband was going to file for divorce?" he asked finally.

"Yeah, she knew."

"You're sure?"

Hayley nodded. "She said one night that when she got the papers, she was gonna go stuff them up Brian's ass."

"Brian? Brian Brenner?"

"Yeah. You know him?"

Louis shook his head. "So Candace didn't want a divorce?"

"Nope. She was perfectly happy playing the game."

That bitter tone had returned to her voice again.

"Did Spencer tell Candace why he wanted a divorce?" Louis asked.

"If he did, she didn't tell me."

Hayley was looking at the house. Louis followed her gaze. The maid was standing at the French doors, staring at them.

"God, I hate that woman," Hayley murmured. "She

speaks Spanish because she thinks I don't know what she's saying. Shit, I learned what *tortillera* meant in ninth grade.''

She looked back at Louis, shielding her eyes. ''You mind sitting down? You're blocking my sun.''

Louis sat on the edge of the lounge chair next to hers. At least he had found out Candace knew about the divorce. But he had the feeling there was more and that Hayley, for whatever reason, was willing to talk.

''Your landlord told me to tell you not to expect your security deposit back,'' he said.

She laughed. ''I got all the security I need now.'' She took a big gulp of her drink. ''So, what did you do to piss Candy off?''

''I don't know. Maybe I didn't smell nice enough.''

Hayley laughed again, a big whoop this time. ''Yeah, she's big on smells.''

Louis looked at the house. The maid was still there, watching him. He had the feeling that if he didn't leave soon, he was going to end up in jail for trespassing. Candace could show up any minute.

''I think I better get going,'' he said, rising.

''Wise choice,'' Hayley said. She took off her sunglasses and laid back in the lounge, closing her eyes.

He started to leave, then turned back. ''Why did you call Spencer Duvall 'sad'?'' he asked.

Hayley looked at him. ''Because he was.''

''Why? Because his wife was cheating on him?''

A slow smile came to Hayley's face, and Louis had the feeling that she was humoring him, like she might a boy who had just figured out what sex was.

''Spencer was gay,'' she said.

Louis was dumbstruck. Which made her smile even more.

''And he didn't want to be,'' she added.

He could think of only one thing to ask. ''Did Candace know?''

"What do you think?"

She was grinning, enjoying his bewilderment. "Candy was his beard," she said. "Or he was hers. I'm not sure how it worked, to be honest. All I know is that they found each other in college and kind of struck a bargain to prop up each other's lies."

"So their marriage—"

". . . was pretend," Hayley finished. "You know, like a fairy tale." She let out a whoop of laughter again.

Louis couldn't conceal his surprise, and that made Hayley laugh even harder.

"So who was Spencer . . . ?" he asked.

"Sleeping with?" She smiled. "I don't have a clue. Do you?"

Louis's eyes wandered up over the huge white house, across the glistening pool and out over sparkling San Carlos Bay.

He couldn't think of one more damn thing to ask. Except maybe to Brian Brenner. It was definitely time to go back and talk to the lying divorce lawyer. He looked back at Hayley.

"Why are you telling me this?" he asked.

Hayley wiggled down into the lounge and brought her arms up behind her head. She gave him a big smile.

"Because I'm out and I'm not going to let her put me back in."

Chapter
Twenty-Two

Brenner, Brenner and Brenner. Louis stood in the lobby, looking at the gilt letters on the door. He knew that Brian Brenner had a brother named Scott. The third had to be the father, he guessed.

His eyes caught a portrait on a far wall. It was of three men, all wearing gray suits. Brian was on the left, his somber doughy face made thinner, his wispy hair thicker by the artist's kindness. The man on the right was about Brian's age, with thick hair the color of coffee beans and eyes to match. Had to be the older brother, Scott. The artist had given Scott a small smile, but God had obviously given him the looks in the family.

The older man in the middle had to be the father, a distinguished looking white-haired man of about sixty. His eyes were so blue they jumped off the canvas. It was the only spot of real color in the painting.

"What are you doing here?"

Louis turned.

Brian Brenner stood at the door to his office. His suit coat was off, and the collar of his white shirt open, the blue tie loose. He was holding a wadded-up tissue in one hand and a file in the other.

"I was hoping you could see me for a minute."

"I'm a busy man."

"So am I."

Brian tossed the file on the secretary's desk and went back in his office, leaving the door open. Louis followed him in.

Brian's office was stacked with files and storage boxes. A conference table near the large window was covered with papers. The two women at the table both looked up at Louis. Brian waved his hand toward his door.

"Give us a minute, would you?" he said to the women.

The women rose slowly and disappeared while Brian noisily blew his nose. He looked terrible.

"Allergies acting up again?" Louis asked.

"Something in bloom," Brian said, waving a hand at the window.

Another door opened and a man emerged from a bathroom. Louis recognized him from the portrait outside and quickly extended a hand, hoping to warm up Scott Brenner before he assumed the same cool posture as Brian.

"Scott Brenner? I'm Louis Kincaid, private investigator."

Scott offered his hand and a warm smile.

"He's working for Outlaw and Jack Cade," Brian said.

Scott laughed softly. "Chill out, little brother. Everyone has to make a living, even defense lawyers. What can we do for you, Mr. Kincaid?"

"I just have a few questions."

Brian came back to his desk, still clutching the tissue. He looked like he was choking. Or maybe just having an asthma attack.

Scott perched on the edge of the large desk and leaned a forearm on his knee. It looked like a pose out of a Paul Fredricks catalog. Louis found himself staring at Scott's gleaming oxblood wingtips. Before he could talk, Scott took the lead.

"Brian told me you asked about Spencer's divorce. How did you find out about it?" Scott said.

"People talk."

Scott offered a ten-thousand-dollar smile to match the three-hundred-dollar Bally shoes.

"Yes, they do. Fortunate for us, isn't it?" he said. "How else would we ever win a case?"

"People lie, too," Louis said, looking at Brian.

Brian was dabbing at his nose with the tissue. He looked up at Louis.

"Why did you tell me Candace Duvall didn't know about the divorce?" Louis asked.

Brian frowned, looking at his brother before he came back to Louis. "What are you talking about?"

"I was just over at the Duvall house," Louis said, not adding that he didn't talk to Candace.

"I told you the truth," Brian said. "Candace told you different?"

"No, her lover did."

Brian's mouth dropped open. "Candace has a lover?"

"Now you're going to tell me Duvall didn't know that?" Louis said.

Brian looked at Scott and shook his head. "Spencer couldn't have known. He would have mentioned it to me."

"Did he forget to mention that he was gay, too?" Louis asked.

Brian blinked. "That's a lie."

"I don't think so."

Scott rose off the desk slowly. "Somehow I don't think this is what you came here to talk about, Mr. Kincaid. What does this have to do with your case?"

"Maybe nothing, but things like affairs, divorce and sexual secrets make interesting reading for a jury, don't you think?"

Scott nodded. "Most definitely. Throw enough bullshit at a jury and they'll acquit every time. Is that Susan Outlaw's plan?"

Louis was watching Brian Brenner. He had sat down and was pulling at the Kleenex, his eyes on the floor.

"It might work," Scott said. "Worth a try, anyway. Who do you plan on throwing out as a possible suspect? Candace? Her lover? How about *his* lover?"

Brian was sitting there like a rock, shredding the Kleenex.

Scott nodded. "Maybe that's why Spencer was divorcing Candace, to be with his lover. Have you considered that?"

"It occurred to me, yes," Louis said.

"But you haven't found Spencer's friend, I take it."

"Not yet."

Scott opened a drawer, pulling out a Hershey's bar. He unwrapped it slowly, breaking off a piece. He held it out to Louis. Louis shook his head.

"The other woman . . . or maybe man," Scott said, eating the chocolate square by square. "Not bad, not bad. The jury ought to eat it right up, given the way most people look at gays. Homophobia . . . what a great defense strategy. Give the good folks of the jury someone even more disgusting than Jack Cade, right?"

Scott was baiting him. Louis was about to reply when he remembered something Brian had said the first time they spoke back at the Brenner mansion: "There is no other woman in Spencer's life."

Shit, Brian knew Duvall was gay.

Louis looked over at Brian again. He was just sitting there, watching his older brother, his hand massaging his brow like he had a headache. Louis suddenly remembered a cop back on the force in Ann Arbor, a bigot who was too afraid to say what he thought about blacks but thought nothing of telling Louis that he "could spot a faggot a mile away."

Louis studied Brian, his clothes, his hair, his posture. He had known a few gay men in college, but they were all guys who were open about it. What about the ones who weren't?

Brian suddenly met his gaze and Louis looked away.

Shit, Kincaid, there's no way you can tell from just looking at him.

"Mr. Kincaid?"

Louis looked back at Scott.

"I asked you what it was you wanted to talk about? Why you came here?"

Louis needed to find a way to switch gears. He had a feeling Brian was hiding something, but there was no way to get anything out of him with the big brother here protecting him.

"Jack Cade was planning to sue Spencer Duvall," Louis said.

Scott nodded. "I heard. Legal malpractice. Fascinating . . ."

"Susan Outlaw told me your firm specializes in malpractice cases. I was hoping you could shed some light on it."

Scott smiled. "Well, I can try."

"You're familiar with the details of the Kitty Jagger case, I take it," Louis began.

"Not all of them. Just what the newspapers have been dredging up lately."

"Scott, we've got work to do," Brian said tightly.

"In a minute, Brian. Christ, go take an Alprazolam or something."

Brian got up and left the office. Louis watched him, then came back to Scott.

"I'm trying to find out if Cade had a chance of winning his suit against Duvall," Louis said.

"It would have been very difficult," Scott said.

"Because of the statute of limitations."

"Theoretically."

"Theoretically?"

"Well, a smart lawyer could argue that the statute of limitations begins when the victim—or client in this case—came to believe malpractice actually occurred."

"So assuming Jack Cade discovered this last year, he could still sue?"

Scott nodded. "He could make a legitimate attempt, yes."

"What could he get?"

"He would have to show a tangible economic loss and sue for things like breach of contract, negligent misrepresentation and of course fraud. But the client would have to prove it was intentional."

"And not just stupid," Louis said.

"Right. But let me assure you, Spencer Duvall was not stupid."

"So what could Duvall have done to sabotage Cade's case?"

"Theoretically?"

"Theoretically."

"Duvall would have had to deliberately withhold or alter evidence, or provide Jack Cade with information he knew not to be true or commit some other act that cost Jack Cade his right to a fair trial or intentionally force an action that would not have otherwise occurred."

Scott smiled. "Sorry, let me know if I'm talking over your head."

"I'm still with you."

"Has Cade told you Duvall did anything like that?"

Louis shook his head. "Cade gave up on the lawsuit when Duvall ended up dead. He said you can't sue a dead man."

Scott ate another square of the chocolate. "Well, that's not really true. You can bring suit against almost anyone or anything. Like I said, that's how we pay the rent here."

"So Cade could have sued Duvall's estate?"

"And his law practice, most likely."

Scott wadded up the Hershey wrapper and tossed it into the trash.

"Two points," he said. "The crowd goes wild."

Louis's beeper went off and he turned it off without even looking at it.

"Need to use the phone?" Scott asked.

Louis shook his head. "No, but I better get going."

Scott walked him to the door and opened it. Louis extended his hand. "Thanks for your time. You've given me a lot to think about."

Scott shook his hand. "Any time, Mr. Kincaid. Glad to be of help." He paused. "You know, even if Jack Cade is convicted, he can still bring suit against Spencer Duvall."

He saw the look of surprise on Louis's face and added, "The law is a hocus-pocus science."

Louis shook his head grimly. "Susan Outlaw says no judge will ever look at Jack Cade's suit now."

"Well, let's just say Miss Outlaw is not a malpractice attorney."

Louis could see Brian out in the lobby, pouring water from the cooler into a paper cup. Louis turned back to Scott.

"Mr. Brenner, would you consider representing Jack Cade's family in a civil suit against Spencer Duvall's estate?"

"Now there's an intriguing idea."

"Would you consider it?"

Scott's mouth tipped up. "Let's just say I'd be interested in seeing the evidence first."

The beeper went off again.

"Sure you don't want to use the phone?" Scott asked.

Louis switched the beeper off. He was eager to call Susan, but he didn't want to do it here. He finally had something to take back to her. Lyle Bernhardt, Candace, Hayley Lieberman—any of them had something to lose if Jack Cade had sued. He also had something to take back to Ronnie—that one of the top malpractice lawyers in the state was willing to take a look at his father's civil case.

"Thanks, Scott, I'll keep you posted," Louis said.

"We'll be talking, detective," Scott said.

Chapter
Twenty-Three

He was on the road to Immokalee first thing the next morning. It was Saturday and traffic was light, so he opened the windows and pushed the Mustang up over seventy, heading east on Corkscrew Road.

It didn't take long for the small subdivisions to fade away, and then he was out in the scrub lands that formed the northern border of the Corkscrew Swamp. As he passed through a preserve, the light grew dimmer and cooler, filtered through the canopy of slash pines and ancient live oaks. He was only about thirty miles east of Fort Myers. But out here, away from the coast and in the vast nothingness of Florida's gut, it was another world. Or maybe just another time, before man had left his mark.

He slowed, seeing signs warning: PANTHER CROSSING: Only 60 Left.

He thought of Susan and how happy she had been with what he had found out about Hayley and Brian

Brenner. He had called this morning, catching her and
Benjamin just as they were going out the door to Benjamin's Bible study group. She had been so pleased, she
told him to take the day off.

Orange groves lining the road led him into town,
where a Rotary sign declared "Welcome To Immokalee, 'My Home'." The air grew ripe with the smell
of rotting fruit. He had never been to Immokalee before,
and had heard only two things about it: It was a farming
town of Mexican migrants who worked for big fruit
cooperatives, and that you didn't want to pick a fight
in the bars on Friday nights.

The directory had listed Stan Novick's address on
Armadillo Drive. A guy at the Sunoco station directed
Louis west of town toward Lake Trafford. Louis found
the house, a small but well-kept ranch house, its yard
facing the entrance to a cemetery. He went to the door
and rang the bell.

Someone was screaming. Louis could hear it through
the closed front door. He rang the bell a second time,
then opened the screen and knocked hard.

Finally, the door jerked open and a woman peered
out at him.

"What?" she demanded.

She was in her mid-thirties, a shag of flaming red
hair around a pale freckled face. Except for the lines
around the eyes and thirty extra pounds, Joyce Novick
looked pretty much the way she had in Kitty's old
snapshot.

"Mrs. Novick?"

"Yes?" she said warily.

"I'm Louis Kincaid, a private investigator."

She used her forearm to brush her hair back from
her face. "Is this about Sean?" Her voice sounded
tired.

Louis shook his head. "No, Kitty Jagger."

Her pale blue eyes widened slightly, then she blinked

rapidly several times. "Kitty . . . good God," she said quietly.

"Do you have time to talk?"

She hesitated. "I . . . Christ . . . Kitty."

Joyce Novick had gone even paler, if that was possible, as if a ghost had just knocked on her door. *Maybe it had,* Louis thought.

"I'm working," Joyce Novick said finally, gesturing weakly behind her.

"I'd appreciate it if you could take a few minutes," Louis said.

Joyce wavered. It was obvious she didn't want to talk.

"Please, Mrs. Novick. I wouldn't bother you if it wasn't important."

She hesitated, then nodded. She opened the door wider so Louis could come in. "I have to finish up," she said. "Do you mind waiting?"

"No problem."

Louis followed her through a small living room decorated in the country style that mandated plaid sofas, stuffed roosters and the cloying smell of cinnamon potpourri. In the tiny kitchen, two boys were sitting at the table, eating peanut butter and jelly sandwiches. The smaller one's face was tear-streaked; he must have been the one screaming. They eyed Louis as he followed Joyce out a door and into the garage.

Off in one corner was a teenage girl, sitting in a swivel chair in front of a big mirror. Her body was covered with a green smock and she had big rollers in her hair.

Joyce Novick saw Louis staring at her. "I do hair," she said.

The makeshift beauty salon was stuffed in one corner of the dark garage. An old a/c wall unit wheezed away above the mirror, trying to defuse the garage's odor of mildew and car oil.

Joyce Novick moved in behind the girl and picked up a brush and a big pink foam roller. "How did you find me?" she asked cautiously.

"Ray Faulk told me about you," he said.

"Ray . . . I haven't thought about him in years," she said softly, winding a strand of hair.

"It took me a while to track down your address."

Joyce smiled wryly. "Immokalee isn't exactly the center of the universe."

"You moved out here after high school?" Louis asked.

She shook her head. "I dropped out before senior year. Moved out here right after I got married. My husband Stan's a foreman over at one of the cooperatives."

Louis looked into the mirror and caught the eyes of the girl in the chair. She was looking between Louis and Joyce, trying to figure out what he was doing here.

"Time for the dryer, Rachel," Joyce said.

The girl let Joyce deposit her under the dryer, wedged next to a tool bench. It was only when Joyce was sure the girl couldn't hear anything that she turned back to Louis.

"I'm sorry I acted so weird at the door," Joyce said. "I thought you were here about my oldest kid, Sean. He's eighteen and been in some trouble. I haven't heard from him in a while."

"Can we talk about Kitty?" Louis asked.

She began to pile the pink rollers back in a box. "What do you want to know?"

"Anything you can remember."

Joyce nodded. "I used to think about her all the time, even though I didn't want to. Then the years went by and it got easier to forget."

"I'm sorry I have to bring it all back."

She looked at him. "Oh, it wasn't just you. It was that man, seeing him on TV after all this time."

She was talking about Jack Cade, but Louis knew she didn't want to say his name. He slipped a notebook out of his pocket. "I just have a few questions, Mrs. Novick. What can you tell me about the night Kitty disappeared?"

She sat down in the swivel chair, holding a hairbrush. "God, I can still remember that night like it was yesterday."

Joyce's pale blue eyes grew distant. "It was April 9th. And it was hot and sticky, like summer was coming early that year. All the kids were out cruising. We were very busy, I remember."

"Do you recall anything out of the ordinary?"

Joyce shook her head. "Kitty punched out at eleven, just like always. I waved to her as she walked toward the bus stop. She turned and waved back. That's the last time I saw her."

"She didn't leave with anyone?"

Joyce shook her head slowly.

Louis pulled up a stool and sat down opposite the swivel chair. "How long did you know Kitty?" he asked.

Joyce was staring at something on the opposite wall. Louis followed her gaze, but all he saw was a bunch of tools hanging on a pegboard.

"Mrs. Novick?"

She looked back at him.

"How long did you know Kitty?"

"We met in sixth grade. I remember the first time I saw her." For the first time, Joyce smiled. It transformed her, made her look younger. "Kitty was in the girl's john ratting her hair and making spit curls. I was in awe of her. None of the other girls ratted their hair in sixth grade."

"That's when you became friends?" Louis prodded.

"Yeah, I lived a couple doors down so we walked

to school together, slept over at each other's houses. We were like sisters.''

She smiled as another memory came to her. ''When we were thirteen, Kitty came up with this big plan to run away to London, because she was in love with Paul McCartney and I was in love with George. But she decided she couldn't leave her father. We used to talk with English accents and make up false identities. Kitty wanted to be called Lady Kitrina Jaspers. I was Lady Joy Heartsfield. Joy . . . Kitty came up with that for me.''

Joyce's smile lingered; she was still lost in the past. Louis waited, not wanting to interrupt.

''What was Kitty like?'' Louis asked finally.

Joyce blinked, coming back. ''Like? Oh, geez, she . . .'' She shook her head, like she didn't know how to answer.

''She loved to swim, especially at night,'' Joyce said. ''Once, when we were in eighth grade, she made me sneak out of the house and we rode our bikes over to the municipal pool. It was closed, but Kitty just climbed the fence. I was so scared we'd get caught. But Kitty wasn't. I can still see her laughing and jumping off the high-dive board.''

Louis had a vision of the two girls giggling in the moonlit water.

''Kitty wasn't afraid of anything,'' Joyce went on. ''But I was. That night at the pool, I was afraid to jump off the high board so I kind of scooted down and hung from it. I was hanging there, scared stiff and she was yelling up at me, saying, 'Don't be afraid, Joyce, just let go!' ''

Joyce fell silent. The only sound was the wheeze of the air conditioner and the steady hum of the hair dryer.

''I never figured out what she saw in me,'' she said. ''She was so pretty and I was, well, I was kinda plain and a little chubby.'' Joyce blushed slightly. ''I figured I could just get her rejects.''

''Her father told me Kitty didn't date.''

''That's right,'' Joyce said, nodding. ''I haven't seen Mr. Jagger since—'' She hesitated. ''I was going to say since the funeral, but he didn't come. He spent a fortune on the coffin, mahogany with these beautiful brass handles. But then he was so upset, he couldn't even come to see her.''

She looked at Louis. ''How is he doing?''

Louis thought a moment before he answered. ''Still confused.''

Joyce nodded slowly. ''I should go see him. I always meant to afterward, but I got pregnant with Sean and we moved out here. Twenty years . . . goes by before you know it.''

Louis thought of Mobley's words about the greasers, the ''wild crowd'' girls: They got pregnant.

Joyce glanced over at the girl under the dryer. ''Excuse me a moment.'' She went over, checked the dryer and came back.

Louis wasn't sure how to phrase the question that was in his head. ''Ray told me boys tried to come on to Kitty all the time. You never saw her go with anyone?''

''Ray would drive her home once in a while, but she never went with anyone else.''

''Was there any boy who was more aggressive than others?''

Joyce frowned. ''Well, they all flirted with her, especially the football players. They'd cruise in after a game in their cool cars, all puffed up with themselves. Lonnie Albertson, Jeff, Tony Cipolli, Lance . . .''

''Lance Mobley?'' Louis asked. ''Did Mobley come on to her?''

''Lance came on to to anything that breathed, even me once. I think he thought we were easy, you know, because we were from Edgewood.'' Joyce's eyes grew distant. ''Lance Mobley . . . he was a good-looking boy. He's sheriff now, isn't he? I guess he did all right for himself.''

''Did any of these boys get angry when she rejected them?''

Joyce shook her head. Louis could tell she was miles—and decades—away from the dingy garage.

''Ray told me Kitty was saving herself for a rich guy,'' Louis said. ''So Kitty was . . .'' He wasn't sure how to make this sound anything but judgmental.

Joyce looked up abruptly. ''Kitty was smart, she could've gone to college if she had some money. But she knew that wasn't going to happen.''

''So she wanted someone to take care of her,'' Louis said.

''Don't we all,'' Joyce said softly.

She noticed Louis writing in his notebook. ''Look, Kitty wasn't a gold digger. She just wanted nice things. She wanted to go live in England someday, meet a guy with manners, like James Bond or something.''

Louis remembered the poster of *Goldfinger* on Kitty's bedroom wall.

''Tell me more about Ray,'' he said.

Joyce let out a sigh. ''Poor Ray. He had such a crush on Kitty. It was kind of pathetic. We were mean to him. We teased him behind his back.'' She hesitated. ''I remember one of the other girls told us he copped a feel behind the grill. She was afraid to tell his Dad because she thought she'd get fired.''

She looked up at Louis. ''Why are you asking me all these questions about Ray?''

Louis debated how much to tell her. ''You said Ray had a crush on her. It might be helpful to me to know about anyone like that.''

''But why now? What's the point? Kitty's dead. Why are you bothering with this now?''

She was looking at him strangely, like she suddenly could read his mind, or like he was some weird voyeur, like poor old Ray Faulk.

"It might have some bearing on Jack Cade's present case," he said.

She stiffened at the name and something flashed over her face, like she had remembered something she had tried very hard to forget.

"I saw him once," she said softly.

"Cade?"

Joyce nodded. Her eyes went to the girl who was sitting under the dryer, absorbed in her *Cosmopolitan.*

"When I was walking to school," she said. "I was walking past this house, one of those pretty places over near the park." She stopped, her eyes downcast. She was playing with the brush, rubbing the bristles over the palm of her hand.

"Was Kitty with you?"

Joyce nodded. "His truck was at the curb, an old beat-up red Ford with that landscaping sign on the door. He was pushing a lawn mower and he saw us walk by on the sidewalk."

She stopped again. The air conditioner droned on.

"I looked up," she said, "and I saw him watching us."

She was gripping the brush, pushing the bristles into her palm. "He looked at me and . . . he touched himself."

Louis looked up from his notebook. Her head was still down, the brush gripped in her hand. When she finally raised her head, her eyes were bright, her face red.

"Did Kitty see him, too?"

Joyce shook her head. "I don't think so. I didn't say anything to her. It was too . . ." She hesitated. "I thought about it later, after . . ." Her voice trailed off again.

There had been no mention of this in Ahnert's report of his interview with Joyce. "You didn't tell the police," Louis said.

She shook her head slowly. "A detective came and talked to me, but I didn't think about it until later, when I saw Jack Cade on television after he had been arrested."

Louis's pen was poised over the notebook as he looked at her stricken face.

"I never told anyone. I guess I was embarrassed," Joyce said. "I should have, but I never did."

"Mrs. Novick?"

They both turned to look at the girl, who had ducked out from under the dryer. "I'm done, I think, Mrs. Novick."

Joyce looked at Louis, then got up to rescue her young customer. When the girl was sitting back in the swivel chair, Joyce turned back to Louis.

"I've got to finish this," she said. "I got another one coming in five minutes. Winter Fest dance tonight at the high school. Big event." She looked wistfully at the girl in the mirror.

Louis rose, putting his notebook away. She followed him out and stood by the door.

"Thank you for your time," Louis said.

"Are you talking to others?" she asked.

"Others?"

"From the school or the drive-in, I mean."

"Should I?"

She was chewing on her bottom lip. "What you said about Ray, about him having a crush on Kitty . . ."

"Go on."

She ran a hand through her hair. "It made me remember Ronnie Cade."

Louis felt something in his chest, like a sudden extra heartbeat.

"Ronnie used to come to the drive-in a lot in that

old red truck," Joyce said. "The guys laughed at him because the truck had that landscaping sign on it and dirt and bags of fertilizer and things in the back. Ronnie always smelled like that truck."

"Did Kitty laugh at him?" Louis asked.

"No. But I remember he used to watch her and sometimes he used to stick around when we were closing and ask her to go for a ride." Joyce's eyes were steady on his. "Kitty turned him down."

"Was he at the drive-in the night Kitty disappeared?"

"I don't remember," Joyce said. "It was awful busy that night."

She was standing there, arms folded over her chest, staring at something off in the distance.

"Mrs. Novick!" The girl with the rollers in her hair was calling.

Joyce looked back at her. "They don't know," she said softly. "They don't know how fast it all can change. One minute you're singing along to the radio, then something happens and your whole life spins off in a different direction."

Her eyes welled. "One minute you're fifteen, the next minute your life is over. You know what I mean?"

But Louis didn't hear her. His mind was racing, thinking about Ronnie Cade, Jack Cade and the broken connections between fathers and sons.

"I have to go," he said quickly, starting away. "Thank you for your time, Mrs. Novick."

"It's Joy," she said.

But Louis was already gone.

Chapter
Twenty-Four

He drove like a madman, the Mustang racing as fast as his brain. He saw it now, saw it clearly. He saw the answer to the question that had gnawed at him from the first day he met Jack Cade.

Why did you take that plea bargain?

I figured it was the better deal. Blood is thicker than water, man.

The scrub land bordering the highway sped by in a blur. The drive from Immokalee back to Fort Myers would take about an hour. Too much time to think, too much time for his anger to boil.

God damn Ronnie Cade.

He had lied. Worse, he had run his own little con game. Conning him with that *I lost my father for twenty years* shit, conning him into believing his life was ruined because his father went to prison. His life had been *saved,* for chrissake.

Blood is thicker than water. Damn right it was, in ways that Ronnie Cade couldn't begin to understand.

He cut across downtown and picked up 41 North. He was thinking about Joyce and Kitty swimming in the moonlight, thinking about how both their lives had ended twenty years ago, thinking about the man who in one instant, had changed everything for them.

It was near three by the time he made his way across the causeway to Sereno Key. He was trying to figure out how to approach this. He told himself to do it like a cop, put Ronnie on the defensive, confront him with evidence, play head games with him and get him to say something incriminating.

But he wasn't a cop. And maybe for once that was good. He didn't have to worry about privilege and Miranda. And the more he thought about Kitty and Ronnie, and the twisted branches of the Cade family tree, the more he was ready to throw procedure out the window and just beat the shit out of the pathetic asshole.

The sun was low in the sky when he pulled into J.C. Landscaping.

Louis shoved the Mustang into park and got out, looking around. The yard was deserted, the still, humid air heavy with the stink of fertilizer.

"Ronnie Cade!" Louis shouted.

Eric came around the back of the trailer.

"Eric! Where's your father?"

"Around back."

Louis started around the shed. Jack and Ronnie were working with potted palms, lifting them from small black pots into larger ones. Both were shirtless, their skin brown and wet. Ronnie looked at him, his hair matted against his forehead, his face smudged with dirt.

Louis was staring at both of them. Ronnie must have seen something in his face because he stepped toward him slowly, pulling off his gloves.

"You've found out something," Ronnie said.

"I sure did," Louis said.

Jack Cade reached in his back pocket for a cigarette. He watched Louis while he lit it, cupping his hand around it. "So say it," he said.

Louis glanced at Eric, who was standing there, staring at all of them.

"Tell him to go inside," Louis said.

Eric looked at Ronnie and Ronnie motioned toward the trailer. Louis waited until Eric was gone before he turned to Ronnie.

"Ever since I met your father," Louis said, "I wondered about two things. Why he didn't want to talk about Kitty Jagger and why he took the plea bargain if he didn't kill her."

Louis glanced at Cade. He hadn't moved a muscle. "You want to tell him, Cade, or do you want me to?"

"I told you to leave it alone," Cade said softly.

Ronnie moved toward his father. "What's this all about?"

"He was protecting you, Ronnie," Louis said.

"What?"

"Shut up, Kincaid," Cade hissed.

Louis shook his head. "No, I'm not going to shut up." He turned to Ronnie.

"You want to tell me what happened that night, Ronnie?"

"What night?"

"April 9, 1966. The night you asked Kitty to take a ride with you."

Ronnie took a step backward. "What?"

"You cruised the drive-in with your father's truck.

You asked Kitty to take a ride with you. What did she say to you, Ronnie, when she turned you down. What did she say that made you snap?''

Ronnie was shaking, looking back and forth between Louis and his father. ''I—''

Louis looked at Jack Cade. ''You knew all about this, didn't you? That's why you took the goddamn plea, to protect him.''

Cade didn't answer.

''Blood is thicker than water, that's what you said,'' Louis said. ''You knew they could trace the semen sample to Ronnie if they looked. You knew it and you did it to protect him.''

''What is he talking about?'' Ronnie said, his eyes frantic. ''Dad, what the fuck is he talking about?''

Cade looked away.

''Dad?''

Louis hit Cade's shoulder, spinning him around. ''What happened, Cade?'' Louis pressed. ''What did Duvall have on Ronnie?''

''I don't know, he never said,'' Cade said, his voice flat. ''He just said that if I didn't plead he'd offer up another suspect that had the same opportunity and same access to the truck and to the garden tool.''

''Jesus,'' Ronnie said in a strangled voice. He turned away, hands over his face.

''What was I supposed to do, Ronnie?'' Cade shouted. ''What was I supposed to do? I found those panties in the truck! I knew you took it out to the drive-in the night before! I mean, what was I supposed to think? You never brought home any girls. You never even seemed interested in pussy! Christ, I figured you were a fucking virgin or something worse!''

Cade took a deep breath, but he didn't even see the stricken look on his son's face.

''And then I see on TV about the dead girl. What

the fuck was I supposed to do? What was I supposed to *think?!*'' Cade yelled.

"You should have asked me! Why didn't you just ask me?'' Ronnie yelled back.

"Fuck . . .'' Cade jerked out of Louis's grip.

"I didn't kill her!'' Ronnie shouted. "She was never in the truck! I swear! Why didn't you just ask me?!''

Cade spun back to face Ronnie. "Because you're my son! You hear me, you're *my* son.'' He stabbed a finger at his own chest. "Jack Cade's son! You get it?''

Ronnie just stared at him.

"You got my blood in you,'' Cade said.

Ronnie's eyes darkened. His hands curled into fists at his sides.

"You want to hit me,'' Cade said softly.

"That's enough,'' Louis said.

"Stay out of this, Kincaid,'' Cade said. He took a step toward Ronnie. "You want to hit me. Go ahead.''

Ronnie's eyes suddenly welled. "Twenty years,'' he said. "Twenty years I've been living in your stink because I thought you killed Kitty. And now you tell me you did it for *me?*''

"We've both been living in it, son,'' Cade said.

"Don't call me that!'' Ronnie shouted.

Suddenly, Ronnie's fist shot out. Cade dodged and it clipped his chin. Lightening quick, Cade's hand came up and smacked Ronnie hard on the face, sending him falling back against the shed.

"Stop!'' Louis shouted, jumping in front of Cade. Cade was breathing hard, staring down at Ronnie. Ronnie was just lying there, holding his bleeding lip.

"You ungrateful little bastard,'' Cade said.

Louis put up an arm to push Cade back, but Cade swatted it away.

"I told you to leave it alone,'' he said. He walked off toward the trailer.

Louis looked down at Ronnie. He wasn't watching his father; he was looking over at the corner of the shed.

Eric was standing there. Louis could tell from the hard line of his mouth that he had heard every word.

Chapter
Twenty-Five

The picture of Kitty was lying on his dresser. He picked it up, looking at it. His anger at Ronnie Cade was still simmering. And his imagination was kicking in now, too, flashing ugly pictures across his mind. Pictures of Ronnie Cade, the red truck, and Kitty's bloody body lying in the back of it with the dirt and fertilizer.

He stuck Kitty's picture in the wood frame of the mirror.

Pulling on a clean sweatshirt, he went back out to the kitchen.

It was all there, spread out for Susan to see. The autopsy reports and the police files covered the kitchen table. The newspaper clippings were taped to the walls along with crime scene pictures of the dump. Colored note cards detailing aspects of the case were stuck on the doors of the kitchen cabinets.

He had called Susan's office as soon as he got back

from the Cade place. He didn't tell her anything, just that they had to talk. He was surprised when she easily agreed to come out to his cottage.

His eyes swept over everything he had collected. Susan wouldn't be able to put him off now. She wouldn't be able to turn a blind eye to the idea that whoever killed Kitty also killed Duvall.

But she still wasn't going to like it. Especially when he told her about Ronnie. It was going to throw a major wrench into her defense. To get Jack Cade off, she was going to have to make his son a suspect. If Cade didn't fire her first.

A crunch of gravel on the drive drew Louis's eyes to the open window. He recognized the diesel wheeze of Susan's old Mercedes and went to the screen door. The headlights went out and he saw her door open. He was shocked to see Benjamin get out of the passenger side.

"Okay, I got here as quick as I could," Susan said, coming onto the screened porch.

Louis couldn't hide his annoyance as he nodded at Benjamin, who was hovering behind Susan, looking around at the cottage with bored eyes.

"I had to pick him up from his saxophone lesson after work," she said.

Louis shook his head, as he led her inside the cottage.

"I'm really tired and I wasn't about to drive all the way home and back out here," Susan said. She motioned to Benjamin to sit. He flopped down on the couch.

"We need to talk about Kitty," Louis said, lowering his voice.

She sighed. "Kincaid—"

"I found out why Cade took the plea."

She stared at him. Then she turned to Benjamin. "Ben, Mr. Kincaid and I have to talk. You mind waiting out on the porch?"

He gave her an exasperated look. "What am I supposed to do out there?"

"Go get your sax and practice."

"I just got done playing. My lips will fall off if I play anymore."

"You have two choices, Benjamin. The porch with your sax or lifelong groundation."

Benjamin slunk off toward the car to get his saxophone.

Susan slipped her purse strap off her arm and dropped it into a chair. "Okay, talk," she said.

"Cade took the plea to protect Ronnie," Louis said. "He thought Ronnie killed Kitty."

Her face registered astonishment, then something else that Louis couldn't quite decipher. Irritation, probably, just as he expected.

"How did you find this out?"

He told her about his meeting with Joyce Novick and what she had revealed about Ronnie. When he told her about his visit to the Cade place, her expression turned from irritation to exasperation.

"You should have gotten some proof before you went storming over there," she said. "You have any idea what a bad spot you've put me in?"

"I'm sorry," he said.

She turned, smoothing her hair, frustrated. "Why would Cade think his own kid killed Kitty?"

"Duvall told Cade that if he didn't plead, he would offer Ronnie up as a suspect. Cade must've gotten nervous and pled to keep his teenage son from going to prison."

She drew her lips into a line. "You're telling me Duvall forced Cade to plead, knowing he had another suspect? No lawyer would do that."

Louis nodded. "It explains why he never submitted the vaginal report."

Her eyes flared. "Maybe Duvall never submitted it

because it was the same as the damn panties—
O-positive.''

''The prosecution never submitted it either and if it
was O-positive, it cemented their case against Cade.''

''How do you know they never submitted it?''

''I read the trial transcript.''

She looked at him, stunned. Then she shook her
head. ''Do you believe Ronnie killed Kitty Jagger?''
she asked.

''Yes, I do.''

''Do you believe Ronnie killed Spencer Duvall?''

Louis drew in a breath. ''I don't know.''

''You're blowing your theory,'' Susan said. ''I can't
use any of this and all you've done is rip that poor
family apart even more.''

Louis started to strike back, but he saw her looking
at the files spread on the table. He watched her eyes
as they swept up to the cards taped to the cabinets and
all the photos taped to the walls. Then they came back
up to Louis's face.

Susan picked up Kitty's autopsy report. ''God, Louis,''
she said quietly. ''What are you doing here?''

''My job,'' Louis said.

She set the report down, without looking at Louis.
The low wail of a saxophone drifted in from the porch.
Susan rubbed her eyes.

''Where's your john?'' she asked, not looking up.

Louis pointed toward the bedroom. She got up and
left without saying a word.

He went to the refrigerator and got himself a beer.
He stood at the window, listening to the moan of Benjamin's sax mingle with the rustle of the wind in the
palm trees.

When he tipped his head back to take a swig of beer,
he saw Susan standing at the door of his bedroom. She
was holding something, her brows knit. It was the
snapshot of Kitty Jagger in the pink bathing suit.

"This is her, isn't it?" Susan asked.

"Kitty," he said. "Her name is Kitty."

He felt a twinge of annoyance, like Susan had somehow violated his privacy by taking the snapshot off the mirror. He held out his hand.

When she hesitated, he took the picture. He looked down at Kitty's face. It was easier than looking at Susan's.

"I have something to tell you," she said quietly, sitting down at the table.

"What?"

"Sit down, okay?"

He slipped into the chair across from her.

"I was going to tell you tomorrow at the office, but when you called, I thought I'd better come out here tonight and tell you in person."

Louis leaned back in the kitchen chair, his grip tightening around the beer bottle.

"Jack Cade wants you gone," Susan said.

"Gone? What, fired?"

She nodded. "He said—"

"What did you tell him," Louis demanded.

"Kincaid—"

"What did you tell him, damn it?"

"When he called me, I asked him why, but he wouldn't tell me. Now I know." Susan looked away. "I'm sorry, Louis, this is Cade's call, not mine."

Louis slammed the bottle on the table and jumped up. "You're firing me? I don't fucking believe this."

The saxophone playing stopped suddenly. Susan glanced out toward the porch, then looked back at Louis.

"I don't have any choice," she said, her voice low. She paused for a second. "It's better this way."

"Better for who?" Louis said.

"Don't yell at me, Kincaid."

"Better for who?" Louis repeated.

"Everyone. Cade, me. And you."

Louis shook his head. "Don't you see what Cade is doing, Susan? He's protecting Ronnie again! He doesn't want me going after him."

"Louis," she said firmly. "It's my job to protect Jack Cade. And that is what I have to do."

"So you're going to just ignore everything I just told you?"

She was looking at the door. Benjamin was standing in the doorway, holding his saxophone, watching them both.

"Go get in the car, Ben," Susan said.

"We going home?" he asked hopefully.

"Yes. Go wait in the car."

Ben glanced at Louis, then turned. Louis watched him pack the sax back in its case and head out to the Mercedes. Susan rose, went to the chair and picked up her purse, taking out her keys.

"I'll try to get my boss to pay you through the end of the month," she said.

"Don't bother," Louis said.

Susan hesitated in the doorway. "Look, you did good work for me. That stuff about Hayley and Candace, I can use it."

"Winning the case, that's all it's about to you, isn't it?" Louis waited for her to fight back.

But she didn't. There was no fight in her eyes. All that was left was something perilously close to pity. Her gaze dropped to the picture of Kitty still in his hand.

"You can't save her, Louis, it's too late."

Louis tossed the picture down on the table. But he still couldn't look Susan in the eye.

"Your son's waiting," he said.

She started to say something but didn't. He didn't see her leave, just heard the slap of the screen door.

Save her? She was already dead, for God's sake. He

knew that. Didn't he? Or was he starting to hear her talking, just like Bob Ahnert had warned?

He heard a ringing somewhere in the back of his mind and it took him several seconds to realize it was his phone. He grabbed it.

"Louis? It's Vinny."

"What do you got, Vince?" Louis asked.

"I got nothing. No report, no sample. They said the policy back then was to return or destroy everything after a few years."

"Damn it."

"Yeah. Sorry, Louis."

Louis hung up, letting out a long breath. He went out on the porch. Through the gray mesh of the screen, he watched the red taillights of the Mercedes disappear down the dark island road.

Chapter
Twenty-Six

It was rare when he drank alone anymore. Since leaving Michigan, he had slacked off, and when he did drink, it was usually over at Timmy's Nook, where Bev treated him like a son and there were plenty of people to talk to. People who kept a man from thinking about the parts of his life that drove him to the bar in the first place.

But he wasn't in Timmy's now. He had wanted to go someplace where no one knew him and he didn't know anyone. So he had found his way over to Sereno Key and to the scarred wood bar of the Lazy Flamingo.

Louis picked up the Heineken and finished it off. He considered leaving, but didn't want to go home to the empty cottage. There was a ripple of laughter from the group in a booth as Billy Joel's "Innocent Man" came on the jukebox.

Louis waved at the bartender, a thin man with a

shaggy mustache. "Hey, bring me a shot of brandy, would you?"

Louis's eyes drifted to the two men at the end of the bar. One was chubby, with a trim gray beard and a colorful tropical shirt. The other was younger, his blond hair pulled back into a ponytail. He wore a neon green tank top. They were laughing, the older man's arm on the younger man's shoulder.

The bartender set the shotglass in front of him. Louis reached for it, gulped it down and closed his eyes, giving a slight shiver as it burned its way down to his belly.

He was about to get up to go home when he felt a slap on the back and spun around.

Dan Wainwright's beefy face was grinning at him.

"Hey, Dan." The words came out in an edgy breath.

"Jeez, you're jumpy. What the hell's the matter?" Wainwright said.

"Sorry. Thought you might be Jack Cade."

"Cade? Why?"

"He's real pissed off at me right now." Louis waved for the bartender. "What are you drinking? My treat."

"I wasn't. I just got here and saw you sitting here. Bud's fine."

Wainwright waited until the bartender brought their drinks. "I heard you're working for Cade's defense."

Louis waited for the look of reproach, but there was none in the Sereno chief's eyes.

"I was. He fired me today."

"What did you do to piss him off?"

"Long story," Louis muttered.

Wainwright didn't press it. Instead, he gave Louis a smile. "It's good to see you," he said. "I've been meaning to call you."

"Same here," Louis said.

They fell into an awkward silence that was broken by a trio of laughing women who had squeezed up next to Wainwright. Wainwright tapped Louis on the shoulder and motioned toward a booth, walking away.

Louis sucked down the second brandy, then picked up his water glass and followed.

Wainwright settled into the booth and Louis slid in across from him, his gaze drawn to the window. It was a pitch-black, moonless night, and the green and pink floodlights cast a surreal glow on the fluttering palms.

"So why'd Cade fire you?" Wainwright asked.

Louis rubbed his face. "I accused his son Ronnie of murdering Kitty Jagger."

Wainwright's expression didn't change, but his eyebrow twitched. "Can you prove it?"

"There was a semen sample and it's disappeared. I can't prove shit without it."

Wainwright took a drink. "What semen?"

"The shit inside her," Louis said, irritated. Then he realized that Wainwright didn't have a clue as to what he was talking about. Susan was right. No one gave a rat's ass about the Kitty Jagger case. It was ancient history, yesterday's papers.

He let out a breath. "Sorry, Dan," he said. "Bad day."

Wainwright put up a hand. "No problem. Tell me about this sample thing."

Louis hesitated. He wanted to talk about Kitty, but no one had wanted to hear it. Maybe Wainwright would understand.

"Two semen samples were taken," he said. "One from Kitty Jagger's panties, the other vaginal. The results from the vaginal sample are missing from the original police files."

"The state lab?"

"No record. I tried. No one has a record anywhere."

"The prosecutor's office would have it."

"Yeah, Vern Sandusky is just going to hand it over. Right."

"He might."

"Give me a break, Dan. There isn't a prosecutor in the world who would voluntarily reopen a case where there's been a conviction. You know that."

"What about Spencer Duvall's records? He would have it too."

Louis looked up, his mind trying to work through the slosh of the brandy. "Mobley has that."

"What?"

"Jack Cade's old legal file. It was on Spencer Duvall's desk when he was shot, so the cops took it."

Wainwright took a long swallow of beer. "Kiss that idea goodbye. Mobley's an idiot."

Louis shook his head. "Maybe not. I might be able to convince Mobley to let me take a look."

Wainwright leaned back in the booth, considering Louis. "I got to ask you this, Louis."

"What?"

"Why bother? Why bust your balls on a closed case?"

Louis stared at him. "Because someone has to, damn it."

Wainwright drew back ever so slightly. And the look on his face was the same as the one Louis had seen on Susan's, like he was nuts or obsessed or something.

Louis rose abruptly and went to the bar. He returned with another shot and a beer. He didn't look at Wainwright as he sat down.

"Look, Louis," Wainwright said. "Cade probably did you a favor. He's a loser, so is his son. So's the case."

Louis took a breath. He didn't want to be angry at Wainwright. He wanted him to understand. "Dan, it's important to know who killed her," he said slowly.

"To who, Louis? The girl's dead twenty years and I hear her old man is just a walking zombie. Who cares?"

Louis reached for the shotglass, hesitated, then brought it to his lips. It went down easier than the last.

"A piece of advice, Louis," Wainwright said. "Let it go."

"Can't," Louis said, his eyes on the scarred wood tabletop. He knew Wainwright was looking at him. He heard him let out a sigh.

"I gotta take a piss. Be right back."

Louis watched Wainwright trudge off to the rear of the bar. He leaned back, shutting his eyes. Shit, maybe he was going nuts. He was seeing things in his head, that much was clear. He was seeing the lonely confusion in Willard Jagger's eyes. He was seeing the shadow of sadness in Joyce Novick's eyes. He was seeing the question in Eric Cade's angry eyes as he watched his father and grandfather: Which one of you killed her?

And he was seeing her. She was in his head, day and night now, walking around like a ghost, pink cheeks and peppermint lipstick, whispering to him.

"Louis?"

He looked up. Wainwright's face was green in the neon light.

"You okay?"

"Yeah." He sat up, pulling the beer bottle toward him.

Wainwright slid back in across from him. A new song drifted above the murmur of the bar, Van Morrison singing about his Tupelo honey. Louis watched two young guys and their dates playing the ring-toss game over in the corner. The two guys were drunk and weren't coming even close to swinging the ring up to catch the hook. The girls were doubled over with laughter.

"They don't know how fast it all can change," Louis murmured.

"What?"

Louis glanced at Wainwright. "Nothing."

They sat in uneasy silence for a long time. Finally, Wainwright cleared his throat. "So, you talked to Farentino at all?"

Emily Farentino had been the Miami FBI agent who had worked the Paint It Black case with them. Louis had promised to keep in touch, but he hadn't.

"No," Louis said. "Have you?"

"Yeah, I called her awhile back. She's doing okay. She asked how you were."

The conversation stalled again. Louis ran a hand over his eyes. What the hell was the matter with him? Why was he always pushing people away? Farentino, Wainwright, even the Dodies. Why was he afraid to let anyone get close?

He glanced at Wainwright, who was gazing out over the bar. Shit, he knew why he hadn't called Wainwright in the last six months. It was because he had never worked up the guts to tell him the truth about what had happened up in Michigan. He had been too damn afraid of another cop's censure. Especially a cop he liked and respected.

"Dan," Louis said.

Wainwright looked back at him.

"There's something I need to tell you." Louis drew in a deep breath, shaking his head. "Man, this is hard," he said softly.

Wainwright just waited.

"I never told you what I did when I was working up in Michigan," Louis said.

"I already know, Louis," Wainwright said. "We all do."

Louis sat back in the booth. "You don't condemn me?"

"Sometimes you gotta do what you gotta do. Even cops."

Louis saw something pass over Wainwright's eyes. He remembered the case that had caused Wainwright to crack when he was with the FBI—the Raisin River serial child killer, Harlan Skeen. Wainwright had cornered Skeen in a bathroom and shot him to death.

"You talking about Skeen?" Louis asked.

"Yeah. I took things into my own hands that day. It was the only way there was going to be any justice." He took a drink of beer. "I don't regret it."

Louis was quiet. He couldn't tell Wainwright what he was thinking. Wainwright had done more than take justice into his own hands; he had broken the law. It wasn't the same as what he himself had done in Michigan; he had killed another cop to save a kid nobody cared about. But he hadn't broken the law.

Louis studied Wainwright's creased face. Even through the brandy haze, he could see that something had changed since he had last seen Wainwright. The Paint It Black case had stirred up a lot of hard memories for Wainwright. But he looked better now, almost peaceful.

"How things going for you lately, Dan?" he asked.

Wainwright looked at him surprised. "What do you mean?"

"I haven't seen you in a while, that's all. Just wanted to know how things have been."

Wainwright shrugged. "Same old shit. Job's good. Things are real quiet." He took a drink of his beer and set the bottle down. He was tapping his fingers lightly on the table.

"I went back to Michigan and saw my son over Thanksgiving," Wainwright added suddenly.

"Oh yeah?"

"Yeah. I called him, and he seemed open to a visit. So I went up there."

Louis nodded. He remembered that Wainwright had not seen his grown son in years, not since the death of Wainwright's wife. He could only imagine how hard it had been for an emotionally constipated guy like

Wainwright to make an overture toward an estranged son.

"So, it went okay?" Louis asked.

"Yeah," Wainwright said. "It was . . . good."

Louis picked at the label on the Heineken bottle. "What made you do it?" he asked.

Wainwright just looked at him.

"Sorry. It's none of my business."

"What made me call my son?"

"Yeah."

Wainwright put his arm across the back of the booth, making a poor attempt to look cool.

Louis raised his beer bottle. "Never mind. Forget I asked."

"No, I want to answer you, I'm just trying to figure out how."

Wainwright drew his arm off the booth. "I don't know why the fuck I finally did it," he said. "I think it was because deep down I knew I had been a lousy father, that I hadn't been there for my kid."

Louis blinked slowly, trying to clear his mind. It was weird hearing personal stuff come out of Wainwright's mouth.

"I mean, I knew I couldn't change the past," Wainwright went on, "but I wanted to try to do something about the future. My son has his own son now. I didn't want him not knowing me, not knowing who he came from."

A man should know what kind of blood flows through his veins.

The beer and the brandy were making his stomach churn. Louis leaned his head back against the wall and closed his eyes to steady things. For a moment, he just sat as still as possible, trying to let the room catch up. When he finally opened his eyes, Wainwright was gone. Louis saw him at the bar getting two more shots. He sat down, setting one shot in front of Louis.

"I was a foster child," Louis said suddenly.

Wainwright seemed to go stiff and his eyes wavered. Then he dropped his gaze to the table, his fingers drawing the cocktail napkin into his fist.

Louis could feel his heart pounding. He wanted the words back. It was like admitting he was a fucking leper or something. Shit, talk about emotionally constipated.

"Did you know your father?" Wainwright asked.

"No."

Louis started to reach for the shot, but drew his hand back, wiping his mouth. He didn't need any more. His belly burned and he wanted to move, get up, go home, but he wasn't sure he could stand.

"What's his name?" Wainwright asked.

"Jordan Kincaid."

"You ever try to find him?"

Louis shook his head slowly. The jukebox sounds seemed dull and distorted. The neon lights above the bar began to quiver and the palm fronds were flapping against the window.

"You want me to try?" Wainwright asked.

Louis didn't trust himself to look at Wainwright. He just shook his head and stared at the palm fronds beating against the dark glass.

He heard Wainwright let out a heavy sigh, then ease himself up out of the booth. He could feel Wainwright's eyes on him.

"You ready?"

Louis looked up.

Wainwright picked up his shot, took one last swig and set it down. "Come on. I'll drive you."

"I can get home."

"You'll put that Mustang of yours in the bay, if you try. Let's go."

Louis struggled to his feet, reaching back for the shotglass, but Wainwright put a hand on his arm.

"Let it go, Louis."

Louis stumbled, catching the back of the booth for balance. A ripple of embarrassment moved through him. God, he hated getting sloppy.

"I'm sorry, Dan," Louis whispered, hoping no one could hear him. "I didn't mean to get this drunk."

"Yes, you did," Wainwright said, taking his arm.

Louis closed the door on Wainwright's cruiser and stumbled into the darkness toward his cottage, hearing Wainwright holler out a goodbye.

He brushed aside a palm and tripped over the rocks that lined the path. He squinted, trying to pick his way in the dim light thrown off by the Branson's On The Beach sign.

His stomach was starting to churn. He needed a bed. Now.

Something snapped behind him. He jumped and spun.

"Where ya been, Louie?"

Louis stared into the shadows of the swaying palms. "Cade?"

He heard the rustle of the wind in the sea oats but still couldn't see anyone. He staggered, almost falling, but pulled himself up.

"Goddammit, Cade. Come out where I can see you!" he shouted.

"I ain't hiding."

Louis scanned the dunes and dark trees, but all it did was make him nauseous. Finally, he picked out Cade's silhouette.

"I told you not to come here again," Louis said.

"You told me not go in your house. I didn't."

Louis closed his eyes. He couldn't fight it anymore. He turned and threw up in the bushes, grabbing onto the palm.

"You done?" Cade asked.

Louis wiped his mouth and looked back at Cade, using those few seconds of clarity that come immediately after vomiting up half a bottle of brandy. His heart kicked an extra beat.

Cade was holding something small and dark in his arms. It was Issy.

"Let her go," Louis said slowly.

Cade had the cat clamped under his elbow, holding its front paws tightly with his left hand. He was stroking the cat's fur with his other hand.

"Let her go!" Louis said.

Cade's hand hesitated at the cat's neck. Then, suddenly, he let go. Issy sprang away and ran into the shadows.

"I wasn't gonna hurt her, Louie," Cade said.

Louis struggled to focus on Cade's face. "What are you doing here?" he demanded.

Cade was silent. Louis waved a dismissive hand at him and started toward the porch. Cade moved quickly, catching Louis's arm. When Louis pulled away, he stumbled.

"You fucked me and my family," Cade said.

Louis pointed at him. "Tell it to someone else. You fired me. You're crazy. Your kid is crazy."

"I told you to leave it alone and you didn't."

Cade came closer and Louis thought he saw a flash of silver. A knife? Louis felt his heart quicken and he tried to stand up straight and focus. It was dark, they were away from the street, no one in the other cottages would hear or see a thing.

Make a move and you're dead. Think . . . bluff.

"What?" Louis said. "You come here to put a hole in me? Like . . . fuck, what's his name, that Haitian guy?"

Cade took a step closer.

"What are you going to do, Cade? Kill me and jump bail?"

"That's not a bad idea."

"You gonna take Ronnie with you? What about Eric? You wanna trash his life too?"

Cade had stopped moving at least. Louis couldn't see the knife anymore. Maybe he had imagined it.

"I found out something," Louis said. "Something about Kitty that could help you."

Cade didn't move.

"There's a lab report that's missing."

"So what?"

"It shouldn't be," Louis said. "It should be there and it isn't."

"You're talking like a drunk, Louie."

"Listen to me, Cade," Louis said. "The report could prove you didn't rape her, that someone else did it."

Cade was silent. "How?" he asked finally.

Louis knew there was no way to explain it right now so Cade could understand it. "Blood, Cade," he said. "They can tell by your blood."

"What if it has Ronnie's blood?"

"Fuck, Cade, what if it doesn't?" Louis asked.

Louis couldn't make out Cade's face, but he had heard something change in Cade's voice. Louis tried to see Cade's right hand, tried to make out the glint of the knife. He wanted to be ready if Cade made a move.

"What about it, Cade?" Louis said.

"You're asking me to put my kid's balls up on the block and hope no one chops them off. You're asking me to trust you."

"I'm asking you to trust your own fucking son."

Cade said nothing, but Louis could hear the rustle of his clothing. Suddenly, there was another glint of silver and Louis heard something hit the sand at his feet.

He looked down.

The butt of a knife was sticking out of the sand, only an inch from his foot. He looked up.

Jack Cade was gone.

Chapter
Twenty-Seven

The small reception area outside Mobley's office was crowded. Louis guessed that the young woman and the disheveled man were reporters, but he didn't recognize the two blue-suited black men who stood solemn-faced near the Amazon's desk. The Amazon herself was on the phone, scribbling on a pink message slip to add to the pile at her elbow. She gave Louis a harried look as he wedged himself in near her desk.

The room was stuffy. Louis massaged his temples, hoping the aspirin would kick in soon. He knew he should have just stayed in bed this morning, but the nagging voice in his head had drowned out the hangover.

Let it go, Louis.

He was tired of hearing that. Okay, maybe he was obsessed, but damn it, someone had to be. He was on his own now, fired, dismissed with a knife at his feet.

He looked at Mobley's closed door. But he was still in need of an ally.

The Amazon hung up the phone. She looked at Louis and cocked her head toward Mobley's door. Louis didn't even look to see if the others were pissed that he was going in ahead of them.

He closed the door, shutting out the ringing phones.

"You've got two minutes, Kincaid."

Mobley shoved aside a stack of papers and began rifling through his messages, obviously irritated.

"I need something from you, Sheriff."

"What?"

"After Jack Cade visited Duvall threatening to sue him, Duvall asked his secretary to pull Cade's 1967 trial file. The secretary says it was still on his desk when she left just before Duvall was shot. Your guys picked it up as part of the crime scene."

"And you want to look at it."

"Yeah."

Mobley shook his head. "No way. It would raise all kinds of questions that I don't need right now."

"Sheriff—"

"Forget it. I don't want to piss Sandusky off, Kincaid. Especially for you and some moldy old case." Mobley leaned back in his chair. "Besides, I heard Outlaw fired you, that true?"

Louis ignored the question. He rubbed his brow, catching sight of the evidence box from Kitty Jagger's homicide on Mobley's credenza. Vince had said the old sample was either destroyed—or returned.

Louis motioned toward the white box. "Can I look through that box again?"

"Look, Kincaid. I've already got my ass in a sling because you're out asking questions about Kitty. From her father, her high school friends—"

"That's what I do—ask questions," Louis said. "Just let me take a look, okay?"

Mobley raked a hand through his hair. "Make it quick."

Louis put the box on Mobley's desk and began taking out the evidence bags. When he got to the Clot Buster, he carefully set it aside.

Mobley's phone rang and he picked it up. "I told you no calls." He slammed it down and looked back at the Louis.

"What are you looking for?"

"A slide."

"What, like a lab slide?"

Louis nodded. Mobley stood just as Louis pulled out a large yellow envelope with the Florida Department of Law Enforcement seal, postmarked 1977. Just as Vince had said, the samples had been returned to the police ten years after Cade's trial. He turned it over. It had been opened once.

Mobley was reading over his shoulder as Louis pulled out a letter from the lab. The phone on his desk started to ring again, but Mobley ignored it.

> *TO: The Lee County Sheriff's Office. As per our policy, we are returning the following items to you for your case file #4532, Homicide, LCSO, Florida, May, 1966, Jagger, K.*
>
> *Please be advised that we will no longer be able store items for cases that have a final disposition. Please let us know if we can be of service to you in the future.*

Louis emptied the envelope's contents onto the desk: a half-dozen slides, some fingerprint cards, and a small heart-shaped locket, everything still sealed in plastic.

He glanced at the locket, thinking of Bob Ahnert, then began sorting through the slides. He stopped at the one labeled R-24, Vaginal. It had Ahnert's initials on the seal.

"This is it," Louis said.

"What is it?" Mobley asked.

Louis turned to him. "There were two semen samples taken from this crime. One off the panties, which the cops assumed came from Cade, and one from her body."

Mobley looked down at the slide. "They match, right?"

"I don't know. That's why I wanted to see Duvall's old case file because the report on the second one is missing from what *you* gave me."

Mobley turned away, looking at his ringing phone with venom. "I gave you everything, Kincaid. I wouldn't hold anything back."

"You never had the report. I think someone removed it from the case file twenty years ago."

"Why?"

"Because it didn't match Cade's O-positive and someone wanted to keep the prosecution's case simple."

"Who? The prosecutors themselves?"

"It's missing from *your* files, Sheriff. I think maybe it was Dinkle. I think he did it after the trial so no one would ever ask questions again."

The phone started again, and Mobley walked to it, knocking the receiver off its cradle.

"You sure like to sling mud on the uniform, don't you, Kincaid?"

"No, I don't."

"The hell you don't."

Louis tightened, the pounding in his head growing stronger. He knew he didn't owe Mobley an explanation. But he was tired of the looks from the deputies, tired of groveling for their assistance when he needed it on something as simple as tracking down a deadbeat dad. He was tired of being looked at like a leper when he walked into O'Sullivan's, for chrissake.

"I've shown you and your department every respect in this case," Louis said.

"Respect? Don't talk to me about respect," Mobley said, his voice rising. "What about last March? You and Dan Wainwright butt-fucked me in front of the whole city. Shut me out of the biggest case this county ever had."

Mobley went back behind his desk and sank into his chair. Louis resisted the urge to put his hands on his temples.

"Leaving you out wasn't my call," Louis said. "It was Dan's."

"They laughed at me, dammit."

Louis knew he needed to say something else, but an apology wasn't it. Mobley had blown it on the Paint It Black case. They *had* laughed.

Louis picked up the slide. "Maybe we can turn it around with this," he said. "Let me have this typed again. Discreetly. I'll take it to Vince myself."

"I don't know."

Louis took a breath. He knew Mobley had no business letting a civilian take evidence, even from a closed case.

Okay. Start lying. You're getting pretty damn good at it.

"Look," Louis said, "if you don't agree to this, Susan will eventually subpoena Sandusky for any copies he has."

Mobley's eyes jumped to Louis's face. His expression took on a whole new look of frustration.

"It's us against the lawyers, Lance."

Mobley swung his chair slightly. "All right. But I get to see the results first. If that slide comes back O-positive, it goes back in the box and neither of us ever touched it. Agreed?"

Louis nodded. "What if it doesn't?"

Mobley picked up the Clot Buster and bounced it

lightly against his palm. "Maybe it still goes back in the box," he said.

Louis sat on the bench outside Vince Carissimi's office. He could hear Vince inside, talking to someone. Across the hall, through the glass door to the autopsy room, he could see a green bulk moving slowly around. It was Octavius, the diener, finishing up a cadaver. Louis leaned his head back against the cool tile.

He had called ahead, but the receptionist told him Vince was busy. Louis had come over to wait anyway. His eyes drifted up to the wall clock, then to the sign above the autopsy door.

Mortui vivos docent. "The dead teach the living."

He reached back to the pocket of his jeans and pulled out the picture of Kitty. It was starting to get creased from all the handling and he ran his palm over it, trying to flatten it back in shape. Finally, he reached back again for his wallet, opened it, and carefully slipped the picture in between some bills.

He heard Vince's door open and jumped to his feet, slipping the wallet back in his pocket.

A strange man came out, followed by Vince, who looked at Louis in surprise. "Hey, Louis, what gives?" he asked.

"Vince, I need your help," Louis said, picking up a manila envelope from the bench.

"Gotta be quick, man, I am up to my ass in alligators today," Vince said, starting down the hall with long strides.

Louis was at his side, holding out the envelope. "I got the sample."

Vince stopped, frowning at the envelope.

"The missing vaginal semen sample," Louis said.

Vince hesitated, then took the envelope. He dug inside and pulled out the slide, still in its twenty-year-old plastic evidence bag. Vince held it up to the florescent light.

"Can you type it?" Louis asked.

Vince sighed. "Won't know 'til I get it under the scope."

"Can I wait?"

Vince gave him a look, then glanced at his watch. "All right, come on."

In the lab, Louis hovered in the background while Vince slipped the old slide under the microscope. He knew this was a long shot. What were the chances that anything could survive twenty years in some municipal storeroom? His fears were confirmed when Vince turned. He could read it in the M.E.'s face.

"It's totally disintegrated," Vince said. *"Memoriae,* Louis, nothing but a memory now."

Louis let out a sigh and watched as Vince pulled out the slide and slipped it back in the plastic. He handed it to Louis.

"I'm sorry, man," Vince said.

"I appreciate you trying, Vince."

Vince cocked his head. "You okay?"

Louis nodded, looking at the slide in the plastic evidence bag.

"Look, I understand how this can be," Vince said. "I had a little girl on my table once, an abuse case. I didn't sleep for weeks until they finally put her stepfather behind bars. A case like the Kitty Jagger thing, it can get under your skin."

Louis looked up at him. Maybe it was the way Vince had said her name, maybe it was just the look of compassion on Vince's face. But something pulled inside Louis's chest.

"I've got to get going," Louis said. "Thanks again, Vince."

Outside, Louis paused to slip on his sunglasses. His gaze drifted over to Page Field, where a small plane floated down to the runaway and rose again, the pilot practicing touch-and-goes.

Dead end. Like Vince said, there was nothing but memories of Kitty now, memories that the decades had rendered useless. Joyce Novick's rose-colored reminiscences, Willard's fading echoes, none of that could help him now.

Bob Ahnert . . .

Louis watched the plane circling. But Bob Ahnert remembered clearly, remembered things he didn't want to tell. Kitty was still talking to him. And he was still listening.

Chapter
Twenty-Eight

"I figured you'd be calling sooner or later," Ahnert said.

"We need to talk," Louis said.

There was a silence on the other end of the line. "All right," Ahnert said. "I'm on duty. You'll have to come out to the substation." He gave directions and hung up without another word.

Louis was an hour's drive into the wasteland of the Corkscrew Preserve before he saw the radio tower that Ahnert had told him to watch for. It led him to a sun-bleached cinderblock building set in the flat gray-green scrub land, land that looked untouched by the recent hard rains. There were no trees, nothing to give shelter from the sun. The only break in the monotonous landscape was the line of electrical towers marching like skeletons to the horizon.

Louis parked next to the Lee County Sheriff's

Department cruiser in front. As he got out of the Mustang, he saw Bob Ahnert emerge from the building.

Why was Ahnert wearing the standard green uniform? He was a detective, wasn't he? Louis's eyes dipped to the name tag on Ahnert's shirt. SGT. AHNERT. Had the guy been busted in rank? Is that why he was sitting out in a substation in the middle of nowhere?

Ahnert removed his glasses, drew out a handkerchief and started to wipe them.

"You must want something pretty bad to drive all the way out here," he said, putting his sunglasses back on and resting his hip against his cruiser.

"I know now what was missing from Kitty's homicide file," Louis said. "The second lab report. That's what you were talking about, wasn't it?"

Ahnert drew a cigar out of his breast pocket and lit it. He didn't have to cup a hand; there wasn't one whiff of a breeze out here.

"Did you find it?" Ahnert asked.

"No."

"So that's why you're here. You want me to tell you what it said," Ahnert said.

"Yes."

Ahnert drew on the cigar. Louis could see his reflection in Ahnert's sunglasses.

"Is she talking to you yet?" Ahnert asked.

Louis stiffened slightly. "Yes," he said.

For a moment, Ahnert didn't move. Louis could hear the faint hum of the electrical lines above. He could feel the sun on his neck.

Ahnert took the cigar out of his mouth. "The semen inside her was blood type AB-negative," he said.

"That proves Cade didn't rape her," Louis said.

"You're not going to prove anything on my memory," Ahnert said. "You're going to have to find that report. Why haven't you gone back to Duvall's old defense records?"

Louis shook his head. "I can't get access."

Louis waited for Ahnert to say something, but he just chewed on the cigar, watching Louis through the sunglasses.

"I have reason to believe that Duvall buried the semen report and let an innocent man go to prison," Louis said.

"Duvall was a winner. Why would he do that?"

"I don't know."

"What about two killers? You consider that?"

Was Ahnert talking about Cade and Ronnie acting together? It was sickening, the image of Ronnie raping Kitty and then Cade killing her to shut her up. Was that what Cade meant by blood being thicker than water?

"Cade and Ronnie . . . together?" Louis asked.

Ahnert said nothing, just moved the cigar to the other side of his mouth.

"Sergeant," Louis said, "was that where you were going with this twenty years ago?"

A lone white egret took sudden flight and Ahnert watched it rise and disappear against the bleached sky. "April 9th. That's the day she was killed. I remember it was hot, like summer was coming early." He paused. " 'April is the cruellest month, breeding lilacs out of the dead land, mixing memory and desire, stirring dull roots with spring rain.' "

He looked back at Louis. "It doesn't matter where I was going twenty years ago."

"It mattered. It still does," Louis said. "I think you still want to solve this case. I think you're the only one who does."

"Besides you, you mean."

"Yes."

Ahnert was silent for a long time, looking out over the desolate landscape.

"It's over for me," he said. "She's yours now."

Louis was surprised to hear a hint of relief in Ahnert's voice. What the hell had happened to this man twenty years ago? Had he been so obsessed with finding Kitty's killer that it had destroyed his career and the rest of his life?

He suddenly heard Mobley talking to him as he leaned over the bar at O'Sullivan's.

He stole an item that belonged to the victim. A gold necklace. Some kind of heart-shaped locket. Guess Ahnert needed the money.

Ahnert hadn't needed the money a cheap gold necklace would have brought, and he wasn't obsessed with finding Kitty's killer. It was *her* he was obsessed with.

"Why did you stop investigating?" Louis asked.

"I was told to."

Louis shook his head. "I don't believe that."

Ahnert finally looked back at Louis. "I was hung up on a dead girl." He looked away. "It's sick, isn't it?"

Louis ran a hand over the back of his neck. It wasn't the sun that was making him sweat.

"I'm just trying to give her justice," Louis said quietly.

Ahnert didn't answer. He tossed the cigar into the sand and squashed it out with his boot. Then he picked a bit of wet tobacco off his lips and flicked it away.

"Forget justice," he said. "Give her some peace."

Chapter
Twenty-Nine

It was on the drive back to Fort Myers that Louis remembered something Ronnie Cade had said the very first time he had gone out to J.C. Landscaping. Ronnie had mentioned that his father had bailed him out of jail when he was a teenager. That meant Ronnie probably had a record. And there was a slim chance that the record could lead to a blood type on file somewhere. But he needed Mobley's help to get it.

The reception area outside Mobley's office was empty when Louis got there. He looked at the wall clock. Past five. Mobley's door was shut, the lights off. He was about to leave when the Amazon came in, carrying a freshly washed coffeepot.

She smiled at him. "What are you doing back here?"

"I needed to see the sheriff."

"Too late. He cut out early today. He won't be back 'til Monday."

"Damn," Louis said under his breath.

"Can I help?" she asked.

Louis almost told her no, but nodded. "Yeah, maybe you can. Can you check to see if someone has a record?"

"Sure. What's his name?"

"Ronnie Cade."

She gave him a look, but went to the computer terminal at the back of the room. Leaning over the chair, she brought the monitor to life and looked back at Louis.

"Got a social or a birthday?"

"Sorry."

She typed in the name, then looked back at him. "I got two. Ronald John or Ronald Walter?"

"Hell, I don't know. Do you have birth dates or anything elsc there?"

"I got one in nineteen-forty-nine and one in nineteen-thirty-two."

"It's got to be forty-nine."

She pecked at the keys, then the printer in the corner started pumping out a piece of paper. She ripped it off and brought it to Louis.

Ronnie Cade had one charge: a DUI from 1976, the result of an accident with injuries. Finally, a break. Any accident victim who had been treated at a hospital was always tested for alcohol. And they were routinely blood-typed.

"Excuse me," Louis said.

The Amazon had been putting away the coffee filters and she looked back at Louis over her shoulder.

"Is there any way you can check to see if the hospital records for this accident are in his file?" Louis asked.

For the first time, she gave him something other than a smile. "Hey, I've clocked out. I gotta go pick up my kid at the baby-sitter."

"I wouldn't ask—"

"But you *really* need this . . . yeah, yeah, yeah."

She heaved a big sigh. "We don't usually have hospital records."

"Sometimes they're put in the files. Can you check?"

She took the computer printout back. Louis paced while she made the call. He was looking up at Dinkle's portrait when she called his name.

"This must be your lucky day. We've got them," she said.

Louis came toward her quickly. "I just need to know his blood type."

She spoke into the phone and looked back. "O-positive."

Louis let out a sigh. He was relieved for the sake of Ronnie and Eric.

The Amazon had hung up the phone and was now stuffing things into her big purse.

"Can you tell me how I can reach the sheriff?" Louis asked.

"No way. He would kill me."

"I doubt that. Come on, it's important."

She hesitated, then shrugged. "Okay, but don't tell him I told you. He's a partner in a supper club down in Naples—La Veranda. He'll be there tonight and tomorrow night. I've been there. Fancy place. Men gotta wear ties to get in." She smiled. "I can drive you down, if you want, after I pick up my kid."

Louis smiled. "Maybe some other time."

Outside, he paused on the sidewalk. He knew he needed to call Susan. The fact that neither Cade nor Ronnie had raped Kitty could still be important to her defense. If he could tie Kitty and Duvall's deaths together. And if she would listen.

But there was something else, and it bothered him when he recognized it. He just plain wanted to talk to her.

He turned and walked a block to a café, ducking inside to a pay phone in the back. He dialed her office number and it rang ten times before she picked it up, breathless.

"Susan, don't hang up," he said.

She hesitated. "I wasn't going to."

"I want you to listen to me without saying a word."

There was another pause. "Okay."

Louis took her through his day, laying everything out for her, from the unreadable slide to Bob Ahnert's revelation about the AB-negative sample. He finished up with the fact that neither Jack nor Ronnie Cade raped Kitty.

She said nothing.

"Well?" he asked.

"I'm a little stunned," she said softly. "I'm trying to figure out what I can use." There was a pause. "Can you bring me this report that says Kitty's rapist was AB-negative?"

"Not exactly."

"Can I subpoena it from someone?"

"No."

A long pause this time. "Where *is* this report?"

"It's in Jack Cade's trial file from 1967, which was on Spencer's desk when he was shot. The cops picked it up along with everything else."

There was another pause. Louis could hear papers rustling. He was about to tell her that he was going to see Mobley when she interrupted.

"It's not here," she said.

"What?"

"I have the evidence sheet from Duvall's office right here in front of me. There's no mention of Jack Cade's trial file. It's not here."

"It has to be. You're sure?"

"I'm looking at the list, Louis. They took other files, but nothing about Jack Cade."

Louis shifted the receiver to his other ear. "Then where the fuck is it?"

"How the hell should—"

"Wait," Louis said quickly. "Ellie told me that she gave Duvall the file. It was there. So whoever killed Duvall must have taken it."

They were both silent for a moment.

"Susan, I have to go see Mobley," Louis said. "Come with me."

"Why?"

"I need to convince him to reopen Kitty's homicide."

"You don't need me for that."

"Yes I do. I need him to see you're with me on this."

Susan was quiet for a moment. "If I decide to use this in a new defense, I don't want to tip my hand. Mobley is a cop, Louis, with a cop brain. I can't trust him."

"Susan, listen to me. You're going to have a hard time making this believable. You need Mobley to reopen Kitty's homicide for credibility. You need the cops on your side this time."

Susan was quiet.

"Trust him, Susan," Louis said. "And me."

He heard her sigh. "Okay. Give me an hour. Pick me up at home."

Chapter
Thirty

Susan jerked open the door and stared at Louis.

"Damn," she said.

"What?" Louis said.

She waved a hand at his blue blazer and tie. "Why didn't you tell me this was dressy?"

Louis's eyes traveled down to Susan's blue jeans and back up to her face. "I'm sorry," he said. "We're meeting Mobley at a restaurant down in Naples."

Susan let out an impatient snort. "Give me ten minutes," she said over her shoulder as she disappeared down the hall.

Louis came into the living room. Benjamin was tossing foil icicles on a Christmas tree, helped by a teenaged girl Louis assumed was the dreaded April.

"Hey, Benjamin," Louis said.

"Hey." He eyed Louis's striped tie. "Ricco Tubbs wouldn't be caught dead in that tie."

"Well, when I get my Masarati, I'll upgrade."

"You taking my mom on a date?"

"Nope. Just work."

Benjamin went back to throwing wads of icicles. Louis stood there watching him until a flash of red made him turn.

Susan was there, dressed in clingy red silk, leaning against the wall as she struggled to put on her high heels.

Oh man . . .

He tried not to stare as she came forward. She was cramming stuff in a small black purse and it was a moment before she looked up at Louis.

"What?" she asked, frowning.

"Nothing . . . nothing," he said.

"Well, let's go," she said, heading out the door.

Louis glanced back at Benjamin.

"Sure looks like a date to me," Benjamin muttered.

La Veranda was a candle-lit womb of a place on the water. Someone was playing "Fly Me To the Moon" on the piano as Louis followed Susan and the maitre d' to a table near the window. It wasn't until he heard the singer's voice that Louis turned to look at the man seated at the piano.

Fuck a duck. It was Mobley.

Louis looked over at Susan. She was staring at Mobley too.

"I can't believe it," Susan said.

"I know," Louis said.

"No, I mean, I can't believe he's good."

Suddenly, Mobley spotted them. He didn't miss a beat as he finished and then leaned into the mike.

"Okay, here's a special song for two special friends of mine," he said. He launched into "Hello Young Lovers Wherever You Are."

Louis was watching Mobley, trying not to let his

gaze drift over to Susan. On the ride down from Fort
Myers, they had talked only about the two cases, bouncing things off each other in a mad tango of ideas. They
had made a commitment to back each other up in front
of Mobley. For the first time, they were on the same
track.

But now, the heat of the work talk had tapered off,
and they were left with only the votive candle flickering
between them.

Louis looked over at Susan. How had she managed
to do her hair up like that so quickly?

She felt his eyes on her and looked at him.

"You look really pretty," he said.

She blinked several times, like she hadn't heard him.
"Thank you," she said softly.

Mobley finished singing. He announced he was taking a short break, rose and came to their table.

"Well, if it isn't the Lone Ranger and Tonto," he
said. "What are you two doing here?"

"We're here just for you, Lance," Louis said.

"How'd you find out I was here?"

Louis pulled out a chair. "Hard to keep a talent like
yours secret for long," he said.

Mobley looked at Susan, who was grinning. Finally,
he sat down and a waiter immediately appeared with
a scotch and water. Mobley glanced at the table, and
seeing their empty glasses, motioned toward the waiter
to fill them up. When he was gone, Mobley took a
drink, then sat back.

"Didn't know you moonlighted," Susan said.

"It pays for all the piano lessons my mom made me
take," Mobley said. He looked at Louis. "I thought
it was us against the lawyers, Kincaid," he said.

Louis could feel Susan's eyes on him. "I had to tell
Susan. She's Cade's lawyer."

Mobley took a drink of his scotch. "Forget it. Just

tell me what you found out. Did the second sample match or not?''

"It didn't match. It was AB-negative."

"Any chance Ronnie Cade did it?"

"Nope. I checked his blood type. He's O-positive, just like his father."

"Son of a fucking bitch," Mobley whispered. "I guess I will have to go pull Cade's old defense file out of my evidence room."

"You don't have it," Louis said.

"What?"

"You never had it. Whoever killed Duvall took it."

Mobley leaned back in the chair. In the flicker of the candle, Louis could see something pass over Mobley's eyes, like the sheriff was watching his whole career go down the toilet. Mobley reached up and, with a hard tug, undid his black bow tie.

"Lance," Louis said quietly. "We can't put this back in the box. You've got to reopen Kitty's homicide."

Mobley looked at Susan. "I hate lawyers," he said. "I fucking hate lawyers."

Susan glanced at Louis but said nothing.

Mobley got slowly to his feet. "I've got to do my second set. Order whatever you want, dinner's on me."

He drained his scotch and set the glass down hard. "Goddamn, I liked being sheriff," he muttered, walking away.

Susan looked at Louis. "Is he going to reopen?"

"Yeah," Louis said, watching Mobley resume his place at the piano. "I think he will."

Louis looked down at his drink, thinking about Jack and Ronnie Cade and what they would do when he told them they would be cleared. This whole thing had kicked up so much mistrust between them, so much bad blood. Twenty years was a long time to wait for the truth, and it might be coming too late to repair the damage that had been done between them. Damage that he himself had helped cause by his accusations.

He looked at Susan. She was stirring her drink, her dark eyes intense with thought.

"Susan, what are Cade's options now?" he asked.

"It's going to depend on the investigation, but assuming it favors Cade, a motion for a new trial would be first, I suppose," she said. "But it's always a tough road."

"You can do it."

Susan looked at him, then played with the swizzle stick in her drink. "Not me, Louis. I never had a case like this one. I'd be in over my head."

Louis let a moment pass, looking at her in the soft light of the candle. He knew how hard it was for her to admit that. She had fought hard to get the Cade case in the first place, and once the news broke that Kitty Jagger's case was being reopened, there was a good chance her bosses would take it out of her hands. Innocent man does twenty years for a murder he didn't commit? The press would be all over it. And Susan would be cut out.

Louis glanced back at Mobley. He was playing "Yesterday."

"Who would've thought," Susan said softly.

"Thought what?"

"That for twenty years, this whole town looked at Jack Cade like a piece of garbage. And he's probably innocent." She shook her head. "I'll go see Cade the first thing in the morning and give him the news."

Louis thought about how Cade looked last night, standing in the dark, Issy in his arms, making threats. He thought of the knife Cade had thrown at his feet.

"Do you mind if I tell him?" he asked.

She frowned slightly. "Why?"

He took a drink. "We have some unfinished business," he said.

Chapter
Thirty-One

Louis swung the Mustang into the gravel drive of
J.C. Landscaping and stopped. He could see Ronnie
and Eric loading plants on the truck. Black clouds were
rolling in overhead and he could hear the distant rumble
of thunder.

Louis turned off the engine, picking up Cade's knife
from the passenger seat. He got out and started toward
the truck.

Ronnie saw him coming and nudged Eric. Both of
them stopped working, waiting for Louis to get closer.

"You've got no business here," Ronnie said coldly.

"I need to see your father."

Ronnie's eyes dropped to the knife in Louis's hand.
"Why? He fired you."

Louis hesitated, knowing he needed something to
say to Ronnie.

"Look, Ronnie, I owe you an apology. I know you

didn't kill Kitty and I shouldn't have accused you without cause. Especially in front of your son."

Ronnie glanced at Eric, and his face softened. He ran an arm across his forehead and pulled off his work gloves.

"Okay. I appreciate that."

"And I think we can prove your father didn't kill her either."

Ronnie's eyes widened, then he broke into a slow smile. "That's great," he said. "I mean, that's really great. Did you hear that, Eric?"

Eric's sour expression didn't change.

"Where's your father?" Louis asked.

Ronnie motioned toward the trailer. "He's over there, on the porch. He's sick."

"He's hung over," Eric muttered.

Louis headed across the yard toward the front of the trailer. He could see Cade sitting in a plastic chair, his feet propped up on the wooden spool table. Cade took a drink, and set the beer can on his knee, watching Louis approach.

Louis came up to him and stopped. He brought Cade's knife from his side and stuck it hard into the top of the wooden spool. Cade glanced at it.

"What do you want? I fired you."

"We need to talk," Louis said.

Cade's eyes flicked beyond Louis. Louis turned to see Ronnie and Eric coming up behind him.

"Dad, did he tell you?" Ronnie asked.

"Tell me what?"

"Louis says he can prove neither of us killed Kitty."

Cade didn't move.

"Dad?"

Cade slowly pulled his legs off the table and set the beer down next to the knife.

"So now you believe I was set up. Took you long enough."

Louis started to say something but stopped. First, he just didn't like agreeing with anything Cade said, but there was something else too, pulling at him.

"I'm waiting, Louie. You believe now that somebody stole my tool and threw those panties in my truck?"

Louis ignored him, trying to focus in on what it was that was bothering him. He could accept that the real killer had found Cade's tool and used it on Kitty. But how could the killer have known the semen on the panties would match Cade's blood type? He would have had to have been damn sure—or damn lucky—to set Cade up.

Cade was talking about money now, but Louis wasn't listening. He was seeing Joyce Novick, and hearing how she described Jack Cade.

He looked at me and . . . he touched himself.

"So, Louie. Who can I sue?"

Louis looked back at Cade. He was standing there, scratching his stomach.

"We can sue? I thought you told me we couldn't," Ronnie said. "How much can we get?"

"Millions," Cade said, looking at Louis. "Right?"

"Forget that for now," Louis said. "I need to talk to you, Cade. Alone. Let's take a walk."

Cade followed Louis toward the front gate. When they had gone about halfway, Louis stopped and turned. He was facing the sun and he moved so that he could see Cade's face clearly.

"So," Cade said, "what do we have to talk about?"

"The panties in your truck."

"What about them?"

"How did the semen get on them?"

Cade shrugged. "Well, that's obvious, ain't it? That girl's killer left it, you know, as part of the setup."

Louis shook his head. "The killer would've had to

know that those stains would match your blood type. How did he know that, *Jack?*''

Cade scratched his chest, then looked off across the yard. ''You already know the answer, don't you?'' he said.

''I want to hear you say it.''

Cade hesitated. ''I found the panties on the floor of the truck in the morning when I was leaving for work. I knew Ronnie had taken the truck out the night before. I figured he just got lucky.''

Louis shook his head. ''You said he was a loser around girls, a virgin. Try again, Cade.''

Cade shrugged. ''Okay, so he was a horny kid who couldn't get laid. He found the panties and jacked off in them. He didn't do nothing wrong.''

Louis stared at Cade. ''You lying sonofabitch. You found those panties that morning and *you* jacked off in them.''

For a moment, they just stared at each other. Then Cade wiped his mouth with his arm. ''You're going to believe what you want about me,'' he said. ''Just like everyone else.''

Louis turned away, walking toward his car. Thunder rolled overhead as shadows from the clouds moved across the ground.

''Hey, Louie,'' Cade called. ''Who's going to handle this lawsuit thing for me? That bitch lawyer?''

Louis didn't turn. He was finished here. ''She can't. Find someone else.''

''I don't know any fucking lawyers,'' Cade hollered, hurrying after him. He grabbed Louis's arm, spinning him around. ''You need to find me someone.''

Louis jerked his arm free. ''I don't need to do *anything* for you.''

Cade glared at him, then turned, heading back to his trailer. Louis started to get in the Mustang, but paused. He could see Ronnie and Eric over Cade's shoulder as they tried to load a large potted plant onto the truck. It tipped, scattering dirt at their feet.

Louis shook his head slowly. Damn, he wasn't finished. He did need to do something.

''Cade!'' Louis called out.

Cade turned and waited.

''I'll find a lawyer,'' Louis said. ''But for Ronnie and Eric, not you.''

Cade gave him a wave of his hand and kept walking.

Chapter
Thirty-Two

The Guilty Party was packed with lawyers, a smokey blur of white shirts and loosened ties. Louis spotted Scott Brenner in the back, a pool cue in his hand.

As Louis wove his way through the crowd, Scott saw him and waved him closer. Scott extended a hand, which Louis took.

"Give me a minute here, would you, Louis? I'm about to kick some very expensive ass."

Louis watched as Scott sank the last of the striped balls, then snapped the eight ball into the side pocket. His opponent, a small man with thin brown hair handed Scott some bills and moved to the bar.

Scott turned toward Louis. "You want to play?"

"No thanks. Like I said when I called, I need to talk to you about Jack Cade."

"We can talk and play. Just for fun. Let me get you a drink first. Name your poison."

"Brandy and water."

Scott handed Louis the billiard rack. "Rack 'em while I'm gone, would you?"

Louis racked the balls and picked up a cue stick, trying to remember the last time he held one. Had to be years. He was chalking it when Scott came back. He set both drinks on the table.

"I like to break," Scott said. "Do you mind?"

Louis motioned toward the table. "Be my guest."

Scott broke, sinking the six. He circled the table, looking for another. He paused behind the two ball, eyeing the angles. Louis noticed there was an easier shot with the ten.

Scott gave Louis a grin then took aim at the two. It rolled toward the pocket and stopped short. Scott shook his head, his grin never fading.

"You had a sure thing with the ten," Louis said.

Scott picked up the chalk. "The victory is sweeter when the odds are greater. Your turn."

Louis took a shot and missed. Scott started circling again, deciding finally on the fourteen ball. He bent over the table, his arms extended, his stick poised behind the cue ball.

"So, what about Jack Cade?" Scott asked.

"I thought you might be able to do something for his family."

Scott's eyes flicked up to Louis, then back to the table.

"And that is?"

"Make a motion for a new trial."

With a crack, Scott sent both the fourteen and the twelve balls zipping across the table. Both hit their pockets.

Scott came over to Louis, resting the butt of his stick on the floor. "I like a challenge, but I like winning even more. Give me a reason to believe I could."

"He didn't rape Kitty Jagger and we can prove it."

A flick of interest lit up Scott's eyes and his lips

tipped up in a slow smile. He set his cue back in the rack. He picked up his drink and started toward the rear of the bar, nodding for Louis to follow.

Scott slid into a wooden booth, moving aside a small unlit candle. He leaned back, his fingers around his glass, the smile still on his face. Louis slid in across from him.

"You have my attention," Scott said.

Louis quietly gave Scott the whole story, starting with the AB-negative blood in the report and ending with the theory that whoever killed Kitty shot Spencer Duvall and took the 1967 Redweld in an attempt to protect himself.

Scott reached for his drink, saw that it was empty and set it back down. He sat back, his gaze drifting to some far place of the bar.

"What do you think?" Louis asked.

Scott's fingers were tapping lightly on the empty glass. "We called him Creepy Cade back then. Everyone did. We all thought he did it." He paused. "God, twenty years of his life down the drain."

"Will you consider taking this on?"

"I'm not a criminal attorney, but I can make a motion for a new trial. If it gets that far, I can either pass it off or take on a second chair."

"The Cades don't have any money."

Scott waved his hand. "I wouldn't expect any for this. Jesus Christ, Louis, there comes a time when you just have to do something human. This poor man wasted twenty years."

"But there is something you want, right?" Louis asked.

Scott leaned forward, the alcohol shimmering in his eyes. "You know what I want, Louis? I want a shot at lawyers like Spencer Duvall, who treat the legal system like their own personal toilets. And prosecutors who would walk over their mothers' bodies if they thought they could convict. And the fucking state of Florida that doesn't give a damn how many innocent men they fry.''

Louis had a feeling it was the potential publicity and not any real sense of altruism that was getting Scott Brenner fired up. But he didn't care. He knew that Scott Brenner, with his connections and experience, could help Ronnie and Eric.

"Besides," Scott said, "if we pull this off, I want the civil suit." He was trying to catch the waitress's eye. "Lot of potential for big money."

"What about the chances for a new trial?"

"Before we go any further, can I ask you a question?" Scott said.

"Sure."

"You want to be in on this?"

Louis took a drink. "Yeah, I do."

"Okay, this is how it is. The whole key is *new* evidence," he said. "The vaginal semen sample you mentioned isn't new."

"But it was never submitted in trial."

"The law doesn't care," Scott said. "If Duvall had that report and didn't use it, too bad. Having had a stupid lawyer won't get you a new trial, either. Nor does the probability of innocence. We've got to find something new."

For the first time since he had started talking to Scott, Louis felt a twinge of discouragement. "There isn't anything, Scott," he said. "Believe me, I've been over all the files, all the records. There isn't anything we can dig up."

Scott took a long, slow drink of his vodka. He leaned back in the booth and leveled his brown eyes at Louis.

"Oh yes, there is," he said. "Kitty Jagger."

Chapter
Thirty-Three

The mechanical clamor stopped and the quiet rushed in. The hush stretched over the cemetery and then was broken by the chirp of a bird. Then came the *beep-beep-beep* drone as the backhoe crept away from the hole in the ground.

Louis watched as two men jumped down and secured the straps around the concrete vault. He looked up, his eyes traveling over the knot of people standing in the shade of a tree a few yards away. There were a couple of Lee County uniforms and a guy Louis assumed was the detective Mobley had just assigned to the case, all with the usual stone cop faces. There were also two men in suits. The shorter one, the cemetery administrator, wore the benign expression of a man used to watching the dead unearthed. The other was Scott Brenner. He was standing a few yards away, his eyes locked on the hole, his expression determinedly stoic.

Over by the road, a small group of reporters and

rubberneckers were cordoned off by yellow crime tape. He saw someone standing off by himself away from the crowd, under a tree. It was Bob Ahnert.

The vault was hoisted out and carefully set down. Gray concrete, mottled with mud and mold. The workers took out crowbars.

Louis had never been to an exhumation before. It was all so . . . business-like. He had not expected that. There was something disturbingly commonplace about it, like the dead were routinely taken from their graves, like children rousted from sleep to get up for school.

The smell was terrible. Louis had not expected that either. He looked up, as if for relief. The tree's canopy stretched for about fifty yards. The branches were heavy with flowers that looked like lilacs. It made a beautiful umbrella of lavender over Kitty's grave site.

They lifted the casket out. The dark wood still had a sheen to it, but the brass handles had gone green. He thought of what Joyce had said about Willard. *He spent a fortune on the coffin, mahogany with these beautiful brass handles. But then, he was so upset he didn't even come to see her.*

Louis was staring at the casket. Why wasn't he feeling anything? He should feel something—sorrow, regret, at least a sense of propriety. But he was dry inside.

The thud of a car door made him look up. A green uniform ducked under the yellow tape. Mobley ignored the reporters' questions and came up to Louis's side.

"Thanks for coming, Sheriff," Louis said.

"I had to get out of the office," Mobley said. "They won't leave me alone. Between the damn reporters and Sandusky, I don't have enough ass left to take a shit."

Louis nodded slightly, his eyes going back to Scott Brenner. He was staring at the casket now, his eyes narrowed, his hand clasped over his mouth like he was going to be sick. Suddenly, Scott turned away and walked off.

"Excuse me, Sheriff," Louis said.

Louis went over a small rise and saw Scott standing, head bowed, hands in his pants pocket.

"You okay?" Louis asked, coming to his side.

Scott looked up. "What? Oh yeah . . . yeah." His voice dropped off and he looked away.

Louis followed his gaze down to the large granite headstone in front of them.

BRENNER
Charles 1914–1981   Vivian 1919–1953

"Your parents?" Louis asked.

Scott nodded.

"Your mother was a young woman when she died," Louis said.

"Yeah, I was seven," Scott said quietly. "At least I remember her. Brian doesn't at all."

Louis looked back at the headstone. "But you had your dad."

"It was just the three of us," Scott said. "Dad was away most of the time in Tallahassee and we were raised by the housekeeper. I ended up watching over Brian." Scott looked back down at the headstone. "But my father was there when it counted."

They fell silent. Louis looked at the Brenner headstone. It was only then that he noticed the three small markers set down in the grass.

Geraldine   Infant Baby Girl   Infant Baby Boy
1942–1944   1945 Stillborn   1948 Stillborn

Scott noticed Louis looking at the small markers. "Dad always wanted a big family, but my mother— she had a difficult time with her pregnancies." He paused, looking at the marker. "Dad always called them blue babies," he said. "That's what they called stillborns in those days."

The sound of a car door made Louis look back toward the grave site. They were loading Kitty Jagger's casket into a county van. Louis turned back to Scott.

"Thanks for getting this done so quickly." He extended his hand and Scott shook it.

"No problem," Scott said.

Louis looked over at the crowd behind the tape. Bob Ahnert had disappeared.

"Aren't you going with her?" Scott asked.

Louis turned to Scott. The sympathy in his voice had surprised him.

"Yeah," Louis said quietly. "I guess I better."

The door to the autopsy room opened and Octavius walked out.

"She's on the table, Vince," he said. The diener went back into the office, leaving Vince and Louis standing at the door. Louis was looking at the window, but he couldn't see the table.

"Are you sure you want to do this?" Vince asked.

"Yes."

Vince wasn't wearing his Walkman or earphones. It was the first time Louis had seen him without them. But other things were different today too, like the whole place was muted somehow. No sounds, none of the usual numbing smells. Even the florescent lights seemed dimmer than usual.

"I don't know what we're going to get here, Louis," Vince said. "If there was a lot of water damage or if the—"

"Her father bought her the best casket," Louis interrupted.

Vince just looked at him for a moment, then pushed the door open. Louis followed.

A spot of pink. That was the first thing he saw. He moved closer.

She was wearing a dress. Pink, with a high white collar. White shoes. He hadn't expected her to be dressed. He had expected . . .

It hit him now. He had been expecting decay, putrified flesh and bone, like the corpses he had seen pulled from mangroves, or at least a shattered shell, like the bodies lifted from car wrecks.

Not this . . .

Her skin was waxy and sunken, her long hair limp and bleached to ash from the decades of laying in darkness. But as she lay there, hands folded over her chest, Kitty Jagger looked almost as if she were asleep.

Louis felt a dullness in his chest, but he couldn't look away.

"Man, whoever did this was a hell of an embalmer," Vince said. "They don't usually come out of the ground this well preserved."

But Louis did not hear him. He was staring now at her hands. Small fingers, a silver ring on the right hand. She was holding a pink rose. It was shriveled but still intact, like a cherished prom corsage.

Louis realized he had been holding his breath. He let it out. Bones . . . if it had been just bones, he could have stood that. He had seen bones before, like Eugene Graham, the young black man whose skeleton he had found in a Mississippi swamp with a noose still wrapped around the vertebrae. Eugene had been violated and brutally murdered just like Kitty. But this was different. Kitty was still here. A ghost of herself, but she was still *here*.

He stared at the pink rose. Something so beautiful . . . so damaged. Something so alive . . . so wasted.

He felt his throat tighten. A whisper in his head: *Don't be afraid, just let go.*

Something broke deep in his chest. He was hearing her, just like Ahnert. God, he was hearing a dead girl talk to him.

Oh Jesus, am I going crazy?

"Send me your report when you're done, Vince," Louis said. He turned quickly and left.

Chapter Thirty-Four

When he got back to the cottage, Louis got a beer and went out to sit on the porch. He watched the waves curl in from the gulf, letting his mind drift. Issy rubbed up against his leg and, without thinking, he reached down and scratched the cat's head.

There was an emptiness in his chest, and he couldn't figure out where it was coming from. He took a long, slow drink of the beer.

It was Kitty. She wasn't just his anymore. Now that her case had been reopened, other people would be involved—Vince, Mobley, Scott Brenner and who knew who else. He would still be a part of it. He was officially working for Brenner, Brenner and Brenner now, hired to help find evidence against Spencer Duvall to reopen the Cade case. He had signed a contract this morning and Scott had given him a check for $2,500 as a retainer.

Louis finished off the beer. He needed the money.

And the fact that Scott was going to pick up Jack Cade's civil case made him feel like he had helped Ronnie and Eric put their lives back together. But he still felt an emptiness, like he had left something incomplete.

He rose and went inside. The table still held the mess of papers, photographs and files he had accumulated from Kitty's case. He picked up the blurry black-and-white class picture of Kitty.

Give her some peace, Ahnert had said. But it wasn't up to him anymore.

Setting the beer bottle down, he went to the bedroom and came back with a cardboard box. He began to pack everything up, taking down the photos and note cards he had taped to the walls and kitchen cabinets. He slipped the picture of Kitty in a folder and put it away.

When he got to the old copy of *Gulfshore Life* magazine, he paused. He opened it to the paper-clipped page, the one with the society picture of Spencer and Candace Duvall.

How different Duvall looked to him in light of what he now knew about the man. Duvall's expression no longer looked merely dour; now it looked cold and calculated.

What had happened? Why had he done it? Who was Spencer Duvall? The sand-in-the-shoes crusader revered by Ellie Silvestri—or a status-seeking shyster who bargained away Jack Cade's life?

Louis looked at the society picture again. This time he focused on Candace Duvall. Her expression looked different now too—almost predatory.

There were eight other people in the photograph. There was a man standing next to Duvall, a man whose face looked vaguely familiar. Louis read the names in the caption.

Shit . . . why hadn't he noticed this before? He stared at the man's face, and at the pained expression on

Spencer Duvall's face. He flipped over to the magazine's cover to check the date: December, 1973. Maybe it was just a coincidence that the two of them were in the same picture. But his gut was telling him it wasn't.

There was only one way to find out. He had to talk to Candace again. And Ellie Silvestri. If anyone knew if there was a connection between Spencer and this man, it was the two women in his life.

The maid opened the door and frowned at him.

"Tell Mrs. Duvall I want to see her, please," Louis said before she had a chance to say anything.

The maid shut the door. A few minutes later, it opened and she nodded Louis into the cold, white foyer. "She's out at the pool," the maid said, pointing at the far glass doors.

Louis tucked the magazine under his arm and went out to the patio. Candace was lying in the shade. Hayley was sitting in a chair close by, her feet propped on the end of Candace's chaise. Both women wore bathing suits and had wet hair, like they had just gotten out of the pool. Hayley had a big tan towel wrapped sarong-like around her. They both looked up as he came toward them.

Candace took off her tortoise-frame sunglasses. "Hayley says I should be nice to you."

Louis glanced at the other woman, who gave him a small smile, then went back to flipping through her *Vogue*.

"I'd like to talk to you about your husband," Louis said.

"We've already covered that."

Louis pulled over one of the chairs. Candace looked at him like he was a reptile that had slithered into her yard, then slipped her sunglasses back on.

"I'd like to know about the early years," Louis said.

"What do you mean?"

"You and your husband, what it was like. You met in college?"

Candace glanced at Hayley, then looked out over the glittering water of San Carlos Bay. "At a frat party," she said with a bored sigh.

"I understand you were broke in the beginning."

"Where'd you get that idea?"

"Spencer's secretary, Ellie."

"That old bag," she said flatly. "Yeah, we were broke. I taught elementary school to put Spence through law school. Third grade. I hated every minute of it."

"I take it things got easier after Spencer set up his practice?" Louis asked.

Candace gave a short laugh. "Oh yeah. Ten-thousand dollars in law school loans, start up costs for the practice, rent on that dump of an office downtown. A cozy little duplex overlooking the tracks. Yeah, it was peachy keen."

"Not exactly what you dream about when they're putting the Miss Quincy Cucumber Queen crown on your head, huh?" Hayley chuckled.

Candace shot her a look. Hayley went back to her magazine.

"When did things get better for you?" Louis asked.

Candace was twirling a strand of her hair, looking out over the bay again. "Years," she said quietly.

Louis held out the *Gulfshore Life* magazine. "Did any of these people have anything to do with it getting better for you?"

Candace lowered her sunglasses and looked at the society picture. Then she raised them and looked back out at the water. "They all did. We scratched each other's backs."

Louis glanced at Hayley. She had put down the *Vogue* and her green eyes were fixed on Candace.

"You were the one who scratched, Candy," Hayley said. "Tell him what you did for that man."

"Yeah," Louis said. "Tell me, Candy."

Candace was quiet.

"Tell him," Hayley prodded. "Tell him for the same reason you told me, hon. Deep down, you like this rags-to-riches shit. You're proud of it."

Candace looked at her, then smiled. "Maybe."

"You're proud of your achievement," Hayley said, giving the last word a bite.

"Damn right I am," Candace said. "Spencer never would have gotten anywhere without me."

Louis's eyes went between the two women, trying to understand the dynamic. It was obvious Hayley held some power here, maybe the threat of outing Candace to her society friends. Status—that was Candace's button and Hayley knew it.

Suddenly, he understood that morose look on Duvall's face in the society picture.

"You pushed him," Louis said.

Candace shrugged. "Someone had to. Spence would have been happy wearing his Sears suits, defending those wetbacks in Immokalee for the rest of his life."

Louis leaned forward on his elbows, letting his eyes drop to the patio stones. He pulled in a slow breath before he went on.

"Well, they say behind every successful man there's a good woman," he said.

Candace sat forward. "You got that right. I picked out his clothes, showed him what to eat and what to drink. He wouldn't leave that dump office downtown, so I made him remodel it." She waved a hand at the big white house. "I picked out every faucet and piece of tile in this house. Do you think he cared?"

She slumped back in the chaise. "That man was socially backward. I dragged him to parties, taught him how to schmooze. About the only thing I didn't do was manicure his damn toenails.''

Hayley laughed.

Louis drew in another slow breath. ''So you got him into the right circles.''

''Yes. It wasn't easy.''

Louis hesitated. He wasn't sure where to go with this now. ''What about his work, his clients?'' he asked. ''Did he talk to you about it?''

''He did in the beginning,'' Candace said. ''That's why I knew I had to step in and get him on a better track. I told him he had to upgrade his clients, I told him to hire Lyle. Once the money started coming in, I didn't really care. I had done my work, so I retired.''

She started twirling her hair again. ''The law bores me to tears,'' she said. ''Spence bored me to tears.''

Louis was quiet for a moment. There was one last question and Candace was probably the only one now who might tell him the answer.

''I know your husband was gay,'' Louis said. ''Was Brian Brenner his lover?''

Candace looked at him, then laughed. ''Brian? God no. Brian may not be a charmer like his brother, but he is definitely not gay.''

''Do you know who your husband was seeing?'' Louis asked.

Candace shook her head slowly. ''No one. I mean, there were guys in the beginning, but Spence just kind of . . . lost interest. He was depressed and I told him to get help. When he went on the Trazodone, it killed what was left of his sex drive.''

Candace gave a soft sigh. ''Spence wasn't a bad man. I mean, I liked him and we kind of took care of each other in the beginning. That was part of the deal. But then, it was like Spence just kind of . . . I don't know, dried up.''

She was looking at Hayley and Louis followed her gaze.

"Like I told you," Hayley said, "Spence was kind of sad."

Candace wasn't smiling. But Hayley had an amused smile tipping the corners of her lips. With her green eyes and sleek dark hair, she looked like a cat sitting there, a smug, pampered pet sitting by her mistress's feet.

Louis rose. He had had enough.

"I'll find my own way out," he said.

Chapter
Thirty-Five

Louis took a sip of his coffee and scanned the pedestrians. He was sitting in a café a block away from the courthouse, waiting for Ellie Silvestri.

He had not wanted to see her in Bernhardt's office. He was hoping that, here, away from her memories of Spencer Duvall, she would talk about him openly. She hadn't asked what he wanted to talk about, but he had the feeling she knew and even wanted to talk.

Ellie was coming toward him, a blur of blue and white weaving through the lawyers and shoppers. He stood, pulling out a chair. Ellie sat down, setting her purse on her lap.

"It was nice of you to come, Miss Silvestri," Louis said.

"You had me intrigued, Mr. Kincaid," she said. "With all the stuff in the paper about the Kitty Jagger case, I don't know what to think anymore."

Louis waved to the waiter. Ellie ordered an iced tea.

"Why did you want to see me?"

"My role in Spencer's murder has changed since we last talked, Miss Silvestri. I'm not working on Spencer's homicide anymore. I'm working for Scott Brenner."

Ellie drew in a deep, slow breath. "Scott Brenner ... he's the one trying to get a new trial for Jack Cade." She paused, the creases in her face deepening. "I've heard things. They think Spencer did something wrong, don't they?"

He knew this was coming, but it was still hard to meet her eyes. "Yes," he said. "That's why I'm here. I was hoping you could help me figure out why."

The waiter brought Ellie's iced tea and she took a sip. She still looked distressed. When Louis drew out his notebook, she looked down at it, then back up at him.

"What do you want to know?" she asked softly.

"Tell me what was going on during Cade's trial. How was Spencer doing during that time?"

Ellie sat back, her hands clasped over her purse. "Spencer was working really hard. We couldn't afford investigators, so he was doing the legwork himself. There was a point early on, that he seemed optimistic, but that didn't last. It seemed that the longer the trial went on, the more depressed Spencer got. I think he felt he couldn't help Jack Cade and he took it really hard."

"Candace told me Spencer was taking antidepressants. Did you know that?"

"Not at first. I thought he was just sick ... you know, from working too hard. He was almost living at the office and he began to look ill. I remember one night, I begged him to get a checkup."

Ellie seemed to draw away, and her eyes became teary. "A few days later, he came out of his office in the middle of the day and told me he was going to see a doctor. I was so relieved.''

"Did he tell you this doctor's name?''

"I'm not sure . . . Dr. Mufisso, I think it was. Yes, that was it. I remember he came out of his office and he looked really pale. He said, 'Cancel everything, Ellie, I'm going to see Dr. Mufisso.' ''

Louis wrote the name down, knowing he would have to follow up on it later, although he doubted the doctor would break confidentiality.

"I guess he was a psychiatrist,'' Ellie said. "I found the antidepressants in his bathroom.''

"Did Spencer get better after that?''

Ellie nodded. "A little. The trial ended with the plea bargain and Spence was more himself. Lyle joined us shortly after that and we got really busy, especially with the Kermit case. That lasted for months.''

Louis was about to ask her more about Spencer's state of mind, but Ellie was off in memories again. "George Kermit,'' she said. "He was the president of Florida State who was charged with misappropriation of alumni funds. He ended up losing his position, but Spencer kept him out of jail. It was a big deal.''

Louis looked up from his notebook. "Florida State, that's in Tallahassee, right?''

She nodded.

Louis pulled out the copy of *Gulfshore Life* magazine and opened it to the society photo of the Duvalls. He pointed to the face next to Duvall.

"Why, that's Senator Brenner,'' she said. "My, he looks young there.''

Louis already suspected the answer to his next question, but he needed to be sure. "Did the Senator refer Kermit to Spencer?''

Ellie hesitated. "Yes, I remember the Senator did call. And after we won, he sent me flowers and Spencer a box of cigars. I had forgotten about that.''

Louis had a feeling the rewards went way past cigars. The Cade and Kermit cases probably weren't enough to make a career, but together they would have been a helluva launch.

"Did the Senator send other business Spencer's way?" Louis asked.

Ellie nodded slowly, like she was beginning to understand. "And sometimes favors."

"So Spencer and Senator Brenner were friends?"

She shook her head vigorously. "Oh, heaven's no. I mean, they saw each other at all the things Candace dragged him to. But truth be told, Spencer disliked the Senator. He disliked the whole family."

"Why?"

"I don't know. They just weren't his type."

Louis set down his coffee mug. "Tell me about the Brenners. Tell me their history."

Ellie hesitated. Louis knew she was wondering where he was going with this, but he had to hope she would just trust him. Or maybe trust Spencer.

"Well, let's see. The Brenners have been in Fort Myers for generations. Charles was a big attorney here in town for many years, then went on to become a state senator. That was just after his wife, Vivian, died."

"What did she die of?" Louis asked.

"I'm not sure, but the girls in my garden club back then always said it was pure exhaustion." She leaned close and lowered her voice. "We used to say it was her husband's fault, making her have all those babies just so he could have a bunch of sons. He was always going around town talking about how his sons were going to run his firm someday."

Louis was about to interrupt when she went on.

"After Brian was born, we said maybe the poor woman would finally get some rest," she said. "You know, because the senator finally had his heir and a spare." She paused, shaking her head. "But Vivian had another miscarriage and died. Brian was only a baby."

Louis remembered the Brenner family plot and the infant tombstones. "Scott told me the babies were called blue babies or something," he said.

Ellie ran her paper napkin along her glass, rubbing away the condensation. "Blue babies . . . I haven't heard that term in years. Of course, they weren't really blue. That's just what they called stillborns in the old days."

She was off on a tangent again, and Louis was just about to pull her back when she said something that made him listen.

"It was because of the Rh-negative thing," Ellie said.

"Rh-negative?" Louis said.

Ellie nodded. "My sister was Rh-negative, so that's why I know about it. Well, poor Vivian, she just kept on having miscarriages and stillborn babies. Back then, doctors couldn't do much about it."

Louis didn't know what he was hearing, but he knew there was something important in Ellie's meanderings.

"My sister Cecile lost two and she wanted to stop," Ellie said sadly. "But then she got lucky and the next one was negative. That's my nephew Alan. He's a dentist in Houston."

Louis was trying to make a connection in his mind. "Only the negative babies survive?" he asked.

She looked at him, like she was coming back to the present. "It depends on the mother. If the mother is Rh-negative, like my sister Cecile . . ."

"Or Vivian Brenner?" Louis interrupted.

She nodded. "Yes, if the mother is negative and her baby is positive, her body responds to the growing baby like . . . well, something foreign and attacks it."

She paused again. "How sad it was for poor Vivian . . . thinking her own body was killing all those babies and she couldn't stop it."

Louis sat back. He was thinking again of all those little markers in the Brenner plot.

"So that means that *any* baby that survived had to have Rh-negative blood?" Louis said.

Ellie paused. "Not exactly."

Louis sighed in frustration. "Ellie, this might be important. Explain this to me slowly."

Ellie looked at him oddly. "Well, if the mother is negative, the babies have to be negative, too, to survive. Except the first baby. That one can be positive and live."

"Why does only the *first* positive baby survive?"

"It has something to do with the first pregnancy triggering the antibodies to attack any other positive babies."

Louis set down his pen, his mind working.

"Ellie," he said, "is Scott Brenner the oldest?"

She stopped to think. "There was Scott, a couple of stillborns, and then Brian came along."

Louis sat back, looking out across the street, the granite buildings and gray sky seemed to blend together in a milky pool. Things were coming together, connections being made. A negative-blood baby. A teenage boy with no parents to watch him. A powerful client seeking out a backwater lawyer. A weak man with an ambitious wife.

He looked back at Ellie. She seemed to sense that he had been inside himself and she was waiting patiently for him to say something.

"Ellie," Louis said, "the doctor Spencer went to see, the one you thought was a psychiatrist?"

She nodded.

"Could his name have been Mephisto?"

She looked surprised. "Yes, come to think of it, I believe it was. Why, do you know him?"

Louis closed his notebook. "No. But I know someone who did."

Chapter
Thirty-Six

On the elevator up to the Brenner offices, Louis tried to put the pieces together in his head. All he had were some suspicions, a connection between Duvall and Senator Brenner and a gut feeling that Brian Brenner had something to hide. Maybe he just wanted to see Brian's face when he said Kitty's name.

The elevator doors opened and Louis stepped into the reception area. The receptionist recognized him and told him Scott was due back soon. When Louis told her he wanted to see Brian, she waved him past with a smile.

Brian's door was open. He knocked but didn't wait for an invitation to come in.

"You got a minute?"

Brian looked up. He was sitting behind a mountain of files at his desk. He looked paler than normal, his big bland face blending in with the stacks of manila folders on the desk. There were dark circles under his eyes.

"Scott isn't here," Brian said.

"I can wait," Louis said.

Louis came further into the office. He could feel Brian's eyes on him as he moved to the window.

"Ah, maybe you'd be more comfortable out in the reception area," Brian said.

Louis ignored him, pretending to look down on the street and river below.

"Nice view," Louis said.

Brian didn't answer.

"You know, I'm getting to like Fort Myers," Louis said, perching on the edge of the sill. "It's a nice town, big but not too big. A place where everybody knows everybody else."

His eyes went up to the diploma on the wall behind Brian. He did the math and figured out that Brian had been sixteen or seventeen when Kitty was killed.

"You grew up here, right Brian? Went to high school here?"

Brian looked like a cornered cat.

"Oh, yeah," Louis said. "That's right. Your family has that big old crumbling house over on Shaddlelee Lane. Have you unloaded it yet?"

Brian reached for a tissue and wiped his nose. "No, we just got it appraised."

Louis smiled slightly. "I like old houses."

"You already told me that," Brian said flatly.

"Yeah, but your family's place, it has . . . charm. Why did you decide to sell it now, after all these years, Brian?"

"It was time."

Louis shook his head slowly. "Too bad you've got to let it go. How does your brother feel about selling it?"

"He thinks it's worth saving," Brian said tightly. "But Scott likes all lost causes."

"Yeah, me, too," Louis said.

Louis went toward Brian's desk, Brian watching him closely. Louis pulled a chair close and sat down. Brian looked uncomfortable, like he wanted to tell Louis to leave but didn't know how. He plucked another tissue from a walnut box on his desk and blew his nose.

"I'm not interrupting anything important, am I?" Louis asked.

Brian threw the tissue hard into the trash can near his feet. "What do you *want?*" he asked.

"I just came by to run a few things by Scott about Kitty Jagger." Louis paused a beat. "You remember Kitty don't you?"

"Of course."

"Maybe I could run them by you."

"I'm not part of that case," Brian said, moving papers. "That's Scott's project. I don't know anything about it."

"Do you think he did the right thing?" Louis asked.

Brian looked at him questioningly. "What do you mean?"

"Exhuming the body."

"I don't know," Brian said flatly.

Louis leaned back in the chair, crossing his ankle over his knee. A part of him didn't really want to talk about this, but he was getting angry, sitting across from Brian and thinking about what he might have done.

"I saw Kitty the other day," Louis said.

Brian just stared at him.

"She looked good," Louis said. "All dressed in pink. Had a rose in her hand. For a minute, I thought maybe I could just walk over to her, wake her up and ask her who murdered her."

Louis paused. Brian looked like had stopped breathing.

"I wonder what she would say," Louis added.

Brian reached across the desk, grabbing another Kleenex. Louis watched him snort into it, then toss it away. Louis stared at the tissue, sitting on top of crumpled paper.

"Something's in bloom again, huh Brian?" he said.

"I don't know. Look, I have work to do. I think you should go."

Louis rose. He glanced at a closed door. "Can I use your john first?"

Brian started to protest, but finally just waved his hand.

Louis went into the adjoining bathroom, closing the door. He turned on the light and picked up the brass trash can. It was partially filled with used tissues. He glanced around. Paper cups. He picked out what looked like a thickly stained tissue, and slipped it in a cup. Folding the cup flat, he put it in his pants pocket. Then he flushed the toilet and went back out to Brian's office.

Brian was standing by his office door. "You need to leave now."

Louis threw up a hand. "Hey, I understand. You're a busy man, Brian. I'll catch Scott tomorrow."

Louis walked out and Brian shut the door behind him.

When Louis reached the reception area, Scott Brenner was just coming in, carrying his briefcase. Scott smiled broadly when he saw Louis.

"Louis! Perfect timing. Come on in, I have some great news."

Louis hesitated, but Scott had already gone into his own office, leaving the door open. Louis followed and stood at the door.

"God, what a day," Scott said, tossing the briefcase on his desk. "Sandusky tried to get a prohibitory injunction to stop the sheriff's office from reopening." Scott yanked off his tie. "Of course, this dealt more specifically with who actually had control over the old evidence—''

Scott stopped, smiling. ''Shit, you don't want to know all that. Bottom line was, Sandusky didn't want the old evidence reexamined.''

''You won the argument?'' Louis asked.

''Yes!'' Scott said, pumping his arm. ''Sandusky looked like a man who had just had his tongue pulled out through his ass. It was magnificent. We need a drink. Brandy, right?''

Louis nodded, leaning against the doorjamb. He was watching Scott, but thinking about Brian in the next office. He had to be sure first; he couldn't do to Scott what he had done to Ronnie. He couldn't make an accusation until he had proof. But once he did, how was he going to tell Scott that his brother might be a murderer?

Scott pulled open the doors to a built-in bar and made two drinks. He brought Louis his glass, then held up his own in a toast.

''Let justice be done,'' Scott said.

Louis hesitated, then clinked his glass against Scott's.

''Though the heavens may fall,'' Louis said softly.

Chapter Thirty-Seven

Louis dropped two quarters into the vending machine and punched at the button. The can of Dr Pepper tumbled to the bottom and he pulled it out.

As he took a drink, he looked down the hallway to where Octavius was loading linens into a closet. Louis looked up at the clock, then in the window of the autopsy room. There was a body laid out, but it wasn't Kitty. Vince must have put her in storage until the Sheriff's department released her.

Louis walked the hall, slumped down in a plastic chair, then rose again, walking the other way. What the hell was taking Vince so long?

A door opened and he saw Vince coming toward him, carrying some papers. He was wearing jeans and a polo shirt instead of his usual green scrubs, but still had earphones looped around his neck. As he grew closer, Louis could hear the tinny whine of Marvin Gay singing "Ain't That Peculiar."

"First you bring me fossilized jism, and now you bring me a snotty Kleenex," Vince said. "Louis, this has got to stop."

"I know. I'm sorry. Were you able to type it?"

Vince nodded. "AB-negative."

A strange mix of emotion passed through Louis. The excitement of knowing he was closing in on Brian was tempered by the knowledge that one more person was going to get hurt by all this. He still had to face Scott.

"Louis, you want this too?" Vince was holding out the papers.

"What is it?"

"Kitty's updated autopsy report. You want to take Scott Brenner his copy?"

Louis nodded, taking the report from Vince. He opened it, then saw Vince moving out of the corner of his eye.

"Wait a minute, Vince."

Vince turned, throwing his arms out. "Louis, Louis, Louis. Unlike the rest of the people around here, I have a life. Let me live it."

"Just tell me, did you find anything new?"

"Yeah, one thing," he said. "We found clay in her hair."

"In her hair? Why didn't the mortician wash it out?"

"Well, she had the blunt trauma wound on the back of her head. I guess whoever did her couldn't get it all."

"Clay," Louis said slowly. "Why the hell would she have clay in her hair? Did she get it in the dump?"

"I doubt it," Vince said. "It had traces of silica quartz and vinyl acetate mixed in. It wasn't clay, like dirt. It was like what they use for cement work."

"Cement work?"

"Yeah, you know, the stuff they use to stick tiles on the wall."

Louis was quiet, thinking.

"One more thing," Vince said. "Remember I told you I thought that the head wound was not what killed her? I was right. She died from the stab wounds and she almost bled out. She was very dead by the time the body was moved to the dump."

"So wherever she was killed, there was a lot of blood," Louis said.

"It would have left a mess, I would think."

Vince started away. Louis rubbed his brow, trying to think. This couldn't be all there was.

"Vince," Louis called. "If she was already dead when the killer put her in the landscapers' dump, how did she breathe in the fertilizer?"

Vince turned. "What fertilizer?"

Louis flipped through the report as he walked to Vince. "Here. Right here, the potassium monopersulfate."

Vince took the report and looked at the listing. "Who told you this was fertilizer?"

"We looked it up."

"Well, potassium is in fertilizer, but when you add monopersulfate to it, it's a different chemical compound."

"What is it used for?" Louis asked.

"Pools. They use it to chemically balance swimming pools." Vince handed him back the report. "I'd guess your girl probably went swimming just before she was killed and took some water into her lungs."

Louis ran a hand over his brow. *Shit, one little mistake.*

Vince mistook his contrition for fatigue and put a hand on his shoulder.

"Louis, give it a rest. Go home."

Louis nodded, folding the report. He watched Vince disappear down the hallway and leaned back against the cool wall. He was thinking about Brian and he was seeing the Brenner house. Not as the rotting place it was now but as Kitty must have seen it twenty years ago. A beautiful mansion where she could swim in a moonlit pool, pretending she was Lady Kitrina Jaspers.

He knew now what had happened. Now he just had to find a way to prove it to Mobley.

Chapter
Thirty-Eight

Louis searched O'Sullivan's for Mobley and when he didn't see him, he looked at his watch. Mobley had said eight o'clock. Where was he?

Then, through the smoke and bodies, he saw him sitting in his usual booth in the back. The glass in front of him was empty and Louis stopped at the bar before going back. Sticking his manila folder under his arm, he carried Mobley a scotch and water and brought a Heineken for himself.

Mobley looked up at Louis as he sat down, but then his gaze dropped to the fresh scotch. He picked it up, downing nearly all of it in one swallow. His face looked drawn, and there was something in his eyes Louis couldn't quickly place.

Two men came by the table, heading toward the restrooms. Mobley looked up at them.

"Hey, guys," he said.

They kept walking.

Mobley's eyes drifted down to the glass in his hands. It hit Louis at that moment that what he was seeing in Mobley's face was the sting of exclusion. And maybe even a little fear that he wasn't going to survive this.

Mobley drank the last drop of scotch and settled back against the booth. "Okay, what was so damn important?"

"I know who killed Kitty and I know where," Louis said, sitting down across from him.

Mobley eyes narrowed. "I just got the damn case reopened and you've got it all solved."

Louis put the folder on the table. "I think Duvall sold Jack Cade out in 1967," he began. "Sometime during the investigation and trial, Duvall latched onto Brian Brenner as a suspect—"

"Brian Brenner? Give me a fucking break, Kincaid."

"Stay with me for a minute. I think Duvall was afraid of the fallout if he accused the sixteen-year-old son of the city's most prominent family of murder. So he went to Senator Brenner and struck a deal to protect Brian. Jack Cade got twenty years in prison and Spencer Duvall got rich."

Mobley stared at Louis. "You got proof of this supposed deal?" he asked.

"No."

"I didn't think so," Mobley said. He motioned to the waitress for another drink.

"The vaginal semen sample taken from Kitty was AB-negative blood. Brian Brenner is AB-negative."

"How do you know that?"

Louis hesitated. "How I know isn't admissable. You'll have to test him yourself when you arrest him."

"Arrest him? What are you talking about?"

Louis searched through the folder and pulled out Kitty's original autopsy report. "There was potassium monopersulfate in Kitty's lungs. Vince told me it's a common pool chemical. Kitty's friend Joyce told me

Kitty liked to go swimming at night. Then when Vince did the second autopsy he found silica quartz and vinyl acetate in her hair. That's a cement mix they used to put up tiles.''

"So?"

Louis pushed another paper across the table.

"What's this?"

"A building permit. I went over to the planning department and pulled it. It's for the Brenner house on Shaddlelee Lane, specifically to renovate the pool cabana.'' Louis pointed to a date. "It was pulled by Leyland Brothers Construction November 1, 1965.''

"Kitty wasn't killed until April 9th of the following year, right?" Mobley asked.

"Maybe the work got stalled or something. We can call Leyland Brothers to find out. But that isn't what's interesting. Look at this.'' Louis slapped a second permit in front of Mobley. "A new permit was pulled for the same job by a different contractor, Delacarpini and Sons.''

Mobley was looking at the date on the second permit. "April 30, 1966.''

"I think the cabana was still under construction when Brian killed Kitty there,'' Louis said. "That's why she had cement powder in her hair. And then, after Brian dumped Kitty's body, the second permit was pulled and the cabana work was completed.''

Mobley looked up at Louis.

"Maybe Brian got scared and told his father. That's why Charles Brenner made the deal with Duvall to set up Cade and then he hid the evidence by bringing in new workers to finish the cabana.''

Mobley was rubbing his temple, looking at the permit. "I was in that house once, for a party in high school,'' he said quietly.

"Brian's been trying to sell it," Louis said. "He

knew this might all come out if Cade brought suit against Duvall.''

Mobley looked up. ''So you think Brian killed Duvall too?''

Louis nodded. ''Duvall was treated for depression right around the time of the Cade trial. I think he always felt guilty about what he did, and when Cade got out and threatened to sue him, it all came back.'' Louis paused. ''Maybe Duvall was going to come clean, maybe he even told Brian. Brian had no choice. His father wasn't around to clean up his mess this time.''

Louis finally picked up his Heineken. It tasted good, and for a second, that surge of adrenaline he had been expecting with Vince came forward.

''But why Jack Cade? Why'd they set him up?'' Mobley asked.

But before Louis could answer, Mobley spoke again. ''Never mind. I can guess. Cade did the Brenners' lawn, right?''

Louis nodded slowly. ''I called Cade and asked him. Cade was always losing his tools. Brian probably found the Clot Buster in his yard and realized he could make it look like Cade did it.''

''What about the panties? They had Cade's blood type on them, not Brian's,'' Mobley said.

''Cade told me he found the panties in his truck the next morning and figured Ronnie left them there. He used them to jack-off in. I think Brian put the panties in Cade's truck to set him up.'' Louis paused. ''The semen inside Kitty was AB-negative. It's a rare blood type, Lance, only five percent of the population. That's what is important.''

Mobley was quiet, looking down at his glass.

''Jack Cade was the perfect murderer,'' Louis said. ''He was the man any jury would love to hate.''

Mobley took a long, slow drink of his scotch, then

looked off across the bar. It was a moment before he looked back at Louis.

"What about Scott? Is he involved?" Mobley asked quietly.

Louis shook his head. "First of all, he was away at school at Florida State. And second, he's the wrong blood type."

"What is he?"

"I don't know, but I guarantee he's not negative." Louis paused. "I don't think Scott knows anything. My guess is the old man never told Scott, just in case something ever did come to light. If Brian went under, at least the favorite son wouldn't. The heir and the spare."

"What?"

"That's what Ellie Silvestri called Scott and Brian."

Mobley's shoulders slumped slightly as his gaze drifted over all the evidence Louis had laid before him.

"Jesus H Christ," he said. "Why the hell would Duvall do it?"

"Money, success, status." Louis paused, deciding not to bring up Candace right now. "He knew what he was doing."

"Faust selling his soul to the devil," Mobley said, shaking his head.

"He sold it to Dr. Mephisto. I looked it up."

Mobley just stared at him. Then he picked up his glass, finished off the scotch and set the glass down. The laughter of the bar floated around them. Mobley ran both hands across his face.

Louis watched him, not knowing what to say. There was nothing he could do now. He had taken things as far as he could. It was all up to Mobley now.

"Sheriff?" Louis asked.

"Scott and I have known each other a long time," Mobley said, without looking up. "I want to talk to him first. Before we go after Brian."

Louis tensed. "Look, I like Scott, but Brian's his brother. If we tip—"

Mobley's head shot up. "This is *my* call, Kincaid. You want to be there, fine. But we handle it my way."

Mobley started gathering up the papers. When Louis tried to help, Mobley jerked the folder away. "I can do it, goddamn it," he said.

Louis sat back in the booth. *Jesus, don't let him blow this.*

Mobley rose, picking up the folder. His eyes traveled over the crowded bar and came back to Louis. "Five P.M. tomorrow," he said. "Brian Brenner's office."

Chapter
Thirty-Nine

Louis waited in the first floor lobby of Brenner's office building, watching the glass doors for Mobley. It was ten minutes after five. Where was he? A Lee County cruiser pulled up and Mobley got out. Louis held the door open for him.

"You ready for this?" Mobely asked.

Louis nodded.

At the elevator, Mobley jabbed at the button. His dark green uniform looked fresh from its dry-cleaner plastic. He looked rested but grim. Louis's eyes dropped to the folder in Mobley's hands. He wished he knew how Mobley was going to handle this. What the hell did he plan to say?

The doors opened and they stepped into the Brenner reception area. The receptionist's desk was empty; Mobley led the way past it, down the short hall to Scott's office. The door was open.

Scott was picking up his suit coat and paused, his

eyes moving from Mobley to Louis. Louis knew he was trying his damndest to figure out what they were doing here together.

"Evening, guys," Scott said, shrugging on his coat. "Something I can do for you?"

"Is Brian here, Scott?" Mobley asked.

"No, he left early," Scott said, looking again at Louis. "Is there something wrong?"

Mobley hesitated. "We need to talk to you."

Scott looked puzzled, but motioned to the chairs in front of his desk. "Please, sit down."

Mobley didn't move. "There's been a couple things come up in the Kitty Jagger investigation I thought you should know about."

Scott's face brightened. "Oh, well. Good. I need all the leverage I can get for the motion to retry."

Mobley drew in a breath. "Scott, we think Brian raped and murdered Kitty Jagger."

Scott froze, his eyes locked on Mobley's face. Then placing both hands on his desk, slowly sat down.

"Lance, you've known Brian and me since high school," he said quietly. "You know he couldn't have . . ." Scott's voice trailed off.

Mobley glanced at Louis, then stepped forward. "Scott, listen to me."

"No," Scott said, shaking his head. "You're wrong."

"We're not wrong," Mobley said. "We think Brian picked Kitty up after work and took her to your house. Then something went wrong."

Louis resisted the urge to cut in. *Jesus Christ, how much was he going to tell him?*

"After he killed her," Mobley went on, "he threw her body in the dump, and tossed the panties in Cade's truck, which we know he saw every morning in your neighborhood."

Scott tightened, closing his eyes, trying to hold himself together.

"Scott, we need your help on this," Mobley said. "Brian was a kid. We understand that."

"He didn't do this," Scott said, his voice stronger.

"Then ask him to submit to a blood test."

Scott's head was down and his eyes were closed. It was quiet enough that Louis could hear the ring of a telephone out on the secretary's desk. It rang for a long time before the person finally gave up.

Scott pushed himself up from his desk. Slowly, he straightened his lapels and touched his tie. A change came over his expression, like he had suddenly slipped on a mask that didn't quite fit.

"Since I am the attorney of record for my brother, I am ending this conversation now," he said.

"Scott, c'mon," Mobley said. "You're a civil lawyer. Get him somebody who can help him, for chrissake."

"Brian and I have a standing retainer with each other. He's my attorney and I am his. Now get out. Now."

Mobley shook his head. "Not yet, Scott. I have search warrants here."

"For *what?*"

Mobley stepped forward and laid them one by one on Scott's desk.

"For Brian's office. For his apartment. And for the house on Shaddlelee Lane."

Chapter Forty

The sun was going down by the time they got to the Brenner mansion. The circular drive around the fountain was crowded with squad cars from the Sheriff's Department and Fort Myers Police.

The deputies and detectives, waiting near the front door, turned to look as Louis got out of Mobley's car. Scott's gray Mercedes pulled up and he got out. The three of them went up the steps to the old wood door.

Mobley turned to Scott. "You got the key?"

Scott unlocked the door and stepped back. Mobley pushed it open and went through first. Louis followed.

The smell of mildew and must swirled up like a cool vapor in the close, dark foyer.

Mobley turned to Scott. "I told FP&L to turn on the power. Where's the light switch?"

Scott hit a wall and the foyer lit up. Louis looked up at the wrought iron chandelier. Only a couple of the bulbs still worked and the weak light followed the black chain up, disappearing into the shadows three stories above.

"How many rooms, Scott?" Mobley asked.

Scott hesitated. "Five bedrooms upstairs, the baths . . ." His voice trailed off. He was looking around, solemn-faced, like childhood memories were crowding out all other thoughts. Louis watched him carefully, wondering if he was seeing Brian in his mind, his young brother bringing Kitty into their house.

"Len, take a couple guys and go upstairs," Mobley said to one of the deputies. "Chris, you start on the downstairs rooms."

The men split up, leaving the three of them in the foyer. Mobley's eyes were traveling over the cracked plaster walls. Without a word, he walked slowly into the dark living room. The thud of his boots on the old wood floors echoed through the empty room. He punched a wall switch and one of the two sconces over the fireplace lit up, bathing the room in a sickly yellow glow.

Louis saw Scott's eyes take in the obscenity the vandals had scribbled on the wall.

Mobley was on the move again, and Louis followed him through the dining room, where a crystal chandelier hung dark and the china cabinets stood empty. In the stale air of the kitchen, Mobley punched another light. The florescent bulbs gave out a feeble flicker that made the place look unnervingly like Vince's autopsy room. Louis scanned the kitchen, with its scarred wood counters and old black and white tiles, veined with age.

Louis heard a creaking sound above his head and looked up. It was just the footsteps of the deputies searching the bedrooms. Louis looked back at Mobley's face. He knew what he was thinking. The old house was filled with mold and decay, but it held no secrets. Whatever had happened that April night twenty years ago had happened out in the cabana.

"What else is down here, Scott?" Mobley asked.

"Just my father's study," Scott said.

"Point the way."

Scott led them back to a closed door off the living room. It opened with a groan and Scott found a wall switch. A chandelier came to life, illuminating a wood-paneled room. Mahogany bookcases lined three walls, broken by windows with dusty old plantation shutters. The third wall was papered in a dusky blue. The plaster ceiling was cracked, with bits of it laying on the old wood floor.

The study reminded Louis a little of Spencer Duvall's law office. And he could almost see Duvall sitting across from the old man's desk, striking his Faustian bargain. He could even make out the outline on the dusty floor where the desk would have been.

Louis's eyes wandered up the blue wallpaper. What he first had thought was a pattern he now realized were just darker spots on the blue paper. He turned to the windows. They faced the east and he could imagine that when the shutters were open, the morning sun fell full-force on the opposite blue wall, fading the paper over the decades.

He looked back at it. The darker blue patches were silhouettes. Silhouettes of guns.

"Scott," Louis said, "did your father collect guns?"

Scott was looking at the outlines on the wall. "Yes, he did."

Louis looked back at Mobley and could tell he was thinking the same thing.

"Where are the guns now, Scott?" Mobley asked.

"We sold them to a dealer after Dad died," Scott said.

He noticed Louis and Mobley exchange glances. "Duvall was shot with a collector's gun," he said quietly. He drew in a quick breath. "Wait a minute, if you think Brian—"

Mobley held up a hand. "Let's take this one step at a time, Scott."

A couple of the deputies came in at that moment. Mobley turned to the tech guy. "I want photos of this wall," he said, pointing, then he looked at Louis.

"Let's go look outside," he said.

They exited the house by the French doors that Brian had taken Louis through on his first visit. For a moment, the three of them just stood on the coral rock patio. The night was ripe with the brackish smell of the river and night-blooming jasmine. At the end of the long yard, Louis could make out the white boathouse and the red lights of a boat making its way down the black ribbon of the Caloosahatchee River.

Mobley led the way down the crumbling steps to the overgrown path. The only light came from a half moon low in the night sky, and as they picked their way toward the cabana, Mobley flicked on a flashlight.

"Remember that party you had here, Scott," Mobley said. "Homecoming, senior year. We snuck down to the boathouse with a six-pack of Pabst."

Scott didn't answer him.

They stopped. The pool was a gaping gray hole in the faint light, the cabana behind it a dark outline against the tall ficus hedges.

Mobley swung his flashlight beam into the pool. The dark green water was filmed with scum. The smell of decay hung in the still, humid air.

Louis looked back at the house. The deputies were searching the second floor, and the play of their flashlights on the palm trees looked almost festive. For a moment, he could see in his mind what the Brenner house must have looked like once, when boys in madras shirts and girls in gold paisley necked on the lawn and snuck off to sip beers in the boathouse. He could see what an outsider like Kitty must have seen that night.

"Any lights out here, Scott?" Mobley said.

"I . . . I don't know if it still works." Scott disappeared and, a moment later, a spotlight came on, illuminating the decrepit cabana and the cracked patio. The pool light had come on too, sending a beam out into the ghastly green water.

Louis moved toward the cabana and tugged on one of the French doors. It stuck, and Louis had to pull it open, scraping it across the patio stone.

He went inside.

It was dark, except for small lasers of light that came in through the shutters. He felt for a light and turned it on.

It was a simple room, about twelve-by-twelve. Old wicker furniture was piled against one wall, and over in one corner was a shower stall with a rusty shower head. The floor was cement painted gray, the walls tiled in blue and peach.

Len, one of the tech guys, came to the door, holding a plastic bottle and a portable light. "Is this the place?"

"Yeah," Mobley said, coming in.

Len slipped in behind Louis and Louis heard Mobley let out a sigh. "You know what a long shot this is, right Kincaid?" Mobley said.

Louis nodded.

Len started in one corner, spraying the first wall, from the floor to about four feet above, with luminol. He nodded at Mobley, standing near the door.

Mobley hit the switch and the cabana went dark. Louis anticipated the glow of the phosphorescent blue that would have signaled the smallest speck of blood. Len flicked on the portable luminol light.

Nothing.

"Do the others," Mobley said, flicking the lights back on.

Len sprayed the second and third walls. Again nothing. After the fourth wall, Mobley hit the lights again. Len ran the light over the tiles in a slow caress. Nothing.

Mobley turned on the light and looked at Louis.

"Check the ceiling," Louis said.

Len glanced at Mobley. Mobley nodded. Len pulled an old wicker chair to the middle of the floor and climbed on it, spraying the ceiling. Again, there was nothing when the lights were turned off.

Louis was staring at the floor, his eyes drawn to the drain near the shower. "Try the shower stall. Near the drain."

Just as Len was flicking on the portable light, Scott appeared at the cabana door. Louis looked back at him but couldn't read his expression in the dark. A man came up behind Scott. It took Louis a moment to recognize Brian. Louis watched as Scott leaned over and whispered something to his brother. Then they stepped outside.

Louis watched. They had stopped by the pool. Brian was shaking his head; Scott was doing all the talking.

"Nothing here, Sheriff."

Louis turned back to Len, who was on his knees by the shower stall holding the portable light. Mobley was kneeling next to him. When he looked up at Louis, his face was grim in the ghostly blue light.

"There's nothing here, Kincaid." He got to his feet and went to hit the wall switch. "Twenty years is a long time."

Louis paused, looking at the wall. He was thinking about the ugly green tile in Susan's kitchen and the cracked black and white tiles up in the mansion. He ran a hand over the peach and blue tiles and in the grout crevices between. These tiles looked clean in comparison.

He was remembering what Vince said: *She had almost bled out. It would have left a big mess.*

A mess that Brian had not been able to clean up. So his father had ordered all the old tile ripped out and new tile installed. Louis looked at Mobley.

"This isn't the original tile," he said.

He pursed his lips, then turned to Len. "Go get the axe from your cruiser, Len," he said.

When Len returned, Louis held out a hand. Len looked at Mobley, who nodded. Len handed him the axe. Louis took a step back and aimed at a section of the wall near the shower.

"What the fuck are you doing?"

They turned to see Scott standing at the cabana door. "You can't tear up walls," Scott shouted.

"Read the warrant, Scott," Mobley said.

Louis swung the axe. It cracked into the tile, scattering chips at his feet.

Louis swung again, and this time the axe cut through the wall and lodged in the empty space behind it. Louis pulled the axe free and looked at the sheet rock. Using the sharp edge of the axe, Louis began to pry off the tiles. Mobley came up next him and started popping them off with his pocket knife. When they had cleared a couple square feet up from the floor, Mobley waved Len to come over with the luminol.

Nothing. They moved onto another section, popping tiles, spraying the luminol and lighting the sheet rock. Still nothing. The sheet rock was clean.

They went on to the next wall, then the third, chipping out sections of the tiles and spraying the sheet rock beneath. Finally, after a half-hour, they stopped. The air was heavy with dust and the sound of ragged breathing.

A coughing sound made Louis turn. Brian was holding a Kleenex over his nose. Scott was just standing there, leaning against the doorjamb, his arms crossed, his mouth pulled in a tight line.

"I think you're done here, Sheriff," Scott said.

Mobley nodded at Len, who started to pack up. Louis

was staring at the walls, at the gashes, the gray sheet rock and the jagged tiles. He turned when Mobley put a hand on his shoulder.

"Enough," Mobley said quietly. "There's nothing here."

"Damn it, Lance, she was stabbed twelve times," Louis said tightly. He threw the axe down in frustration. "Not one fucking drop of blood on these walls."

Mobley moved away, talking quietly to the other deputies who had gathered near the door. Louis could hear him giving orders to start packing up. He could hear Scott and Brian too, whispering.

Louis stared at the ravaged walls. She was *here* damn it. He knew she was here. He could almost feel her presence, almost see what had happened. He could almost see—

Walls. *No walls.*

He took a step closer, staring at a torn piece of sheet rock. *Maybe there were no walls here when she was killed.*

Louis grabbed the edge of a torn piece of sheet rock, and jerked backward, ripping off the entire board. There was nothing beyond it but studs and the old lath and plaster backing. No blood stains.

He heard Scott call to Mobley, but he didn't turn. He moved to the next piece of sheet rock, curling his fingers over the side edge.

"Sheriff, this is fucking crazy," Scott said.

Then he felt a hand on his back.

"Kincaid—" Mobley said.

Louis shrugged Mobley off and yanked at another piece of sheet rock, breaking it off. He threw it down and pulled again.

"Louis!"

The wood groaned and the rest of the panel popped off, sending Louis stumbling backward.

A flash of red caught his eye and he struggled to

gain his balance. The cabana fell silent, a film of white dust in the air.

He moved closer.

Fabric. A billow of red. And a yellow cloth that seemed suspended in the air between the two-by-fours.

Then he saw the bones. It was a full skeleton, bent in a fetal position. The arm and leg bones had dropped away but most of it was still intact, the skull lodged against a stud, balanced on top of the vertebrae.

A strange cry pierced the silence and Louis spun around.

Brian was staring at the bones in the wall, his face white.

"I left her in the dump!" he shouted. "How could she be here? I left her in the dump!"

Scott grabbed his brother's shoulder. "Shut up," he hissed, pushing him backward. "Shut up!"

Louis and Mobley followed them from cabana. Brian was muttering Kitty's name, waving his arms. Scott finally grabbed his shoulders, drawing Brian so close he had no choice but to walk with him. Scott led him toward the grass, and eased him down.

Brian was crying.

Mobley started toward them, but Scott waved him off. Scott knelt in front of Brian, leaned close and said something to him. After a moment, Brian shuddered and gently placed his forehead against his brother's.

Mobley gave them a few seconds, then walked over.

"Stand up, Brian. You're under arrest."

Brian didn't move. Finally, Scott helped his brother to his feet. Brian stood there, wavering, his face streaked, his eyes panicked. Scott took his brother's face in his hands, looking him in the eyes.

"Brian, listen to me," Scott said. "Don't say a word, not one damn word. I'll be there as soon as I can. Do you hear me?"

Brian closed his eyes.

Scott shook him. "Brian! Do you hear me?"

Brian nodded weakly. Scott let go.

Louis watched as a deputy led Brian away, Scott following. Mobley was giving orders to the deputies. Louis turned and walked back into the cabana.

He went back to the hole in the wall. He stared at the skeleton. The tilt of the skull made it look almost like it was in mourning.

He moved closer. He could see it was a female.

The red fabric was a skirt, deep brown stains of dried blood running down the front of it. The yellowed cloth was streaked with brown splotches. There was a pink band around the skull and a necklace of some kind hung between the clavicle and sternum.

Louis squatted down so he could see the necklace. *Dear God.*

He heard the crunch of Mobley's boots on the broken tile behind him.

Mobley let out a slow breath. "Who the hell is that?" he said softly.

Louis couldn't take his eyes off the necklace. "I know who she is."

Chapter
Forty-One

The bones were laid out on the steel table.

She had been tall, Louis thought, as he stared at them. Just like her father, Bob Ahnert.

Louis sipped his coffee, his eyes going to the items that Vince had carefully laid out on a table nearby. A ragged red skirt, the yellowed blouse stained with brown blood. A beaded pink headband they had taken from the skull. The small white puka beads taken from around her vertebrae.

Louis stared at the skull, at the crack, high on the cheekbone. Vince had told him someone had hit Lou Ann Ahnert hard, hard enough to crack her face open.

Shit. He threw the empty styrofoam cup in the trash.

He thought he had it all figured out.

He had spent hours at the house, watching the techs dismantle the wall, carefully sorting the bones and scraping the hard dried blood off the plywood behind them. He had stayed as they went back through the house, searching for anything that might have been missed. They were working two homicides now—Kitty Jagger's and Lou Ann Ahnert's. They still had found no evidence that Kitty had been killed there. And they didn't know who had killed Lou Ann Ahnert. But at least they knew now that Brian Brenner had something to hide.

A sound behind him made Louis turn. Christ, it was Bob Ahnert.

He was standing at the door, his beefy face drawn, his eyes red. Louis knew that Mobley had already told him that remains had been found and that it was suspected the puka beads belonged to Lou Ann. It could all be confirmed through dental records later. But Louis had not expected Ahnert to show up here.

Damn. Mobley had gone down the hall for a cup of coffee. Louis started toward Ahnert.

"Is that her?"

Ahnert's words stopped Louis in his tracks. Something told him to just step aside. Bob Ahnert's eyes were fixed on the table. He came forward slowly.

He stared at the bones for a long time, his face slack, his eyes empty. There was nothing there, nothing in his expression.

"Detective—" Louis said.

Ahnert was shaking his head slowly. "That's not Lou Ann, it's just bones," he said. "Just bones."

Then, his eyes skittered to the table where the clothes lay.

He went to the table. Louis moved to his side. Ahnert was looking at the clothing. Something in his expression changed, shifted slightly, like he was focusing in on one small thing.

"Oh, Jesus," he whispered.

He started to reach for the puka beads, but Louis grabbed his wrist.

"Don't," he said gently. "It's evidence."

Ahnert looked at Louis. His eyes teared and he moved away. Louis let him go.

Louis stood there, looking down at the clothing. He heard weeping. He turned and went to Bob Ahnert, putting a hand on the detective's shoulders. Ahnert continued to sob softly until they both heard the snap of Mobley's boots in the tiled hall way.

Ahnert turned, wiping at his face, drawing quick breaths.

The door opened and Mobley stopped, seeing Ahnert. He sized things up immediately and cleared his throat.

"Bob, I'm sorry—"

Head bowed, Ahnert brushed past him and was gone.

Mobley watched him go, then turned to Louis. "How'd he take it?"

"Hard."

Mobley walked to the table, looking down at the bones. Louis came up next to him.

"Hard to believe it about Brian," Mobley said. "You think you know people."

Mobley moved away. When Louis turned to look, Mobley had sagged into a chair, hands on his knees. Louis went to sit down next to him, leaned his head back against the wall and shut his eyes. For a long time, neither spoke.

"The heir and the spare," Mobley murmured.

Louis looked over at him.

"I keep thinking of that, what you called them," Mobley said. "It was true. Brian was always kind of . . . an afterthought." He let out a tired sigh. "I remember he used to come and watch us at football practice, this chubby zit-faced kid standing out by the chain-link fence by himself, watching his brother. He always wanted to hang with us afterward. We didn't want him around. But Scott, he'd drag him along anyway."

Louis was thinking of Kitty and what Brian had done

to her. And what he might have done to Lou Ann Ahnert. He didn't want to hear anything about how tough Brian had it.

"It must have been hard," Mobley went on. "Your mom's dead, your father's gone all the time. And your only role model is a brother who's smarter, more popular, better looking, than you ever had a prayer of being. Shit, do you love him or hate him?"

Louis closed his eyes, fatigue beginning to take over his body. Mobley nudged him.

"You okay?"

"I just want to go home."

"Brian will be home before we are."

"He made bail already?"

Mobley shrugged. "He will in a few hours, you watch. Come on. I'll drive you back to your car."

Louis followed Mobley outside and they headed toward his cruiser. It was past three in the morning and the air was wet and still, enveloping him like a warm blanket.

Louis settled back in the seat and closed his eyes, lulled by the squawks and chattering from Mobley's radio. But even that did not stop the snapping in his brain.

The images were fast-forwarding like a high-speed slide show, propelled by Mobley's talk of Brian Brenner. He saw Kitty's empty grave. Willard Jagger's worn face. A pink dress on a lifeless body. Bones in a cabana wall. And the tortured look on Brian's face when he saw them.

The car stopped and Louis sat up. They were in the parking lot in front of the Brenner law offices. Mobley mumbled something about getting some sleep and Louis got out. As Mobley drove off, Louis stopped in the street, looking up at the top floor of the granite building in front of him.

I put her in the dump.

Why the hell did Brian say that? Had he been so terrified and confused that he simply mixed up his victims?

Louis unlocked the Mustang and got in. And why had Brian shown up at the mansion during the search? He wasn't the type of man who hid his feelings easily. He hadn't even seemed nervous at the cabana—until they had found Lou Ann's bones.

Louis started the car. The slides were still moving in his head and suddenly he could see Bob Ahnert's face showing him Lou Ann's picture.

She ran away from home Thanksgiving night.

College kids came home at Thanksgiving.

They also came home at Easter. And Easter was almost always in April.

Louis leaned on the steering wheel, staring straight ahead. The slides were forming a new picture now. Onc bathroom shared by two law offices. One secret shared by two brothers. And a father who was never there—until it counted.

Louis jerked the Mustang into gear and made a U-turn across the deserted street. He needed to see one thing to be sure, before he said anything to anyone. He headed north, toward the cemetery.

The darkness disoriented him. He swung the flashlight beam over the headstones, stepping gingerly on the soft, wet grass. Finally, he spotted the black outline of the huge lace-canopied tree and found his way to Kitty's grave. From there, he was able to retrace his steps to the Brenner family plot.

He flicked the beam over BRENNER and down across CHARLES and VIVIAN. On the ground, the beam picked up the three tiny markers.

| Geraldine | Infant Baby Girl | Infant Baby Boy |
| 1942–1944 | 1945 Stillborn | 1948 Stillborn |

Louis focused the beam on the first baby girl. He was remembering now what Ellie had told him about the Rh-factor. She had told Louis that the first positive child was the one who triggered the antibodies that killed all the positive babies who followed. Vivian's first child wasn't a stillborn; she had a name, Geraldine, and she had lived two years. That meant she was positive and the one who triggered the death of the second baby, a stillborn.

So Ellie had been wrong. Scott wasn't the firstborn— he was the third. And he had to be Rh-negative.

A sudden image came to his mind—Scott at Kitty's exhumation, standing over the grave, holding a hand to his mouth, a hand that hid not nausea but a smirk.

God damn him. God damn him to hell.

Louis turned and walked quickly back to his car. He jammed the keys in the ignition and roared the engine to life, jerking the Mustang into reverse.

He was almost to the entrance when he saw oncoming headlights. He slowed to let the car pass. It was a black BMW.

It was Brian.

Louis turned around, cut his lights and trailed the BMW. He gave Brian enough time to park and walk away from the car before he pulled up behind. When he got out, Brian had disappeared.

On top of the rise, Louis looked toward Kitty's open grave, but Brian wasn't there. Louis started off toward the Brenner plot.

Brian was standing there, head bowed, staring down at the headstone. Louis hesitated, knowing if he took one more step, he would beat the shit out of the pathetic bastard.

Brian looked over at him. Louis could barely see his face in the darkness.

"I hardly knew my father," Brian said softly.

Louis unclenched his fist and moved closer.

"When Scott came and got me tonight," Brian said, "he told me to just go home. I couldn't. I had to come here. I had to talk to him. I had to apologize."

"To who?" Louis asked.

Brian nodded at the headstone. "My father. I had to tell him I couldn't keep our secret anymore."

Brian was staring at the headstone.

"Brian?"

He looked up at Louis. There was something in his face, a piteous look, almost a forewarning, that for a moment made Louis want to turn and walk away. But he knew he had to hear it.

"Tell me what happened that night, Brian."

Chapter
Forty-Two

"I remember it was really warm that night, like summer was coming early."

Brian raised his face to the dark sky, closing his eyes. When he opened them, he was looking across the cemetery but not focusing on anything in particular. The tombstones were just gray shapes in the weak pre-dawn light, like silhouettes of people waiting patiently in line for something to begin.

"I had a new red Corvette. It was my first car, and I remember I wanted to show it off."

He fell quiet. Louis waited.

"You went to the drive-in that night," Louis said finally.

Brian gave a slight nod. "It was crowded. Everyone was there." He blinked several times, like he was trying to bring the picture in his head into focus.

"She hung the tray on my window. Her hair was pulled back in a ponytail and she was wearing this silly red and white hat on her head. She smiled at me and said she liked my car." He paused. "God, she was so pretty."

Louis looked down at the ground for a second, then back up at Brian.

"I had seen her before," Brian went on softly, "but I didn't have the guts to talk to her. But then when she said she liked my car, I guess I felt a little braver. I don't know . . ."

He was quiet again. The silence was broken by the first faint birdsong of the morning.

"I asked her if she wanted to go for a ride," Brian said. "She said she had to work. I asked her if I could wait and give her a ride home."

Louis couldn't resist. "She turned you down," he said.

Brian looked over at him and gave a wan smile. "Yes," he said. "But I was used to it. I wasn't like Scott. Talking to girls was hard for me."

The breeze lifted Brian's wispy hair down over his forehead. For a second, Louis thought he looked like he was twelve, but then the illusion was gone.

"I parked down the block and waited until the drive-in closed," Brian said. "It was about eleven-thirty, I think, when I saw her come out and start down Linhart. I followed her to the bus stop. She saw me and we started talking. I remember sitting there at the curb and she came over and leaned in my window to look inside the car. She smelled like . . . chocolate, like a chocolate malt."

Louis rubbed the back of his neck. "What happened next?" he asked.

"She said her feet hurt. I asked her again to let me give her a ride home. I told her I would put the top down. I thought she was going to turn me down again. But she didn't. She got in the car."

Brian stopped, his eyes going up to the trees and

then down again. He took a few steps away and sank onto a stone bench facing the Brenner headstone. He pulled a Kleenex out of his pocket and quietly blew his nose.

"I had a hard time watching the road," he said. "I remember we were driving down McGregor and the top was down and it was warm and the wind was blowing and she was laughing and her hair was blowing back. I had a hard time watching the road . . ."

Louis leaned against the tree, watching as Brian's features took shape with the quickening light.

"She said it was almost warm enough to go swimming," he said softly. "I told her my family had a pool."

Louis crossed his arms. "She went with you willingly?"

Brian nodded. "I could tell she was worried about it and I remember she said something about her father. But I told her I lived really close and I would take her home right after. So we went to my house."

Louis looked away to the pink-edged horizon. He could see the Brenner mansion and everything it must have represented to Kitty. When he looked back at Brian, he was sitting, elbows on knees, head bowed.

"You gave her something to drink?" Louis asked.

Brian's head came up slowly and he nodded. "One beer. She had a few sips, but she said she didn't like the taste and gave it to me. I didn't like beer either, but I drank it anyway."

When Brian fell quiet again, Louis prodded him. "You went out to the pool."

"Yeah. We weren't supposed to use it because it was getting redone. So I told her to be quiet so no one up at the house would hear."

He stopped, like he just remembered something. "There must have been a full moon, because I could see her standing there and I was too scared to turn on the lights. But I could see her really clearly. She took off her tennis shoes and sat down on the edge, dangling her feet in the water. I sat down next to her, drinking the beer. She was so damn pretty sitting there and I was so damn nervous.''

Louis felt a twinge of anger, but he said nothing.

''She said she didn't have a bathing suit so I showed her where we kept the spare suits for the guests,'' Brian said. ''She went in the cabana to change. I stripped down to my underwear and sat there, waiting. I drank up her beer.'' He paused. ''Oh god, when she came out . . .''

Louis shut his eyes. He heard Brian pull in a deep breath.

''I had to get in the pool quick. I . . .'' he hesitated. ''I had a hard-on and I didn't want her to see it.''

Brian's voice had gone soft. ''She got in and we started swimming. She was laughing and I was feeling so good. I was splashing her and we were playing around. I could feel her skin, so warm and wet.''

''When did things start to go wrong?'' Louis asked.

Brian balled the Kleenex up in his hand. ''I dunked her and she came up coughing. I didn't mean to be so rough. We were just playing. But she got out of the pool and said it was late and she'd better get home. She went into the cabana to change.''

The pink in the eastern sky was deepening. ''What did you do?'' Louis said slowly.

Brian didn't answer. Louis could see that his eyes were closed.

''Brian, what did you do?'' he said, more firmly.

''I stayed in the water for a minute,'' he said softly. ''I felt . . . I didn't want her to leave, so I got out and went in the cabana. I don't know, maybe I was going to apologize or maybe I thought I could talk her into staying, I don't know . . . but when I went in, she was standing there. She was standing there in her panties and bra and she looked . . .''

Brian looked up suddenly at Louis, as if for understanding. "I was sixteen. I was a fucking virgin. I didn't know . . . I didn't think . . .'' He stopped, pulling in a deep breath and the rest of the words came out in a torrent. "I grabbed her and tried to kiss her. She was trying to pull away and all I wanted to do was kiss her. And then she screamed.''

He stopped abruptly, looking away.

"What did you do?" Louis said.

"I slapped her.''

Louis took a slow breath to calm himself.

"She looked at me, then started screaming again. I think I put my hand over her mouth, I'm not sure. I was so scared someone up at the house was going to hear and come down.'' Brian stopped. "Then suddenly, Scott was there.''

Louis pushed off the tree and came closer.

"He was home for Easter, and I remember how embarrassed I was, Scott seeing me in my underwear with her there. I was afraid he would call me stupid or something in front of her. But he wasn't looking at me, he was looking at her.''

Louis could see it in his head; he could see Scott looking at Kitty.

"She was crying, holding her cheek,'' Brian said, "And then she went to Scott and started begging him to take her home. She was yelling that I tried to rape her.''

"What did Scott do?"

Brian closed his eyes. "He locked the door.''

Louis felt his fist clench.

"Then Scott shoved her backward. She fell on the floor, against the wicker chair. There was some bags of stuff the workers had left in a corner. She was curled up against them in a ball.''

Brian's voice cracked. "Scott looked at me and he said 'I'm going to show you how it's done, little brother.' "

Louis turned away.

Brian looked up at him, his eyes red. "Do you want to hear all of it?"

Louis nodded.

"He was on her before I could move," Brian said, "I didn't want to look, I didn't want to . . ." Brian had wrapped his arms around himself. "He pulled off her bra and panties and held her down. I couldn't . . ." He was rocking slightly. "He was grunting and pushing at her and she was crying. It seemed to last forever."

Brian drew in a shuddering breath. "Then it was quiet. I looked over at her. She was behind the wicker chair, curled up in a ball, naked. Scott picked up her uniform and threw it at her. He said something about how she smelled like grease."

"What were you doing through all this?" Louis asked.

Brian shook his head. "Nothing . . . nothing."

"What happened next?" Louis said tightly.

"She got dressed. I could hear her trying to hold back her sobs and I wanted to go help her but I couldn't . . . I just wanted to get away from there." Brian hesitated. "That's when she said it."

"Said what?"

"She looked at us and said, 'I thought you were better than us.' "

Jesus . . .

"Scott spun around and backhanded her and she fell down hard." Brian stopped suddenly. "And she just laid there."

Brian had shredded the Kleenex. "I guess she must have hit her head against the bag of cement. Scott rolled her over with his foot, but she didn't look like she was breathing. I was so scared. I . . . I puked up the beer, and when I looked up Scott was gone. And then he came back and he was carrying that thing, that tool. He said we had to make it look like a sex murder and that we had to stab her.''

Louis could see Brian's face clearly now. His eyes were fixed on the headstone. ''I just stared at him and he told me it didn't make any difference because she was already dead.''

Louis thought of what Vince had told him, that Kitty had not died of the head wound. For a second, he thought of telling Brian that Kitty had been alive before she was stabbed. But he couldn't; he needed to hear all of it.

''I wouldn't do it,'' Brian said in a whisper. ''So . . . so . . .''

He squeezed his eyes shut. ''Scott knelt down, I saw that, but then I closed my eyes. I kept them closed, but I could hear the sound it made. I could hear it.'' He took a breath. ''I can still hear it.''

Louis looked up at the sky, deepening to a coral as the sun broke the horizon.

''When I opened my eyes, I didn't look at her,'' Brian said. ''But I could see the blood. It was everywhere. I was just sitting there on the floor and Scott was talking, telling me what we had to do. But I couldn't move.''

Louis couldn't look at him. He just keep staring at the sky.

''I guess that's when he pulled down the shower curtain and wrapped her up in it. I don't remember, I was just sitting there. Then Scott was shaking me and yelling at me to get up, get dressed, telling me I had to help.''

''What did you do?'' Louis asked.

Brian shook his head, like he wasn't sure. ''We carried her out and put her in the trunk. Then we went back to the cabana. There was blood everywhere and Scott said we had to clean it up. I saw something and picked it up. It was her gold necklace. I remember she had it on in the pool. I put it in my pocket."

Brian stopped again.

"What did you do next?" Louis prodded.

"Scott was mad at me because I was just standing there staring at the blood. So he told me to go get rid of her."

"Did he tell you where?"

Brian nodded woodenly. "The gardener's dump. He said it had to be the gardener's dump."

He let go of the shredded Kleenex and it fluttered to the ground. "It was way across town. It took me a long time to get there. Then I had trouble carrying her. She was heavy and I dropped her." He paused. "Then I set her down in the . . . I set her down and I ran. I ran back to my car and when I went to get my keys out of my pocket, I felt the necklace. I went back. I went back and laid it around her neck."

Brian closed his eyes and bowed his head. He covered his face with his hands. It was quiet except for the chirping of the birds overhead and the faint sound of a lawn mower starting up somewhere far off.

"Things were different after that," Brian said quietly. "We never talked about it, but it was like we shared something, like we were closer somehow. More like brothers."

Louis stared at the Brenner headstone. All the feelings that had been churning inside him for the last hour were now settling into one deep ache.

Brian looked up, tears in his eyes. "She was so pretty," he whispered.

The quiet was broken by the thud of a car door. Louis turned. A figure was coming over the rise toward them. It was Scott.

Chapter
Forty-Three

Scott paused on the top of the hill, a silhouette against the rising gray mist. Brian looked up at him, tears streaking his face.

"I should have known you would come here, Brian," Scott said quietly. "It took me a while to figure it out. But I should have known."

Scott came toward them, looking over at Louis, then back at his brother.

"What did you tell him, Brian?" Scott asked.

Brian shook his head.

Louis was watching Scott. His face was composed, almost serene. Standing there in his perfect gray suit, he seemed almost a part of the morning vapor, like a benign spirit.

But he was a man. And Louis could see him, his body covering Kitty's. He could see him thrusting at her, his grunts mixing with her sobs.

Louis looked up into the tree's canopy, feeling his chest tighten. *God, don't let me kill the bastard.*

"What did you tell him?" Scott said.

"Everything," Brian said.

Scott came over to Brian and stood in front of him. Louis thought he was going to hit or slap him, but Scott didn't lift a hand.

"You stupid sonofabitch," Scott whispered.

"I didn't know about the other girl," Brian said softly. "I didn't know. I thought you were . . . . Oh, Jesus, Scott."

"I told you," Scott said. "I told you that you don't talk, you don't admit anything. I told you, it's just a *problem,* something to be fixed."

Scott turned from his brother and crossed to his father's headstone.

"You're not going to be able to handle this problem, Scott," Louis said.

Scott looked at him. "I can handle it."

"I know what you did to Kitty," Louis said.

Scott pointed a finger at Louis. "You don't know *shit.* And neither will anyone else."

"You killed two girls, Scott. How do you expect to walk away from that?"

Scott walked behind the headstone, looking down. "Do you remember what you signed the day after I hired you?"

"That confidentiality agreement doesn't include you, asshole. Only your clients."

Scott looked over at his brother. "Brian, poor bastard that he is, *is* a client. You knew he was my client before he allegedly confessed to you."

"What about you?"

"I am *his* client," Scott said. "Privilege belongs to the client and I'm not waiving mine. And I'm sure when he thinks about it, neither will Brian. And since I never fired you, our agreement is still in place."

Louis took a quick step toward him. "Fuck your privilege!"

Scott's face was emerging in the light and it was near a smile. "Okay, let's do that. How about hearsay? That's always a good one. Or I could argue you were acting as an agent of the sheriff's office and you had no right to talk to my client outside of my presence."

"I'm not a cop!"

"You sure looked like one tearing my cabana apart."

Louis glared at him. Scott's face relaxed and now the smile emerged.

"I have one more argument too," Scott said. "But I think I'll wait to see if it pans out."

"Argue your ass off if you want, I'll tell my story anyway."

"And you know how you'll come across? Like the lovesick dick you are, obsessed with a dead girl."

Louis took another step toward Scott, and Scott backed up quickly, but the smirk never left his face.

"Self-control is an admirable trait," Scott said.

Louis drew in a breath, pointing at Brian. "How much self-control does *he* have? What makes you think he won't break down again and tell a jury the same story he told me?"

Scott glanced at Brian. "Because he knows what I did for him. He knows that I'm the one who got him through law school. I'm the one who made him a lawyer. I'm the one who was always there to clean up his mess. He's my brother and he owes me."

Louis looked back at Brian. He looked like a beaten animal, sitting with his hands between his knees, head down.

"Blood is thicker than water," Scott said.

Louis looked at the grass, his jaw was clenched tighter than his fist. The only thing that kept him from killing Scott was the thought that some way, some how, Brian's confession could still be used.

"Besides," Scott added, running his hand along the rough edge of the marble headstone. "Brian wouldn't want to disappoint Dad. Would you Brian?"

Brian's head shot up.

"You made a promise to Dad that night," Scott said. "You remember? After Duvall left and Dad came up to your room? You remember what he said to you?"

Brian's eyes teared up again.

"He told you that you could never screw up again. He told you he had made a deal to save your ass. You remember, Brian?" Scott said.

Brian didn't move.

"Do you *remember?*"

Brian nodded slowly.

"And you promised him you wouldn't. You promised him you would try harder."

Louis's muscles were so tense they burned.

"I did try," Brian whispered.

"You failed!" Scott yelled. "You failed Dad and you failed me."

Brian started rubbing his hands back and forth across his knees.

"But you can still make things right, Brian."

Louis faced Scott. "You sonofabitch. You're going to ask him to plead, aren't you?"

"It keeps him off the witness stand," Scott said, leaning against the headstone.

The graveyard fell silent. Louis couldn't move, his eyes locked on Brian, who was just sitting there, *just sitting there,* ready to take the blame for everything again. What kind of man was he?

Scott suddenly laughed.

Louis turned to look at him.

"Jesus Christ," Scott said. "I just realized something. Do either of you see the irony of all this?"

"Scott, stop," Brian said. "Just stop."

Scott rose off the headstone. "No, listen. Let's say,

twenty years ago, I have sex with the daughter of a cop. When she cries rape, I get angry and kill her with a kitchen knife. Her father is then assigned to handle the case of the next stupid bitch I rape and kill. But he's too pissed at his dead daughter to do a decent job." Scott paused. "That *is* how you explained it, right Louis?"

Louis didn't move. He couldn't believe this. Scott was telling him everything.

Scott gave a small smile and went on.

"Wait. It gets better. An innocent asshole is convicted and twenty years later, he hires *me,* the killer, to help him prove his innocence and sue the state so we can both get a lot of money."

Scott spread his hands, looking at Louis. "Surely you can appreciate the irony?"

Brian was staring at his brother in disbelief.

"You talk too much, Scott," Louis said slowly. "Brian may be protected by privilege, but you're not."

Scott laughed again. "Jesus Christ, Louis. Don't you see? I can tell you whatever I want. No one will believe you."

"Don't bet on it."

Scott shook his head slowly. "You are outclassed here, Louis, outclassed and outsmarted."

"Fuck you, Scott," Louis snapped.

He spun away, drawing on every ounce of strength he had. He started walking.

"Louis! Where you going?" Scott called out.

"To the sheriff's office."

"To do what? We'll deny everything. We were never here and we never talked to you."

Louis spun back. "I'll kill you before I let you get away with this!" he shouted.

Scott laughed, coming toward him. "Jesus, Louis, I think you're more hung up on her than Brian was."

Louis turned away. *Don't do it . . . keep walking . . . don't do it.*

Scott came up behind him. "Let it go, Louis," he said softly. "She wasn't all that good."

Louis spun and hit him, hard and quick. Scott stumbled backward, but Louis came at him again, taking another swing and connecting solidly against Scott's jaw.

Scott stumbled again, grabbing onto a headstone to keep his balance. He wiped his lip, looking back at Louis.

"Feel better now?" Scott asked.

Louis hit him again, sending Scott toppling over a stone bench. Scott sat on the grass, looking down at the blood on his hand.

"Get up!" Louis shouted.

Scott didn't move and Louis stepped forward, dragging him to his feet by his lapels. Louis slugged Scott again, but before he could fall, Louis grabbed his suit coat to keep him upright.

When he was steady, Louis hit him again, then again, each punch driving him backward over a small rise in the grass. Louis could hear someone yelling in the background—Brian, yelling Scott's name.

Scott threw up his hands, choking, his face smeared with his own blood.

"Enough . . . enough," Scott gasped.

"It's nowhere near enough!"

Louis stepped into another punch, this time knocking Scott to the grass, where he sat huddled, his bloody hand on his mouth. Behind him Louis could see the backhoe that sat near Kitty's open grave.

He looked back at Scott. "Get the fuck up."

Scott shook his head, holding up a hand.

Louis grabbed Scott's coat and started dragging him toward the open grave. Scott fought to twist loose, cursing as he tried to untangle himself from his suit coat.

"You're going in the ground, you sonofabitch," Louis said, jerking him toward the grave.

Brian was following slowly, his mouth moving, but Louis couldn't hear him.

Scott saw the open grave and for the first time, his face registered fear. He began to struggle harder to get out of Louis's grip.

Louis dragged him closer. Scott was screaming now, and Brian's voice was somewhere in the background.

At the lip of the grave, Louis stopped. He pushed Scott's face into the dirt, then picked him up by the back of his coat. He held his face over the gaping black hole.

"You ready, motherfucker?" Louis said.

Scott spat out a mouthful of dirt. "Stop! Stop!" he screamed. He twisted frantically, wrestling himself out of his coat and Louis's grasp. Louis let him go. Scott scrambled away on his knees, backing up against the backhoe. He sat there, heaving, wiping his dirty face.

Louis still had the coat in his hand. He threw it to the ground. A flash of red caught his eye. He bent down and picked up the paper that had fallen out of the coat. It was an Air France ticket envelope.

Louis looked over at Scott. "You sorry sonofabitch," he said quietly. "You were going to fucking run."

Scott was crumpled against the backhoe, his white shirt streaked with red. He lowered his hand from his mouth and squinted up at Louis.

"You were going to run out on your own brother," Louis said tightly.

"Fuck you," Scott said, coughing on his blood. "Fuck you and him and that girl."

Louis saw Brian out of the corner of his eye, staring

at his brother. He threw the ticket at Scott. Scott flinched but did not get up.

"Her name was Kitty," Louis said. He turned and walked away.

Chapter
Forty-Four

Louis examined the knuckles of his right hand. The skin was broken and something hurt, like he had cracked a bone. He glanced up at the wall clock. It was after one; he had been here since seven this morning.

After leaving the cemetery, he had gone right to Mobley. He told him what Brian and Scott had said, but not what happened afterward. Mobely had looked long and hard at Louis's swollen hand but had not asked the obvious questions. Then Mobley had called Scott, asking him to come in for questioning. Scott had come willingly, bringing Brian. They had been in the interrogation room for more than an hour now.

A door opened and Louis looked up as Mobley came out. He saw Louis sitting there and came over.

"You look like hell," Mobley said.

Louis realized Mobley had the same beaten look he had the last time Louis had seen him at O'Sullivan's. Something hadn't gone right in that room.

Mobley sank down onto the bench next to him. "They've denied everything," he said. "Scott says they were at the cemetery mourning their poor dead father and you just appeared and started harassing them."

"Did he tell you the rest?"

"No. Why don't you give it a shot?"

Louis drew in a deep breath. "I tried to walk away, but Scott kept talking. He laughed about her. He said it was ironic that he was hired as Cade's lawyer. Ironic, for chrissake."

"So you beat the shit out of him."

Louis nodded, flexing his hand. "I lost it. And he just stood there while I beat the crap out of him. Just stood there with that fucking smile on his face like he wanted me to keep hitting him."

"He did."

Louis started to ask Mobley what he meant, but suddenly it hit him. Scott knew exactly what he was doing; it had been part of his game strategy. He knew that if Louis attacked him, Louis would lose all credibility and any testimony that might get admitted wouldn't be believed. That why he was so willing to show up at the station; he wanted everyone to see his face.

Louis leaned his head back against the wall.

"If you push this so-called confession," Mobley said, "I get the feeling he'll counter with assault charges. And we're not talking thirty days here, Louis."

"I don't care. I'll tell it to anyone who will listen."

"I don't think it's going to do you any good."

Louis stared at the closed door to the interrogation room. "So Scott was right? It's all privileged?"

Mobley shrugged. "I don't know about that, but between the privilege, hearsay and coercion issues, I do know we got one big fucking legal cesspool that will take years to clean up."

Louis sighed, dropping his gaze to the floor.

"It gets worse," Mobley said. "They've hired a big time lawyer from Miami who's already on his way here to file a motion to try Brian as a juvenile. Sandusky says we've got to go by the 1966 laws, and it was general practice back then to try kids as kids. If they do that, Brian will walk away completely because he's already over the maximum age you can punish juveniles for."

Mobley hesitated, watching Louis. "And without Brian facing charges, we got no leverage to ever turn him against Scott."

"I don't believe this."

"And even if the juvenile thing doesn't work, Scott's claiming everything we found in the search is inadmissable because the warrants were based on information you gave us—"

"And that makes it privileged," Louis said.

Mobley nodded. "And without the warrants, we can't even use Brian's statement."

"That's fucking crazy. There's no way a lawyer can claim privilege when one of his employees discovers he's committed a crime."

Mobley sighed heavily. "I don't know about that, but I do know this case is going down the toilet real quick. Even if we could use the evidence, what else do we got?"

Louis didn't answer. He knew what was coming.

"Hell, we got a shaky statement by Brian that some lawyer will get thrown out because we didn't Mirandize him when he showed up or some shit like that," Mobley went on. "And we have no way to put Scott at the house when either girl disappeared."

"We can look deeper," Louis said. "We can find witnesses, housekeepers—"

"All the housekeepers were illegals. Long gone, Louis."

"What about the cabana itself. Prints, blood—"

"We got some preliminaries on the cabana and we're still looking, but the drywall was clean. Not a single print. Nothing on the wood behind it or on Lou Ann."

Louis felt suddenly very tired.

"What about college friends?" Louis asked.

"Can you remember which holidays your college friends went home and when they didn't?" Mobley said.

"Okay, then, what about Brian's red Corvette? People keep cars like that. It still might be around, there would have to be blood in the trunk somewhere."

"We checked. He wrecked it in sixty-eight. It was scrapped."

Louis rubbed his face, and spoke softly. "Maybe Scott told someone else over the years."

"He didn't and you know it," Mobley said. He let a few seconds go by. "He's probably going to walk, Louis. I'm sorry."

The hallway fell quiet. Louis stared at the floor, the pit of anger in his stomach now an ache that he was dangerously close to getting used to. He knew he needed to let her go. But not yet. "Lance, Scott is a killer."

"I know that, Louis," Mobley said, exhaustion in his voice. "But what do you want me to do? There's nothing to even hold him on until we finish processing the cabana."

"He's got a plane ticket to France in his pocket," Louis said.

"Fuck," Mobley muttered.

A deputy came up. "Sheriff, Detective Jensen said to give this to you asap."

Louis watched as Mobley thanked the deputy, then he leaned his head back against the wall and closed his eyes. He could hear voices behind the interrogation room door, voices that sounded almost like laughter, but he knew his head was playing tricks now, that it was probably only his own anger he was hearing, something he knew he was going to hear for a long time.

"I'll be a motherfucker."

Louis looked over at Mobley.

Mobley was reading something in the file the deputy had given him.

"What?" Louis asked.

"Remember all those prints I told you we took out of Duvall's office?" Mobley said. "Guess whose name showed up? Our boy Scotty."

"He's a lawyer, Lance. He must have been in that office at some time."

"Yeah, but no one can ever remember seeing him there. Not even that old bag Ellie. Jensen double checked."

Mobley was reading something else.

"And we've got a phone call from Duvall to Scott's direct line in the Brenner law office that afternoon, just after Cade left."

Louis waited, while Mobley read more.

"And get this . . . that old trial Redweld that we thought was taken by Duvall's killer? Guess where we found it?"

"Scott's office?"

"Yup, in a search we did this morning of Scott's office. Scott's prints are all over it and on damn near every paper inside it," Mobley said. "Plus, that AB-negative report you were looking for was found in his desk drawer."

Mobley was grinning.

"What else?" Louis asked.

"Our homeless witness, Quince? He was shown a photo line-up this morning. He identified Scott as someone he saw going into Duvall's building just before nine P.M. Said he remembered him because Scott gave him a buck."

Louis was dumbfounded. "How'd you get all that together?"

Mobley closed the folder. "After I left you at O'Sullivan's, I got to thinking. So I asked Jensen to poke around, see if he could connect Brian to Duvall's murder. We got Scott instead."

"They can't suppress that, can they?" Louis asked.

"Not a chance. This was information we had all along, none of it came from you."

Louis looked up at him, knowing that wasn't entirely true.

"At least that's how I remember it," Mobley added.

"Did you find the Tokarev?"

Mobley shook his head. "We're still looking. When they sold off the gun collection after the senator died, the old guns got scattered across the country through antique dealers. It would be nice, but we don't need it. We know Charles Brenner had a collection, we can put Scott in Duvall's office and we know he had motive to protect his brother."

"Scott shot Spencer Duvall," Louis said quietly. "Jesus."

Mobley nodded. "Guess Scott isn't going to make his plane."

A strange feeling came over Louis, something faintly resembling satisfaction, but it was dull. He had found Duvall's killer, brought Bob Ahnert home his lost daughter and he even knew what happened to Kitty. But there was one thing missing.

"It's not enough, Lance," he said quietly.

"It has to be." Mobley closed the file. "Scott's still in there with Brian. I think I'll arrest him while he's here. Want to watch?"

"Yeah, I do."

Mobley rose and opened the door. Scott was just coming out, Brian trailing. Scott's face was purple and patched with two butterfly bandages. He had a thin red split in his lower lip.

"We're going now," Scott said.

"You're under arrest," Mobley said.

Scott's swollen eyes moved from Mobley to Louis. "You're kidding, right? What for?"

Mobley turned Scott around. Scott didn't resist as he looked back over his shoulder.

"Hey, come on, Lance. What's this about?"

"Scott Brenner, you're under arrest for the murder of Spencer Duvall."

Scott tried to spin around, but Mobley jerked him back, pressing him against the wall.

"Christ, Lance," Scott said. "Ease up here. I barely knew Duvall. I had no reason to shoot—"

Mobley spun Scott around to face Louis. Louis expected to see at least some flicker of fear on his face, but there was nothing.

"Tell me what you got," Scott said. "The old file, right? Okay, I had it. Duvall called me over there after Cade's visit. He wanted me to take a look at what he was up against—"

Mobley yanked on the cuffs.

Scott's face suddenly went cold. "Hell, I'll be out in an hour."

Mobley reached in Scott's jacket and pulled out the Air France ticket. "No, you won't. You're a flight risk."

Scott jerked his face toward Louis. "You just won't let it go, will you?"

Mobley stepped between them quickly. "Wait outside, Louis."

Louis didn't move.

"Outside. Now." Mobley said.

Louis walked stiffly down the hall to the lobby. He shoved open the door and stepped into the sunlight.

He stood for a minute, forcing himself to breathe

slowly. Then he walked over and sat down on the edge of a concrete planter. He looked down at his hand, flexing it slowly.

It wasn't near enough, but it was all he had.

A strange image to came to him. A child killer cornered in the dark and his friend, Dan Wainwright, pulling a trigger, making his own kind of justice.

It was the only way I knew it would happen.

A few weeks ago, Louis had condemned Wainwright for it. Cops didn't make their own justice. Not good cops. But sitting here now, knowing Scott would never be punished for what he did to Kitty and Lou Ann, he understood. And he wondered, had he known last night what he knew now, would he have been able to walk away from the graveyard?

"You okay?"

Louis looked up. Mobley was standing over him, a silhouette against the sun.

Louis nodded. "Just thinking."

"Sorry I threw you out. One dead prisoner a month is enough."

Louis suddenly remembered the Haitian prisoner. "You ever find out who killed that Haitian guy?" he asked.

"Yeah, another prisoner. They were fighting over cigarettes. The guy admitted it."

Louis was staring at the ground. Another assumption about Cade he had gotten wrong.

"The Duvall charges will be dropped against Cade," Mobley said.

Louis still said nothing.

"Why don't you go get some sleep."

Louis shook his head slowly.

"Then go call Tonto. Give her the good news."

Louis looked at Mobley. "Yeah, okay."

Mobley was standing there, hands in his pockets. Louis wanted to say something to him, to thank him for coming along on this, for putting his ass on the line. But they both turned at the sound of a van pulling up to the curb. The side read WINK-TV FORT MYERS.

Mobley watched the cameraman get out. He reached in his pocket and pulled out an Altoid tin. "I guess I better go do my thing," he said.

Louis nodded.

Mobley started toward the van, then turned back to Louis. "Next time you're in O'Sullivan's, I'll buy you a drink."

Chapter
Forty-Five

He let Susan drive, not sure he could handle the roads as tired as he was. She was quiet, but he sensed she was happy. This miserable case was over and her client was absolved of murder, including Kitty's.

Susan pulled up in the drive of J.C. Landscaping and cut the engine. "By the way, thanks for coming with me," she said. "I hate coming out here alone."

"I don't blame you."

He followed her to the trailer door and waited while she knocked. He didn't see anyone working in the yard, but Ronnie's truck was parked near the shed. Eric opened the door and let them in.

Jack Cade was sitting in a worn chair, dressed in his boxers and a T-shirt. A beer can sat on the table next to him. Ronnie was in the kitchen and Louis could smell hamburger cooking. Eric slumped back down into the couch and trained his eyes on the television. They were watching an old version of *Star Trek*.

"Jack," Susan said. "We have some good news."

"Don't tell me," Cade said. "You got me off."

Susan glanced at Louis. "Yes. They've dropped the murder charges for Spencer Duvall. They're charging Scott Brenner."

Cade's eyes jumped to Louis. "My lawyer? Fuck, don't that beat all? What about my new trial thing and the money? Who's going to handle that?"

Louis came further into the room. "Brian Brenner has been arrested for killing Kitty Jagger. When he's convicted and the story comes out of how they set you up, lawyers will be beating down your door to represent you."

Cade stood up slowly, the beer can in his hand. "That snotty little bastard . . ."

Eric and Ronnie looked at Cade.

"You mean to tell me that piece of shit killed that girl," Cade said. "And he stole *my* fucking tool? And then put the panties in *my* truck? Those cocksucking bastards!"

Cade flung the beer can toward the kitchen. It smashed against the wall, splattering beer.

Ronnie had flinched and was still half-cowering at the stove. Louis glanced at Eric. He was staring at the beer dripping down the wall.

Eric rose slowly and went to pick up the beer can.

"Leave it the fuck alone!" Cade yelled.

Eric dropped it and looked up at his grandfather.

"What are you looking at?" Cade spat. "Get out of my face."

Eric started toward his room, and Cade caught his arm, spinning him around. "Go outside. Get the fuck out of here."

"Cade, leave him alone," Louis said. "Jesus."

Eric jerked free and ran out the front door. Cade stood there for a moment, his eyes unfocused. Then he looked at Susan, who was standing there, stunned.

"How long before I get my money?" Cade asked.

Susan started to explain about how long lawsuits took, but Louis was looking beyond Cade, into the kitchen where he could see Ronnie wiping up the spilled beer. He turned and looked out the window. Eric was in the front yard, wiping his face, kicking some rocks through the dirt.

Cade's voice drew his attention back. "I think I'll ask for five million." He smiled at Susan. "But you can settle for three. That ought to be enough to get me the fuck out of here."

Ronnie turned from the stove toward his father. "What?"

"Mexico," Cade said. "A man can live cheap there. Three mil will last me a lifetime."

Ronnie came forward. "What about the business?"

Cade stared at him, but it was almost like he wasn't even seeing him anymore. "Who the hell wants it?"

Ronnie stared at his father, then turned and went back to the stove. Cade plopped back down in his chair. Susan was trying to explain something to him, but he was barely listening.

Louis flexed his aching hand. *The hell with this. . . .*

He turned and left the trailer. Eric was still out front, tossing rocks, trying to hit the pile of plastic containers stacked against the shed. He looked up at Louis and then his eyes went back to the trailer door. Louis walked up next to him.

"So he's not going back to jail, huh?" Eric asked, tossing another rock.

Louis hesitated. "No, he's not."

Eric stared out across the rows of plants, his jaw set. Louis tried to think of something of comfort, something that would tell Eric things would get better. But he knew they wouldn't.

Eric looked up suddenly. "Can a kid get in trouble if he knows something?"

Louis couldn't read Eric's dark eyes.

"Are you trying to tell me something, Eric?"

Eric hesitated, then dropped the stones and started toward the shed. Louis followed. Eric went around the back, stopping at a group of potted palms.

He looked back at Louis, then lifted one of the palms from the pot.

"I hate him," Eric whispered. "I just hate him."

Louis looked down. The gun in the plastic bag looked like a hundred others he had seen. But he knew it wasn't. It was the Chinese Tokarev.

Louis looked back at Eric. "Does your father know about this?"

Eric shook his head.

Louis rubbed a hand over his face. "Go back inside, Eric," he said. "Don't say anything about this. Just tell Miss Outlaw I'll be in the car."

"No, no," Eric said, shaking his head. "I can't go back in there. He'll kill me if he finds out." Any bravado that had been in Eric's face was gone; he looked terrified.

"Eric, listen to me. You can't say anything, do you understand?"

"No—" Eric started to back away. Louis grabbed him by the shoulders.

"Eric, just go back inside and be quiet. Trust me, okay?"

Eric was close to crying, but he nodded. Louis let him go, his hand lingering on the boy's shoulder. He was shaking.

"Don't worry," Louis said. "I'll take care of you."

Chapter
Forty-Six

When he dropped Susan off at her house, she asked
him if something was the matter. He told her nothing;
he knew there was no way he could explain it to her.
He wasn't even sure he could explain it to himself.

Back there at the Cade place, looking at Eric's face,
he had made a decision. It hadn't come from that place
Susan called his cop-brain. It had come from some
place deeper inside him.

He headed the Mustang due west into the low slanting
sun. The Tokarev was hidden in the trunk. He showed
his resident badge at the causeway and drove on to
Sanibel.

This time, when he appeared at Candace Duvall's
door, the maid let him in without a word.

He found Candace and Hayley having drinks on the
patio. Hayley saw him coming and set down her glass.
Candace had her back to him, but turned when his
shadow moved over the table.

She moved her sunglasses down the bridge of her nose and looked at him, then turned her back. "What do you want now?"

"Money."

Candace spun around in her chair, pulling off her sunglasses. "You've got to be kidding."

"Twenty years ago, your husband covered up the identity of Kitty Jagger's killer and allowed Jack Cade to go to jail," Louis said.

Candace's eyes flickered and she put her glasses back on. Louis had the feeling that what he had just said was not a surprise to her.

"You're nuts," Candace said.

"I know how he did it and why he did it," Louis said. "And I'm on my way to tell Jack Cade."

"And why should I care?"

"Like I said, money. The Cades will sue your husband's law firm. Then they'll go after his personal assets, like this pretty house."

Candace was sitting very still.

Louis moved around so he could see her face. "I might even suggest to them that you were behind your husband's scheme. Then they can come after you too."

"I committed no crime," Candace said.

"You want to tell that to a whole courtroom?" Louis asked. "With your girlfriend sitting right there in the first row?"

Candace looked over at Hayley. "How much?" she said.

"Fifty thousand, and I promise you that you'll never hear from me or the Cades again," Louis said. "Think of it as a gift."

Louis stared down at her. He was blackmailing her, but a part of him didn't care. Blackmail would be the least of it, if the rest of his plan worked.

Candace got up and went inside. Louis glanced down

at Hayley. She was looking at him with a small smile on her lips.

Candace came back with a check, made out to cash. "How do I know you won't come back for more?"

"You'll just have to take my word for it, lady."

Chapter Forty-Seven

It was dark by the time Louis got back to J.C. Landscaping. Ronnie's truck was gone, but Louis could see the blue light of the TV flickering in the window of the trailer.

Louis cut the engine and opened the car door. It was quiet for a moment, then came the buzz of insects flailing against the dome light. Louis looked down at the small blue gym bag on the passenger seat, then up at the trailer.

He grabbed the bag and got out.

At the trailer door, he knocked. The TV was turned up loud to a sitcom, the one about the alien Alf, and the shriek of the canned laughter pierced the night silence. Louis waited until a lull and banged hard on the door. It opened and Jack Cade peered at him.

"Louie . . ."

"Come on outside, Cade," Louis said.

Cade rubbed a hand over his face. "What you want?"

"I want to talk." Louis walked away. Cade followed, closing the door behind him. He stood on the patio, bare-chested, old jeans riding low on his flat stomach. His sweaty skin gleamed in the blue light coming from the television inside.

"What's up?" Cade asked.

"Where's Ronnie?"

"Went down to the Circle K. Why?"

"Eric go with him?"

"Yeah." Louis could see Cade's eyes narrow. "What's up, Louie? What you doing back here?"

"We're going to strike a bargain, Cade," Louis said.

Cade arched an eyebrow. "Bargain? What kind of bargain?"

"I'm going to give you money, Cade, and you're going to walk away forever."

Cade's teeth flashed as he laughed. "Walk away? From what?"

"Your son, your grandson. And this place."

Cade gestured to the desolate land. "This piece of paradise? Now why would I want to do that, Louie?"

"Because I have your Tokarev automatic."

Cade froze. He was still smiling, but it had turned twisted in the blue light. Canned laughter drifted out of the trailer's jalousies, mixing with the whine of the mosquitoes in the humid night air.

"That little shit," Cade whispered.

Cade turned away. He walked in a slow, tight circle around the patio. "That little shit," he said louder. "I knew something was going on with that—"

"Cade," Louis said sharply.

Cade looked back at him.

"You're going to take the money and you're going to leave," Louis said. "You're going to leave Ronnie and Eric alone, you hear me? That's the bargain."

"Why should I leave? I'm going to sue! I got big money coming," Cade said. "They owe me, goddamn it, they owe me!"

"It isn't going to happen that way," Louis said.

Cade's jaw was clenched. And his fist was too. Louis could see it in the blue light. He braced for Cade's swing, but then, suddenly, Cade seemed to go limp, almost swaying on his feet.

"You're right," he said, shaking his head. "It ain't gonna happen. I knew it. I always knew it. That's why I shot the fucker."

He was talking about Duvall. "You knew about the statute of limitations, didn't you? You knew you couldn't sue?" Louis said.

"Not until he told me that day I went to see him," Cade said. "He told me I would never get a dime."

Cade cocked his head at Louis. "And then you know what he says to me? That cocksucker lawyer was just sitting there behind his big desk, sitting there looking up at me, and you know what he *says?* 'I'm sorry this had to happen to you.' "

The blue light flickered over Cade's face. "That's why I went back and shot him. If I wasn't gonna get money, I was gonna get some justice."

A splash of headlights on the trees made Louis look out toward the dark road. But it wasn't Ronnie's truck. Louis looked back at Cade.

"Make a decision, Cade," Louis said.

Cade had been staring at the ground. When he looked up at Louis, his face was slack. "How much money?"

"Twenty-five thousand dollars."

"Twenty-five . . . for twenty years," he said quietly.

"That and your freedom."

Cade stood there for a moment, his eyes taking in the dark grounds and the decrepit trailer. "So I go free and that cocksucker lawyer does my time?" A slow smile tipped Cade's lips. "I like your style, Louie."

"You going or not?"

"I'll go tomorrow."

"You go tonight, before Ronnie gets back."

Cade shook his head sharply. "Fuck that. I'll go when I'm ready."

"You'll go tonight. Right now. Go get whatever you need and get out. Now."

Louis could see Cade's muscles tense. Louis braced himself again. But then Cade's eyes drifted down to the gym bag under Louis's arm.

He turned and went back into the trailer. Louis waited, watching the dark road, hoping Ronnie didn't come back. When Cade came out, he was dressed and carrying a small canvas bag and a jacket.

Cade held out his hand. Louis tossed him the bag. Cade caught it against his chest. He unzipped it, poked inside, and zipped it back up.

"It's there," Louis said. "Start walking."

Cade slung the bag over his shoulder. "See you around, Louie."

Cade started walking. Louis watched him turn down Mantanzas Trail and disappear into the darkness.

Chapter
Forty-Eight

He was sitting on the ground, under a gumbo limbo tree, a few feet from his front porch. He was digging a small hole, scooping out the cool sand with his hand.

It was one of those perfect Florida days he had come to appreciate. Sun-drenched but humidity free, a fine, tangy breeze blowing in from the gulf. He could have given himself over to it, lost himself in the feel of the sun on his neck and the rush of the waves breaking on the beach, but his head was too full of things.

When he thought the hole was deep enough, he reached back for the Tokarev.

It was still wrapped in Jack Cade's clear plastic bag. Louis picked up a second plastic bag, a thick-ply evidence bag. He placed the gun inside, then added an envelope. Inside, was a letter, explaining everything.

He put the bag in the hole and started pushing back the sand. He took his time, hoping that maybe he would begin to feel as if he was burying more than just the gun, but it didn't come.

"Louis?"

He turned to see Susan standing by the side of his cottage. She was wearing a blue cotton dress that swirled with the breeze. She looked different. Brighter, softer. He had to squint to look up at her.

"What are you doing?"

"Just burying something."

"Good God. Did your cat die?"

"What? No, no."

Benjamin ran up next to her. "Can I go swimming?" he asked.

"Not in your shorts," Susan said. "Don't go in the water and stay where I can see you."

Benjamin ran off. Susan was still looking at the fresh mound of sand.

"What are you doing out here, Susan?" he asked, standing up and dusting the sand off his hands.

"I came to ask you about something."

Louis nodded toward the porch and they went to sit down on a step. Susan was looking out at the beach, keeping an eye on Benjamin, who was playing tag with the waves. She hiked her billowing skirt up over her knees and slipped off her sandals, digging her toes in the sand.

"I went out to the Cade place yesterday," she said. "Ronnie told me Jack ran off. Did you know about this?"

Louis stared off at the water, watching Benjamin play.

"No."

"He didn't tell me either," Susan said. "But then Ronnie told me Cade left them twenty-five thousand dollars. They found it in Eric's bedroom, in a dresser drawer. Funny, isn't it? A man like Jack Cade having any money, let alone leaving it to Ronnie and Eric. Where do you think he got it?''

Louis drew up his knees.

Susan reached into her bag. ''Ronnie asked me to give you this,'' she said, handing Louis an envelope.

Louis took it and looked inside. There were five hundred dollar bills inside.

''I don't need this,'' he said.

Susan pushed the envelope back. ''He needs you to have it. It makes things right for him.''

Louis closed the envelope. ''How'd Eric seem?'' he asked.

Susan shrugged. ''He was fine. He was talking about getting a Nintendo.''

''Did he seem happy?''

''Yes. Seemed like a different kid,'' Susan said.

He could see Benjamin picking up shells. Maybe Eric had a chance now. Maybe he could somehow rediscover the hope and innocence kids should have, the things Benjamin had.

''Susan,'' Louis said suddenly. ''You've done a good job with Benjamin.''

She seemed surprised at his comment. ''Well, thank you, but sometimes I don't think I do enough. It's hard being alone.''

He looked at her profile. She was staring off toward the beach.

''You don't have to be alone all the time,'' he said. ''You could bring him back here. I mean, any time he wants to come.''

She looked at him quickly, then away just as quickly, blinking. He knew she understood what he meant. Not just to come back and let Benjamin play in the water, but for her to come back and spend time with him.

''Maybe,'' she said.

Louis didn't press it. They fell quiet, watching Benjamin.

"Oh, I saw something posted in the courthouse the other day that might interest you," she said.

"What?"

"Fort Myers is hiring three officers next month."

Louis turned away, looking out at the gulf.

"Are you going to apply?"

Louis shook his head.

"I thought you liked Chief Horton. I heard he likes you too."

Louis was thinking about Ellie Silvestri. He had gone to her office yesterday, to tell her about Spencer Duvall. He had tried to make Duvall sound misguided, but wasn't sure she had bought it. She had taken him back into Duvall's office and shown him one of the pictures on the wall. He had noticed it the first time; it was the picture of the Victorian beachfront cottage among the photographs of old Fort Myers. Ellie told him it was a real place, in a town up in the panhandle called Seaside. It was a new development, a fabrication of an idyllic twenties village, complete with a bandshell in the town circle and rockers on the pastel porches. The motto of the place was "Remembering how nice the world can be." Duvall had planned to divorce Candace, leave her everything and move to Seaside, Ellie told him. He wanted to open a small law practice and start over.

But Spencer couldn't go back, not after what he had done. No more than he himself could.

"Louis?"

He looked at Susan. "I think I'll wait," he said.

"But why? I thought you hated this PI stuff."

Louis shrugged. "You get used to it."

They fell quiet, watching Benjamin chase the gulls.

"Do you think they'll get a conviction on Scott?"

"If they don't," Louis said, "it was all for nothing."

She was looking at him, hearing the hollow sound in his voice. "The system *worked* this time, Louis."

He didn't comment. She sighed and picked up a shell. He saw her looking at the mound in the sand.

"Louis, what did you bury?" she asked.

He hesitated, his gaze dropping to the ground. He opened Ronnie's envelope, pulled out one bill and held it out to her.

She looked at it. "What?"

"Just take it."

She accepted it. "Why?"

"I want to hire you as my attorney."

"What for?"

"I don't know yet. It's a retainer."

She eyed him, then looked down at the bill.

"Am I now your client?" he asked.

"I don't know how much a hundred bucks will get you, but yes, you're my client."

Louis nodded.

She looked back at the sand. "Now are you going to tell me what you buried?"

"I didn't bury anything."

"But you told me you buried something."

He looked at her. "And what I told you is now privileged."

She stared at him, then turned away. "Technically, you told me before you hired me, but I can get around that."

"I thought you could."

"Do I *want* to know what you buried?"

He shook his head.

Benjamin came running up, his shorts and sneakers wet.

"Ma, this is so cool," he said. "There's a really cool dead fish out there, and some seaweed. And look what I caught!" He held out a shell. There was a tiny crab in it. "Can I take him home?"

"No, Ben."

"Aw, why not? Please, Ma, please?"

"No, now go put it back."

He plopped down on the sand at her feet. "But you said I could maybe get a fish tank. I could keep the crab in it. Can I, Ma?"

"We need to buy a tank first. You can come back and get another one," Susan said.

Louis glanced at her. *Come back?*

She saw his expression and quickly looked away. She slipped the hundred dollar bill in her pocket and rose.

"So, show me this really cool dead fish," she said.

Ben scrambled to his feet and took Susan's hand. He looked back at Louis.

"You coming?" Ben asked.

Louis hesitated, then got to his feet, dusting the sand off his hands. "I guess I am," he said.

Chapter Forty-Nine

It took him a while to find his way back. He was lost until he spotted the towering tree and he used it as a landmark, walking through the headstones until he found Kitty's grave.

There was a fresh mound of dirt. They had already put her back in the ground. The dirt was covered with lavender flowers.

Louis looked up. The canopy of the tree was bare. Not one flower was left on the branches.

He moved closer. For a moment, he just stood there, staring at the dirt. He looked up at the bare tree, then down at the grave.

"I had to do it the way I did," he said.

The sound of his own voice was startling in the silence. He hadn't meant to speak. And for a moment he was tempted to look around to see who had heard. But he keep his eyes on the grave.

"I know now," he said.

Knew what? How everything could change in one split second? How one decision could alter the course of a life? How precious it all was?

One split second, one decision, and the road of his life had taken an unexpected turn. He would never wear a uniform again; how could he now? He had done what he had to do. And because of it, Eric's road had taken its own turn. But that wasn't why he had done it.

He heard a sound and turned. Two people were coming over the rise, an old man and a younger woman. He was surprised to see Joyce Novick and Willard Jagger walking toward him.

Joyce smiled when she saw him. Willard did too, but Louis wasn't sure it was from recognition.

"How you doing?" Joyce asked.

"Good," Louis answered.

Joyce had her arm linked through Willard's. "This is it, Mr. Jagger," she said, nodding toward the mound.

Willard looked down and frowned slightly. "There's no headstone," he said.

Joyce looked at Louis. "I think someone just forgot to put it here, Mr. Jagger. But we can get one, if you want," she said.

Willard was looking at the grave. Louis paused, then reached in his pocket.

"Mr. Jagger?"

Williard looked up at him. Louis held out the picture of Kitty. "I think you should have this back," he said.

Willard stared at it for moment, then took it.

"That's my girl," he said.

Then his eyes went blank and he turned to Joyce, holding out the picture. She took it and slipped it in his shirt pocket. Willard's eyes went back to the lavender blanket of flowers. Then his eyes drifted up to the tree's canopy.

"Jacaranda tree," he said, pointing. "Two weeks every year. That's all they bloom."

Louis followed Willard's finger, looking up at the bare branches. They were quiet for a moment. Then Willard turned to Joyce.

"I'm ready to go home now," he said.

She looked at Louis and he nodded, telling her there would be another time for talk. She led Willard back over the rise.

Louis's eyes were drawn back to the grave. It was so quiet. Not a sound, not a bird, not a human voice, just his own heart beating slowly, steadily in his chest. For a second, it terrified him, this silence. Then he knew it was all right. She was quiet now, and it was all right.

It was time to go. His eyes went from the mound of lavender flowers up to the bare branches. Then he turned and walked back over the rise. He would come back when the flowers did.

ABOUT THE AUTHOR

P.J. Parrish has worked as a newspaper reporter and editor, arts reviewer, blackjack dealer and personnel director in a Mississippi casino. The author currently resides in Southaven, Mississippi, and Fort Lauderdale, Florida, and is married with three children, three grandchildren and five cats. P.J. Parrish is currently at work on the next Louis Kincaid thriller. Please visit the author's Web site at www.pjparrish.com

"Book 'em!"
Legal Thrillers from Kensington

Grab These
Kensington Mysteries

___**Blowing Smoke**   1-57566-723-1   **$5.99US/$7.99CAN**
by Barbara Block

___**Dead In The Water**   1-57566-756-8   **$5.99US/$7.99CAN**
by Carola Dunn

___**The Confession**   1-57566-672-3   **$5.99US/$7.99CAN**
by Mary R. Rinehart

___**Witness For The Defense**   1-57566-828-9   **$6.99US/$8.99CAN**
by Jonnie Jacobs

___**Mad As The Dickens**   1-57566-839-4   **$5.99US/$7.99CAN**
by Toni L. Kelner

___**Stabbing Stephanie**   1-57566-729-0   **$5.99US/$7.99CAN**
by Evan Marshall

___**Shooter's Point**   1-57566-745-2   **$5.99US/$7.99CAN**
by Gary Phillips

Call toll free **1-888-345-BOOK** to order by phone or use this coupon to order by mail.

Name _____

Address _____

City _____ State_____ Zip_____

Please send me the books I have checked above.

I am enclosing $_____

Plus postage and handling* $_____

Sales Tax (in New York and Tennessee only) $_____

Total amount enclosed $_____

*Add $2.50 for the first book and $.50 for each additional book.

Send check or money order (no cash or CODs) to: **Kensington Publishing Corp., 850 Third Avenue, 16th Floor, New York, NY 10022**

Prices and numbers subject to change without notice. All orders subject to availability.

Check out our website at **www.kensingtonbooks.com**.

Scare Up One of These Pinnacle Horrors